Dragons of Venosta

Book 1
A Novel by
Fred J. Hoyle Sr.

Dragons of Venosta
Book 1
By
Fred J. Hoyle Sr.
Copyright © Fred Hoyle 2018
Cover and Design Copyright © Jack Hoyle / T-Rex
Studios

ISBN-13: 978-062072202
ISBN-10: 0692072209

Special Thanks to:
Jody T. Washington

and

Tim Marquitz

Prologue

Long ago, before man dominated the earth, the wilderness of Venosta was vast and full of life, but death lurked in her shadows, waiting to provide a meal to any creature that was more cunning or powerful. Even her vegetation, with beautiful flowers and sweet-smelling buds were in constant battle as they chocked and climbed over one another in their endless quest for sunlight.

Armed with fire and intelligence, men and dragons arose to dominate both creatures and plants. The dragons were large, strong, and guided by instinct. Nature armed them with bone crushing teeth and claws, but their greatest gift was that of flight. Fortunately for man, the dragon's instinct called on them to be allusive.

Toiling desperately for untold generations, men never knew that dragons existed. Thousands of years pass and dragons remain hidden. But man, whom nature armed with very little has learned much the hard way forcing his intelligence to grow. He begins making tools and weapons, spurring his creativity and curiosity. Men begin searching the wilderness for wealth and adventure.

Deep within the wilderness a metallic *plink* echoes through the trees resounding over and over again, blending with chopping and laughter, it creates an environment of unnatural noise. Men are stomping about with purpose. They saw and chop, tree after tree, until they come crashing to the earth with a thunderous sound that echoes into the wilderness.

Creatures in the forest and in the sky watch in fear as the hole in the canopy grows wider. Campfires burn, smoke swirls to the heavens, marking the spot where men are digging for silver.

<>

Sailing high above the wilderness four young dragons become intrigued when they see an ashen cloud hanging over a hole in the canopy. They circle for a moment, then one of them dives toward the meadow below. They all follow, but when they see unfamiliar creatures milling about, they land in the cover of the forest. They cautiously creep closer and scoff when they get a good look at the men. "These creatures look frail, walking around on two little legs, and why are they so busy?" asks one of them. Another points to a man leading a donkey burdened with a heavy load. When it resists, the man whacks him with a stick and it trudges on. A donkey brays in the distance. They turn and see more donkeys cooped-up in a lean-to, swatting at flies with their tails, and looking sad. "I will free those little four-legged creatures tonight," says one of the dragons.

Thinking this will be exciting they all agree and return to the woods.

When darkness falls they sneak back toward the donkey's shelter. The donkeys sense their presence and chaos erupts as they bray and kick the walls.

Men pour out of the mine shooting arrows toward the shelter.

The dragons run into the forest and catch their breath. Then one of them, shaking uncontrollably sinks to the ground with an arrow sticking out of his side.

The others grab his arms and tail and thrash through the trees as they wing their way into the air, desperately trying to take him back to their cavern.

<>

Jeb, the miner's leader steps out of the mine shaking his head. "Stop wasting arrows, there's nothing out there. Go back to your blankets."

As the sun rises the next day they anxiously wait for Jeb to pick three of them to be this week's hunting party. Jeb enters smiling. "Good morning, men." He looks around and Lec, the youngest catches his eye. "Lec, go get Jay and Spah. You three haven't been hunting lately. Lec leaps to his feet. His smile brightens and he runs to where they are stacking bags of ore. "Do you two want to go hunting with me today?" he asks, still smiling.

"Am I really that lucky?" marvels Spah.

"Grab your bows, and let's get out of here before someone changes their mind!"

They slide quivers over their shoulders and playfully carry bows as they walk toward the meadows to the north of the mine.

The three young men step lively as they enjoy each other's conversation.

"The donkeys were too restless last night. I'm worried that something evil is lurking near the mine frightening them," says Jay with a scowl.

"I will build the fire next to their lean-to bigger tonight. Maybe that will make them feel safer," suggest Lec, winking at Spah.

Shadows flash over the men abruptly stopping their conversation.

"Did you see that?" gasps Jay.

"Stop worrying about a shadow. We need to get serious about finding a good piece of meat for supper," says Lec.

Quietly, they stalk through the knee-high grass. An occasional wild flower's bloom peaks above the grass, soaking in the sun and advertising its nectar to the bees. Jay halts and raises his hand. Lec and Spah stop. Not far ahead, a large black boar with long tusk roots in the meadow.

Slowly, they set arrows and take aim.

As they pull the bowstrings back, a deafening *smack* and tremendous jolt slams them from behind. Wracked with pain they can't even look at each other as huge claws dig deeply into their flesh, crushing bones, and squeezing tightly, snatching them off the ground. Rising helplessly higher and higher, blood trickles down their backs, dripping off their dangling legs as they sail away.

At midday, the camp begins to wonder what has happened to the hunting party. The cook is restless. He should already be preparing the evening meal.

"Cid, you and Tab, go find the hunting party. They should be back by now," orders Jeb. He notices Dragn, the cook fumbling with pots and pans. "It will be a while before you have meat. Why don't you go find some vegetables to go with our meal?" The cook nods and heads into the woods with a sack.

Cid and Tab grab water bags and weapons. They step out of the lean-to the instant a large shadow streaks across the clearing in front of the mine. Looking up and seeing nothing, Cid kneels to the ground searching for tracks, he rubs his chin. "They went this way," he says.

Hurrying into the trees, they jog in the direction of the meadows. In minutes, they find the hunting party's bows and arrows strewn about. Cid spies a drop of blood in the grass and stands quietly. He takes another quick look into the forest, frowns, then sprints toward the mine. Tab is in front as they break free of the canopy and enter the clearing in front of the mine. A large shadow falls over them, blocking the sun. They grab their bows and nock arrows, turn, and gasp.

"Two giant flying lizards are after us!" screams Tab. The creature's eyes are squinted and fixed on them and they can hear them breathing. The harrowing sight of glistening black claws extended and aiming for them rattles their senses, and their hands shake as they try to shoot. Two arrows *zing,* instantly sinking into the front lizard, dropping the beast to the ground. It skids on its stomach, shrieking in agony and slides to a stop. Tab frantically leaps into the entrance. The second lizard, raging with anger, bellows as its claws slice into Cid. The sound of crushing bones and Cid screaming sends chills down the spines of the men nearby. Turbulence from its wings furiously flapping sends leaves and dirt swirling over them. They cover their eyes and tremble.

Filled with determination, it lifts into the air with Cid's body dangling beneath and disappears over the trees.

The wounded lizard howls as blood oozes around the arrows protruding between its scales. It crawls aimlessly in front of the mine, gasping for air, immersing the camp in chaos. Several men hiding outside dash for the safety of the mine. Two men standing in the entrance, with bows ready, step back to let them dive inside. Then cautiously step out, pull their bowstring back and release their arrows. They plunge into the scaly creature. It jerks as its eyes turn white. The silver and yellow lizard wilts to the ground. Suddenly an aimless gush of fire blast toward them, and they cower back into the mine. All is quiet for a moment. Curious they peek out at the creature. Its unlike anything they have ever seen. Seeing no movement, they are drawn to take a closer look. They barely step into the sunlight when suddenly another giant lizard drops from the sky landing with a *thud*. Screaming, they spring to the sides of the entrance as it spews blue and yellow flames into the mine. Fire washes across their backs, scorching their clothing and singeing the hair off their heads.

The creature doesn't enter the mine, moving instead to examine his fallen companion. An evil look grows on his face as he looks at the corpse. He snorts and stares into the mine with squinted eyes. He springs into the air, spreads his wings, and with powerful strokes, lifts into the sky and disappears.

Jeb rushes to the burnt men, grabs two that are hurt and muscles them deeper into the mine. They scream as he drags them along.

Four frightened men crouch behind rocks deep in the mine, crying in fear as the two burnt men whimper.

Jeb shouts at them. "Get a hold of yourselves, men! Two of you grab your bows and move up to the entrance! Guard us while I think about what to do!"

Evening passes and there's no giant lizards to be seen. As the sun sets, the men gather around a small fire in the mine. They are quiet as Jeb stares into the flames. "Hopefully those creatures are done with us and tomorrow we can make a run for home, he says."

Late that night, loud noises wake the men in the back of the mine. The fire is dying, and the light is dim as they peer toward the entrance. The guards are fumbling with their bows. Loud banging and thuds echo into the mine from outside. The guards don't dare look outside until a crashing sound causes one to steal a peek. He jumps back and catches his breath. "More giant lizards have arrived and they're destroying the lean-to, letting the donkeys go! Why aren't they hurting any of them?!"

Both guards set arrows and step to where they can shoot at what looks like the silhouette of a giant lizard. One arrow sails harmlessly into the woods, but the other finds its mark, landing with a dull *thunk*. The wounded lizard shrieks. It turns and fixes its eyes on the men. In agony it slowly limps toward the entrance.

The guards scream for everyone to get ready for fire to be spewed into the mine. They bravely step out and continue to shoot at the huge creature, but it keeps coming. Tab runs up and joins them. They step back as the dying creature's head plunges into the mine. Their hearts beat madly as they shoot again.

The creature collapses and releases a blast of fire as its heart stops. The flames cover the men and they stumble to the ground with flames dancing over their bodies.

"We're hopelessly trapped!" mutters Jeb, as he looks at the two injured men hiding with him.

"I can still shoot a bow," responds one of them gritting his teeth.

As the sun rises, the three men are startled by the sound of the dead creature being dragged out of the entrance.

Quietly, they slip to the entrance and wait until the corpse is out of the way.

Jeb jumps out, fires an arrow, then the other two men's arrows fly. They plunge into a surprised lizard and it bellows an ear shattering shriek as it stumbles to the ground beside the corpse.

Hearing its anguish, another giant lizard explodes with anger and bursts into flight, darting toward the men. Jeb and the men scramble back into the mine.

The creature crashes through the entrance and charges fearlessly spewing fire over them.

Quiet returns to the wilderness.

<>

The donkeys wandered aimlessly in the wilderness to never be seen again, except for the one Dragn found a week later as he was fleeing. He had hidden in the woods and saw his friends perish. Dragn returned to his tribe, clinging to the donkey, delirious, and half dead, ranting about giant flying lizards breathing fire and killing his friends. Days later when he dies, the tribe births a legend when they began telling stories about Dragn's giant fire breathing lizards hidden in the wilderness.

<>

Hundreds of years pass.

Chapter 1

On a beautiful morning deep in the wilderness of Venosta Land, the sun shines brightly on the entrance of a cavern occupied by a small den of dragons.

Leath, a young female, approaches. Her smooth, trim body gleams dark blue as the sun dances across her beautiful scales. She stops to pick up a remarkable yellow stone from a pocket in her cavern entrance wall. The pocket faces south; assuring the stone is filled with warmth from the sun. This is a dragon hatching stone and is slightly larger than her egg. The stone is so warm today that it's uncomfortable to carry. She places it in a small bundle of straw and carries it to her family's special place in the cavern. As she enters, her mate, Aram, smiles at her. He is cloaked with dark blue scales that are slightly larger than hers. Like the other male dragons, he's tall and muscular. There's a pleasant look about his face even though he's adorned with two dark-colored horns protruding above his bronze, cat-like eyes. They tilt toward his back, curling up slightly just before they come to a point. Larger than two full grown grizzly bears, he is still very agile, and capable of soaring high above the wilderness on his powerful bat-like wings that are normally out of sight until they are unfurled. They are black and leathery with a hint of blue outlining the front edge. Aram, like his entire den, walks upright on strong hind legs leaving his small front legs free to hold and carry things.

Leath pleasantly smiles as she places the stone in her family's nest next to their egg. Aram moves closer to her as she carefully covers it with grass to keep in the warmth. The hatching stone begins to slowly release life-giving warmth as it has for hundreds of years.

Aram and Leath are part of a den of twenty dragons living in a vast wilderness high atop a plateau. The terrain on one side of the plateau is hilly and slowly flattens out. The other side is filled with mountains as far as the eye can see.

When it's time for the egg to hatch they stay close together near the nest. They hear a tiny scratch and Leath gasp and her mouth pops open. "I can hardly wait," she says, cuddling against Aram. As the scratching grows stronger she looks up at Aram with a smile on her face and a tear in her eye. He gently slides his wing around her, but soon he's holding her tight as the shell begins to fall apart.

Many den members have gathered and they beam as Aram and Leath's son pushes away the broken pieces of shell. To everyone's surprise his body is covered with dark blue fuzz, except for a tiny red patch on top of his head.

The den is amazed. No other dragon is fuzzy!

"I think he is wonderful!" exclaims Aram. "The fuzz is probably only temporary and will fall off as he grows." He pulls his wing from around Leath. She glances toward him with troubled eyes wishing he had thought a little longer before saying anything.

The other dragons are kind but they affectionately start calling the hatchling "fuzzy" that night.

"I don't care about our son's different appearance. I see a healthy male dragon," says Leath gently touching her son.

Aram is too quiet, and she can tell the smile on his face is not genuine. When he starts to move away she calls to him. "Aram, come over to me." Leath wisely holds the damp ball out to him.

"Why are you giving the hatchling to me?"

"You need to hold your son."

He reaches cautiously as if he were picking up a butterfly. Nervously, he holds the hatchling. For a few seconds, he feels uncomfortable, and wonders why this is so important to her. As moments pass, he holds the fuzzy ball closer and begins to see a helpless hatchling that needs his love. And he has Leath's eyes. Deep inside he feels a warm sincere love growing, not for a hatchling, but for his son. As his love grows stronger, it fills places in his heart he never knew existed.

Leath can see his expression changing. "You feel it?"

"I do." Aram wipes tears from his big eyes.

"Love for your son will never stop growing until your heart is completely filled. That's just the way dragon fathers are."

They agree to name him Fuzzy and lovingly care for him.

<>

Three years later his blue fuzz has grown thicker and the patch on top of his head is as red as ever. In Aram and Leath's eyes, he is a pretty dragon, but unfortunately, he doesn't look like the rest of the youngsters.

One sunny fall evening Leath happily makes her way to where a large walnut tree has been found. Its full of nuts ready to be gathered. Some of the other mothers are already hard at work picking them, and she joins in. One of the mothers nearby speaks to a friend next to her. "We need some of the younger den members to help carry these nuts to the cavern."

"I will ask Lester and Leonard to come back with me and help," says Lib, Lester's mom.

"Tell Fuzzy to come and help, too," Leath interjects.

Lib looks at Leonard's mom and replies. "Our two young dragons are friends. They're hardly know Fuzzy, and they might not want to help if he comes."

Leath feels a painful sadness inside, but she doesn't rebuke the other mothers. That's not her way of handling problems.

Later that evening, when she and Aram are alone, she speaks softly to him. "I feel sorry for Fuzzy. He looks so different. The younger dragons hesitate to be his friend or ask him to do things with them."

Her humble tone and the pleading look in her eyes tell Aram that she's hurting, and he hugs her.

"I know. He tries so hard to be accepted by the others. They can't see past his appearance to realize he has good judgment and is learning fast."

Several days later, on a cool evening, Fuzzy finds all the young dragons playing together. He is hurt that no one told him to meet there, and when they don't ask him to join in. He runs away.

That night while alone with his mother, he tells her what happened, and she hugs him, shutting her eyes as she feels his pain.

"I don't know why all the other young dragons treat me different and make fun of me. I can do anything they can," he says with a meek little voice.

Leath puts a pleasant face on and smiles. "Don't worry, Fuzzy. They will feel different once they really get to know you. The most important thing to remember is to joke with them and be as much fun to be with as you can."

"I know, Mom, but it's hard for me to joke around when they're calling me a four-legged woolly worm."

"Now that *is* funny," Leath grins slyly, reaching over tickling him. Fuzzy laughs and pulls away.

"Don't let them know they are hurting your feelings and it won't be long until they stop doing it."

His mother's advice helps him cope with the pranks and soon he learns to use the humor in them to make friends.

<>

A couple years later, winter storms engulf the wilderness, holding it in their grip and it's colder than it has ever been. No one is able to leave the cavern long enough to gather fish. The den is famished and everyone is edgy.

Aram thinks about the den's plight as he sits near Leath in their special place. "I can tell by the way Fuzzy likes playing outside in the winter that his coat of fuzz helps keep him warmer than the other dragons," states Aram.

Leath is worried. There's only one reason he would say such a thing.

"I think it's time to tell the den that Fuzzy can go out in the cold and gather fish for them."

"No! He's too young. I would rather try myself than take a chance with our son," begs Leath.

"Neither you nor I are able. Nature made him the way he is to do this for us. I have watched him play in the cold and have seen him catch fish. He has a knack for it. This is his chance to finally be accepted by our den. I will worry just as much about him as you, but I know he can do this."

Leath looks into his eyes and concedes with a gentle nod. They walk to the cavern entrance. "Ureeeeee," he beckons. Slowly Sixteen hungry and cold den members gather to hear him.

"I know my son is young, but he's dependable. I believe because he is covered with a beautiful coat of fuzz, he will be able to withstand the cold and gather enough fish to get us out of this predicament."

"I'm too worried about his safety to ask you to do this," interrupts one of the mothers.

Aram looks at Fuzzy feeling a little fatherly pride. "Fuzzy, what do you think? Would you be afraid to go out alone and catch fish to bring back to the cavern?"

The den isn't as sure as Aram until they see Fuzzy's big smile and hear his reply.

"I'm honored that my den has faith in me. I'm sure I will be able to help, and you won't have to worry. If I start getting too cold, I will turn around and come back before I'm too far away. I will make you and my den proud."

The den bows in respect, and the proposal is accepted.

Fuzzy is full of energy as he departs on his first fishing trip.

The wind ripples through his fuzz and makes his eyes water as he tromps through knee-high snow. He finds the stream and brushes the powdery snow off the ice-covered water. The wind whips the powder away and he's surprised to see ice thicker than he has ever seen. He searches for a stone. It's the only way he'll be able to break through. Good fortune is with him, and soon he finds one with his foot, and quickly digs it out. It's just the right size. He strikes the ice several times before it cracks open. The water is frigid, and he gets frustrated splashing and grabbing at fish. He stops for a minute to calm himself.

He remembers a trick a very wise old dragon had shown him. He places his hand in the water and hums.

The fish feel a vibration in the water and they come to his hand. He slides a claw into their gills and picks them up. He catches three quickly, and returns to the cavern a cold, happy young dragon. The den cheers when they see him approaching with fish.

He ventures out again and again, returning each time with enough fish to provide for the den until the cold snowy weather ends.

<>

When summer arrives, he discovers the cavern sits in the midst of a beautiful landscape, begging to be explored. Playing with Leonard and Lester he discovers a mother bear has chosen a cave near the cavern to raise her cub.

One day Leath catches him peeking into the bear's cave. She runs over and pulls him away. "I know you are curious, but you must leave these bears alone."

A couple days later he finds the cub alone in the cave, and it's whimpering. Fuzzy persuades it to follow him back to the dragon's den.

Aram and Leath meet him at the entrance. "Fuzzy, what are you doing? You could get some of us mauled by the cub's mother," says Aram.

"The cub feels so much safer here, he's almost stopped crying. You understand don't you mom?" says Fuzzy as he looks at Leath, with his big eyes.

"I believe your father is right. What you're doing is risky. I'm glad that you want to help the little cub, but you must take him back." She follows as he returns the cub to its cave, then motions for him to follow her to a safe place where they can watch for the mother to return. Late that night the mother bear ambles to the cave and goes inside.

Fuzzy and Leath are happy and tired as they return to their cavern.

The next day, before the sun sets, Aram has to stop what he's doing and listen as Fuzzy tells him all about two birds having trouble with their nest on the other side of the plateau.

"I worry about Fuzzy. He is so concerned about the other animals around the den," says Aram.

"Fuzzy is just a little kinder than most dragons," replies Leath.

Sometimes the young dragons tease him for being so kind. They don't realize he has a valuable gift for gaining the trust of other creatures.

Chapter 2

After Fuzzy's eighth birthday, his desire for adventure grows stronger every day and he's independent enough for Aram and Leath to let him do as he pleases. They don't worry about him flying away from the cavern on his own. They think he's spending time with the other young dragons. However, savoring his new-found freedom he travels far into the wilderness alone. On a beautiful summer day when berries are ripe he's further from the cavern than his parents would approve. He's intrigued with a whole new world he has found where the landscape is flat, and the discovery fills him with enthusiasm. He sails along, watching a green canopy unfold below and it stretches south as far as he can see. An occasional hole appears in the canopy, and they look like a perfect place for a dragon to land. Fuzzy soon discovers they mark the spots where meadows are thriving, and that's where his favorite fruit grows.

Curious and always hungry, he flies lower where the smell of ripe berries bursting with juice drifts into the air. As he sails below the tree line he sees it's full of delicious berries. He lands to find out if they taste as good as they look. As he fills his mouth with juicy ripe fruit, he hears a sound he has never heard before.

Curiosity wells and he carefully tiptoes in the direction the sound is coming from. He slips behind a fallen tree where he can easily hide. Slowly and carefully, he peeks over to see what's making the sound.

Below, he sees two strange creatures, nothing like he has ever seen. They aren't very large, and they stand upright on two legs. He marvels, seeing how easily they can pick things up and throw them.

They're young, and something about them overwhelms his curiosity, making it impossible to take his eyes off them. The two creatures chase each other and make sounds that excite him. Recognizing they're having fun overwhelms his judgement and he forgets to stay hidden.

The two creatures stop and stare with caution and curiosity at the beautifully colored animal looking in their direction. They move closer to one another and gaze for a moment. Fuzzy feels there is no danger and a broad smile fills his face giving him a friendly demeanor. Something about him is appealing, like a puppy, and his gift for making new friends is winning their trust.

They look at each other again and smile, then motion for him to join them.

Fuzzy is excited! Filled with anticipation, he climbs down to where they are.

Slowly, they play again motioning for him to join in. He watches for a few minutes, then claps with joy—he knows how to play hide and seek.

The three young creatures play for an hour. They're lost in the magic of childhood playing when they hear a loud cry in the distance.

"Cap! Jackson! Where are you?" a voice echoes. "You better listen to your mom and come here right now!"

Shocked, he wonders if their mother is on her way to protect them, like he had been warned the bear cub's mother would do.

The children stop playing and stand still. She sounds angry so he runs and hides.

"I told you children not to get out of my sight. You haven't picked any berries and now it's time to head home." She is much bigger than his new friends, and the look on her face is not pleasing, as she scolds them.

Filled with fear, his instinct warns him to never let any of these creatures other than the young ones see him. He's sad to see his friends leave.

As soon as he feels it's safe to come out, he flies back to his den, but playing with these new friends called "children" was a lot of fun, and he is still intrigued. He continues to think about them and hopes to return one day. Deciding to stay out of trouble for flying further away from the cave than his parents would approve, he never tells anyone about his encounter. A year later, he returns to the meadow where he played with the children, but he's thinking about the mouthwatering berries he found before. In the distance, he hears the children playing.

He crawls under some bushes and moves closer to the sound so he can take a peek and see if this could possibly be the children their mother calls Cap and Jackson.

They're there, helping their mom and other adults pick his berries.

"You boys are old enough now to pick as many berries as the rest of us." He recognizes their mom's voice. She looks the same, but Cap and Jackson are bigger.

"Can we at least look around for a few minutes?" asks Jackson.

"Not this time. We need to finish and head home."

His curiosity is raging now that he has seen his new friends again, and he is determined to see the cavern where their den lives.

Very carefully he follows them and is surprised to see their family doesn't live in a cavern! He's puzzled. Why would any creature want to build a shelter like theirs? It's made of wood!

Looking around, being careful not to be seen, he discovers a lot of animals live there, too. Cap and Jackson's family have built shelters out of wood to protect animals from the weather, and they feed them, too.

Seeing all the shelters and fences makes him wonder why their family has to work so hard to have the things they need.

He realizes how lucky he is to be a dragon, but now he is more curious than ever, and he wants to know about Cap and Jackson and their way of life.

The sky turns a beautiful red and orange as the sun is setting, and it's time to fly home, but he promises himself that one day soon he will come back for an adventure. The next day, Fuzzy sees Lester and Leonard chasing each other. "Let's play hide and seek!" He is eager to play the game again.

"Okay. You count first," replies Lester.

Fuzzy smiles as he starts counting.

Lester opens his wings and sweeps into the sky flying north while Leonard heads south.

When he opens his eyes, they're nowhere to be seen. He forgot how hard it is to play hide and seek with other dragons.

He looks for them for a little while and gives up. All he can do is wait until they have their fun and return.

"Couldn't find us, could you?" jokes Leonard, hours later.

"Sure, I could! I was just tricking both of you."

"Now, Fuzzy, we can tell when you're not telling the truth," says Lester.

"I'm just kidding. Let's go find something good to eat."

They run and sail along, having fun with each other until they find a meadow filled with fruit trees.

"Lots of animals are scampering around, eating in this meadow. I'm surprised not one of them is acting as if they're afraid of us."

"I will show you how to get their attention," says Leonard.

He hops onto a large boulder, takes a deep breath, squints his eyes, puckers his cheeks, and releases a blast of red and yellow flames into the air, followed by a deafening roar that sends chills down Lester and Fuzzy's spines.

The roar echoes in the trees. Birds flutter away precariously, while every animal that can darts out of sight.

"Wow," says Fuzzy, feeling his heart race. "That's amazing, but don't you feel sorry for all those animals you just frightened?"

Lester shakes his head, "Fuzzy, look at us. We're meant to be respected by the other animals. Nature made us content to be peaceable but also equipped us with fire, teeth, and claws to protect ourselves. Sometimes we need to remind ourselves and the other animals how powerful we are."

"You'll be glad you're this powerful when you have to protect our den someday," says Leonard.

Playing with his friends is fun, and he's learning things a young dragon needs to know. He's content to stay around the den and play with the other young dragons for the rest of the summer.

When spring arrives, he's fascinated when he realizes he can leave the cavern for a day or two without his mother worrying about him. She knows dragons his age can take care of themselves in the wilderness. This freedom is important to build the confidence needed by a young dragon.

He decides it's time to visit Cap and Jackson. Taking the risk of flying too far away fills him with zest and a feeling of freedom. His only worry is finding just the right place to land where he'll be hidden from the children's mother.

He lands and carefully creeps up to one of the wooden shelters. Cap is feeding pigs when he catches a glimpse of Fuzzy peeking out from behind the barn. Cap's startled and puts his hand over his throbbing heart when he first sees him. It takes a few seconds for Cap to calm down. A smile fills his face, and he runs toward Fuzzy. "What are you doing here?" he asks softly.

Fuzzy cocks his head trying to understand. Cap smiles and shakes his head, then motions for him to follow him into the woods. "Go home boy," he says, and after Cap gestures for him to skedaddle, Fuzzy understands. Looking back as he prepares to leave, he sees Cap is sad and realizes he is only concerned for his safety. An unexplainable feeling of trust is present as he takes to the air. Flying home he is satisfied that Cap will have a plan next time he visits.

Cap is thrilled by the experience, and he's filled with nervous energy. He runs around searching for Jackson and when he finds him he's too excited to talk. He stops and catches his breath before he tells him about the fuzzy dragon coming to the farm.

"Why didn't you come find me so I could see him, too?" asks Jackson.

"I was worried someone would see him, and the only thing I could think to do was send him home."

"I guess that was the best thing to do," says Jackson, looking sad. "We need to think of a plan so we can visit with him without worrying, in case he returns."

"I'm sure he will come back! I can't explain why but I just know he is going to come back," assures Cap.

They talk about the dragon all evening as they work, and they begin to call him Fuzzy.

That night in their room, they scheme. They're two little boys lying in their beds with visions of dragons in their heads as they excitedly discuss the possibilities. They agree the safest place for him to hide is in the corn crib when he returns. It's further from the daily activities than any of the other sheds, and it's next to the woods.

<>

Fuzzy curls up in his grassy bed and ponders Cap's reaction to his visit. As he relives the moment, he feels sure Cap's only concern is for his safety. He lies there, wondering if he really is beginning to understand what Cap is thinking. The possibility of a real friendship with another creature that appears to be as intelligent as any dragon fuels his desire to return.

<>

"I hope Fuzzy will return now that we have a plan," says Jackson the next day when they're alone playing.

"It won't be long. I can't explain why, but I can feel he's just as curious about us as we are about him," assures Jackson.

The boys wonder why there are so many evil legends and stories about dragons. They will have to be careful. They don't want the young dragon to be hurt just because he wants to play with them.

<>

Looking out over the landscape from the cavern entrance, Fuzzy is contemplating his next trip to the farm when a friend walks up.

"Want to play hide and seek?" asks Leonard.

"Not really," says Fuzzy. He's tempted to say that hide and seek is more fun with his new friends, but he realizes he can never mention them to Leonard and Lester. They would want to go with him to see what he's talking about. He shudders at the thought of Lester jumping up on one of the farm buildings and spewing fire into the air and roaring.

Lester interrupts. "Let's go see who can catch the biggest fish. We can take what we catch back to the den and everyone will think we've been working."

Fuzzy and his dragon friends enjoy the day fishing, and soon they're making plans to explore and play together every day for a while, and he doesn't venture to Cap and Jackson's farm.

<>

Cap and Jackson are playing in the barn loft, pretending they can fly like Fuzzy as they jump into a pile of straw below. The bell rings for supper, and they race to the kitchen. As they enter, their mother, Inez, is setting the last bowl of food on the table. Miles, their father, is already sitting at the table discussing farming problems with his brother, Matt. When the boys run in hungry and excited they stop talking and smile, waiting for Inez to make them go wash their hands first. When they return the family eats and enjoys casual conversation.

"Dad, have you ever seen a real dragon?" ask Jackson calmly.

He can tell by the look on Cap's face that he's surprised and concerned his brother is going to get them into trouble. His jaw drops.

"I don't believe there is such a thing," Miles says with a little laugh and a big grin on his face. He doesn't even stop chewing.

When Cap sees that big grin, he relaxes and is no longer worried.

"There are stories about dragons, but no one ever has any proof," Miles continues, still smiling. "Dragons are kind of like Yeti. Lots of people talk about seeing one but no one ever brings proof to the village or sees one when others are around to witness what they say is true."

Uncle Matt perks up and grins. "I know better! I hear they're fierce creatures that can blow fire from their nostrils hot enough to cook a bear in a minute! They have sharp teeth and long sharp claws!"

Jackson and Cap look at Matt with their mouths open.

"Matt," says their father, urging him to stop talking.

"It's true! Dragons are fierce creatures and very dangerous. Some people in our village have told me they're sure they have lost cows and chickens to dragons."

"Now, Matt, no one ever saw a dragon do any of those things. Don't get the boys worked up over something that doesn't even exist. They'll be afraid to go out at night and tend the animals."

Matt only smiles. No more is said about dragons. Several weeks pass. Cap and Jackson wonder if Fuzzy is ever going to return. It's mid-summer and the farm work shifts into a slower pace as the crops grow. The brothers have more time to play together.

Jackson is playing alone near the corn crib when he hears footsteps behind the crib and thinks it's Cap. He jumps around the corner to scare him.

"Aaah!" he yells.

"Umph!" snorts Fuzzy, stumbling backwards.

Shocked, the boy and the dragon jerk away and start to run. When they realize what's happening, they fall in the grass, rolling in laughter and relief.

Jackson has an uncanny feeling Fuzzy will understand what he says so he tells him to hide behind the corn crib while he looks for Cap. Fuzzy crouches behind the building. Seeing Fuzzy do as he asks makes his eyes almost pop out. He takes a deep breath and takes off running.

"Cap, Cap!" he hollers.

Cap steps out of the barn just as Jackson reaches the door. "What's wrong now?"

"Fuzzy is here, and I can talk to him!" he says, gasping for air, and looking around to see if anyone else can hear them.

"Are you telling the truth? I think you're fooling."

Jackson smiles triumphantly as he leads Cap to the corn crib. Cap looks behind the building, and there sits Fuzzy. The three of them smile broadly. They're glad to be together again. Sitting behind the corn crib, they begin to realize a strange magical feeling is present when they're close together.

"I'm glad Fuzzy has come to visit! I like the feeling I get when he's near. I think the feeling helps me understand what he's thinking," says Jackson.

"I get the same feeling too," replies Cap. "Watch him, I bet he understands what we're saying to each other just like he does when we talk to him."

Fuzzy smiles and moves into the light as he listens to them. They're spellbound by his beautiful colors as the sun makes his fuzz radiant. The round red spot on the top of his head and shiny dark blue fuzzy body glistens. A short little horn grows on each side of his red spot, making him look mythical. However, those beautiful colors cause them to worry. It will be hard to keep Fuzzy from being seen, especially that bright red spot.

"He's studying us, too," says Cap.

Just then the boy's mother calls out loudly. "Boys, it's time to come in for the night."

So, you're called 'boys'? thinks Fuzzy.

"Did you hear him?" Cap asks Jackson.

"I did," answers Jackson.

Cap looks at Fuzzy. "Will you allow me to lock you in the corn crib so we can safely hide you for the night?"

"I will. I'm not going home tonight, and I know you want to keep me out of the weather in a wood shelter like you live in." The boys hear him reply without speaking.

In the morning, Cap and Jackson return to let Fuzzy out, but he is already behind the corn crib where they usually meet. "I opened the latch and came out."

"We can play for a while, but we must stay out of sight. We should play in the woods," suggests Jackson.

"Lead the way," says Fuzzy.

They run toward a creek the boys like to splash in. Fuzzy steps up to a clear pool of water and submerges his hand. Seconds later, he catches a nice fish.

"Wow! Did you see that, Jackson?" says Cap.

"How did you do that?" blurts Jackson.

"Catching fish is easy for me. I place my hand deep in the water and hum. The fish swim to me, and I scoop them up."

"I don't believe you. Are you trying to trick us?" asks Jackson.

"Come stand beside me and see for yourself."

Jackson looks into the water as he stands beside Fuzzy. He appears to be humming, but the boys hear nothing.

"There he is," says Fuzzy. "Quick! Get him!"

Jackson grabs the fish but it wiggles loose and swims away. "I can't believe that just happened," says

Jackson excited and placing his hands on both sides of his head.

In the distance, the porch bell rings.

"That means mom has fixed our lunch. Don't go away. We'll come back after we eat."

"I'm hungry, too." He eats the fish and finds lots of fruit and vegetables. After he feasts, he lies down to wait for his friends to return. "I'm really glad you're still here!" says Jackson.

"Look at all those muscadines way up in the top of that tree you're lying under. I bet you could fly up there and get us a bunch of them," suggests Cap.

"I would be glad to help you." Fuzzy smiles and hops into the air. With two gusty flaps of his wings, he's at the top of the tree. With one claw, he shakes the vine and muscadines rain down.

"Look out!" yells Cap as he covers his head and runs out from under the tree. Jackson laughs and lets the fruit fall on him.

Fuzzy glides gently to the ground.

Playing and eating, they eat until they don't want to ever see a muscadine again. It's so much fun playing with Fuzzy that time just slips away.

Cap looks toward the sun to see what time it is, but it's already behind the tree line. It's time to start their evening chores.

"You can explore out here in the woods while Cap and I work," says Jackson sadly. The boys don't want to leave, but they have no choice. They finish the chores, eat supper, then return. Fuzzy is waiting behind the crib.

"Just to be safe, I am going to lock you in the corn crib again tonight," Cap tells him, adding a wire to the latch this time, to be sure Fuzzy stays inside where he will be safe.

The next morning, Fuzzy is playing behind the corn crib. He smiles at them as he chews on an ear of dry corn.

The boys worry that someone, especially Uncle Matt, will see him. They feel it's up to them to do a better job of locking him in the corn crib, but nothing they do stops Fuzzy from leaving when he's ready. Opening the latch is a game to him, and he always wins.

"I give up, Fuzzy is as smart as me," concedes Cap.

"We shouldn't lock up a creature as smart as Fuzzy," remarks Jackson.

From that day on they treat Fuzzy as they treat each other, and they respect him too much to lock him up, or ever consider him a pet.

The three friends play together for a whole week. Then one evening, Cap and Jackson's mom is curious about where they're playing. She can hear them out near the corn crib and decides to take a look.

Fuzzy's instinct tells him someone is coming. "I must hide," he tells Cap and Jackson. He hides under the corn crib and holds his breath long before she gets close.

"What have you boys been doing all week? I have missed not getting to see you as much as usual." The boys hug her but give no answer. She smiles contently and goes back to her work.

Fuzzy crawls out from under the corn crib. He realizes he has been away from his den for a long time, and he misses his family. "I have had a lot of fun playing with you, but I have to go home." The boys nod sadly.

"When I come back, I will have a gift for each of you. It will be a symbol of our friendship. If another dragon sees it, he will know you're a dragon's friend."

The boys watch as Fuzzy flies away in the direction of the dragon den.

The next day, they overhear their father talking with Uncle Matt. The men are unhappy as they talk about someone stealing apples off the trees near the woods and taking vegetables out of the garden.

"I will catch whoever did this, even if I have to watch the garden every day," says father smacking his right fist into his open left hand.

"I miss Fuzzy but it's a good thing he left for home," says Cap.

"Hopefully by the time he comes back, father and Matt will have forgotten about the fruit and vegetables," replies Jackson.

<>

Fuzzy lands in the cavern entrance and everyone he passes smiles and greets him. He heads for his family's special place and as he enters, he feels the love and safety he can't find anywhere else.

Leath smiles. "Fuzzy, I have missed you so much! Don't stay gone this long again." She hugs him like the boys' mom hugged her sons.

He doesn't mention going to a farm or playing with children. He hopes they will think he's adventurous and busy exploring the world around the cavern.

Lying in his grass bed near his family, he remembers how pleasing it is hearing everyone tell him that they miss him when he's gone, and his loyalty for the den grows. He misses his friends, but he's content playing with the other young dragons and helping his den prepare for winter. Winds and snow come and Fuzzy is content to stay close to his family while it's cold and stormy. As soon as flowers begin blooming again, he can hardly wait to head back to the farm. A beautiful spring day fills him with irresistible need for adventure, and soon, he's behind the corn crib, waiting for his friends. Jackson sees him.

"Fuzzy!" he hollers and runs toward the crib. Both boy and dragon are glad to see each other.

Cap walks up, showing a little less excitement. Fuzzy wonders what's on his mind.

"I have something really important you need to know. It's more dangerous this time for us to be together. Our father and Uncle Matt will be watching the orchard and garden to be sure nothing happens to our apples and vegetables like last year."

"Am I in trouble?"

Cap and Jackson explain the importance of gardens and fruit trees, and how hard the farmers have to work plowing, planting, and harvesting their food for winter.

"Farmers even have to plant and harvest the feed the farm animals depend on, too. Soon, you will understand how a farm works. Don't worry," says Jackson.

Just then, Uncle Matt calls out. "Where are you, boys? I need help putting straw in the chicken house."

Cap, Jackson, and Fuzzy flinch at the sudden call.

"We will be back in a little while," whispers Cap. "We will have to be more careful than we have been."

Fuzzy hides behind the crib thinking about what the boys had explained to him, and then he quietly crawls into the woods.

The three are back together at the corn crib a little later that day.

"I brought both of you a gift as I promised." Fuzzy gives Cap and Jackson two small, round yellow stones. "Take care of these and keep them with you at all times. They have a mystical effect on dragons. They're small pieces of hatching stone and will protect you if you show them to a dragon. When he sees the stone, he will know you have an understanding of us."

Cap and Jackson are in awe as they take the stones that feel strangely warm and look like the center of a dragon's eye. "Thank you. We're honored that you care for our safety," says Cap, turning the stone taking in its beauty.

"I'm glad we're friends. I enjoy being with you and learning about farming and your family. I can tell your family works hard to provide for you and the animals."

Cap is captivated by the stone. "I wish we could see and learn about your den and explore your cavern," he says.

"I wish you could, too. It's safe when it storms and never too hot in the summer or too cold in the winter. It's vast and filled with many chambers, each one is different. We could run, hide, and explore together for days in it. The ceilings are amazing. They're covered with colorful rock spikes draping toward the floor. The floor is so far below the spikes that you could set your barn inside and not even be close to touching them."

"I wish we could see where your cavern is. I know we could never go inside, but it would be fun to at least see the entrance," says Cap, not noticing Jackson looks concerned.

"If you can spend one night hiding with me in the forest, I can keep you safe, but be absolutely sure you have the pieces of hatching stone with you."

"Do you think one night is all we will be away from our home?" asks Jackson gritting his teeth.

"I can't wait. I will ask our dad tonight," says Cap energetically.

<>

After supper Cap is excited as he approaches his father. Jackson is by his side, but his stomach is queasy.

Miles relaxes on the porch, thinking how nice it is to be alone without a care in the world.

"Father, Jackson and I want to go camping overnight in the edge of the wilderness by ourselves," explains Cap, smiling and bright-eyed.

"I wouldn't let you go camping in the edge of the wilderness with me much less by yourselves," he says in no uncertain terms. "I can tell I have to teach you boys to respect the wilderness."

They're disappointed, realizing their father is right.

The next day, they tell Fuzzy it will be several years before they can go with him to see the cavern.

"I understand. Your father loves you. I can tell human children aren't as capable of surviving in the wilderness as a young dragon like me." They play until evening and as the sun begins to set, Fuzzy seems sad. "It's time for me to return to my den. I'm taking a chance staying here too long. I promise next time we get together, I will take each of you for a ride you will never forget. Hopefully, next time Uncle Matt and your father won't be watching so closely."

"I won't forget!" says Cap.

Fuzzy gently flaps his wings and rises into the sky as the boys wave goodbye.

<>

When he lands at the cavern entrance, his father is nearby.

"I have been looking for you for days. Where are you going and staying so long?"

Fuzzy knows he has to tell him the truth. He has always let the den presume he is gone a lot because he is curious about the wilderness. This time he must tell the whole story. He will not risk losing the respect of his father, whom he loves too much to tell a lie.

"I have been flying out of the wilderness to a farm where I have made friends with two young boys. We have fun playing together."

His father gasps. "Son, I have failed to teach you the most important lesson of all. Think of all the pain and suffering you could bring upon our den. We need to have a long talk. Do you realize what you have done? Please, never tell any of the other dragons about this, especially your mother."

Fuzzy's eyes fill with tears. He has disappointed his father and done something the den would disapprove of.

"How old are your friends?" asks his father.

"They're my age, or maybe younger," replies Fuzzy, his head bowed in shame.

"Has anyone else seen you?"

Fuzzy shakes his head. "No one, except my two friends. I promise."

His father's frown fades. "Never go back. When humans grow older they change and will not want to be your friends anymore. All children can be friends and play together but grown up dragons and grown up humans cannot."

Fuzzy thinks about what his father says and realizes Uncle Matt and the boys' father are grown up, and he's afraid of them.

"When you're older you will understand better, but it's important that humans don't believe there is such a thing as dragons. You need to enjoy your life around the den and live like a dragon. The only way you can live like a dragon is to keep humans away from the den and our hunting grounds. Fuzzy, what you did was a bad idea. I know you're curious and concerned about every creature you meet. I forgive you, but you must promise to remember what I've told you."

"I promise, Father." Fuzzy is very humble and respectful.

"Humans are very curious creatures, and the only way to keep them away is to never let them know we exist."

Chapter 3

Two years pass and the boys see no sign of their dragon friend. They stop thinking he may show up and wonder what has happened to him.

One day after lunch, Cap and Jackson are working in the barn with no one else around. Jackson is scooping hay with a pitchfork and tossing it into a leather tarp. When the tarp is full, Cap pulls it up and dumps it in the loft. After a while, Cap climbs down to rest. He's quiet and wrinkles his brow. He pulls a straw from the pile and chews on it for a moment, then jerks it out flipping it to the floor.

"I can't stand it any longer. I have to tell mom and dad about Fuzzy. I even wonder sometimes if we just imagined him."

"Oh, he was real alright. It was amazing. If he wasn't real, we wouldn't each have a piece of hatching stone," states Jackson leaning back in the straw. "The only thing I still wonder about is if he tricked us when he showed us how to catch fish by humming."

"That was too real to be a trick," replies Cap. "I'm going to tell the family tonight. It's time they knew about part of our lives they know nothing about."

That night, as the family sits around the supper table, Cap gathers his wits. "Jackson and I have an unbelievable story to share with you. It's about something that happened to us when we were children."

Everyone stops talking. Jackson is apprehensive. He wishes Cap would quit worrying about Fuzzy and leave well enough alone.

"Several years ago, even though we were only children, you took us to the wilderness to help pick berries. We were more trouble than help and you didn't notice when we slipped away. While we were playing, we spotted a young dragon watching us. He looked friendly so we waved for him to come over. In no time, we were playing together."

Uncle Matt asks the first question. "How big was this *friendly* dragon you played with?"

The boy's eyes brighten, they have wanted so long to share their experience with their family.

"The dragon was young like us, but he was a foot taller than me," answers Cap.

"He was two feet taller than me," replies Jackson.

Miles hasn't taken a bite since he heard the word "dragon." He spoons a bite and asks his question. "What kind of games did you play?

Jackson is getting braver. "We played hide and seek," he explains, talking faster he continues. "Later, he came to visit us here at the farm. We went fishing and picked muscadines." He stops abruptly when Inez gets up and starts gathering dishes to wash. The boys look at each other, the adults aren't taking their story seriously. Miles and Matt are chewing happily with big smiles on their faces.

"What did this dragon look like?" asks Uncle Matt taking a bite of pie.

"He had red fuzz on his head and dark blue fuzz covering rest of his body," answers Cap.

The adults burst into laughter.

Miles looks at the boys still smiling broadly. "That is a good tale, boys. But it would be a good idea not to mention it to anyone else."

Cap and Jackson are embarrassed but also relieved. Their conscience is clear. They tried to tell their family about dragons, and if anything ever happens, they can say, "we tried to tell you."

That night in their bedroom, they agree not to ever mention Fuzzy to anyone again.

Two years pass and they have grown into young men. Cap is still slightly taller than Jackson. They long for adventure, as would any strong young man who has worked hard since he was a child. Full of energy, they're the picture of health.

One evening as they stack corn in the corn crib, they hear a noise behind the building.

"Fuzzy maybe?" says Cap, cutting his eyes toward Jackson.

They run to see, but nothing is there.

"I just knew that was going to be our old friend hiding where he always did," says Jackson.

They stroll back and return to work.

"I have to admit, I thought he might have been there, too. I often think of all the fun we had playing with him," says Cap

They only have each other to share dragon talk with. They're too old now to mention dragons to anyone. The time has come for the young men to reason out on their own what dragons in the wilderness will mean for them and their family's future.

"Let's promise each other that as soon as we get permission to go camping in the wilderness, we will try at least one time to find Fuzzy's cavern," says Cap.

A year passes. Cap is eighteen and Jackson is sixteen. They yearn more than ever for adventure and a chance to find Fuzzy before they have farms and families of their own to take care of.

One evening, as they're riding around the farm, they stop on a knoll that looks out over the wilderness.

"Look at the beautiful green world out there. Can you imagine how many wonderful places must be hidden beneath those trees?" asks Cap. "There could be a better place for a farm just out of sight." He pauses, in thought. "I know what we need to do if we're going to talk father into letting us go on our adventure," he says, bright-eyed. "We will tell him we want to explore the countryside along the edge of the wilderness so we can find a good place to build our own farms someday. Then, as we work hard all summer, we will mention the adventure to him every now and then. In the fall, when the harvest is all put up, we will make him feel obligated to let us go."

They work hard all summer and keep hinting about going on their camping adventure.

One evening after supper, when the last of the harvest is stored away, the boys sit on the porch talking to their father. It has been a long, hot summer and the cool evening air on the back porch puts Miles, Inez, and the brothers into a good mood. The sunset is dying as darkness creeps toward the porch.

"Father," says Cap. "We have worked very hard this summer, and we're growing up. It's time for you to let us go on our adventure we have talked about.

"I still don't think you boys are ready for the wilderness," says Miles with a slight grimace.

"Time doesn't stand still for any of us. This could be the last time we will have a chance to go together and explore for our future. You were my age when you, mom, and Uncle Matt came out here and started homesteading this farm, and this was wilderness," argues Cap.

"But that was different…" Miles starts but wrinkles his brow and abruptly stops. He sits quietly for a minute, looking toward the wilderness. "Your mother and I will worry, and not rest until you return safe and sound," he finishes.

Inez is shocked and tears trickle down her cheeks. She remembers how frightened she was until the log walls of their cabin stood between them and the wilderness creatures.

"How can you let these boys go like this?" she asks.

"These boys are young men now. I feel obligated to give them a little freedom. They're old enough to make their own decisions," he replies with a long face.

Cap and Jackson experience a flood of emotions. "Mom, we love you so much it breaks our hearts to see you cry. Please, have faith in us so we can enjoy our little bit of temporary freedom," pleads Cap.

Jackson walks over and hugs her. She grips him tightly.

"Thanks, dad, we will be careful. You don't need to worry," says Cap. Seeing the sadness in his father's eyes tames his enthusiasm.

They quietly retreat to their room, excitement slowly growing again as they make plans. Filled with confidence and youthful energy they can't wait to hunt, fish, and camp for a couple months. Living beside the wilderness has taught them something new every day about its cruel beauty, and they know how to take care of themselves. They also have the two little pieces of hatching stone Fuzzy gave them.

<>

Inez looks at Miles with tears welling in her eyes. She leans her worried head on his shoulder, and they drip on his shirt.

He puts his arm around her. "Don't worry, dear. I don't think they will be gone more than a couple weeks. I know from experience that the fun of camping in the wilderness wears off quickly."

Inez is no less worried. "Are you sure they will be safe?"

"Sure, they will. I have watched them shoot their bows, and they can outshoot me. They have their knives. Remember how I used to play with them when they were learning how to use a loadstone pointer? They figured it out much faster than I did. They can't get lost," Inez cocks her head; she knows he's trying to sound confident. The whole house is too quiet the rest of the evening.

That night Inez cries softly until she drifts off to sleep. Miles's heart aches as he lies next to her. He has been pretending he's not worried, but his stomach is tied in knots. He knows how unpredictable the wilderness can be.

Soon, the morning the parents and Uncle Matt are dreading arrives. The brothers are leaving in a few minutes and reality hits hard. Everyone looks worried, and their emotions are on edge.

"My heart will hardly be able to bear the pain, when you walk away from this porch," says Inez, crying.

"I wish your father could handle all the farm work by himself so I could go and look after you boys," says Uncle Matt, smearing tears across his face with his fingers.

"Please be careful and wise in your decisions. Don't get too confident or horse around having so much fun that you aren't aware of what could happen at any moment. And don't be too proud to come back early. I love both of you so get this thing done so we can all stop worrying," states Miles.

"We will be careful. We love all of you, too," says Cap hugging his mother, then his father.

Jackson can only wave goodbye he doesn't want to cry in front of them.

They're hardly out of sight and Miles is already experiencing deeper remorse. He tries not to walk around frowning, but smiling is going to be a task until his sons are home again.

<>

After walking a little while, Jackson speaks for the first time. "Mom and dad broke my heart as we were leaving. Now I feel guilty for being excited about this adventure."

"It's time for us to have a taste of freedom and enjoy our trip," replies Cap confidently. A cool day filled with abundant rays of sunlight adds to the thrill the young men feel as they taste more freedom than they have ever experienced. Going is easy in the countryside near the farm, explorers and hunters have cleared paths in the forest, but soon the paths fade, nature has repaired her wounds, and hard work replaces leisurely walking as they hack limbs, briars, and underbrush so they can continue. To their surprise, it's harder work than farming.

"If something happens to me, I want you to know I realize how lucky I have been to be your brother," says Jackson

"You're just homesick. Don't get all mushy on me, we're going to be fine," says Cap, feeling a closer bond with his brother.

"Well, that may be true, but don't you find yourself checking your bow and arrows more often the further from home we get?"

Cap laughs, realizing Jackson is right.

The first week is filled with discoveries and fun, even with all the hard work. Inez lovingly filled their packs with dried beef, rolled oats, bread, and honey to help with their meals. Every time they come upon a river or lake, they try to catch fish. They don't want to take a chance of running low on food.

One evening after sitting and fishing for a long time without getting a bite, they give up on catching their supper and talk.

"I wish Fuzzy was here. We would already have more fish than we need," says Jackson, throwing a skipping stone. It hops three times.

"Yeah, and then he would start a fire for us so we could smoke them," replies Cap as he carefully rolls up his twine and hook for later.

"I hope mom and dad aren't too sad thinking about us tonight," says Jackson, watching the sun sink below the trees.

"I wish mom was here now. I miss her more all the time. We're spending so much time mending our clothes and preparing food we can't go far each day." Cap sighs.

"You forgot about washing our clothes. That's what I get tired of. It's pretty cold out here changing clothes, and then we have to wait for them to dry," complains Jackson.

There are no fish to smoke this evening, but they enjoy talking. Some days, the campsite doesn't move. It takes all day to fix things they must have before they travel again.

The weather is growing colder and takes a lot of energy out of the young men. They spend more time building campfires and cooking. They're always hungry now and have to hunt and fish more often.

"I still want to find Fuzzy, but this is getting to be a lot of hard work," complains Jackson. "Some days, I find myself wondering if this adventure is going to be worth all this trouble."

"Trust me, if we give up now we would regret not finishing our trip for the rest of our lives," replies Cap.

"You're right. It's almost time to bed down for the night, and that's when I get depressed, missing home."

"When the sun goes down, I feel guilty knowing how much mom is worrying about us. But during the day, I feel sorry for father and Uncle Matt. I hope things are going well at the farm so they don't have to work too hard," says Cap, pulling a blanket out of his pack.

Chopping through the thick underbrush is so laborious they only travel twenty miles in fourteen days. On the fifteenth day, at midday they find a cave that looks inviting. It fills them with intrigue, and they can hardly wait to go inside.

"I can't believe how lucky we are to find such good shelter," says Cap, a big smile on his face as he drops his pack and looks around the opening.

"I will go in first. You stay outside. I want to be sure it's empty. This could be some creature's den." He looks in cautiously and sets an arrow, and then he steps in. He's blind, and his heart races until his eyes adjust to the dim light.

Jackson stands outside with an arrow set in his bow. He squats, trying to see Cap. He bites his lip nervously when his brother disappears in the darkness.

He doesn't have to wait long.

"Come on in!" yells Cap, satisfied there are no animals inside.

"It's pretty dark in here," says Jackson as he steps inside."

"It will be too easy to get into trouble until we know all about this place. We need to be able to see better in here," says Cap, and he heads outside to gather fire wood

They don't mention it to each other, but they know too well that even a harmless injury could mean the difference between life and death this far from home.

As the fire grows, it lights up the cave, and the warmth is tantalizing.

"Now that I can see where I am walking, I want to look around to see if this could have once have been where Fuzzy lived," says Jackson.

After a good look, they know the cave is too small for a dragon's den, and there aren't any dangerous places to worry about, but something just doesn't seem right. They look closely at the walls and find marks where picks and chisels have hewn away the rock and dirt. They are struck with the same realization at the same time

"This is an abandoned mine," they blurt out in unison.

They begin searching for treasures. At the entrance, they see where campfires had been built long ago inside a ring of rocks surrounding a little pit. It sits waiting for a fire to be rekindled.

"I wonder what the miners found in here," says Cap, looking closely near the ring of rocks.

"Let's move our fire here where the old campfires were once built and burn all the leaves and trash that's lying around. We may find a clue," suggests Jackson.

The roof of the mine is lower over the fire than the entrance so the smoke rises and drifts out the entrance.

"I found something," says Cap as he tries to pick up an old pack that's too rotten to stay together. They find a lot of old rotten packs lying about filled with small rocks. All the rocks are broken into pieces the size of a man's thumb.

"Whatever is in these packs is what they were after," suggests Cap.

"Don't you think it's kind of spooky these were abandoned?" asks Jackson.

"Anything could have happened. I know most of the reasons aren't good, but obviously that was long ago," replies Cap.

"I guess you're right, but someone did a lot of work to just up and leave." Jackson scratches our several stones. "They just look like rocks to me. I'm going to take a handful of these stones back with us when we start home."

Cap thinks for a moment. "Why don't we put two stones in each pack, just in case? Something could happen and we wouldn't be able to come back. Two stones are plenty and will not slow either of us down," suggests Cap

"Good idea. I really want to know what these miners were taking out of here," says Jackson as he throws two stones into Cap's pack.

"I think this will be a good place to call our home away from home for the rest of our adventure," says Cap.

They are Immersed in the clutches of the wilderness where Nights come early, and the wilderness changes as the curtain of darkness settles in. Insects thirst for a taste of blood, while predators prowl in search of food. Cap and Jackson have from the beginning relished the warmth and security their campfire radiates around them.

Unfortunately, the beautiful dancing flames and ascending swirls of smoke can be seen for miles around and tells the dragons exactly where the creatures of civilization are spending the night. Feeling safer than ever in the mine, it never occurs to the brothers that Fuzzy's den has been watching their progress for days.

Chapter 4

Things are different at the den now that Aram surrendered to old age and passed. The den believes he, like all their ancestors, soars in the heavens of eternal peace, watching over them.

While the den respects and loves Fuzzy, his different appearance is too much for them to accept, and he is not chosen to be their leader. Lester, one of Fuzzy's childhood friends is chosen to lead. Fuzzy is pleased with the den's choice because Lester always shows him respect and relies on him to help with decisions that require wisdom and kindness.

Fuzzy is no longer the young, freehearted dragon Cap and Jackson once knew. He is fully-grown now, with a mate, Liz; a son, Lee; and a daughter, Kim. He's still kindhearted and wise and cares deeply for his den.

As evening approaches, Lester turns to Fuzzy with troubled eyes and a grimace on his face. "I can't ignore the threat these fires moving in our direction pose." He paces back and forth in front of the cavern entrance.

Fuzzy nods in agreement. "Let me fly out close to the campsite tonight. I will hide in the woods and see if I can figure out what's happening."

As the last of the evening's sunset fades away, Fuzzy walks to the edge of the plateau, leans forward, drops into the darkness, opens his wings, and sails in the direction of the last campfire.

He looks to the heavens, watching the stars twinkle as the moon peeks over the neighboring mountains. The rushing air sweeping over his face is refreshing and he sucks in a deep breath to help keep his mind off what he's about to do. Closing his eyes, peacefully sailing along, he hears his father's words run through his mind. *Never let them know we exist.*

He opens his eyes and looks intently into the distance. Something is different. There doesn't appear to be a fire. There has been one every evening for many days. "I don't want to go back and tell Lester I can't find the camp," he tells himself, beginning to feel uneasy.

Maybe something has happened to the men, and there will be no more fires. He circles around and is about to give up when a flash of fire light catches his eye, then disappears.

After several tries to find it again, he discovers the men have built the fire in a cave, and it's only visible when he's in front of the entrance.

He carefully studies the landscape, looking for a place where he can land without being heard. A meadow comes into view and he quietly lands. Time doesn't matter, so he slowly makes his way toward the cave's entrance. He creeps silently and gently, putting his weight on one foot at a time. He must not crunch leaves or break limbs. He inches into a place where he can see inside the cave. Smoke curls out of the entrance, rising into the night sky. Patiently watching, he sees two men, one inside at the fire and the other gathering wood. The smell of fish smoking drifts by, and it smells good. He decides to creep even closer hoping to get a better look at the men. He can't help wondering if this is Cap and Jackson, even though the chances are slim.

Curiosity drives him dangerously close, and he hears them talking.

"Jackson, don't you think that's enough fire wood for one night? Come over here and help me finish hanging these fish."

These are his old friends! Fuzzy is tempted. He wants to go into the cave and greet them, but he wonders if that is betraying his den's trust. The old feeling of guilt fills his conscience. He leans back and remembers all the good times they shared, and then worries about what is the right thing to do.

Uncertainty wins out. He's afraid to make contact. Life for him is more complicated now, and he needs to think about the trouble that could cause.

Hesitating to leave, he ponders his next move. He can see they're grown, and he remembers what his father had said. For tonight, the best thing he can do is slip away into the dark. Part of him hopes Cap and Jackson have the two small pieces of hatching stones with them. Seeing them again stirs his feelings of friendship, but it would be best if they don't meet.

From now on, he will need to check on them each night. He wants to know why they're here, and keep his den safe, too.

As he flies back, he doesn't enjoy the beauty of the fluffy white clouds lit up by the full moon. He's too busy wondering if the brothers are looking for him. Had his father been right about boys when they grow up? Why was he so foolish when he was young? If he had brought them to the cavern, something terrible could have happened, and the den would have known they could find their way back when they grew up.

That night, as he lays awake next to Liz, he tries to remember if the boys watched him fly toward his den when he left their farm. If they had, then they would know to head north. He has little doubt this is his fault, but how could they find their way in the wilderness?

Fuzzy can't rest. He needs to share his feelings with Liz. He tells her about the brothers and how he had played with them as children. Even though she's surprised and has a lot of questions, she just lets him talk.

"I knew after playing with them they're very intelligent, but I can't understand how they managed to come this close to our cavern. They can't navigate out here like me. I can see for miles in every direction when I am high in the sky. Even when it's too dark to see, I have an instinct for direction that humans don't have."

"Are you sure they don't have some of that instinct, too?" questions Liz.

"I'm sure they don't. Men have been out of the wilderness too long, they have lost almost all of their instincts."

"Young men like this will suffer and learn a lot of things the hard way on a trip out here," replies Liz.

"I guess that's why this is bothering me so badly. I think they have gone to a lot of trouble to find me, as a friend would do."

"Sounds to me like you still have feelings of friendship for these men?"

"When I was young, I gave each of them a small piece of hatching stone to show our eternal friendship. Even after all this time, I'm still concerned about their well-being."

"I know you too well, Fuzzy, you kindhearted dragon. Deep down, you want to visit again with your old friends." She smiles.

"Yes and no. I don't want to cause trouble for my den or for them. I don't want anyone hurt because of what I did when I was young."

"You may not have anything to worry about, even though they are close. They may still not find the cavern."

"You're right as always. Dragons live like dragons. We don't build fires or fences or do other things that attract attention. Our den doesn't even have a garden. The wilderness provides what we need and I'm thankful every day for our instinct and simple lifestyle."

Liz puts her wings around him and lays her head on his strong chest. "That's why I love you so much. You're thankful for what we have and care about every living thing."

Fuzzy peacefully closes his eyes, knowing he's lucky to have such an understanding mate.

<>

Waking up the first morning inside the mine feels strange. Cap looks at Jackson. It's dark except for several dying coals where the fire had languished in the night and a small glowing circle on the floor, illuminated by a shaft of sunlight slipping through the trees and streaming into the entrance. Jackson is awake and hears Cap uncovering. It feels strange not to see the sun rising.

"Good morning, brother," says Cap, standing to start the new day. "Last night was the first time in days I have slept peacefully." Jackson turns away his blanket and stands. Cap takes a long drink of water from his pouch and pulls a piece of smoked fish from the rack to share with Jackson.

"Let me guess what we're having for breakfast," jokes Jackson.

"The same thing we had for supper and lunch yesterday."

"Yuck. Somehow, I *have* to shoot a rabbit or squirrel today, or I'm going to go crazy eating fish all the time."

"I think we can spend a little time doing that. But first, let's make plans to continue our search from here," says Cap, sitting to think. "We just came from the south. I think we should fan out from here and travel five miles in each direction, spend two nights in the wilderness, and then head back here to spend a night in the safety of this old mine." Jackson nods in agreement. "Let's go outside, draw a circle in the dirt, and divide it into ten points. Each time we choose a new direction, we will start by drawing a line from the middle point to one of the points on the outer circle. That line will point us in the direction we are to take."

"You know what would really be neat," says Jackson. "We can fetch a big rock and put it in the center of the circle, and then at each of the ten points place a smaller one. That way neither rain nor wind will mess up our original plans."

"You're a genius," Cap laughs. "Let's do it."

Outside, near the entrance, they clear an area and draw a circle five-feet across in the dirt. They gather stones, and build their work of art.

"Someday someone will see this and try to guess its meaning," laughs Cap.

"I'm afraid we haven't thought about the most important part of this plan," states Jackson, holding his chin, studying the circle. "We can't stay out here any longer than we promised mom and dad."

"Right, we'll only go in as many directions as time will allow. The trail heading home is already chopped out making the return trip a lot faster, and with a little luck, we'll find Fuzzy's cavern soon, anyway.

"That only leaves one more problem for today," says Jackson with a big grin.

"Let me guess, you're thinking about going fishing."

Jackson smirks. "Grab your bow and let's go hunting rabbit or anything on legs." Then he laughs.

That evening, they return after a day of hunting and enjoying their brotherhood, carrying two plump pheasants.

"I will clean these birds in the woods. We don't want predators coming into the mine because they smell blood and feathers in here," states Jackson.

While Jackson cleans the birds, Cap kindles the fire, and soon they are relaxing as they cook their supper.

"These pheasants are delicious," says Jackson, closing his eyes savoring a bite. "I wish they hadn't been so pretty. I hated to shoot them."

As they bed down for the night, a thunderstorm rolls in the distance. The trees sway as faint flashes of lightning illuminate the forest. Feeling safe and dry in the mine, they pay no attention to the rain as it begins to fall. They drift off to sleep.

In the morning, the air smells fresh with the scent of trees and flowers surrounding the mine. The forest sparkles as sunrays dance on the dew that covers the trees. The sky is clear, and they're full of new energy.

"I'm really looking forward to these shorter trips," says Jackson as he slides his quiver over his shoulder and pulls back on the cord, testing his bow a couple times.

"We won't be too far from the safety of the mine, and I like the thought of that."

"With a little luck, this adventure will be a lot easier on us from now on." They walk out of the mine to their work of art lying on the ground.

"Jackson, you can have the honor of choosing the route we will take this time."

"Makes sense to me to start out going due west, then work our way around to the east."

"Exactly what I would have said myself," reassures Cap.

"I'm going to enjoy the wilderness today and take more time looking for clues or anything that looks interesting," says Jackson.

With a good night's sleep and a pleasant day to hike, they begin to experience more of the beauty in the wilderness. Pretty rocks along the creek banks beckon them to search for a jewel, and they discover mint growing close to the water. They stock up on the leaves to chew on and make tea. The forest floor is covered with leaves, ferns, and moss as they gently rise to hill tops adorned with boulders. Creeks and springs sparkle as they trickle along the bottom of most of the hills.

Cap moves ahead of Jackson and stops on top of the hill. "Wow, how beautiful."

Jackson quickly moves up beside him to see what has seized his attention, and marvels at the landscape below. The streams flowing at the bottom of the hills empty into a large lake sparkling in the sunlight. At the bottom of the slope, little waves lap at the shoreline. The water is crystal clear at the edge and blue as the sky further out. Large rocks jut majestically out of the water in the middle of the lake forming an island.

"I'll race you to the shoreline!" cries Jackson as he darts down the hill toward the lake. Cap is close behind. They slide to a stop at the edge of the water and look around at unbelievable beauty hidden in the wilderness. Surrounding the shore are several smooth, white, sandy beaches separated by large piles of rocks, making each beach a new place to explore.

"I bet I know what you're thinking," says Cap.

"I can't wait to catch a bunch of fish?" replies Jackson, joking.

"No, I bet you're dreaming of having a farm with a lake like this on it someday."

"Actually, that thought crossed my mind."

Exploring, they stumble upon a cave just large enough to shelter them from the weather and they decide to keep it in mind as they return to the mine. They hate to move on and leave the beautiful lake, but they feel it will be best to continue in their chosen direction as planned.

The landscape changes into grassy meadows, traveling becomes easier, and they set up camp well before sunset, so they have time to relax. "This has been the best day yet. I really love the lake we found. Do you think it's too far from the farm for us to return someday? It would be a great place to camp and fish," says Jackson.

"I'm afraid we'll never have enough free time to travel this far just for the fun of it, but we will always remember it and, someday, who knows?"

The next morning, rising before the sun, they're met with a cold breeze whipping through their clothing, and they shiver as they hurry to rekindle the fire. Slowly it grows, and soon they sit back and enjoy the warmth as mint leaves dance around in boiling water.

"Let's head back to the lake, spend our evening in a beautiful place and sleep in the small cave tonight," says Cap.

"Yes!" shouts Jackson happily. I know we need to smoke some more fish so maybe we can catch some at the lake."

"I can't believe you said that." Happily, they begin their hike. Knowing they will be sleeping beside the beautiful lake makes this a special day from the start. They discover a large sassafras tree, and as they dig at the base of the tree, something blocks the sunlight for a split-second.

Jackson gasps. "Did you see that?" He gazes into the sky.

"I'm afraid I did." Cap is uneasy as he scans the horizon.

They search in their pockets for the pieces of hatching stone. Once they find them, Jackson kneels down and with a little hatchet digs out enough roots to fill a pouch. The fresh roots smell wonderful. They will make a delicious tea to enjoy at the lake tonight.

When they reach the cave, they drag logs from the beaches to lay across the entrance in an attempt to make it safer. Then they gather firewood and kindle a warm fire.

"What could that have been today besides a dragon?" asks Jackson.

"I'm not sure, but one thing I'm sure of is that it didn't intend to do us any harm. Whatever it was went on its way and left us alone," replies Cap.

They curl up close to each other in the cave and sleep peacefully until morning.

The next morning, they brew a pot of fresh sassafras tea. Cap remembers how they felt, seeing the shadow and realizes they're going to be afraid of any dragon that isn't Fuzzy. Neither of them mentions the troubling possibility lingering in the backs of their minds, but they realize Fuzzy may not even be alive anymore.

They look at the lake one last time, then turn toward the mine and begin their hike. Soon, they're making good time. Everything looks familiar and the wilting foliage they cut on the way out helps guide them back.

That night in the mine, a sense of security surrounds them and it almost feels like being home even though there seems to be a few more bats hanging on the ceiling.

The next morning, they hear birds singing outside, but they pull their blankets up to their chins and snuggle under them, staying warm a little longer. Cap throws his blanket back first and rekindles the fire, soon a pot of root tea is bubbling, filling the mine with the wonderful fragrance of sassafras.

"I think we might have time to go hunting for a couple more pheasants," suggest Jackson.

Soon they're hiking into the woods, talking at first, but quiet down as a clearing comes into view.

"I see a big fat groundhog," whispers Jackson.

"I see him, too. Let's both shoot at him at the same time. Surely one of us will get lucky."

Slowly, they move closer, take aim, and let their arrows fly. Jackson's arrow hits the hog. "What a shot," he shouts. He smiles as he picks up his prize and carries the limp animal to a small creek where he skins and cleans it. The water washes all the blood and unwanted parts away, and then he places it on the campfire. It's a perfect ending for a perfect day as they sit around the fire, eating roasted groundhog.

With groundhog left over to eat later and everything ready to head out in the morning, Cap and Jackson spend time sitting around the fire.

"I hope mom and dad are well. We have been gone long enough now something bad could have happened."

"It's just that time of evening when you and I always miss them the most. They're just fine. I'm sure they miss us the most this time of day, too." They say good night to each other and mean it more than ever.

The morning sun has yet to rise, but the brothers are up and looking forward to starting the next trip. Cap picks up the loadstone pointer, holds it over the middle stone of the wheel and, in a short time, they're ready to head north. They hike along for a pleasant half-mile before the terrain transforms the trip into a laborious task. The grade turns upward and the climb becomes an obstacle course as they maneuver around boulders and struggle as they climb over some that are impossible to go around. The steep incline continues all morning. They breathe hard and their shirts drip with sweat as their energy is washed out of their bodies.

"This direction is killing me," says Jackson, panting.

"I agree. If we struggle like this much longer without an extra-long break, I'll not be able to start again."

The trail is tiring, but its character rewards the adventures. A spectacle is displayed for them as they look down at the tops of clouds below. The brothers are higher above the valley floor than the tops of the clouds on their right. To their left, a mosaic of color unfolds. A large grove of trees painted with yellow and red leaves exhibit a breathtaking work of art created by nature's hand. They contrast beautifully with the dark green leafy trees surrounding them and filling the rest of the mountainside. Jackson's senses come alive, surrounded by nature's beauty. He points to a tree up ahead that holds onto the side of rock cliff with clinching roots. They look like a giant claw clinging to the mountain for dear life.

"I can climb no more," says Jackson, walking over to a smooth rock.

Cap is ready to rest, too. He glances at the rock Jackson sits on. "You're sitting in a giant chair."

Jackson stands to look. The rock he chose, and several others around him, look like giant chairs. "This is another work of beauty and wonder hidden in the wilderness," he says.

After resting, they regain their energy and start again. The chosen route continues to climb higher. Just when they think they can't climb any longer, Jackson calls out. "I see a clearing up ahead, and it looks like the landscape is flattening out at last."

"Please, let it be so. When we get there, I want to rest again."

They push through the last of the brush, stepping into a clearing, and their eyes light up. The grass is plush, soft, and green, and the wind dances through the evergreen tree limbs causing them to release an essence of freshness. The brothers stop, close their eyes.

"This is refreshing," says Cap when he opens his eyes. He's overwhelmed as he tries to take it all in. Fir trees tower above them, soaring into the heavens surrounding the meadow on three sides. They stand close to each other and gaze at the trees until they catch a glimpse of the open side. They drop their packs and weapons. The view is breathtaking. They stroll toward the opening with their mouths open in awe. The sensation of flying fills their bodies, and their senses sweep them away. Daydreaming, they soar above the valley below. Green rolling landscapes stretch far away, making the trees look tiny. They gaze speechless as the shadows cast by the clouds above the valley slide effortlessly across the wilderness.

"I have to sit here for a while and take this all in," says Cap, unable to take his eyes off the wonder lying before him. "I can almost see all the way home," he says, gazing into the distance.

Jackson walks back into the meadow and lies down in the soft grass, close to a pit. "Can you imagine the view atop that plateau in the distance?"

"I think we should stay at this clearing for the night and enjoy this amazing place. We will be at the base of the plateau in a few more days," replies Cap.

They search for a place to shelter for the night and find a rock outcropping on the edge of the clearing.

Chapter 5

Fuzzy hangs his head in anguish when the campfire begins to glow. He walks slowly back to his special place to be with Liz. Now, with hindsight torturing him, he knows he should have stopped Cap and Jackson earlier. Why had he struggled with his emotions trying to do the *right thing?*

With a long face and troubled eyes, he approaches Liz. "Something is bothering you. Would you like to talk to me about it?" she asks.

"I just saw Cap and Jackson's campfire. They're too close, and now I have no choice but to talk to them. I will meet with them in the morning and hope they can still communicate with me like they did when we were young."

"Why don't you go talk to them tonight?"

"I don't want to take a chance of being shot with an arrow before they realize the big creature they can hardly see in the dark is me. Nighttime plays tricks on humans. They're easily frightened in the dark. I will go early in the morning. I don't want them to ever see the cavern, and I don't want the other dragons to see them near the den."

"Fuzzy, you're too kindhearted, worrying about the den and your old friends." Liz hugs him.

"They don't understand that no other dragon feels the way I do about humans. In the world of dragons, humans have just as bad a reputation as dragons do in the human world. It's up to me to let Cap and Jackson know what they're getting into. I'm the one who made them think all dragons are like me."

Liz comforts Fuzzy, but he still has too many concerns on his mind to rest.

<>

Cap and Jackson sleep well and are up the next morning before the sun. Jackson goes to gather wood to build a fire and is surprised to find a nice pile right beside them under another outcropping.

As he sips his root tea, he tells Cap about the pile of wood.

"That seems strange. Why would a pile of good, dry wood just happen to be lying in the back of the outcropping?"

"Every piece has been broken so that they're all about four feet long," says Jackson. The wood burns quickly and Cap returns with him to gather more.

"There's something not quite right about this wood pile," says Cap as he picks up a piece to examine.

"It looks like it's spilling out of the wall."

Cap pulls a few pieces out throwing them to the side. "That's interesting." He squints and holds his chin. "I think the more wood I pull out, the further back into the wall we can go." He starts tossing wood faster. Jackson's eyes are glued on the pile as the shape of an entrance appears; it even has an arch at the top.

"We have discovered the entrance to a cave or maybe even a cavern," he says with a laugh.

"I have to see how far back this hole goes," says Cap as Jackson starts carrying wood out into the meadow.

They work several hours, but the men are so filled with excitement, wondering what they will find, that time means nothing. Their excitement spikes when they reach the point where the wood doesn't reach to the ceiling anymore. With renewed energy, they soon finish moving the rest out of the way.

"Well, brother, you may have been right when you said at the lake that we might find something just as interesting in a couple of days!" exclaims Jackson. He and

Cap slide their hands along the entrance walls as they inch along. There is enough light to see the rock is white and it feels smooth and slick as if coated with candle wax. A cool light breeze drifts past them and it's getting darker.

"Do you think Fuzzy could fit through this entrance?" asks Jackson.

"It would be tight but I'm sure he could. This may not be a dragon's den, but it could be a pathway that leads to a much larger cavern." The entrance walls stop and pitch-black surrounds them abruptly. Only a trail of faint light is visible behind them. Cap stops and Jackson peers over his shoulder. They pause in awe and apprehension.

"How large do you think this place is," says Jackson easing around Cap? Tripping, he screams, not knowing if there is a floor to catch him.

"Be careful," says Cap, his stomach churning. "If we get hurt in here we may never see home again."

"I'm ready to build a fire," says Jackson, carefully standing. They gather wood and work to get a fire burning. They fan and blow on the tiny blaze, waiting patiently.

Smoke rises from the entrance and drifts into the sky where the woodpile had been. As the fire flickers and grows brighter, details of the cavern begin to unfold, amazing formations deeper and deeper inside reflect light, and the cavern takes on an alluring character.

"I can hardly wait to explore this place, but I'm not sure something isn't hiding in here watching us build this fire," warns Cap. The look in Jackson's eyes tell him his warning brought his brother's imagination alive.

"Don't worry too much, nothing worse than a dragon is going to be in here." Jackson smirks, but chooses not to be in too much of a hurry.

"Take a look at the ceiling in here!" exclaims Cap.

"Wow! This place is going to be more beautiful than the lake," replies Jackson.

The firelight releases the hidden beauty of the walls and ceilings. They're bejeweled with tiny milky white crystals that twinkle. Even the stalactites draping from the ceiling are covered with crystals.

The men crane their necks to soak in the beauty displayed before them. Rising from the floor are stalagmites stretching thin as they reach to kiss their stalactite partners, but most of the floor is smooth, making it easy to walk around.

"When we tell everyone at home about this place, no one is going to believe us," says Jackson.

"Look at the rock hanging over our path. It looks like a dragon from this angle," says Cap excitedly.

"Here's a turtle with a long neck next to a crystal-clear pool of water!" exclaims Jackson.

"We can't see a tenth of what is in here. We'll need to build several fires to light it all up."

<>

The men are too busy exploring the magical place to notice what's unfolding outside the entrance, where a large, dark blue, scaly dragon is sniffing around their campfire.

The dragon turns his head toward the entrance and sneers. He can hear the men inside talking, and he sees smoke rising from the outcropping. Instinctive anger boils in his veins, preparing him to protect his den.

Stomping toward the entrance in obedience to his instinct, lusting for the kill, he unleashes a deafening roar flooding the cavern with a warning of foreboding death. The sound bounces down shafts, echoes off walls, and is acoustically enhanced by adjacent chambers.

The roar stops Cap in his tracks. Instantly jolted from joy to horror, he shivers. He sees Jackson trembling as he scrambles back and forth, not knowing what to do. Frantically, Cap screams, "hide!"

The dragon pushes through the entrance, its claws clicking and screeching on the rock floor. Coming to the end of the entrance, he pounces into the cavern.

Jackson holds his breath as he hides behind a gigantic stalagmite not too far from the entrance.

Cap is glued to a wall, hidden from view.

The dragon's eyes glow in the firelight. Usually, he could see every little detail in a dimly lit cavern. Luckily for the men, he has been in the sun and his eyes are not adjusted to the darkness as he searches for the intruders. He bellows again, hoping to scare them into moving.

The thunderous sound is unbelievable inside the cavern. The men shake as they cover their aching ears. Cap can see Jackson paralyzed with fear. Cap thinks about his piece of hatching stone, but he too, is so consumed with horror that he's incapable of pulling it out of his pocket.

The dragon stomps around impatiently, snorts, and jerks his head left, then right. Sucking in a deep breath, he raises his head and releases a blast of fire toward the cavern ceiling. It mushrooms out as it hits, forming a gigantic circle of yellowish-blue flickering light. The crystal-covered interior of the cavern is white, and it amplifies the brightness of the flame.

The stream of fire lasts an eternity to the men engulfed in tempestuous fear. The flame is blinding and smells of brimstone as his scorching breath drifts by them. All they can do is shut their eyes and suffer. They don't dare move.

With a snort, the dragon turns and squeezes back thru the entrance.

The brothers breathe a sigh of relief.

There comes a deafening *thud* at the entrance that makes them jump up to see what's happening. They scramble to get a better look.

"No!" screams Cap. The hopelessness in his scream rips Jackson's nerves apart. "He's plugging the entrance with the wood we dug out!"

Another *thud* rumbles as wood tumbles into the entrance.

"What can we do?" screams Jackson with tears of fear streaking down his dusty face.

"Pull out your hatching stone, and let's show it to him!"

They stretch as close to the last bit of opening and hold up the stones. The dragon doesn't look. He's too busy flinging the load of wood, some of which strikes their arms. The last bit of light from outside is gone.

The entrance is sealed and the cavern starts filling with smoke and dust. They can hardly breathe. Cap moves back toward their little fire.

"The dragon is plugging the entrance, trapping us here to die," he laments.

Queasy pangs fill their stomachs every time they hear the *thud*.

"For the first time in my life, I really am afraid of dragons. I know it's too late for me to figure out that Uncle Matt was right all along," confesses Cap, feeling responsible for their demise.

"Stop punishing yourself. I'm the one person in this world who understands why you weren't afraid of them." Jackson pauses. "You can't blame yourself. When we were children, I was there with you when we both saw a beautiful, friendly creature wanting to play with us. I have been fooled all this time, too."

"I think we're victims of an adult dragon protecting his den. There's no doubt in my mind that we're too close now, and this is his instinct," says Cap.

"When we started this trip, I thought we would find the den and Fuzzy would be so glad to see us that he would have his den welcome us, or he would meet us on the trail first," says Jackson.

"Foolishly, I thought the other dragons would be friendly like Fuzzy," says Cap. "I'm sorry for what I have gotten you into."

"Listen, I think the dragon has stopped," says Jackson.

They're quiet for a minute.

"Our only hope is to dig out. We'll have to hope the dragon is gone when we punch through," says Cap.

"We better hurry before our fire burns out," says Jackson.

"I would rather die from the wrath of the dragon than starve or suffocate in this cavern. There's a chance we'll be able to show the dragon our hatching stones and even survive without a fight."

Cap and Jackson begin picking up wood and tossing it deeper into the cavern. They work frantically until they collapse from exhaustion.

"I feel strange," says Jackson.

"I feel it to," replies Cap.

They lie on the floor a few minutes trying to regain their strength. They struggle to return to their task, digging slower and slower. They gasp for air.

"I think it's a bad sign the fire isn't burn brightly anymore," says Jackson.

"We're running out of air. Poor mom, dad, and Uncle Matt, I feel sorry for what we've done to them," remarks Cap in anguish. "No one will ever know what happened to us, and that will make it even worse for them. It's all I can do to stay awake another minute. I think once we fall sleep we'll never wake up again. What have I done?"

"Don't blame yourself for bringing me along. I have grown to love you more out here than I ever did at the farm," replies Jackson with tears in his eyes.

Looking at each other in very dim light for the last time, their eyes tell each other they're glad they had been brothers.

<>

They surrender and lie helplessly their souls are as one and an unexplainable bond unites their fading senses as they share their ascent into the unknown. Tears flow from closed eyes as they long to work just one more day on the farm. It had been such a wonderful, safe place to live with their family always looking after them. All the hard work they had done was little payback for the love their family had given them. A feeling of surrender overwhelms them as they drift, spinning around and around into deep, deep sleep, and they dream.

The dreams are pleasant at first but the light in their minds' eyes begins to slowly darken. Wailing sounds grow louder as souls that never broke free of earth's firmament, cloaked in rotten flesh, and gnashing teeth descend upon them. Pulling and gouging, they try to rip out the essence of life from deep within their bodies. The pulling and jerking inflicts excruciating pain, like strings of flesh being torn, one ribbon at a time from every muscle in their bodies. The brothers struggle to break loose and run, but their arms and legs refuse to work.

Then a purple fog, damp and cold begins to blow, sweeping the specters away and the sound of their wailing fades. A pulsating warmth moves across the brother's cold aching bodies, bringing a release. There is serenity. They float around the beautiful cavern, seeing without light. All is peaceful until they see their lifeless bodies with unfocused, staring eyes.

Horror wracks their souls as wailing comes again. Clearly, over and over, they hear their mother's mournful cry, "Where are my boys?" The sound chills their souls so deeply they shiver. Then their father appears, but he has no face. He picks them up, one in each arm, holding on, squeezing tightly. Tighter and tighter he grips, refusing to let them slip into eternity. Then, a numb *thud.*

Slowly, a sensation like needle pricks tingles across their bodies in waves. They can't move and the sharpness of the pain is maddening.

<>

Cap squints painfully as he tries to see, but a blur of light blinds him as it shines overhead.

The tingling pain lessens and turns into slow, gentle drifting waves. Cap leans his head to the side and sees Jackson's silhouette out of the corner of his eye. He tries with all his might to beckon him, but his head spins and nothing audible comes out of his mouth. Giving up for a minute, he lies still and thinks. *"We're still alive, but we're just going to die?"*

He tries to move. He sees Jackson trying to move his fingers and arms, too. Trying to move again, his muscles ache and resist his will.

Lying there, his awareness grows. Bushes, trees, and then the forest comes into focus around them. A breeze with delicious fresh air is blowing. They're out of the cavern, and he takes a deep breath.

In the dim moonlight, Cap can barely see the out cropping in the distance. The sound of breaking sticks and crushing leaves alarms him. A large creature is nearby, causing fear as strong as before to rush through his body. He's unable to talk or move as the sound comes closer.

The brothers tremble, assuming the dragon is coming to finish them off. Their brains send signals to run, but their arms and legs only wiggle and squirm.

Cap's eyes are glued in the direction the sound of the large creature comes from. Suddenly, eyes high above him come into view. He and Jackson flail helplessly trying to stand.

"Calm down, be quiet," utters the large figure with a familiar voice.

"Fuzzy?" Cap manages to mutter.

"It's Fuzzy," whispers Jackson with a tear sliding down his face.

"Quiet. You will get us all killed," whispers Fuzzy sternly.

When he kneels between them, they see the fuzzy red spot between two long horns.

"How did you get here?" asks Cap.

"No questions or talking now. Get up and follow me," demands Fuzzy.

Cap and Jackson can't help wondering what his intentions are. Still helpless, they have to wait for Fuzzy to help them stand, and they stumble until they regain feeling in their legs.

"Here are your bows and quivers. Put them over your head and across your shoulder so they won't fall off in the underbrush as we travel."

Cap can tell Jackson is light-headed, groggy, and disoriented like him. But fortunately, they can communicate with Fuzzy as well as they could when they were young.

Trudging along for a good while, they're walking better. Fuzzy stops to rest and talk.

"I'm not angry with you. I'm just tired. We must walk hastily. Our lives depend on us being far away from the plateau before the sun rises. We're heading toward your farm. Don't ask any questions now. We must move on."

Cap and Jackson comply with his request and ask no questions. They stand, feeling stronger. With renewed hope, they walk with determination as Fuzzy's instinct leads them in the dark forest.

They walk until the sun paints the southeast sky a pinkish blue-grey. The dew begins to glisten in morning light.

"I think we're safe for now. We can rest," says Fuzzy.

"I thought you were never going to say that. I don't think I can go any further," says Jackson.

Cap and Jackson sit on the ground and lean against a tree waiting to hear Fuzzy's story.

"Several days ago, I discovered you were the reason for the campfires I have been watching in the wilderness. I checked on you each night after that, hoping you wouldn't come too close to our den. Two days ago, I couldn't ignore the danger any longer, and I made my way to your campsite, planning to turn you around. When I approached, I saw Lester sniffing your fire. All I could do was hide and wait for him to leave.

"You saw the whole thing?" asks Cap.

"Yes, I had no choice but to watch. I was helpless. You will never know how hard it was for me to wait until Lester left you for dead. I had no way of knowing if he had killed you and decided to cover the entrance or whether he was burying you alive."

"You had to wait until you were sure he was gone for good?" asks Jackson quietly.

"Yes, and I knew there was a lot of work ahead of me, digging that entrance back out. Enough explaining for now, let's hide in the underbrush and sleep until evening, then I'll tell you what you have to do if you're to make it home safely."

Everyone is tired, and they fall into deep slumber until the sun is setting. When Fuzzy wakes, Cap and Jackson are patiently waiting.

Fuzzy rubs his eyes and looks at the brothers. "I'm hungry, and I know you are, too. I will be right back. Don't move." He returns in minutes with three fish. He hands Cap and Jackson one each.

"I know you like your fish cooked but you will have to eat these raw," he explains.

"Can't we warm them up a little bit?" asks Cap.

"If you want to see your home again, you will not build anymore fires until you're there."

The brothers are starving. They cut the fish into little pieces, and after a couple curious bites, they devour them. They need no more explanation about campfires. They just want to go home.

"By being with you, I'm risking all of our lives and the respect of my den. The other den members wouldn't understand why two humans should be trusted. If Lester ever finds out I dug you out, he will kill me."

"We didn't mean to cause trouble, old friend. We only wanted to see you again," states Cap.

"I understand, but this will absolutely have to be the last time we're together. You can never come this far into the wilderness ever again."

"I can't believe we can never come back. It's so beautiful," says Jackson.

"That's just the way it is. My den cannot live like dragons if humans are around. We can only survive secluded in the wilderness. My den is beginning to feel threatened by civilization eating into our world. Lester was only trying to protect us," states Fuzzy.

The brothers try to understand what he means and will honor his request. They owe him for their lives.

As they say goodbye, they mention the lake in the wilderness with an island in the middle and how it's surrounded by beautiful countryside.

"It's only that beautiful because no human has ever changed it. If humans ever reach the lake, it will be turned into farms all around its shore. After that, dragons and adventures like you will not be welcome. Can you imagine how upset the farmers will be if you or I eat apples or vegetables around the lake once it belongs to them?"

The men remember thinking how beautiful a farm would be at the lake, and they understand.

"Goodbye, old friend," says Cap.

Jackson chokes on tears and bows his head to say goodbye. Fuzzy bows for a second, turns, and vanishes into the underbrush.

Chapter 6

Cap reaches into his pocket and is relieved to find the loadstone pointer has survived the ordeal. The long walk home begins for two brothers who are more bonded than ever. With Fuzzy gone, they start planning what to do. There are only a couple hours of sunlight left. They miss home more than ever and begin walking briskly.

"This has been the best and the worst adventure we could have ever had," says Jackson.

"I know. There's no way anyone has ever had an experience as sinister as our confrontation with the scaly blue dragon and lived to tell about it."

"We're lucky Fuzzy gave us another chance at life. We can never breathe a word about this to anyone. Even if we do, everyone will think we're crazy," laments Jackson. "What are we going to tell our family about this trip?"

Cap thinks quietly as he navigates around trees and undergrowth. They no longer have their long knives to cut a path.

"Just thinking about all the spectacles, we have seen that we can never mention is driving me crazy. We can't describe a dragon or tell of the majesty of the plateau or the beauty of the lake. We have to always be cautious not to mention anything that gives anyone a reason to come out here," explains Cap.

They walk until it's almost dark. Fear of a dark night ahead with no fire turns their thoughts to survival. Cap spies a hickory sapling, strong and straight, in front of him. It will make a good spear. He stops, pulls out his little knife and whittles one end to a point, making it a lethal weapon. As the evening fades, they search for a safe place to spend the night. Luckily, they come upon a small rock cliff that will provide some shelter. Several dead trees lay close by and they drag logs and limbs over in front of their shelter, leaving a small hole to crawl through.

Jackson discovers a limb with a growth forming a heavy bulge. With a little whittling, he turns it into a club. With the last glimmer of light, they pile rocks just the right size to throw where they can be grabbed in an instant. They're ready to fight predators if they must.

Preparing to take first guard duty, Cap slips his bow off and lays it close by. "I will watch the first half of the night while you sleep, and then you can watch until sunlight. Tomorrow, first chance we get, we will have to catch some fish and eat them raw again."

"I thought things couldn't get any worse than having to eat smoked fish all the time. But now I know I was wrong," complains Jackson.

In the morning, they trudge toward home.

"I don't like having to stay up half the night but I have to admit I felt pretty safe taking turns guarding each other behind those logs," says Jackson.

After almost dying, they're more careful now. Seven nights without a fire pass and they're almost home. Late in the evening, two large trees blown over on the edge of their path come into view.

"This looks like a safe spot," suggests Jackson.

"We're only two nights from home now, and I feel it will be safe to enjoy the warmth of a fire again," says Cap.

"I still want to take turns standing guard," replies Jackson. He smiles and searches for a couple rocks to sit on. They're happy thinking about being together around a warm fire again. The fire dances and fills them with warmth they have missed so much. They enjoy talking and stay up a little longer than they did on the dark evenings.

It's a peaceful night standing guard, and the only task is keeping the fire going.

Upon waking, Cap rubs his eyes, and looks at Jackson. "We can try to catch some fish and smoke them this morning if you want to."

"Believe it or not, no thanks, I don't want to waste one second sitting here smoking fish," replies Jackson and Cap chuckles.

They take to the trail before the sun breaks over the horizon. The closer home they are, the more they talk about the farm and the less they talk about dragons.

Stopping early their last night, they decide to hunt rabbits for supper, and after a successful hunt, they're on their way back to the campfire. They stumble across leafy plants that they discovered earlier are tender and delicious when boiled. They pull what they need and return to camp.

It's almost like old times, sitting around the fire as they talk and cook their supper. Jackson is in a rare mood as he throws more wood on the fire.

"That was a good meal, even if it wasn't fish," says Jackson and Cap smiles.

"The wilderness has taught us a lot. I really am sad Fuzzy told us not to ever come back."

"I'm just glad to almost be home. We won't have any reason to go way out there anymore."

The night air is warm and the forest has a familiar feeling, and even the underbrush is thinning out. They pull leaves into a pile, throw a tarp over them and lie down to relax as they watch the fire.

"Everyone will want to know all about what we discovered. The story has to be exactly the same every time we tell it or someone will know something isn't right," says Cap.

"I will forever be grateful to Fuzzy for saving our lives, and I'm as determined as you to keep his den and their hunting grounds as safe as we can. We should tell the story just as it happened until the day we were beside to the plateau. We will only have to leave out the lake," suggests Jackson.

"We might want to call the mine a cave, too," adds Cap. Still thinking, he pauses. "We don't want to intrigue anyone and have to take them into the wilderness to see an old mine."

"Good thinking. We'll say we found a cave that kept us safe and out of the weather, but it wasn't very large. Then we'll mention the lake, saying only that we enjoyed fishing there. We'll emphasize that the best thing about our trip was the satisfaction of making it on our own, and the worst was missing home," replies Jackson. He takes his bow and quiver off and lays it ready to grab if needed. "I will take the first watch tonight. You get some rest."

That night, Cap dreams he's sitting in his mom's kitchen eating her wonderful cooking. It was the most peaceful night he had experienced since their encounter with the dragon.

Cap waits to wake up Jackson until the sun has fully risen. The ordeal is just about over. As Cap packs things up, his eyes are full of tears, just waiting to flow.

"What's bothering you?" asks Jackson. Cap looks his way but gives no reply. "I thought you would be overjoyed today knowing we will be home by supper."

"I feel as if a ton of rocks are on my heart, thinking about all we have just experienced and can never share with anyone. To make things worse, it's our sworn duty to guard Fuzzy's secret and keep others from going into the wilderness. We have not had to deal with that yet, but the minute we arrive home it will be our never-ending duty," says Cap shaking his head.

"It bothers me, too. You have to get a hold of yourself before we return or mom will know something is wrong."

Cap stops, he needs to unload emotionally. Jackson has always depended on him. But now he needs Jackson to listen and understand.

"I feel uneasy about our promise to Fuzzy. What if I mess up our story? Someone might realize we're hiding something."

Jackson tears up too.

"I thought it would be easier on both of us if I hid my fear. We share the same burden. I know now we will be stronger if we're honest with each other. If you stumble, I will be right there for you just as you will be for me."

Cap cries out some of his stress. He hugs Jackson, and Jackson wipes tears from his own eyes.

"This is supposed to be such a happy day," says Cap.

Jackson gives him a tight squeeze, then backs away. The men feel better. They have suffered through so much.

"We will never worry about this again. I will be strong for you and you will be strong for me. We will lean on our resolve to help each other," says Cap.

Jackson's cheeks begin to rise, and he smiles, wiping tears. A wave of fresh energy and confidence fills them from deep inside. They're almost home.

Confidence they gain from the moment lifts their spirits, and they enjoy the last few hours of their adventure. The wilderness is a beautiful and magical place that changes with your emotions. It is frightening and dangerous if you're afraid, but if you're confident and prepared, it can be a refreshing experience with nature's beauty on display.

"We have been away from home thirty-seven days," says Cap.

He stops in his tracks and peeks carefully through the tree limbs. If he stands in just the right spot he can get a glimpse of the top of their barn. It's the most beautiful sight he has seen in days.

"Are you sure it has only been thirty-seven days?" says Jackson.

Jackson watches as Cap pulls out of his pocket a small string full of knots.

"Every night before I went to sleep, I would tie a knot in this."

The men look at each other. Their clothing, shoes, and everything they're wearing is tattered. Only their small knife, bow, and a few arrows are still as good as ever.

"It's a good thing the trip didn't last ant longer," remarks Cap.

Jackson is the first to see their mother. She's sitting on the porch, sewing. She doesn't see them at first, but when she does, she jumps up, spilling needles and thread all over the floor.

She runs as fast as she can to her sons. "You sweet, sweet bad boys how could you stay so long?" She hugs them dearly.

"Mom, it hasn't been that long," replies Cap lovingly.

"When time is measured in worry and motherly concern for her children, even a short period is an eternity. I'm so thankful you two are safe and home. Please, promise me you will never leave me and your father like this again."

Reaching for both of them again, she hugs them long and hard. They understand their mom is satisfying a need deep inside.

"Let's ring the bell so your father and Uncle Matt will come in from the field."

The brothers make the mistake of letting a rejoicing mother ring the bell. She puts a lot of her excitement into it. The bell rings louder and faster than ever before, and when Miles and Uncle Matt hear it, they think something bad has happened.

They're already running when they see the boys standing next to their mother, and they run even faster. Miles reaches them first and hugs them almost as much as their mother had. He tries to hide his emotions, but they're too strong. Long-awaited tears of joy stream down his face. Uncle Matt is just as glad to see them. A tear or two leaks from his eyes. While father hugs one, Uncle Matt hugs the other.

Cap and Jackson feel a new kind of love for their family. They have grown a lot on their trip. The new love has a lot of respect mixed in with it.

Cap and Jackson want to help finish the chores, so there will be extra time for a joyful supper.

"Mom, when you start supper, could you please cook ham and eggs or chicken and dumplings? Anything but fish!" says Jackson.

"This will be the best supper this family has ever had," she replies, smiling.

As the brothers work, the reality of the trip is settling in. They had promised to never go back into the wilderness, but no other man would know that, and they could not tell anyone. Cap and Jackson realize there will never be any peace in the wilderness again. They're the only two men who have surrendered the wilderness to the dragons.

Before supper, Cap and Jackson wash their hair and put on fresh clothing for the first time in weeks. Miles and Uncle Matt wear their best clothes. Inez beams, wearing the prettiest smile she has in two months. To Cap, everyone looks amazingly clean, sitting around the supper table,

Miles speaks first.

"After working without you all this time, I realize how much work you do around here. Uncle Matt and I had to work so hard you would think I wouldn't have had time to miss you, but you'd be wrong. Your mother and I have never been as lonesome in our lives as we were while you were gone."

Cap and Jackson can tell by the tone of their father's voice and his kindness that their father's new found love also includes new found respect for them.

Uncle Matt tries to act as if he doesn't feel quite as enthused.

"Pass the ham, pass the bread," he says, trying to act unconcerned. "I might just take a little trip to get away and rest now that the boys are home,"

Everyone knows how he really feels.

"Let the boys tell us what they found on their adventure," exclaims Inez.

Cap takes the lead and tells the story just like it happened for the first part of the trip. He knows he won't have to change a thing about the first week, and everyone listens earnestly, as he explains what they saw and describes the wilderness.

Jackson tells of the challenges they faced as they were learning new things, especially trying to find food and cooking in the wilderness. He stops for a second. "The hardest part of the trip was missing all of you. We were homesick every time we were ready to lie down. Of course, some nights we were too spooked to miss you much. It's pretty scary out there when you hear things moving around in the woods and you don't have much shelter." He looks at his mom. "We ate fish over and over."

Cap smiles and looks at his father. "Thank you for taking time to teach us how to use the loadstone pointer. We probably would have gotten lost without it."

"I hope you enjoyed your adventure. As long as I'm alive, you're not going back. My heart can't take it again," states Inez.

"We missed you as much as you missed us," assures Cap.

Feeling their story went well, they're satisfied. Mother, father, and Uncle Matt hug them tightly before going to bed.

"Wait," says Uncle Matt. "There's just one more thing to be said before we go to bed. I really did miss you as much as your mother did. Now get out of here and go to sleep. You have a lot of work to do while your father and I take it easy for a couple of days."

He doesn't resist when Cap and Jackson hug him again.

The brothers are looking forward to finally sleeping in their own soft, safe, and warm beds.

"I think the story went okay, don't you?" asks Jackson.

"All I want to do is just snuggle up in this bed and go to sleep. We can talk tomorrow."

In the morning, Cap stacks hay and grain in the barn. Jackson chops wood for his mother to use for cooking. Things are quickly returning to normal. Cap and Jackson are happy working again.

A week later, the adventure seems like it was all just a dream.

Chapter 7

The village near Cap and Jackson is growing, and they're discovering a new kind of adventure can be found there. They can't visit often. It's far enough away to be inconvenient. But when they do, a strange feeling comes over them anytime a lady flirts with them.

Riding home from a trip to the village on horses they washed and curried to look nice for the ladies, they're too busy talking to notice any of the beautiful flowers poking their heads out of the edge of the woods, soaking in the sunlight along the trail.

"I wish I could stay in the village longer. I never have time to become friends with any of the women," says Cap.

"Things have to change. There has to be something more to life than working all the time. Starting next week, I think I'm going to saddle up every Saturday and ride to the village to see what's going on," says Cap.

"If mom and dad will let me, I'm coming with you."

Saturday, Cap is apprehensive as he approaches Miles. "Dad, Jackson and I would like to have your permission to ride to the village."

Miles raises his eyebrows. "Is there something you need there?"

"No. Yes, we need a little more adventure in our lives, and the village always has something interesting going on."

"If you're bored and have a lot of energy, I can find you something interesting to do around here."

"Dad," says Cap with slight grimace.

"I'm kidding! I once was young, I know how you feel. You must promise me you will be careful. You can get into trouble there if you aren't gentlemen. Sometimes you can get into trouble even when you are. You have to be thinking all the time, like you did in the wilderness."

"Thanks! We won't get into trouble, we want to be able to go back again soon," replies Cap, bursting into a smile from ear to ear. He hugs his dad and runs into the house to clean up and put on clean clothes.

It's ten miles to the village. They make their horses trot along, spend a couple of hours there, and reluctantly head home so they will still have time to do their evening chores.

On the way back, they discover a wagon stranded in the middle of the trail. A man shakes his head in despair as he and his wife look at one of the wheels.

They ride up beside the wagon and say hello.

"Hello, young men. One of our wheels is coming apart. My wife and I will have leave the wagon and ride the horses home. I don't have a spare wheel," explains the man, rubbing his forehead.

The couple is friendly and appears to be the same age as their mom and dad.

"I will be glad to ride out to our farm and bring a wheel back for your wagon, if you like," Cap offers. "Our farm is not far from here."

"You're too kind! I don't want to impose on you like this," replies the man.

"I don't mind at all. It's the right thing to do."

"In that case, I will wait here until you return" replies the man, wrinkles fading from his forehead

"You sure are being nice to those strangers," says Jackson as they ride home.

"Like I told them, it's the right thing to do. And, I have a good feeling about them. They're friendly and everything about them—including their wagon—is neat and clean."

Cap heads to the barn and lifts a wheel onto Jackson's horse and ties it down. Jackson stays at the farm while Cap heads back, leading his horse. The wagon is only a few miles from the farm, and soon he and the man replace the wheel. He picks up the broken wheel and lays it on the back of their wagon.

"You have been kind to us, and I want to pay you for your services. Please look on our wagon and pick out one of my tools to pay for all the hard work you have done."

"I can't take any of your tools. You'll need everything you have to build your homestead. Take the broken wheel home or to the village and fix it as soon as you can find time. Then, you can return the borrowed wheel."

"I promise, I will make this up to you soon," says the man.

"Young man, what's your name?" asks the man's wife.

Cap is impressed by her demeanor. She had a smile on her face throughout their ordeal.

"I'm Cap Murray. My family's farm is easy to find. It's on this trail about four miles ahead."

The couple thanks him again as the man flips the horse's reins, and they're on their way.

When Cap rides up at the farm, his father is waiting. "So, you gave away our spare wagon wheel," he scolds. A wagon wheel is hard to come by. He casts a look that lets him know he has to make it up to the family.

"I have a good feeling about these people," Cap tries to reassure his father.

"Even really good people get busy sometimes and forget to keep their promises."

"If they forget, I will work hard and make something I can trade for another wheel at the village." responds Cap confidently.

One week later, Cap is working in the cow barn where there's a good view of the trail coming toward the farm. In the distance, he sees a wagon approaching. It's carrying the man and woman he helped with the broken wheel. He walks to the front of the house to greet them.

When the wagon draws close, Cap notices the woman looks younger than she had the week before. As the wagon stops, he dusts off his clothes. This woman is about his age. Her eyes are hazel and her reddish-brown hair is pulled back and tied with a blue and white cord that compliments a light blue dress she wears. He makes himself stop looking at her so much.

"This is my daughter, Janice. It's such a pretty day I asked her to ride out here with me to bring your wheel back," explains the man.

"Nice to meet you," says Cap, worrying about his appearance.

She looks a lot like her mother, only prettier. There's a wonderful smell of lilac flowers when she's near.

Cap's father joins them. He saw them approaching from the field.

"Hello. My name is Miles Murray. It's a pleasure to meet an honest man."

"The name is Buck Brittain. It's nice to meet you. Your son was good to us. He's a kind man, and I know after meeting him, this is a good family. Let me introduce my daughter, Janice."

"Pleased to meet you, Janice," says Miles, looking at her with more than just a glance. He can tell this woman is confident and full of life.

Cap rubs his chin, thinking about the way his father looked at her.

"Please, sit on the porch for a while."

Mr. Brittain agrees.

Miles takes hold of Cap's limp hand and holds it out to Janice. "Help the young lady down, Cap."

Cap worries he won't do this simple task just right. She smiles, and as soon as their hands touch, he feels a pleasant sensation flowing through her hand into his. When she slips to the ground and stands. Cap takes a quick glance. She's three inches shorter than he is, and she has the most wonderful, genuine smile.

The four of them step up on the porch. Janice sits in the swing and the three men choose chairs. Cap is thinking it would be nice to sit in the swing closer to Janice, but he feels unsure.

"My family is attempting to build a homestead about five miles from here. I'm so proud of my wife— Flavie—and my daughter. They have been working tirelessly on our new place," says Buck.

"I'm glad you're going to be close by. I had no idea anyone was homesteading close to us," replies Miles.

"Please stop by and visit. We're not far. Head toward the village. When you approach the second creek, look to your right and you will see where we are clearing a trail on this side."

Cap is trying hard to think of something to ask Janice. "Are you helping your father build your new house?" he asks.

"So far, we have just built a lean-to. I don't have time to help him much."

"The women are too busy doing things that must be done first. I wish my wife and daughter could help me more but they need to work in our garden if we're going to have enough food to make it through the winter. We also have two cows they tend so they have about all they can do. I have found it's hard to get much done by myself."

Cap, being kindhearted, feels he should try to help these nice people. "If father will let me, I have a little time left over every week after my work here is done. I would be glad to help you then."

Miles looks at Cap and smiles. "We will talk about it later, son."

Cap is embarrassed a little by what his father said. He can't understand why he's so nervous sitting there. Cap is thinking, as he smells the wonderful perfume Janice is wearing, maybe he's old enough to make some of his own decisions. He sits quietly as the older men finish talking.

"It has been a pleasure to meet you, Mr. Murray. Please call on me if I can ever be of help to you. Believe it or not, I make and repair wagon wheels. I just don't have my shop set up yet."

When Janice stands to leave, she speaks to Mr. Murray. "It has been a pleasure to meet you and Cap." She shakes Miles' hand and smiles a beautiful smile at Cap. He's already nervous, and the smile turns his nervousness into a funny feeling he has never felt before. After that smile, Cap can't get her off his mind.

After supper, Cap hurries out to sit beside his father on the porch. He nervously clears his throat before anyone else is around. Miles knows something is on his mind.

"I feel I should help the Brittains. I like Buck and he will compensate me for whatever help I give him," says

Cap, fidgeting. "I don't want my helping Mr. Brittain to burden our family, but can't we work something out?"

His father can't deny his son is growing up. "Son, I talked to Uncle Matt today. We have decided you can help Mr. Brittain every Friday and Saturday."

Cap smiles and quits fidgeting. His father doesn't usually say yes to anything that means he will work less at the farm. Now, he can hardly wait until Friday.

Inez notices Cap is happier than usual on Friday morning. He's full of energy and has a big smile on his face.

"I will see you tonight," he says, then kisses her goodbye.

Anxious to leave, he trots the horse all the way there. Fortunately, Mr. Brittain is home and already working. He waves and walks out to greet Cap as he rides up.

"Good morning, young man. I hope this means you have decided to help me build our cabin!"

"I talked with my father, and he agreed I can work with you on Friday and Saturday. I will enjoy learning how to build a cabin."

"Thank you, Cap. We will both learn a lot. If you work with me every Friday and Saturday until we get the roof on, I will give you a wagon. It will have the best wheels you can find."

Cap feels this is a good deal, and his father will be proud of him. A wagon is something a man needs to get started on his own.

Soon after they finish talking business, Janice returns from the garden. She's wearing an old dress and a bonnet to keep the sun out of her face. The dress is a little dirty because she has been working. She smiles and waves when she sees Cap. He decides it doesn't matter what she wears. Her posture and the smile on her face make anything look pretty. Cap realizes it will be hard to keep his mind on this job, but he's determined to give Mr. Brittain an honest day's work. He knows Janice will be watching to see what kind of man he is, and he's going to keep a clear head and be as good a man as he can possibly be. Cap and Mr. Brittain shake hands and begin their work.

"The first thing we need to do is decide how big the cabin should be," suggests Mr. Brittain.

As they draw the plan, Mr. Brittain and Cap impress each other. They're both good at figuring things out. It doesn't take long until they both know exactly how they are going to build the cabin. It's almost time for lunch when they're ready to start placing the foundation stones.

"Flavie has prepared a good lunch. Come in and eat with us," offers Mr. Brittain.

"My mother sent lunch with me. Thank you, though."

"I insist! Bring your lunch in and we will all share what we have."

Cap is shy around the Brittains, but slowly they begin to talk during the meal. When the meal is finished Cap is ready to head back to work.

The evening passes quickly and soon it's time to quit. "You're more than welcome to stay here tonight," says Mr. Brittain.

"Thank you, but it would be best if I go home. Mom and dad wouldn't know what happened to me, and I don't want them to worry. I'll leave home early in the morning and be back before you start."

Riding home, he has lots of thoughts running through his head. He likes all the Brittains and hopes they feel the same about him.

The moment Jackson sees his brother; he runs over and holds the horse while Cap dismounts. "What's it like working for someone that isn't family?"

"The Brittains are nice just like mom and dad. This is my first day and they seem no different. I do love learning how to build a cabin from the ground up, though."

Jackson stays close to his brother talking about everything he experienced at the Brittains. Cap can tell he had missed him.

Everyone wants to sit next to Cap as they gather around the supper table. Inez fixes Cap's favorite dish, fried ham. Everyone wants to talk about the Brittains. They have a lot of questions for him.

"I can truly say they are very nice and I feel right at home around them. Mr. Brittain told me if I help him every Friday and Saturday until the cabin is dry, he will give me a wagon in trade."

Mile's face brightens. He's glad his son knows how to make a good deal.

"How pretty was Janice today?" teases Uncle Matt. Cap blushes.

"Did Mr. Brittain let you rest every now and then?" asks Miles.

"He works right beside me and tells me to rest while he does," Cap replies, thankful the question isn't about Janice.

"How long do you think it will take to build this cabin," asks his mother?

"I don't really think it will take long. Mr. Brittain will do a lot while I'm working here."

After supper, Jackson finds Cap on the porch. "We need to talk where no one will hear."

Cap wonders what this is all about as they walk to the stables.

"A man came by the farm today on his way to explore the wilderness. He had a donkey loaded with food and gear for camping. He saw me in the yard and stopped to talk. He asked if I knew of anything interesting out there."

"What did you tell him?"

"You can imagine what went through my mind when he asked that question! I told him you and I had gone exploring one time and we went north about twenty miles."

"Surely you didn't tell him about anything encouraging about going that way."

"I told him we didn't see anything except lots of trees. I did say it's all beautiful as long as you're not in a hurry."

"I get nervous now when I hear about people going into the wilderness. Surely, since you told him we went north and found nothing, he will go west or east."

"That's not all. He told me the wilderness is full of hidden opportunities. If one happens to stumble on the right place, there are treasures to be found and a man could return rich. He also had a feisty little white dog with him. It was just the right size to pet and keep him company out there. He said it was a good hunter and would bring small game back to camp to share with him.

"I hope he will be okay out there. You won't see me going into the wilderness alone," says Cap.

"He isn't completely alone. He told me when an animal is lurking close to his camp at night, the dog will bark and by the time he has his bow ready, the threat is gone."

"You should go to the village and find us a pup. I think we will feel better at the farm with a dog around," says Cap.

"He assured me there's no way he's going into the wilderness without his friend."

"I sure hope he goes west."

"No use worrying. There's not much we can do to stop people from going out there like we did." Jackson sighs.

Cap yawns. "Good night Jackson. I'm tired and I want to get an early start tomorrow." He heads toward their house and his bed.

In the morning, Cap can't believe how easy it is to get up and start the day. He's looking forward to getting back to work. He's ready to leave as soon as he can see the trail, even after spending a little more time than usual picking what he would wear. He wants to look as good as possible and be able to work hard, too.

Cap arrives at Mr. Brittain's lean-to before the sun breaks over the horizon.

Mr. Brittain smiles when he sees Cap is raring to work. Janice glances in Cap's direction, smiles and steps outside.

"Good morning, Cap. I'm glad you're here today," she says with a pretty smile.

"Good morning," replies Cap, tipping his hat.

"I hope you're in the mood to do some hard work today," says Mr. Brittain.

"Whatever we need to do, I'm ready."

The men spend the day chopping and hauling trees to where the foundation stones are set. It's exhausting work, but Cap makes up his mind that at the end of the day Mr. Brittain will be proud of him.

Cap fights to keep a smile on his face, but inside he begins to wonder if lunchtime will ever come. Just then, Mr. Brittain plops down on a nearby log and slides his hat off, dropping it next to him. He leans forward and wipes his forehead with his arm.

"I can't do anymore until after a long lunch break. How about you, Cap?" He leans back. "Whew!" A few minutes later, he stands slowly. "I hope you planned to eat lunch with us today."

"I don't want to impose on you."

"Nonsense, young man! Part of our deal from now own will be for you to eat lunch with us every day you work with me."

"Thank you, Mr. Brittain," says Cap with a sheepish smile.

Cap feels more at ease and joins in the conversation without waiting for questions.

As time passes, he gets to know the Brittains, and they enjoy each other's company. For a month, construction progresses as planned, and Cap always looks forward to working Friday and Saturday. Seeing the cabin rise from the ground gives him a sense of accomplishment. He dreams of the day when he will build a house for himself, and he dares to wonder if Janice will be a part of those future plans.

One Friday, while working on the roof, Janice comes out to help. Cap looks down as she measures and cuts planks to hand up to them.

"I'm impressed. You know how to work on things like us. You're just as good at helping your father as I am," says Cap.

"You inspire me, Cap. I want to do things that will please you," she says.

Cap is at a loss for words. He likes what she said and he has to say something. "It's a lot more fun working with you around to help."

She smiles and picks up another board. He worries. Was that the right thing to say?

In the evening, riding home, he has a funny feeling he has never felt before, but he likes it and he's going to burst if he doesn't tell someone. Cap stables the horse, and is on his way to the house when he sees Jackson coming out into the yard.

"Just the man I want to see."

"You're in a silly mood tonight." Jackson smiles.

"I have a feeling inside that's new and quite wonderful. It's also frightening because I never want to lose it."

"I think I might know what people call that."

"Take it easy now. It's a growing respect for Janice, nothing more. But I'm dreaming about a wonderful possibility."

"I hope she will love you, too. I think the Brittains are good people." Jackson's face lights up. "I have a surprise for you that I'm almost as happy about." Cap follows Jackson to the cow barn and in one of the stalls stands a puppy. "You said we would feel safer at the farm with a dog. I happened to be in the village today when a man rode by with the little thing lying in a pile of straw on the back of his wagon. I couldn't resist going over to pet him. When I walked up to the wagon, the man said he was going to trade the pup at the hardware store. I gave him my bow, arrows, and quiver for him. I have already started making another bow. Isn't he beautiful? I named him Homer." Jackson is beaming.

The brothers play with the puppy and for a few minutes Cap doesn't think about Janice. Miles rings the porch bell for supper, and they race to the kitchen.

"How do you like Jackson's dog?" asks Uncle Matt, sitting down at the table.

"I love him," replies Cap.

"Homer's not all he loves," Jackson baits.

"Brother, you better watch what you say."

Jackson fills with guilt. His brother had told him something special, and he couldn't resist a chance to joke around.

The next morning as Cap is leaving for the Brittains', Jackson catches up with him. "I'm sorry about what I said last night at supper."

"I forgive you. We were both feeling good last night."

By lunch, Cap and Mr. Brittain finish drying in the cabin. Cap and the Brittains stand back, looking with pride at the new cabin.

The corners are neatly cut and every wall is straight and plumb. The porch has an inviting appeal about it, and now years of work and play can take place on its floors.

"Well Cap, I guess I owe you a wagon," states Mr. Brittain. He leads him to the shed where his own wagon is parked. "I want you to take this home with you this evening. You've worked hard and you deserve it."

Cap is surprised. Mr. Brittain intended to give him his only wagon.

"I can't take your wagon! You need it more than I do."

Mr. Brittain insists, but Cap shakes his head and will not accept it. "I know you have been too busy to build a wagon for me. When your shop is ready and you have time to build a new one for yourself, I'll take this one."

"Cap, from now on call me Buck. I don't have a better friend than you!"

Cap feels a warm, pleasant feeling inside. He knows he has done the right thing.

"Why don't you and Janice go fishing this evening and bring some fish home for supper. Flavie and I will cook up a fish fry supper to celebrate our new cabin."

Cap is more than happy to go fishing with Janice. When he walks up to the lean-to, he's surprised because Janice is dressed and ready. She has poles, a small rope to string the fish on, and bait in a basket. "How did you know we were going fishing?"

"Father told me you would probably finish early today, and he would invite you to a fish fry. I have to admit I hoped you would stay, so I got ready just in case."

Cap's heart is lighter than a feather, and a happy feeling is growing inside, but he isn't taking anything for granted.

As they walk across the clearing toward the fishing hole, they talk like two old friends.

"This is going to be the prettiest fishing hole you have ever seen. There is a big, beautiful rock jutting out into the creek," she says.

"I am sure it will be beautiful as long as you're there with me."

"I'm serious," she responds. "The rock is pretty and it's just perfect to sit on while we're fishing. Everything is prettier out here. I feel so lucky my family's farm is next to the wilderness and is almost ready to start providing for us."

"Your wonderful family has worked hard to build this place."

"You helped to make it happen, too," she replies with her pretty smile.

When they sit, Janice is so close that they're touching. Cap likes it and wonders if she means to. Or maybe it's a coincidence. He baits his hook and throws it out. He looks at Janice, and she places her hand on his as he holds the fishing pole. He looks into her beautiful eyes. They lean toward each other and share a wonderful kiss.

"I could stay here forever," says Cap.

"I could, too, but we need to compose ourselves and catch some fish."

The fish are biting, and even with them being silly, talking to each other and a couple more kisses, they soon have a string of fish.

Returning from the creek, the passion between Cap and Janice is too strong to hide. The Brittains are watching from the porch, but the two lovers are not intimidated. Their daughter's world has changed. There isn't an inch between the couple and they talk laughingly. It's too obvious to deny.

When they reach the porch, Buck has knives and a bowl waiting. "Cap, let's clean these fish while the women get things ready inside."

Cap works fast as they clean the fish. He's in a hurry to finish so he can be in the kitchen, close to Janice.

Soon, a big pot of lard bubbles around the fish as it hangs on a rod in the fireplace. The table is set ready for supper to begin. Everyone helps with the cooking, and soon it's ready to eat.

The new kitchen comes alive as they sit around the table. There are plenty of smiles at supper this evening.

"I have never enjoyed eating fish as much as I did tonight, Mrs. Brittain."

"Please call me Flavie." Smiling, she reaches across the table to squeeze Cap's hand.

"Thank you, Flavie," replies Cap, his mouth open slightly as he quietly looks into her eyes.

"Flavie, come help me for a minute in my shop," says Buck.

She holds his hand as they walk out to the shop. "I know what you're doing, Buck."

Cap and Janice are alone, and it's time to say good night. For the first time, Cap struggles to say goodbye. They kiss one last time as Cap stands beside his horse. He hops into the saddle and trots into the fading light.

Riding home is a task. He waited too long to leave, and his mind is occupied thinking about the wonderful evening at the rock on the creek.

Glad to be home, he sees Jackson and Homer beside the house. It's getting late so he assumes everyone else is asleep. He dances over to Jackson, singing, "I'm in love, I'm in love! It just happened, and I know she's the one for me."

Jackson smiles. "That's wonderful news! I like Janice, too. I hope someday someone feels the same way about me. I miss not spending as much time together as we used to, now that the Brittains are keeping you away from home two days a week." They enjoy being together for a happy moment.

"I wonder what mom and dad will say when they find out about my feelings for Janice. I dread telling them."

"I don't think it will be too hard." Jackson laughs. "They're on the back porch tonight and probably heard your little song."

Cap blushes and walks toward the back of the house. He peeks around the corner and sure enough, there they all sit.

Miles smiles. "Son, we're happy for you! It's time for you to find your life-long companion. I just have one question... Will we be gaining a daughter or losing a son?"

"I will always be your son, and I will never be far away," answers Cap.

"It's time for Janice to visit so we can get to know her. I would like for her to spend a day every now and then with me," says Inez.

"I will take care of that soon."

Cap is tired and happy. He heads to his room, falls asleep, and dreams happy dreams.

Sunday morning comes with bright sunshine, and he has a feeling of contentment as he begins his usual work around the farm. Jackson is in a good mood, too, and they pick at each other, having fun like they always do. Only now, Cap's mind drifts back to thoughts of Janice often.

At lunch, they're all enjoying their meal. "I would like to ride over to the Brittains and invite them to eat supper with us Friday," Cap says to his mom.

"Wonderful," she replies.

"Why don't you work a couple more hours with your father? Then you can spend the evening with Janice. Goodbyes are better as the sun is going down."

"I don't want you riding home in the dark," reminds Miles.

Chapter 8

Jackson is working alone near the house when movement in the edge of the wilderness catches his eye. He turns to get a better look and his mouth drops open. A wild-eyed man stumbles out of the forest. He stands again, jerking his arms from side to side as if he is still fighting his way through the underbrush. Delirious and trying to flee the wilderness, his injuries and dehydration slow him to a crawl. Jackson drops his tools and runs toward him. The man looks at Jackson and moves his lips, but his words are too soft to understand as he continues toward the farm. Jackson grabs him by the arm, trying to steady his steps. He's bloody and tattered and in shock, having been sliced by razor sharp briars, slapped over and over by tree limbs, and thrown to the ground by roots and stones— all designed by the cruel hand of nature to inflict misery on anyone running in fear.

Jackson recognizes him and sorrow pierces his heart. It's the man who passed by earlier with the little white dog he liked so much. Up close, the torn clothing and gashes across his arms and legs are painful to gaze upon. His face is chapped, his lips are dry and cracked, and blood is smeared over his nose and across his cheeks. He collapses and Jackson carries him to the porch. The poor man's eyes are still open, and he doesn't speak a word. Jackson fears he's dead, but then his eyes move and focus on him. "Water," he faintly whispers.

Jackson runs inside, dashes water in a cup, and wets a cloth to clean his wounds. The man, with hands shaking, gulps the water. He's thirsting so badly that he wastes most of it. Jackson runs back for more, and this time the man drinks a little slower.

"You're very kind," the man says weakly. He rests as he sits in a daze. "My dog, my little dog," he whimpers, and then sobs for a moment. Jackson wipes his wounds, cleaning dirt and dry blood from his arms and face. The man's eyes fill with tears again, and he trembles as he relives his harrowing experience. "It all happened so fast, I didn't have time to think. All that mattered was getting out of the wilderness alive."

Taking the wet rag from Jackson, he rubes his eyes and wets his face. He shakes his head as he takes a deep breath. "My dog is dead and my donkey is gone. He was too stubborn to move quickly. I just left him. I had to get back to civilization, and you're the first person I've seen."

Jackson hands him another cup of water. He takes a sip and pauses for a minute.

"There is something very powerful hiding out there. Something evil took my little dog. We had just settled for the night and built a nice warm campfire. My dog was beside me. As I petted him, he started growling and the hair on his back stood up. His head popped up and he stared into the forest. Then he started barking louder and louder." He wipes the tears streaming down his face. "He was trying to scare that horrible creature away. "As I reached for my bow, he sprang into the woods and out of the campfire light. In an instant, I heard him shriek, then not a sound."

The man stops, trying to regain his composure.

"Without regard for my own life, I ran as fast as I could to find him. Limbs and briars tore at me, but I managed to get close enough to see a large creature in the rising moonlight. My dog was dangling from its claws, blood gushing, and dripping to the ground. It was almost too dark to see, and the sight shocked me so badly. I can't tell you much about the creature, but the thing ran a couple steps and flew away. Suddenly I came to my senses and filled with horror. Running back in the direction we had come from was all I could think about. None of my equipment mattered." He shook his head. "I know this sounds crazy, but it really did happen. It has been almost impossible to sleep since the attack, and the only thing on my mind is returning to my home. There's something wicked, wild, and powerful waiting out there for someone to come its way."

Uncle Matt stands on the porch and hears the man describe the encounter. "I knew there were dragons in the wilderness."

Jackson smirks, shaking his head. "I'm sure it's just a wolf or a bear."

The man shakes his head and Uncle Matt fixes his eyes on Jackson. "The wilderness is a big place. There could be anything out there where no one has ever been."

Inez steps onto the porch just as the talk of dragons starts. "This man needs to stop talking and rest. You can talk in the morning. He needs to eat and sleep before he answers another question."

"Thank you kindly," he replies. Jackson helps him stand, and the man weakly follows her inside.

Uncle Matt takes off to find Miles. He has a story to tell him.

When the man finishes eating, Inez offers him the boy's room. Cap and Jackson will sleep in the kitchen tonight.

The sun is setting. Cap's horse can be heard coming up the trail and Jackson is waiting on the porch. Cap's feelings of love and joy cease when he sees Jackson isn't smiling. The brothers head to the barn.

"We have a problem we can't fix and no one else needs to hear our conversation." Jackson looks around to be sure they're alone. "The man I told you about who went into the wilderness with his dog is here. He's spending the night in our room."

"Did he find something?

"Worse than that. He's telling everyone a large creature grabbed his dog and flew away with it hanging from its claws. Uncle Matt was standing beside him and 'dragon' was the first word out of his mouth."

"There's little we can do, but at least we can act as if we don't believe there is such a thing," replies Cap, gently biting his lip.

The man sleeps soundly, but he wakes up early. Inez hears him stirring and heads to the kitchen. She rekindles the fire and starts preparing breakfast.

Miles and Uncle Matt rise and head to the kitchen. Cap and Jackson are already up. They gather around the breakfast table, talking to him as Inez finishes cooking. They want to hear every detail of his story.

"You are too kind taking care of me like this. I thank you from the bottom of my heart. My name is Bill Williams."

"We're glad to help," says Miles before introducing his family.

"You have a nice family. Every one of you is very kind. I live twenty-five miles south of your village in a place called Water Town."

Uncle Matt interrupts. "From all you have told us, I'm sure you were attacked by a dragon."

"I'm not certain it was a dragon, but I know of nothing else that looks like the creature I saw," his eyes fill with tears.

"Let's enjoy breakfast now," interrupts Inez. "You can talk to Mr. Williams about what happened while you're taking him to the village."

After breakfast, Bill is anxious to leave. "I have seen enough of the wilderness and want no more to do with it. I have had enough adventure. I just want to be with my family."

Uncle Matt longs to talk more with Bill, but he and Miles had set traps the day before, and they have to be checked. They can't leave an animal suffering any longer than necessary.

Jackson hooks up the wagon and volunteers to take Bill to the village. As Bill climbs aboard, Inez hands him a basket filled with jerky and dried fruit for his journey.

"I'm sorry for your loss in the wilderness, but I feel lucky to have the opportunity to take you to the village," says Jackson. "I can't wait to hear more about villages and farms along the trail between Water Town and our farm. I have never been south of our village."

Bill's mood brightens the further from the wilderness they travel. It is a clear warm day without a cloud in the sky, but occasionally he looks up into the sky. Jackson doesn't ask him why. He figures the man wants to be sure the large creature isn't up there following him. Bill reaches for the basket Inez gave him, pulls out a piece of dried apple, eats it, and is ready to talk. "The world south of your farm is an amazing place. You must take time to travel before you get too many responsibilities."

"I'm always too busy around the farm. I'm not sure I'll ever be able to leave long enough to do that," replies Jackson.

"You can't let your life pass by without having a little adventure."

Jackson nods knowingly as his and Cap's adventure flashes through his head. Bill pulls a piece of jerky out of the basket and offers it to Jackson. "No thanks," mom fixed that for you. Bill chews and continues talking. "There are two villages between Water Town and Blade Town. Otherwise, the trail is unsettled. The real adventure starts closer to Water Town. Some farmers there have big farms and raise only cattle. Other farms only raise chickens or pigs. They specialize and are able to produce more that way."

"How can anyone trade enough of one thing to get all the variety of things needed to survive? Our family has always grown and hunted for everything we need."

"You have never even seen a silver coin, have you, Jackson?"

"A silver coin? No, but it sounds pretty. Why do you ask?

"I will show you one when we reach Blade Town."

"It sounds like the world is changing for the better," says Jackson.

Bill smiles, "The world is always changing. Some is good and some is bad. You're young. Be mindful of what's going on around you. Take your time and think things out before you do anything. Especially where silver is involved."

Time passes quickly and soon they're in the village. Bill jumps off the wagon at the public watering trough. "Thank you for not talking about what happened in the wilderness. I would like to forget about it and get on with my life. I do miss my dog. His name was Charlie. He was a good dog."

In the village, Jackson feels excitement in the air and a new adventure is in sight. A new store with a sign over the front door that reads, "Blade Town Hardware and Supplies" is in front of him.

Bill heads into the store and Jackson follows him in. Bill needs camping equipment to finish his trip home. Inside, Jackson is spellbound.

"I have never seen so many different things in one place," says Jackson, walking around, picking wares up and watching the shoppers pick and choose merchandise. Bill smiles as he watches Jackson.

"With a little silver, you can buy almost anything in this store," says Bill, heading for the cashier.

Jackson walks over to one of the people working in the store. "Why is this store named 'Blade Town Hardware'?"

"The village is beginning to be known as the place to buy knives, axes, and metal points to fit on the end of arrows. Everyone wants blades and arrow points made here."

Bill makes his way back to Jackson's side. He has a pack filled with camping utensils and blankets. On his shoulder sits a bow and quiver filled with arrows and a pouch filled with jerky. "I'm heading out now. I have all I need. Thank you and your wonderful family for treating me so kindly." He reaches into his pocket, pulls out a large silver coin and hands it to Jackson.

"You don't owe me anything."

"Take it. If you don't want it, give it to your wonderful mother for the breakfast she cooked this morning. Or spend it in this store and see what silver coins are good for." Jackson hesitates.

"You must take it."

"Thank you. I wish you good luck on your trip home." Jackson looks at all the pretty things in the store and knows he has to get out of there or he'll spend his first coin before he reaches home.

Chapter 9

Jackson climbs into the family wagon, relishing a feeling of freedom he has never experienced before. He's never alone in it with no one to tell him to hurry or which way to go. The feeling is magical and intoxicatingly wonderful. Beautiful weather surrounds him as the sun peeks in and out from behind puffy clouds caught up in a gentle breeze.

"There aren't many days like this," he thinks, taking in a deep breath as if he can inhale the essence of a perfect day for the ride home. Riding contently, he savors the trail's beauty. Mesmerized, he's surprised when he realizes Mr. Brittain's turn off is in sight. As he approaches, a wagon is coming up the trail. He stops and waits to say hello. Janice and her father smile as they come to a stop beside him.

"Hello, Jackson. What a pleasant surprise to see you." says Janice. "Good evening. I'm on my way home from the village. I saw you coming and thought I would stop and say hello."

"I'm so glad you did. If you aren't busy Saturday, you should come with Cap to our house," she says with a twinkle in her eyes.

"Thank you, but I will probably be doing chores until dark, and Cap leaves too early for me."

"That's a shame. I hoped you could come meet my cousin Sandra."

He cocks his head in thought. "Sounds intriguing, if I get the chance, I will. Thanks for inviting me."

He flips the reins and the horse heads home. "What a treat today has been," he thinks as he rides alone on the family wagon. He decides he's going to figure out how to ride to the village alone more often.

Homer lays waiting for Jackson to return. When he hears the wagon approaching, he scampers out to greet him, yipping, and jumping around the wheels.

"Hop up here boy. I'm glad you missed me." Jackson daydreams for a moment as he rubs Homer's head. "It would be nice if someone missed me as much as Homer does." He ponders what Janice said about her cousin coming to visit Saturday.

He starts his chores, working fast to make up for lost time. Then the porch bell rings. Cap reaches the porch and waits as Jackson hurries to catch up with him. Its supper time and they're happy and hungry.

"My trip to the village was amazing today," says Jackson, bubbling with excitement. "The hardware store has been finished and is open. You can't imagine all the things sitting on the shelves ready to bring home and use."

"Sounds like you had a good day. Did Mr. Williams talk about the dragon anymore?"

"No, I was more interested in learning about what he has seen south of the village. Look at this silver coin he gave me." He pulls the shiny silver coin out of his pocket.

"I've heard about these coins." Cap examines the coin. It's the size of a man's thumb, round, and has been pounded smooth. "You better find a good place to keep it," he says.

Jackson drops the coin back into his pocket. "I saw Janice and Mr. Brittain today on my way home, and she invited me to come with you next Saturday to meet her cousin."

"I'm not sure you would like spending your evening at the Brittain's."

"You're probably right. Janice will have her cousin and you to talk to and I won't fit in."

"Wait, now that I think about it, I need you to come along to keep the cousin busy. We'll have a lot of fun together."

Cap and Jackson are in an uncommonly good mood Saturday morning. Time flies by as they work fast to finish their chores.

They saddle their horses after lunch, ride out to the trail, and turn toward the village and the young ladies.

"Hurry up, little brother. I usually go faster than this."

"I'm not feeling so well. Maybe this isn't such a good idea. I wish I hadn't started this whole mess about meeting Janice's cousin," complains Jackson.

"You're just nervous about meeting a girl. That's all."

"What if she didn't come after all? I will be in the way all evening."

"It will be ok."

"What if she is ugly?"

"Jackson, I would be ashamed to say such a thing. Quit worrying."

"You're right. What if she thinks I'm ugly?"

"That's a chance everyone has to take. Just be man enough to take a chance and stop worrying."

"I will try."

"Oh you'll stop worrying soon. We're at the turn off."

"Ha ha, very funny," replies Jackson.

As they ride down the trail, Cap daydreams and Jackson worries.

The ladies are standing on the porch when the brothers ride up. Jackson takes a deep breath as he dismounts. He feels out of place, but now all he can do is hope for the best.

Sandra looks pleasant, and she's definitely pretty. Her hair is light brown, pulled back, and tied in a bun. She stands a little taller than Janice and Jackson is spellbound. Both girls are wearing long blue dresses with ribbons tied like belts around their waists.

"I'm pleased you both came. This is my cousin Sandra," says Janice.

"I'm pleased to meet you," says Jackson.

"Thanks for coming," responds Sandra with a smile that keeps getting prettier.

"Let's sit on the porch and talk," suggest Janice.

Jackson is glad Janice tells him to sit beside Sandra in the swing where the wonderful fragrance she's wearing will drift by. It smells like a bouquet of flowers.

"I love the fragrance you're wearing," says Jackson.

"My mother and I make it in the summer. I like it to," replies Sandra.

As she talks, Jackson feels funny. Being close to a pretty girl with only two other people around is a new experience for him.

"Sandra and I grew up in a little village ten miles south of Blade Town, but my father has always talked about how beautiful it is out here close to the wilderness. One day after visiting Blade Town he pulled up his roots and moved out here. Sadly, that's why Sandra and I don't live close together anymore. She's like a sister to me."

Cap looks at Sandra. "I'm sorry Janice left your village, but I'm glad she's here close to me."

Jackson has yet to say much, and realizes he needs to say something interesting fast. "I have a new pet. A dog named Homer. He's the best friend you can imagine. He's smart and is always glad to see me, especially if we have been apart for a while."

"I think I would like to have a dog like Homer," says Sandra. "I'm only going to be here one day, but when I come back next month, I will be spending a week with Janice and would like to see Homer."

Jackson listens as Sandra talks. Her conversations are pleasant. He's feeling less nervous, especially after she said she wanted to see him when she came back.

Before the evening comes to an end, he and Sandra are lost in conversation and sitting close together.

"I think Jackson and your cousin are in a world of their own. They haven't said a word to either of us in ten minutes," says Cap, sliding closer to Janice.

"They're very content," replies Janice.

It's almost dark and the brothers have to say goodbye. Cap kisses Janice goodnight.

Jackson smiles at Sandra. "I look forward to seeing you when you come back to visit Homer."

"I will see you in a month," she replies, tilting her head and smiling.

It's almost too dark to see as the young men ride home. The moonlight helps, but they have to be careful and ride slowly.

"I never dreamed Janice's cousin would be so pretty, did you?" asks Jackson. "Did you smell how wonderful they smelled when they were close together?" Jackson closes his eyes and inhales slowly like he was taking the fragrance in again. "It's like lavender, roses, and honeysuckle all mixed together. It's heavenly."

"Stop and take a deep breath of fresh air, Jackson. You're talking too much," states Cap, almost unable to get a word in. "We're almost home. Don't ask anymore questions. Just sleep on it tonight. We have all day tomorrow to talk."

When they're close to their house they notice Uncle Matt waiting on the porch. "Our apple thief is back. When your father and I checked the apple trees today they were picked clean."

"Jackson and I will help you catch the thief. You know how much we like apple cider," exclaims Cap.

Uncle Matt is satisfied. He has given them the story and he quietly goes to his waiting bed.

The brothers ride to the barn and put the horses away. They quietly walk back to the house.

"I don't think Fuzzy's getting our apples. We told him all about that long ago," says Cap quietly.

Once they enter their room, they forget about apple trees and remember their wonderful evening. They talk about the ladies until their eyes refuse to stay open.

Everyone rises early for breakfast the next day.

"I'm going to build a blind near the apple trees where I can hide and see what's happening to our apples," says Uncle Matt to Miles.

"That's enough about apples." Inez shushes the two of them. She turns to Jackson. "Did you enjoy meeting Janice's cousin?"

Jackson blushes. "Yes. She seems to be a smart girl and a lot like Janice."

"Are you going to try to see her again?" questions Uncle Matt.

"When she comes back, she wants to meet Homer," Jackson replies, smiling.

"Sounds like there could be more to the story than you're telling," chuckles Uncle Matt.

The blush returns.

"It's not proper to tease a young man about his girl," chides Inez.

Sunday evening and there is not much to keep Jackson's mind occupied. Cap has gone to see Janice, and Sandra is already on her way home. Jackson has a new uncomfortable feeling he will have to learn to deal with.

He whistles for Homer and soon hears the pup's little feet scampering his way. With tail wagging, he looks earnestly to see what Jackson has in mind.

Jackson grabs his bow.

"Homer, we're going hunting. I want to see if you can learn to hunt like Bill's dog."

Jackson enjoys being with Homer and the day passes quickly. He and Homer are relaxing on the porch when they hear Cap returning.

"I have good news for you, brother! Janice asked me to tell you Sandra enjoyed meeting you and hopes when she returns you will come see her and bring Homer."

Jackson lights up all over. Cap even feels good seeing his brother so happy.

"What a wonderful day after all!" he exclaims.

Chapter 10

A week later, as the sun is setting, Homer becomes restless and starts barking. Jackson quiets him and stops his work. In the distance he hears men talking and the clomping of horse hoofs. Stepping out of the barn, he sees four men on fine horses approaching from the south. Jackson walks toward the house, studying them, as he and Homer prepare to greet them.

Every man carries a powerful hunting bow and a quiver full of arrows. Two of the men lead an extra horse with saddlebags strapped on from front to back. It's obvious these men are heading into the wilderness in search of something special. They're wearing shirts and pants so new the soft leather they're made of doesn't even look broken in. Their appearance is very different from most trappers and hunters who wear raggedy and patched clothing. Even their saddlebags are different. They're well-made and bulge with provisions. Whatever they have in mind, they're prepared to stay in the wilderness a long time.

Jackson feels uneasy when he notices two large dogs running around, sniffing here and there. They are much bigger than Homer, and the look in their eyes is of wild animals trained to track and kill.

Homer tucks his tail and stays close to Jackson. One of the dogs darts ahead and sniffs him. It has a piercing look in its eyes. Homer tucks his tail even lower and drops his head, standing perfectly still until the dog moves on. Then he slips under the house and hides.

The men stop in front of the house.

"Hello, young man," says the leader. He acts friendly, but the other men keep looking toward the wilderness, and they can't stand still.

"Good evening," replies Jackson, his mind racing, wondering what they have in mind. Uncle Matt and Miles come up behind him, startling him.

"Welcome, men. My name is Miles Murray; this is my brother, Matt, and my son, Jackson. What can we do for you?"

"Good to meet you. Is this the farm where Bill Williams stopped on his way to the wilderness?" asks the leader.

"Yes, it is. He also came back here when he returned. He was delirious and scratched badly. We took him in so he could recover from whatever happened out there," says Miles.

Hearing Miles's response makes everyone in the hunting party's eyes light up, and they smile at each other.

"If you don't mind, we would like to camp just past your barn for the night."

"You are more than welcome," replies Miles.

Jackson feels sorry for Homer. If their dogs are going to stay this close to the house, Homer will have to sleep in his room.

"When you finish supper, come back to the house. Sit and talk awhile. I would like to hear about your journey," says Miles.

"We may take you up on that, Mr. Murray." They ride past the barn.

Miles waits until they are too far away to hear him. "When these men come back, it will be interesting to see what they're really up to," he says to Uncle Matt. "I'm sure you and I can get them started talking. When they're comfortable with us, they will tell us a lot more than if we ask them questions."

An hour later, the men wander to the porch. Jackson, Uncle Matt, Miles, and Inez are already there and watch as they approach. Jackson studies how they walk and interact. They give the impression, laughing and gesturing, that they're on an adventure they expect to be exciting and enjoyable. The men are sure of themselves and don't show any intimidation posed by the vast wilderness that lies ahead. Jackson remembers what his father told him and Cap long ago—you have to respect the wilderness or the wilderness won't respect you.

"Good evening, Mrs. Murray, gentlemen. My name is Virgil. I am leading this hunting party into the wilderness." He politely nods and introduces the rest of the party as Ron, Jess, and Steven.

Virgil has an air of confidence about him. He looks to be in his mid-twenties. The clothes he's wearing have lots of extra leather sewn in places where they normally wear out and tassels just for looks. He does most of the talking. Ron is a quiet man, several years older than Virgil. He isn't as nicely dressed, and Jackson decides he works for Virgil.

Jess and Steven are the most excited about the adventure ahead. They smile a lot and are about the same age as Jackson. They watch Virgil to be sure they don't say anything he doesn't like.

"We're all from Water Town where Mr. Williams lives. After hearing his story, I had to come out here in search of the creature he spoke about. I asked him how to return to where he was attacked. He told me if I stayed on this trail the last house I would pass on the way to the wilderness would be your farm. He also told us about your kindness, and he sends his regards. Fortunately, I found a group of investors in Water Town, and they're paying me to get to the bottom of the story he's telling. We're going to bring back whatever he saw."

Inez can't wait any longer to speak. "I want to hear all about Water Town first. That sounds more interesting to me than your hunting trip."

"Of course," agrees Virgil. "I will try to give an idea, but you will have to see it to truly understand." He thinks for a second. "Water Town is a big village with lots of people. There are shops there selling everything you can imagine, and my favorite, lots of places to eat. Most of the people work for silver coins. They trade them for things the local farmers raise. People there will even pay silver to see things they have never seen before, like the creature Mr. Williams saw."

"No one in our family has ever traded anything so they could be entertained," states Jackson.

"It's a whole different world than you have experienced out here," says Virgil.

"I can't argue about that. Our world is a lot different in many ways, and I hope you don't end up like Mr. Williams," replies Jackson.

Jess reaches over rubbing one of the dogs as it naps on the porch floor. "We have two hunting dogs specially bred to hunt large animals. There's a big difference between them and the dog Mr. Williams had. They will protect us and help us catch the creature."

"You mean dragon," states Uncle Matt.

The four men slap their knees with joy. They can hardly be still after hearing the word dragon. They smile and nod at each other.

"So, you know about dragons being in the wilderness?" asks Virgil with a half-smile on his face.

"I think Matt got excited. There has never been any proof," says Miles.

"I have talked to several people in Blade Town who say they have seen them," replies Uncle Matt.

"I would like to believe there are dragons. That would be exciting, but with no proof it has to be a story someone made up," states Jackson.

"I believe proof will come. It's just a matter of time," replies Uncle Matt.

Virgil smiles, "Would you trade something to see one?"

"I would feed all of you a fine chicken dinner to see one," exclaims Uncle Matt.

"I can assure you, if there are dragons out there, we will bring one back. And we will take you up on your offer," says Virgil, very confident.

"I will help Uncle Matt with the dinner if you bring a dragon here for us to see, but I wish you would tell us some more about Water Town before you leave," says Inez.

Virgil smiles and chuckles. "Mrs. Murray, I hope one day you can visit Water Town to enjoy and shop for dresses and hats. You wouldn't believe how pretty the women's shoes are."

"The only problem is we don't have any pieces of silver to buy them," states Miles.

"I noticed you have several head of cattle in your pasture." Virgil points to the field. Just pick one you don't need anymore, tie it behind your wagon, and come to Water Town. Someone will give you a lot of silver coins for it."

Miles listens closely.

"You take the silver and go to the shops. You will be amazed how many wonderful things you will see there."

Jackson starts thinking about going to Water Town to buy something pretty for Sandra. He feels guilty, realizing he needs to be more concerned about Fuzzy becoming a victim in man's quest for silver.

"If you ever once come to Water Town to sell your livestock, it will change your lives forever," says Virgil.

Ron speaks for the first time, "I think it's time to settle down for the night. We need to start early in the morning."

Virgil agrees and tips his hat to the Murrays. "Good night. I will be back soon for my fine chicken dinner."

The men fade into the darkness, headed toward a glowing pile of coals. They talk happily as they walk away.

"I guarantee these men think they will get more silver than they deserve, when they return to Water Town with whatever animal they're after," says Miles, starting the conversation again.

"I believe one could get addicted to having silver to buy pretty things. It does sound a lot easier than what we do," says Uncle Matt.

"We have always had all we need," Inez reminds everyone. "It's more important that our family stays close and takes care of each other. We need each other to keep our way of life going, and I wouldn't give that up for a materialistic way of life. I think if you could get too many pretty things, too easily, then nothing would mean much, and families wouldn't stay close like us."

"I still want to see for myself how the people in Water Town live," says Uncle Matt. "I know there's nothing more valuable than a family you can depend on."

In the distance, everyone hears the clop-clop sound of Cap's horse as it trots up the trail. Everyone looks at him as he rides up.

"Why is everyone out here waiting for me to come home?"

"We've been being entertained by four hunters who are camping just past our barn. They came over to talk to us before bedding down. We were surprised to see how many saddle bags they have. And they have two large dogs running along with them. If you look, you can see embers from their fire just past the barn," explains Jackson.

"I wonder what they're up to."

"They told us they're being paid to bring back whatever killed Mr. William's dog," replies Jackson

Cap smirks and shakes his head. "Are you kidding me?"

"He's not kidding. They also told us some unbelievable things about Water Town," says Uncle Matt.

Cap glances toward the dying embers glowing past the barn. "I want to hear all about it in the morning. Now, I'm ready for bed," he says, surprising everyone when he doesn't ask more questions.

In the morning before Cap wakes, Jackson is lying in bed wondering what chain of events is about to unfold. Cap stirs.

"Are you awake?" asks Jackson.

"Yes, good morning."

"You're wrong about the good part. There's nothing but trouble camped near our barn," says Jackson.

"I'm worried, too. These men have no idea what they're about to get into. They think they're going to track some mindless creature down and make the world a safer place for all of us."

Cap slides out of bed and pulls on his trousers. "Get dressed. Maybe I can think of something to say to stop trouble."

"There's nothing you can say to convince a hunting party such as this to give up their quest," says Jackson.

They slip on their clothes, head outside, jump off the porch, and turn toward the barn. The men are gone. They were in such a hurry, they didn't even build a fire to kill the morning chill.

"They're too far gone. We've done all we can," says Cap.

<>

The sun begins to peek over the horizon, and the wilderness wakes, filling the gentle breeze with its fragrance of freshness. The towering trees look welcoming. Virgil leads the way, happy to see his men are enjoying themselves.

"I feel so alive out here. Adventure is in the air, and I have a feeling this is going to be the most interesting journey I have ever taken," says Jess.

"I love the feeling of danger lurking out in these woods, mixed in with the beauty we see all around us," replies Steven, taking a deep breath. He sneezes, but his face is still filled with a smile.

Jess and Steven are eager to reach the excitement they hope lies ahead.

"Ron! Ride ahead and chop some limbs off those trees in front of us so we can stay on this path," says Virgil. He likes being the leader and knows Ron isn't as excited about being on this trip as he is.

Looking to the sides of the path, Virgil sees a battle slowly raging. Vines seize and choke weeds and saplings as they stretch higher and higher trying to escape to bathe in sunlight. The hunting party is immersed in a sea of green, as plants vigorously grow all around, spilling into the path causing it to fade away, but the men make good time the first day.

Once the sun drops below the tree tops, the green fades into gray as darkness creeps into the wilderness.

Virgil looks for a place to camp, and soon finds the perfect spot. They all grab their long knives and hack the saplings and weeds away from around six gray boulders. The rocks are taller than the horse's heads and are situated in a 'U' shape. There is enough room for the four men to nestle between them. With the dogs in front, the fire is only needed for comfort.

Virgil looks at the cleared area. "This will be a great place to spend the night. Jess, you and Steven unload the leather tarps while Ron and I cut saplings to lie across the rocks. If it rains tonight, we will have a dry place to sleep."

Jess and Steven build a fire while Virgil and Ron prepare the meal. The wilderness begins to sing her nighttime lullaby as bugs, frogs, and owls join together in melody. Everyone relaxes around the fire, talking as beans simmer in front of them. They all enjoy camping in the wilderness that night.

The next morning, they warm root tea as they eat jerky. Everyone is eager to start moving again. The wilderness quickly grows treacherous with fallen limbs covered by thick vines and bushes creating a mass of underbrush three feet thick in places.

"You and I will have to start helping Ron. There's too much growth for one man to cut," says Steven, reaching for his long knife.

Virgil overhears them and is glad they understand.

Steven and Jess take turns helping Ron. Before long, they all have blisters. Fortunately Virgil finds a safe place to spend the night before they're too tired and scratched to cut anymore.

Everyone is tired and hungry as they settle down for the evening. They eat early and decide who will stand guard. All but one is asleep before dark.

The next morning, there are lots of groans as the men discover their muscles ache from doing work they aren't used to. Slowly they rise, and before long, they are ready for another day. The sound of chopping and complaining begins again.

Early in the evening on the third day, Virgil sees everyone is tired and calls for them to stop and set up camp. They move close to a large rock where they can protect themselves for the night. Catching their breath, Jess and Steven are thankful they're stopping.

As they sit around the campfire, Virgil is in deep thought. He knows things have to change and he dreads telling the others. He waits until everyone is quiet for a while. "The wilderness is getting too thick. If we keep going like this, we will all be too tired to do any hunting or protect ourselves. We must stop cutting the trail so wide. We have no choice but to leave the horses here. Ron will stay to feed and water them until we return." Ron is shocked. He places his left elbow on his knee, and rests his hand under his chin, as he stares at the ground.

"I think that's a bad idea," says Jess, Steven agrees. They both look him in the eyes. "The horses provide a lot of protection and if we need to get out of here in a hurry, we must have them."

"I understand how you feel about the horses, but we need to travel on foot so we won't have to keep cutting so many trees. The trail need only be wide enough for a man to squeeze through," says Virgil, trying to keep an understanding tone in his voice.

Ron looks up. "I will stay with the horses, but I need a safer place than this, and water has to be nearby," he says without compromise.

"We will find a safer place near water," replies Virgil. "So that leaves Jess and Steven to agree."

"Let's see how we feel when we find Ron his safe place," says Jess.

The hunting party has a restless night. No one talks to Virgil, and they're worrying about leaving the horses.

The next day they discover a good place for Ron to camp next to a stream. There is a large tree growing nearby with limbs close to the ground and a tarp can be thrown over then to provide shelter. If need be, it will be easy to climb.

"Okay, men, this looks like the place we're looking for, what do you say?" asks Virgil.

"It's hard for me to believe we're going to really leave our horses. The three of us will be on foot, chopping limbs and carrying heavy packs," complains Jess.

"This can't come as a surprise to either of you. This is the wilderness and this is what we bargained for from the beginning," states Virgil, feeling defensive.

Steven looks at Jess to see if that was what he understood this trip would be like.

"Men, it's my fault if you have been misled. I wanted both of you to come with me, and I have tried to make this trip as comfortable as I can. I promise you it will be worth all this hard work when we shoot our dragon. We're too far into the wilderness to turn back now."

"It's going to be a lot harder than I thought, but I will go on for another week," says Steven, looking at Jess.

"I will stay as long as Steven," replies Jess.

"Thank you. I promise you won't be sorry," says Virgil.

"Please, tell me you're not going to take both of the dogs," begs Ron.

"I wish you could keep one, but we must have them both. Things could get tricky when it's time to catch the dragon." Ron squints and shakes his head. "Everything will be all right. We will stay here tonight and help you get this camp site set up," assures Virgil.

Ron feels abandoned the next day as the three leave with the dogs. He has little to say as they leave.

The three of them chop and travel along without too much complaining until several days later. Steven is tired and homesick. "This trip just keeps getting harder and harder, and there has been no sign of dragons"

"If you think about it, things aren't that bad. The packs are a little lighter and the dogs are bringing lots of game back for us." Virgil forces himself to look happier than he really is. He's determined to keep their spirits up.

Jess and Steven slowly accept the hardships wilderness travel requires, and they fall into a routine. Things seem better for a while, but with still no sign of any dragons to give them a reason to continue, they feel bitter.

"I can't believe we're sitting out here with no horses. We don't stand a chance without them," says Steven. "We're going to end up like Mr. William's dog," replies Jess, looking straight at Virgil.

"There's no need to worry. We have two well-trained dogs to protect us," says Virgil as he rubs the dog beside him. Jess and Steven don't respond. They feel trapped in their situation. When darkness settles in, their nerves are already frayed. Every time the dogs bark, they reach for their bows. Some nights, they don't go back to sleep after the dogs wake them. They worry and listen intently, opening the door for all kinds of unexplained noises to haunt them.

Listening to Jess and Steven day after day is grating on Virgil's nerves. If he wasn't so determined to come home with a dragon, he would just give up.

<>

Jackson and Cap are happily working on the family's chicken house. Its small compared to their barn, but it's an important part of the farm. They always talk as they work, but today their subject is more interesting than usual.

"It has been three weeks since you saw Sandra. I bet next week will be even harder for you," says Cap, trying to work and talk.

"I have worked hard these last three weeks trying to keep from missing her so much," replies Jackson, reaching for a sapling he had hewn thin enough to fit between the logs.

"If Janice weren't close, I would feel the same way." Cap pounds the sapling into the crack. "I'm more worried about the hunting party. There's no telling what they're doing or how much trouble they're stirring up."

"My biggest concern is that Fuzzy might think we had something to do with these men going out there," replies Jackson.

The next sapling is ready. They pick it up and pound it into the wall. "I think the cracks are all filled," says Jackson.

"Because you have worked so hard trying to keep Sandra off your mind, these chickens have the best house any chicken has ever had," says Cap.

Friday evening, the family is enjoying sitting on the porch. Miles is smiling and holding Inez's hand. "After thinking about what the hunting party's leader said the other day, your mother and I are going to give his suggestion a try. We're going to take a cow to Water Town and see how much silver we can get. We're really looking forward to going; this is a big deal for us."

"You deserve to go. Who knows, maybe all of us will get to go there before too long," says Cap. "Don't forget, next Saturday is when Jackson is coming with me to see Sandra again. That's going to be a big deal, too."

Miles looks at Cap. "How serious are you about Janice?"

Cap doesn't hide his emotions. There is no blushing or hesitation as he replies. "She is the one for me, and I will ask her to marry me soon."

No one is surprised to hear Cap's answer. Jackson feels a lump in his throat when he hears his brother's reply.

Chapter 11

Surrounded by forest so thick they almost never see the sun, and with no clue as to what lies in any direction except for the trail behind them, Virgil, Jess, and Stephen toil from sunup until sundown, and stress is growing between them. Their adventure once guised as fun is turning into drudgery. Every day is spent walking, chopping, and searching for the creature in the wilderness they hope will be a dragon.

They no longer see any beauty within the wilderness. The only thing they enjoy is soaking in the warmth and security they find sitting around their campfires.

<>

High atop their plateau, Fuzzy's den watches the fires. At first, they had occasionally glanced toward the south, where it started as just a flicker of light, but now little groups gather at the entrance every evening, anxious to see where the glow will be. They always leave concerned because the fire marches steadily toward them.

The den hasn't grown much since Cap and Jackson's adventure. Dragons don't reproduce without giving thought to how much nature can provide for them. The wisdom of being obedient to instinct and nature provides them a simple way of life, and they don't live in need. This philosophy has been passed down from Fuzzy's ancestors who lived that way, and the den has called the cavern home for hundreds of years. Things have changed very little. Presently, his den consists of twenty-five members, and they live in contentment. Nature has given them intelligence, but instinct is the most important thing to them.

Fuzzy learned from Cap and Jackson's farm that man has very little instinct left. The less man cares for nature, the less nature freely gives to him, and few men live in contentment.

Lester turns toward the cavern and summons his den. "Ureeeeee," echoes through the chambers. He waits and soon the den gathers around.

"We have all been concerned about the campfires getting closer to our cavern. It's time to see how many men are out there and if they pose a threat."

Fuzzy steps forward and bows. "I volunteer to check on them if it pleases the den." He has no other choice. He worries it may be Cap and Jackson. No one knows why he chooses to go. He has never told any other dragon about meeting humans when he was young. His father told him never to tell anyone, and he has been obedient.

Everyone agrees to let him go.

Lester approaches Fuzzy as the den ambles back into the cavern. "May I share a word of wisdom with you? Remember the man with the dog that barked and dashed into the woods after me?"

"Yes, I know you warned us if men have a dog with them it will sense our presence and bark if we go near."

"Good. Be very careful. It's more important than ever you're not seen. Men are venturing our way too often. We can't let any of them return with stories about dragons in the wilderness."

Fuzzy bows. "I will do my best for our den's sake. Tomorrow morning, I will explain what I find to the den."

Fuzzy flies out the entrance and turns toward the campfire. It's dark enough for him to fly over their camp without the men seeing him. It's easy to see their fire, and it's not far from the cavern as a dragon flies.

Circling high above their camp, Fuzzy smells food and hickory smoke rising into the evening sky. He wonders why man is the one creature that doesn't have the instinct or desire to be hard to find. He hopes these fires won't turn out to be Cap and Jackson's. He wants their promise to him to mean more than this. He lands downwind of the camp. Slowly he slips through the woods, quietly moving to a place where he can spy on them and study every detail. Men are talking in an unhappy tone. The conversations sound very serious and no laughter ever erupts like when he's around Cap and Jackson. It's obvious they aren't having fun.

He watches for a while and counts three men. Two are sitting around the fire and one is practicing his marksmanship, shooting over and over into a rotten tree trunk.

Fuzzy is shocked and fills with anxiety. These men are nothing like Cap and Jackson. They're well-armed with large bows and all kinds of knives in sheaths hooked to their belts. Fuzzy cringes as he thinks about what the knives are used for. He watches with concern as one of the men rubs the blade of his big knife back and forth over a smooth rock. He feels better when the man tests it by cutting limbs and weeds. He frowns when he realizes it will be ready in the morning to cut brush again and they will move closer to the cavern.

Fuzzy turns his attention to the men sitting around the fire, and is shocked. There, among the men, lie two large dogs. Fear overwhelms him and his heart races. This changes everything. He's too close to a very dangerous situation. The dogs add instinct and superior senses to the intelligent human creatures, making them hideously dangerous.

He is disheartened. The situation at hand means trouble for his family. He sits very still, trying to decide what move to make. Slipping away without being detected by the dogs will not be easy. He needs to be much further away before he can safely fly into the night.

As he creeps slowly away from the campfire, he hears a bark and a streak of fear sweeps through his body, turning his stomach upside down and sharpening his senses. He stops and stands perfectly still, but the next bark is louder and more intense. The dogs leap to their feet, growling and barking as they analyze the scent drifting by them.

Fuzzy looks back and sees the dogs sniffing in his direction. Then a bloodcurdling howl, worse than any sound he has ever heard, echoes through the trees, ringing in his ears. The fuzz down the middle of his back stands straight up. Men spring to their feet.

He realizes that howl is not to warn him to run, but to tell him he will soon be their prey. Their bodies are enraged with energy as they obey their killer instinct. They need no light as they zero in on his scent. The race for survival bursts forth.

Fuzzy frantically dashes with all his might through the forest. Making noise doesn't matter anymore. He suffers all the punishment wilderness can inflict as he flees for his life. His heart pumps furiously, as if it will explode, and sweat pours off his brow. He grits his teeth, ignoring the pain. The dogs travel lower to the ground, and their bodies are shaped to slip through the brush easier and run faster than him. The men are right behind them. Their arrows can flash past the dogs so fast they'll make them look like they're standing still. He knows he has a chance if he doesn't trip or fall. He still has enough lead on the pursuers. The second he enters a clearing, Fuzzy leaps into the air, spreads his wings, and, wham! His wing strikes a tree, shooting pain all the way to his chest.

Struggling, he rises into the air, spinning sideways slowing his ascent at a time when any mistake could cost him his life. He panics. He's only a few feet off the ground. Fear triggers an explosion of energy, and he pulls his wings harder, digging into the air above and thrusting it toward the earth.

He can hear the dogs under him now. His body burns every drop of energy it gets. He has to ascend faster so they can't sink their teeth into him. If they can hold him back for even a second, the men will have their prize.

His desire to survive grows stronger. His den needs to know what he has found. Pain and fear disappear as his duty overrides his senses. Breathing deeply, he clears the tree tops. He flinches when he hears a zing as an arrow passes close to his right eye. How much higher does he need to be? He knows another arrow will fly any second now.

The men below scream at each other. Fuzzy's senses peak and he actually hears the next arrow leave the hunter's bow. He flinches, ready for intense pain. But the second arrow isn't as close. It doesn't fly much higher above him before it's spent and falls harmlessly back to the ground.

As the attackers fade out of sight, fear and pain return. Fuzzy's heart continues racing. He shakes with cold chills and nervous energy. He fills with disappointment. At least two men have seen him.

He decides to fly around for a few minutes until he regains his wits. He regrets that the meeting tomorrow will be a serious debate, and he already blames himself. For now, returning to his special place is all he is interested in. He has the rest of the night to put himself back together.

As he safely lands at the cavern, his first thoughts are of his two little fuzzy dragons that trust in him to keep their world safe.

Everyone is sleeping as he quietly makes his way inside. He's thankful to be alive. A little happiness returns when he sees Liz lying next to their precious little dragons. He settles beside them, knowing this will be a sleepless night. Gently, he lays his wing over his mate and is quiet.

Lester is up early and calls out to the den. "Ureeeeee!" He's anxious to hear what Fuzzy has found. Everyone slowly gathers around as Fuzzy prepares to speak. He's still thinking about what he will say as he steps in front of the den.

"I have grave news to share with you." Silence overtakes the den, and parents hold their children still. "Last night, I witnessed three men and two dangerously large dogs camped not far from here. The men are armed with powerful bows and many knives. This is not just a hunting party looking for hides or meat." He pauses. "I'm convinced they're looking for our den."

The strong young dragons look at each other, already bonding in brotherhood, mentally preparing for the fight ahead. The mothers pull their young close as if protecting them already. Lester starts toward Fuzzy. Fuzzy looks at him.

"Wait, there's more." He hangs his head submissively. "With a heavy heart, I apologize for what I foolishly allowed to happen. In my effort to understand what we're dealing with, I got too close. As I was trying to slip away, one of the dogs picked up my scent."

Most of the den feels sorry for Fuzzy. Lester nods. The den is quiet, eager for Fuzzy to continue. They sense his remorse.

"I was lucky to escape with my life. The dogs are very fast and the underbrush didn't seem to slow them as they pursued me. The men were right behind them, running with arrows ready to shoot. Arrows flew by me several times."

Lester gasps. "They could have killed you." He pauses to gathers his wits. "Unfortunately, now they know for sure we are here. They will not rest until they have captured or killed some of us." He looks at Fuzzy.

Fuzzy had thought he couldn't feel any worse before he heard Lester's comment. Now his spirit sinks lower.

"The den must have a meeting to discuss an attack on these men before sun set tomorrow," commands Lester.

Normally, Fuzzy would step in and ask for everyone to be calm and give more thought to what they should do, but in his heart he knows Lester is right.

"I want five healthy adult males to meet here at midday to make a plan. Fuzzy, I'm counting on you to be one of those five." Lester looks Fuzzy in the eyes. "Stop blaming yourself. A dog once discovered me, too."

Lester is tense as he waits to see who will fight these men. Coming from inside the cavern determined footsteps march toward the entrance. He breathes a sigh of relief. In front, striding along is Leo, a thin dragon whose appearance deceives his strength. The den can always depend on Leo. He's the youngest of the five. Next, with determined looks on their faces, come Shim and Tee, walking side-by-side. They always work best as a team. In the rear are Fuzzy and Vic, the quiet one. Lester bows a gesture of thanks and approval to these warriors who are prepared to protect their den. They gather around and wait for him to speak. "Now that these men know we're watching them and understand a little more about us, I'm sure they're thinking of ways to protect themselves. Soon they may try to hunt some of us down to prove to the villagers what great hunters they are. We can't allow them time to prepare. We will study them the rest of the day and attack late tomorrow evening. After the attack, it will turn dark and they will be terrified in the darkness of night. Their imaginations will do battle on them for us," states Lester.

Fuzzy ponders Lester's decision. Lester looks toward him to see if he has his approval. Fuzzy bows in agreement.

"Then we must be strong in our resolve that no man or dog returns to civilization. What these men have seen must not leave the wilderness." Lester looks at the five, hoping for them to commit. Five heads bow.

"It breaks my heart to suggest what I think must ultimately do," states Lester, rubbing his forehead. "Man is a curious creature, and adventures from their villages will never stop searching for us. We must search for a new cavern as soon as these men are no longer a threat."

Leo looks at Shim and Tee. Their eyes say yes. Then he glances to Fuzzy who is deep in thought, but his eyes don't say no. Vic bows in agreement. Fuzzy quietly considers his friends faces, and nods. "I think it's obvious we all agree. This will not be the end of man's quest to expand further into the wilderness. The den will have to move," he assures Lester.

"For now, it's time to come up with a battle plan," says Lester.

"There's little doubt after last night that our first objective has to be killing the dogs," says Fuzzy.

Lester is encouraged that Fuzzy is willing to speak frankly. "You're right indeed."

"Two of us will try to swoop down, undetected and grapple the dogs from behind. Hopefully, no dragon will sustain injuries," says Fuzzy.

"We can carry them far away," says Leo.

"If things work out, the men may never know what happened to them," adds Vic.

"Shim and I want to volunteer to grapple the dogs," announces Tee.

"Does anyone not agree?" asks Lester. Fuzzy, Leo, and Vic bow in agreement. "I'm confident in all of you. We will meet again later this afternoon."

As Fuzzy walks away, he hangs his head in despair. It bothers him that he had suggested something so distasteful. Lester can tell he is in deep though and unhappy.

"Stop a minute, Fuzzy," says Lester, looking at him understandingly. "Sometimes we have to do what's necessary to protect our young and our way of life."

"No one else is as troubled about this."

"Fuzzy, I respect you because you are troubled. Their instinct is in complete control, and told them this has to be done. Your kind heart makes you reason with your instinct. When you're sure it has to be done for your den, you won't hesitate joining the fight."

Midday approaches, and the chosen dragons gather on a flat spot above the cavern entrance. There's always a breeze blowing here and only room for the volunteers to fit into the space.

Shim and Tee explain plans they have discussed.

"We would like to watch the dogs for a while so we can learn their weaknesses. Soon we will be able to pick the best time and place to carry out the attack," says Shim.

"We will follow you and watch. You and Tee decide what to do. When the dogs are dead, we will decide how to deal with the men," says Lester.

Shim takes to the air and spies a hill where the men can be watched as they travel the rest of the day. The others watch as they study the dogs while making sure no one makes a sound. By evening, the men are so close the dragons can hear them talking.

<>

After seeing Fuzzy, the hunting party knows they're close to the den, and they are more cautious. Several times, they nock arrows while looking nervously into the undergrowth.

Virgil talks to them. "As long as we're alert and have the dogs to protect us, we'll be fine. There are probably only a few dragons out here anyway, and we scared one so bad last night we won't have to deal with him again."

"I have been thinking about my shot last night, and I think I hit that dragon. He's probably in no condition to cause us any trouble anyway," brags Jess.

"Sounds like the rest of you are pretty confident, but I'm not," says Steven. "I think common sense says it's time for us to turn around and go back to Water Town. We know there are dragons out here now. Let's go back and get help and supplies. We're not prepared for an attack at night."

Virgil stops. "We have come a long way to go back with no proof."

Steven feels defensive. "What good is proof if it's out here beside our dead bodies? I don't think we have a chance, camping out here like this in the open every night."

"I think Steven might be right, even though that thing last night ran like it was scared to death. I don't think we are prepared to face two or more of them at once."

Virgil smirks and takes a deep breath. He has to regain control. "I know how you feel, but if we don't bring something home as proof, we won't get any silver to pay for our return trip. It's going to cost a lot more to come back next time with all we would like to have. All we need is a little something to show our investors," he pleads. "I promise you, if we don't find something by tomorrow morning, then we will turn around and go back."

For the first time, Virgil is fighting a battle within himself. Part of him realizes this adventure is not as important as staying alive, but he refuses to admit the other men are right.

The dogs don't have any worries. They're having a great time running around. Their instinct is not warning them, and because of the chase the night before, they lust for more excitement.

The men grow quieter as evening wears on.

"I see a great place to spend the night," exclaims Virgil.

Not far ahead stands a large, old oak tree surrounded by tall grass swaying in the wind. Large limbs stretch out from the trunk, and the lower ones dip to the ground. They can pitch their tarps over them and have a dry place to spend the night.

"Is this a good place to defend ourselves if the dragons come back tonight," asks Steven.

"Quit worrying. They're afraid to attack us again after last night," says Virgil.

"I wish we were behind lots of rocks instead of grass that can burn," comments Jess.

The previous night they had been excited and felt confident after seeing Fuzzy running away in fear. Their confidence fades away and is replaced with fear as the evening wears on.

<>

The five dragons watch as the men set up camp. The dogs are running around, chasing each other and hoping to scare a hidden varmint into running.

"This is what we have been waiting for," says Shim. "The men are busy with their camp, and the dogs are running across meadows away from them."

Shim and Tee quietly lift into the sky, gaining altitude as they watch the dogs. When they're high enough to glide, they circle. They will wait for just the right moment to swoop in behind the dogs. They look into each other's eyes. They synchronize their brains. Without saying a word, they will know exactly when to start their dive.

The dogs are running, zigzagging and jumping. They will be a hard target to hit at such speed. Both dragons study the situation. They each must hit their dog at the same instant so neither dog will know what has happened. The dive will only take a few seconds. There's a lot to allow for in those few seconds. Wind direction, speed, and the weight of the dog at impact will determine how much repercussion the dragon's legs will suffer. Everything has to be calculated by instinct, there's no time for thinking.

The zigzag course the dogs run is impossible to figure out and will require good luck.

With a glance at each other, the dragons turn their bodies downward as they begin their dive. They see each other out of one eye as they stay side-by-side, plunging toward their intended targets.

They level out, barely above the ground and close behind the dogs. The dragons are a blur. In less than a second Shim makes his mark with both claws, slashing and tearing into the dog's sides.

The dog yelps, then silence.

Tee slams into the other dog. One claw gouges deeply into one of its legs, but the other misses. The attack is not lethal. The enraged dog turns his head and rips scales and flesh off Tee's leg, inflicting excruciating pain. Tee flinches, and the dog slips out of his clutches and falls to the ground, rolling in the grass. When it slides to a stop, it jumps up quickly, ignoring its pain.

Tee lands limping. Pain floods him with instinctive rage. The dog springs into the air, lurching toward him. Tee gazes deep into the dog's eyes as it closes in and sees the soul of a mindless, viscous creature, oblivious to the fact that it's attacking one of the most powerful creatures on Earth. An instant before the dog clamps his fangs into his face, Tee unleashes an explosion of fire. Blue and yellow flames engulf the dog, flowing like liquid over its body, incinerating the animal.

Flames splatter all around, setting the grass ablaze. Determined to finish his task, Tee is seething and hops into the ring of fire. His claws impale the scorched creature. Fanning the flames into an inferno, he rises in flight and soon catches up with Shim. Together, they fly away with the second dog leaving a thin trail of smoke in the sky.

<>

The men don't see any of the attack because the dogs are too far from their camp, but they hear plenty.

They dash into a clearing, looking in the direction of the sound.

They tremble speechlessly as they gaze into the sky. Terror instantly swoops down, gripping their hearts as they watch the dragons carry their dogs away.

"Run for cover under the trees!" screams Virgil, fearing other dragons are watching them.

"I told you we should have turned back!" raves Steven, running into the woods.

"Shut up and get your bow ready! Blame is of no value now," roars Jess. Lying under bushes, they shake with fear as they brace for an attack. Beads of sweat pop up and slide down their foreheads as their hearts race.

"I smell smoke," says Jess, sniffing. Then the smell grows until it fills the air. Drifting in a heavy cloud, it surrounds them.

"We can't hide. We have no choice but to make a run for it or the fire will kill us before the dragons do!" yells Virgil.

They frantically grab as much gear as they can, stopping for a second to look back they see flames dancing in the tops of the trees, leaping toward the sky.

The men say nothing to each other. In a panic, they run in the direction they came from. After a few minutes, Virgil tries to calm Jess and Steven.

"Stop running before we drop from exhaustion. We must be able to put up a fight if need be. Keep your bows ready, and we'll walk as fast as we can. Be prepared to shoot at any moment."

They walk nervously until it's too dark to go on. Panting, they sit and try to catch their breath. Sweat streams down their faces, and they use their shirt sleeves to wipe it away. Even in the dimness of twilight, they can see worry in each other's eyes.

"I can see the glow of the forest fire far behind us now," says Jess.

As time passes, they feel a breeze growing, and it pushes the fire away from them.

"We should have turned around yesterday!" accuses Steven angrily, looking at Virgil.

"Don't blame me," he shouts, about to jump to his feet.

"Stop it, you two. Don't start blaming each other now. We only need to think about getting home," says Jess.

They sit in the dark, terrified and mad at each other as fear eats at their nerves. Their imaginations run wild, knowing at any moment one of the dragons could pop out of the darkness and rip them apart.

<>

With the dogs dead, and seeing the men fleeing in the direction they came from, the five dragons decide to use the wilderness to their advantage. With night approaching, they leave the men to be immersed in darkness. The cruel hand of the wilderness will weaken them as they lie cold, sleepless, and consumed by fear. Tomorrow when they attack, the men will be weary, lessoning the chances of arrows inflicting cruel wounds and death. There are a lot of mixed emotions at Fuzzy's den. The battle is not over, and no one is celebrating partial success. Quietly they retire to their special places and are thankful they have all returned to be with the ones they love.

<>

After sitting quietly for a while, the men regain some energy, but they're still tense and their tempers are short.

"I think we should try to move further away from the dragons, this isn't a good place to spend the night anyway. Let's walk carefully and find a better place," states Steven.

"In this darkness, it's against my better judgment," replies Virgil.

"I'm not sure that doesn't mean it's a good idea," rebukes Steven.

Jess shushes them, fearing the dragons will hear. Their arguing is eating on his nerves. Quietly he suggests a compromise. "Let's try walking for a few minutes then decide."

They pick up their gear and move on. Jess falls hard in less than a minute, hurting his ankle.

"Well, I told you so. No more walking until daylight. If one of us gets hurt, we'll be slowed down too much and none of us will escape the dragons. We must lie down and rest until we can see what we are doing," says Virgil.

They're overwhelmed with worrisome thoughts after what they have seen. Without the dogs, there's no way to know if something is creeping in the brush and every little sound makes their hearts race. Fear sharpens their senses and tonight their hearing is keener than any night in their lives.

After a while Steven and Jess surrender and plug their ears, hoping to finally get some sleep.

Chapter 12

Virgil sits in the dark with a frown on his face watching Steven and Jess as they try to rest. His mind is made up. He intends to survive and he has no intentions of plugging his ears.

Not long after midnight, they're snoring soundly. He carefully stands and quietly picks up the saddlebag he has prepared for his getaway. Glancing at the two sleeping men, he sighs. He's sure they will be dead by this time tomorrow. Turning, he tiptoes out of camp, moving as quietly as a stalking cat. He knows they're edgy and the slightest flip of a limb or breaking of a stick will wake them. The moon peeks over the horizon, giving a glimmer of light, and to Virgil, it's a sign his escape is meant to be. He will be able to see where he's going. The further he walks, the brighter the moon beams grow. The further he travels, the safer he feels. He begins to regain his confidence. All the dragon problems have been left with Jess and Steven.

Even in all the chaos, he managed to pack his saddlebag well. Food will not be a problem because he stole most of the dried meat. He also made sure he has the loadstone and string so he will have no trouble finding his way south to Ron and the horses.

Still, he's mindful of the dragons and wishes he didn't have to go so slow. There's no doubt they will be looking for men as soon as the sun comes up.

He's obsessed with getting back to the horses. Only then will he allow himself to feel safe. Oblivious to the fact that he is worn out, he quickens his pace. Saw-briars make a rasping sound as they pull past his ankles and arms, tearing clothing and scratching unprotected skin. Blood oozes and dries in streaks down his arms and legs.

He grits his teeth as he pulls through them. The wilderness tests his will. Limbs, vines, and stones lay hidden in the moon shadows, and he trips many times, falling painfully. He always drags himself to his feet and starts walking again.

There's a battle going on in his head between his survival instinct and guilt for leaving Jess and Steven. The more pain and guilt he endures, the stronger his resolve. He will do whatever it takes to return to Water Town. Silver, fame, and his right as a man to have dominion over all creatures spur him on in a dangerous wilderness alone at night.

As soon as the first sunlight breaks over the horizon, completely exhausted he drops to the ground landing in a dip surrounded by briars and bushes. He's so tired his hands tremble as he pulls leaves into a pile and places a small tarp on top to cushion where he will lie. Once settled, he pulls leaves to his sides and then covers his body.

In desperate need of sleep, he closes his eyes. But all the scratches and bruises ache, and in his mind he has to justify what he has done.

The dragons will be looking for movement in the forest, and three men will be easier to spot than two. Even though Jess and Steven are closer to the den, at least now there are only the two of them. They will have a better chance of surviving. If he had stayed with them, it would have lessened their chances. The possibility of three men traveling undetected is slim. His thoughts slow as he drifts into sleep.

<>

Jess wakes first. His dreams have been a parade of creatures and dragons, and he is sure they're waiting in the edge of the woods, crouched and ready to pounce on him.

He moves slowly and quietly over to Steven's side and reaches to shake his shoulder. When Steven's eyes pop open, Jess puts his finger to his lips.

Steven slams his eyes shut. Even after being startled, he's barely awake, his head aches, and he's disoriented. Both men are tired from getting very little sleep.

"I think Virgil is missing," whispers Jess.

Steven squints, trying to look around, but he can hardly see. The light is dim where they're laying. "He's probably searching for water or something. Be quiet and wait a few minutes."

A bad feeling haunts Jess after waiting a short time, and he rouses Steven again. "What if a dragon carried him off and is bringing more dragons back for us?"

Steven rubs his eyes, and sits. "We are out in the open here. Let's move to the underbrush and hide. When Virgil returns, we can signal him."

They move quietly to a location where they can hide under a fallen tree with vines growing over and around it. They peek through the growth and watch where they had slept.

"What are we going to do if we never see Virgil again?" wails Jess.

"Let's be still and quiet for a while. We'll figure something out."

<>

With the dogs dead, and the men hiding in fear, the den awakens to a morning with less worry. They share a feeling of relief, and everyone is confident they can go about their daily activities outside the cavern.

Lester stands in the entrance, bathing in the sunlight that shines on the hatching stone pockets. He has a confident look as he savors the warmth. The den gathers around and waits for him to address them. He turns toward the den, and with a strong and confident look, he smiles.

"Yesterday was a memorable day for our family. The dogs were our worst threat. I take no pleasure in the fact that they died, but it had to be done. The men are still out there, and those who didn't fight yesterday will search for them today."

He looks toward Shim and Tee smiling. "These two dragons fought bravely for our den and have requested permission to search for a new cavern. If there are no objections, I would like to grant their request."

Everyone looks pleased and gestures consent.

"Good. I want them to spend time with their families before they leave. They may be gone for a long time, and we are all indebted to them for agreeing to take on this difficult task."

Lester pauses and looks out into the den. Some members are teary-eyed, realizing the den is really going to leave. He sees their sadness, but he must move on.

"Fuzzy, Leo, and Vic will be entrusted with the task of making sure none of the men return to their civilization. We can't allow them to bring back more men and dogs. If we let them return they will spread their story. Finding us will become a challenge to every man, and they will never rest."

The den bows in agreement. Lester looks toward Fuzzy, Leo, and Vic.

"This may feel like an easy but distasteful chore for some of you, but don't underestimate these men. They are still very dangerous as long as they have their powerful bows. Please be careful. We don't need any dead heroes. Be patient. Time is on our side as long as they're in our wilderness."

Lester looks at Fuzzy with confidence. "Fuzzy, I want you to take the lead on this hunt."

Fuzzy bows in acceptance. "We are honored to do the will of our den."

The den bows in respect to the three of them as they make their way to the edge of the cliff, and with a hop, they spread their wings and sail over the forest in the direction they had last seen the men.

Fuzzy chooses a quiet meadow to stop and talk with Leo and Vic. "I will do my best to keep us all safe from harm. We're in this together, so share your ideas and thoughts."

They decide to sail close to the tree tops to make it hard for the hunters to shoot at them, and they can detect any movement on the forest floor. While two of them fly over an area, one will rest and watch from a distance, hoping the men will make a move right after they pass over. They're all in agreement and ready to begin.

"Leo and I will fly first. Vic, find a high spot. We will watch to see where you land. One of us will take your place later."

<>

Steven and Jess nervously wait until midday, hoping Virgil will show up. They're consumed by fear and a feeling of helplessness. Their emotions torture them as they struggle to understand their situation. One minute they're sad because something could have happened to him, and in seconds, hate and anger wells up as they wonder if he has left them to die. The longer they wait, the angrier they get.

"We have wasted good time waiting for nothing, and I need to find water soon," says Jess.

"It's disgusting, but with dragons looking for us, we will have to crawl like rats under bushes and vines. But you're right; our most pressing problem is to find water. We should make our way downhill. Hopefully there will be a stream at the bottom of this slope," says Steven. He and Jess slowly crawl along, maneuvering around briars and fallen trees. The underbrush and weeds form a thick canopy over them, and there isn't much light except for an occasional shaft that manages to penetrate the leaves.

At the bottom of the slope a small spring bubbles with clear, cool water then meanders out of sight under even thicker vegetation. They dip sand out of the way, making a pocket deep enough to fill their water pouches. The cool water quenches their thirst and with their first problem solved, they lay back to rest and think.

"Do you have any idea which way we should be going to get out of this wilderness?" asks Jess.

"I'm sorry, I have no idea. Virgil always told us which way to go. After running in panic as the sun was going down, I can't tell you anything. Why don't we follow the water flowing out of this spring? It will flow to a larger stream. If we stay close to water, it will be easier to stay hidden under trees and underbrush," suggests Steven.

They move on, being very careful to stay hidden under the brush. Later that day, they watch as a dragon sails overhead, looking for them. They lay speechless and frozen for a moment. Quietly, they close their eyes and sigh in relief when they're not seen. They begin slowly crawling again.

"Thank you for being calm when the dragon passed overhead."

"Are you kidding? I was paralyzed. I couldn't move," replies Jess.

"Thinking about the dragon flying over and not seeing us is encouraging. If we plan every move we make, keeping cover a priority, we may just have a chance to make it out of here," says Steven, crawling along.

The dragons search all day but the men stay hidden.

As darkness closes in, the desperate men pull two ponchos out of the one saddlebag they still have. They pile several rocks they can easily throw, yet big enough to inflict injury next to where they plan to sleep. Then they cut a couple saplings and sharpen the ends, making crude spears. They curl up and huddle under weeds and bushes so thick they can hardly move. It drizzles after the sun sets and they feel miserable.

"If the dragons didn't kill Virgil and I find out he left us like this, I will kill him myself," says Steven, shivering.

"I'm too cold and hungry to think right now. We must find food tomorrow. There's no use hiding from dragons if we're going to starve," replies Jess.

Laying in misery, the men sleep very little. They stay as close to each other as they can, trying not to freeze in the cold rain.

<>

Three days have passed since Virgil slipped away, and he still has plenty of jerky. He's not hungry yet. The dragons still haven't seen any sign of the men, and every night at the den Lester encourages his tired and frustrated dragons.

<>

Steven and Jess learn how to travel a little faster. They force themselves to eat worms and bugs found along the stream that trickles beside them. As long as they stay close to the water, they will not starve. Every day they increase the distance between themselves and where the dragon encounter occurred.

<>

On the tenth day of their search, the dragons fly in a larger circumference around where the men had camped. Luckily for them, Steven and Jess have no choice but to run across an open meadow as they follow the stream.

Fuzzy spots them and watches as they scurry under cover. He wonders why he only sees two men. He assumes one of them is hidden under nearby brush. Their location is all wrong. He realizes they're following the stream and have no idea which way to go.

He returns to the high spot Leo has chosen and lands next to him. Vic follows and joins them.

"I have good news at last! I have seen two men."

"Let's attack," says Leo, a gleam in his eyes, as his lips part slightly showing his clinched teeth.

"Be patient," responds Fuzzy. "I can find them easy enough. I know which way they're going. I want to talk to Lester before we attack."

They return to the den a little happier. Fuzzy lands and heads for Lester's special place. Lester is lying on a pallet of grass held in place by a circle of neatly arranged rocks. His place has a high ceiling covered with long stalactites. It gently slopes to a small opening that lets in light but keeps the weather out. Hearing footsteps approaching, he walks to his chamber entrance. He's glad to see its Fuzzy, looking happier than he has in some time. But there is still concern in his eyes. Fuzzy looks around to be sure they're alone.

"I have found the men following a stream. They're hopelessly lost and moving away from us and civilization. They're headed toward the darkest most dangerous place in the wilderness."

"Do you think they will be of no more threat to us?"

"I think they will perish in the wilderness. Let's watch them for a while. If they're going to perish out there, I don't have the desire to kill them."

"I will call the den together and ask their opinion. Come with me."

Lester and Fuzzy quietly walk to the entrance. The cavern walls along the way are covered with white glistening calcite, reflecting light all the way to Lester's chamber. They wonder if a new cavern can ever be found as special as this one.

"Ureeeeee," calls Lester.

Soon the members appear, moving forward in little groups.

Some are talking to each other as they surround Fuzzy and Lester. Lester raises his wings slightly to quiet them.

"Fuzzy, Leo, and Vic have found the men," announces Lester.

"Yaheee," cheers the den joyfully.

"Fuzzy has suggested letting them perish in the wilderness because they're hopelessly lost and no longer pose a threat."

"No!" shouts Vic. "We have toiled for nothing if we don't finish them off."

Many den members loudly express different opinions. Some don't know what to think. They respect Fuzzy's judgment.

Lester raises his wings, commanding quiet.

"Leo and Vic, you care deeply for our den's safety, and we respect your opinion."

The two dragons are bewildered and some den members are restless. What can be his reason for going along with Fuzzy?

Lester waits until everyone is ready to listen.

"I chose Fuzzy to lead this task because I knew he would do everything in his power to make sure he and his fellow dragons would not be harmed. A good leader cares more for his fellow dragons' safety than for glory. I respect his kindhearted request because of that."

Fuzzy looks surprised. Liz smiles. She's proud of her mate.

The den bows in respect to Lester, and then they turn toward Fuzzy and bow longer in respect for him.

Lester watches as Fuzzy's heart fills with pride and love for the den. Fuzzy places his wing around Liz. A tear falls from his eye. It's obvious the den doesn't care about the fuzzy redheaded dragon's appearance anymore.

Chapter 13

Eleven solitary days in the wilderness have taught Virgil the secret to surviving at night is to assemble and use primitive weapons. Sleeping behind logs and boulders with a pile of rocks and a club lying at his side has proven to be his best defense. After grappling with a couple snakes, an opossum, and several raccoons, he realizes it takes too long to nock an arrow and aim for his bow to be of any use. Many times, he can only get one shot at whatever is after him, if he even sees it. Throwing and bashing can be done quickly and as often as needed.

He has learned a lot, but too many close calls and time alone is getting to him. A reoccurring nightmare tortures him almost every night. Deep in peaceful sleep, he jerks as a scene more real than life unfolds in his mind's eye. A vicious wolf stands on his shoulders, pressing him to the ground. The creature's sharp teeth are so close to his face that the hot air and stench from its filthy mouth stifle his breath. He screams and tries to tear away, but he can never pull its heavy paws loose. Snarling, the beast clamps its teeth into his neck like a vise. Yanking and twisting, it tears his flesh. Pain shoots down his back, paralyzing him. His arms and legs refuse to work. He desperately tries to wake. It's his only hope of escaping, but waking won't come. After an eternity of torture, his eyes pop open, and he screams as he quickly sits up and trembles. Covered in sweat, he puts his hands over his eyes and sobs. More tired than when he laid down, he collapses and tries to understand why it always takes too long to wake when the dream comes.

Waking, he's thankful to see the light of another day, and his heart aches for the warmth of a fire he desperately needs to break the morning chill. He stuffs his gear into his saddlebag and starts aimlessly walking in the direction the loadstone pointer has indicated is south. He shakes his head as he thinks. "Another day, and how much further can it be? How much more wilderness torture can I stand? Am I ever going to get out of these woods?

A chill makes him shiver as a wave of haunting thoughts for Steven and Jess drift through his mind. He wonders if those thoughts are haunting him because at this very moment they're suffering the excruciating pain of tearing flesh inflicted by dragon claws or flames engulfing their bodies. He shivers at the thought that their spirits have just been freed of their bodies and spitefully pass through him on their way to eternal peace. "Too long alone in the wilderness," he thinks to himself. The haunting feeling slowly subsides as he continues to walk.

Stopping at a sparkling stream, he fills his water pouch and looks for a place where he can hop across and stay dry.

His eyes pop wide open. In the distance, he hears the most wonderful sound a lost man in the wilderness will ever hear: the whinny of a horse.

Can it be real? He jumps across the stream without any effort and turns his ear in the direction of the sound. Slowly he walks, trying to be as quiet as possible, desperately hoping to hear another sound. He makes his way in what he thinks is the right direction. Can it be? He holds his breath as he takes a closer look. There in front of him, lying on the ground; is chopped brush and saplings his men had cut on the trip out. All he has to do now is follow the trail back to Ron.

Then a horse snorts. He runs with all his might along the trail. After several turns he sees in the distance a beautiful sight to behold. Six wonderful horses waiting to

carry him back to civilization. The sight gives him a
burst of energy like he has not experienced in weeks, and
he sprints. The spectacle of him running toward them
spooks the horses. They whinny loudly, pulling in all
directions trying to run. They snort and stomp excitedly.

"Easy! Easy boys!" yells Ron, trying to calm them.
He runs over quickly grabbing several of their reins and
fearfully looking for what's scaring them.

There stands Virgil, hair full of twigs and matted.
His clothing is torn to pieces, and he has lost a lot of
weight. He pants, out of breath, but he reaches out to rub
one of the horses.

"You look terrible," says Ron as he pats the horse's
necks, helping to calm them. "Bad as you look, though,
you're the most beautiful sight I have seen in weeks."

Virgil can tell Ron's every bit as happy to see him
as he is to see the horses.

"I'm glad to see you too, Ron."

"It's terrifying out here at night alone." says Ron,
placing a hand on his forehead as he sighs in relief. Ron
moves to peer down the trail. "Are Steven and Jess still in
the woods?"

Virgil has been thinking about what he will say
when Ron asks about them. He looks sad. It's easy for
him. He wishes he could have brought Steven and Jess
back, and he only has to change the story a little to make it
sound believable.

"Dragons attacked us, killing our dogs. In the chaos,
we fled in different directions, hiding in the woods. We
were afraid to talk, so when we lost sight of each other, it
was impossible to get back together." He appears sadder
as he looks back into the wilderness as if by chance
they're not far behind.

He shakes his head and looks at Ron. "We should head toward Water Town. I will explain to you what a terrifying night is really like." He starts saddling one of the horses, getting ready to ride.

Ron reluctantly saddles a horse.

"Should we leave two horses tied up for Steven and Jess?"

Virgil is in a hurry and in no mood to debate what to do. He glances at Ron out of the side of one eye and makes no reply as he continues to throw saddlebags on horses and strap them down. Then he mounts his horse.

Ron looks at Virgil with sad eyes. "You don't really think Steven and Jess are ever coming back, do you? Virgil glares at him. "If we leave these horses tied up, they will be dead in four days. We can prevent that. There's nothing we can do to help Steven and Jess now."

Ron studies his predicament. "I should wait a day or two more, but I have suffered too many nights alone in the wilderness already." He drops his head, and with a frown, he unties two horses.

Ron looks one last time at his camp, and mounts his horse. "I'll never forget all the scary nights I spent there." He pulls the horse's reins toward home, bumps its sides, and they trot toward civilization.

<>

Lester and Fuzzy fly into the wilderness, checking on the lost men from time to time. The men continue to move away from the cavern and civilization. When they're far enough away to no longer pose a threat, Fuzzy and Lester agree to forget about them.

Chapter 14

The Saturday morning Jackson could hardly wait for arrives, and he's feeling so full of energy he can hardly do anything right. He's rushing around, dropping things and forgetting to shut doors and gates.

He and Cap beam as they work, and they work harder than ever to finish early. After gulping down their lunch, they curry and saddle the horses.

"At last we can both go to the Brittain's," says Jackson, pulling himself into the saddle.

"I'm looking forward to seeing Sandra, too," says Cap.

Jackson beams. "I hope she missed me as much as I missed her."

They nudge the horses, and the anticipated journey begins.

"Is it because I'm so happy or is this the most beautiful evening out here on the trail?" asks Jackson.

"It is a pretty evening, even if we weren't going to see our girls."

"Why can't every day feel this good?"

"It sounds like you're in love, brother," replies Cap.

"I know. I hardly know Sandra and have only been with her one evening. Have I lost my mind because I feel this way?"

"Love can do strange things to a young man. I'm only afraid if she's not ready to fall in love, you will get hurt," says Cap.

"I'm trying to be as patient and careful as I can. It's just so uncontrollable."

"I know. I just don't want you to get hurt. She may be the kind of girl that changes as time passes and later not

even act like the girl you fell in love with. Only time
can give you the answer."

He looks at Cap. His brother is his best friend, but
he still doesn't like what he's saying.

"You don't think that's possible, do you?" asks
Cap, understandingly.

"Yes, I have thought about it," replies Jackson a
little snappy.

"If it makes you feel any better, I fell in love too
fast with Janice. To think she wouldn't be in love with me
forever now would kill me."

A smile returns when he realizes his brother is
trying to make him feel better.

As they dismount, the front door opens, Sandra and
Janice saunter out. They're giggling. The brothers smile at
each other. It's a good sign that the ladies are in a good
mood.

Walking toward the porch, he and Cap are pleased
to see the cousins are dressed in pretty clothes. The smell
of lilac perfume the brothers can't resist is in the air, and
their hair is pulled back and neatly braided. Their dresses
look soft and clean. Jackson surmises the girls have done a
little extra to impress them.

Cap steps on the porch and kisses Janice, takes her
hand, and they walk away from the steps.

Jackson's mind is racing as he wonders what he
should do. Sandra holds her hand out to him. "I have
missed you," she says.

Her smile is more beautiful than he remembers, and
the sound of her saying she had missed him melts his
helpless heart.

When their hands touch, he feels a wonderful
tingling. She gently squeezes his hand, giving him hope
she really had missed him. He's in a daze.

"Would you like to sit with us?" says Janice, snapping them back to reality.

"Oh sure," replies Jackson. He turns, still holding Sandra's hand as she sits.

Cap and Janice smile at each other.

As soon as Jackson sits, Sandra tells him about a beautiful grove of flowering trees along the trail. As she points to a vase filled with beautiful red flowers. Flavie appears and invites them to come in and meet Sandra's mother, Mary.

Mary is a small, neatly-dressed woman with salt and pepper hair pulled back in a bun and tied with a ribbon. Jackson takes in everything about her. He knows it will be important for her to like him. Flavie introduces them.

"I'm pleased to meet you," says Jackson, nodding politely.

"I have heard a lot about you and Cap."

"I look forward to getting to know you better," replies Jackson.

The couples excuse themselves and, once outside, they pair up and time flies by.

Flavie rings the bell. Supper is ready.

Jackson is nervous when he first sits at the supper table, but in no time, he forgets about impressing Mary and is his own pleasant self.

Mary talks about her village, and how people from Water Town are beginning to trade silver for the wheels her family makes.

"Things are changing fast." says Mary. "Water Town is close enough to make our little village start changing." Everyone is quiet for a while, but soon the young people become restless. Flavie stands to start cleaning the kitchen. The girls start to help. "You young folks go on outside, Mary and I will clean up."

Cap and Jackson are glad. It's almost time to say goodnight.

They talk a little while on the porch, and then Cap kisses Janice. "I will see you tomorrow evening," he says.

Jackson holds Sandra's hand. "Can I come back tomorrow with Cap?" he asks.

"I would really like that," she replies, her eyes twinkling.

Jackson wants to kiss her, but he knows he will have to wait.

<>

Jackson and Cap enjoy a night of peaceful contentment, but as the sun rises, their minds spring to life before their feet hit the floor. They have every intention of completing their work as fast as possible so they can leave sooner than they had the day before. They eat hastily and run out the door.

Cap hooks a horse to a tree they have cut down and drags it next to the wood pile. The minute the horse is out of the way, Jackson starts chopping as fast as he can. Soon he's too tired to move, and drops the ax, staggering out of the way. Cap grabs it and chops too fast, but they manage to cut it into short pieces. The thick pieces have to be split, and it's a dangerous job when you're daydreaming and in a hurry. Cap almost chops his toe, alarming Miles and Uncle Matt. Concerned about their own safety they move out of the way, and after a few minutes, the older men shake their heads.

"If you two only knew how silly you look trying to work too fast," says Uncle Matt, chuckling. "It's actually taking longer than usual," adds Miles. The brothers shrug and slow down a little.

When the wood cutting is finished Jackson grabs a bucket and dashes toward the corn crib. He's barely in the door when he hears a noise on the side of the building. Tap, tap, tap. Curiously he pops around the building, coming face to face with a full-grown dragon. He gasps and stumbles back, tripping on his own feet. The bucket drops to the ground, spinning. By the time he scrambles to his feet, he realizes its Fuzzy. Out of breath, he leans against the building with his hand on his chest. He peeks around to see if anyone saw him.

"I tried not to scare you," says Fuzzy. "Go get Cap. We must talk."

Jackson begins to smile. "I'm glad to see you, but we need to hide in the woods behind the corncrib. There's a lot going on that makes it dangerous for you to be here. Our father and Uncle Matt are watching to see what is happening to our apples. Not to mention a man running out of the woods ranting about a dragon killing his dog."

Jackson reaches for the bucket lying on its side, and sits it upright.

"Not long ago, a group of hunters wearing fine clothes came by here headed for the wilderness, hoping to capture a dragon.

With an unhappy smirk, Fuzzy shakes his head. "It saddens my heart to hear about all these people looking for dragons. There's a very serious situation developing."

"I regret this for your den," replies Jackson with sad eyes.

"I will be waiting in the woods for you and Cap."

Jackson walks quickly searching for Cap. He finds him hurriedly feeding the chickens.

"Stop what you're doing and come with me."
Cap gives a puzzled shrug, but Jackson has such a sincere look on his face, he sets the feed bucket down and follows him. "Fuzzy is here to talk with us," says Jackson as they walk.

"This is not a good time for him to visit," replies Cap.

"Exactly what I told him."

Jackson stops and looks around to be sure no one is watching before they enter the woods.

As they push through limbs, Fuzzy is waiting where they'd met as children. Cap is shocked and stops to marvel at his old friend's transformation. He's larger than a full-grown bull standing upright, but with a strong tail trailing behind. He still has beautiful shiny blue fuzz covering his body, and the red fuzz on his head is commanding, but now two dangerous yet majestic, shiny black horns crown him. They lay back like armor above his eyes, then turn up slowly, tapering to a point. Standing close to him is intimidating.

"I am glad to see both of you!" says Fuzzy. "I know how dangerous it is to come here like this, but I must know if you have kept your word not to tell anyone about me or what you saw in the wilderness."

"How could you think such a thing?" asks Jackson, looking him in the eyes.

Fuzzy cocks his head slightly, studying his reaction. He and the brothers can still understand what each other is thinking as well as they had when they were children.

"We have been faithfully true to our word," Jackson states.

"I have been true out of old friendship and gratitude for what you did for us," says Cap.

Fuzzy feels the honesty in their words. "I'm sorry, but I had to ask. I, too, still value our old friendship. It's just that my den is having so much trouble with hunters."

Cap and Jackson move closer to Fuzzy, and he opens his wings reaching around them, they share a hug, not a bow. It is a special moment.

"I think the problem started after a man took his dog into the wilderness and it was attacked. He became obsessed and told the story to everyone in his village called Water Town. It didn't take long for his story to catch the attention of hunters. They think they can get a lot of silver for doing something we know is wrong."

"Silver and possessions are what causes most men trouble," remarks Fuzzy angrily. "And now it's causing dragons trouble."

"We're truly sorry for what is happening," says Cap as Jackson nods in agreement.

Fuzzy can tell from the look on their faces that neither of them has a lust for silver. Their family works hard for what they have and enjoys working together like his den. In his dragon heart, Cap and Jackson have a special place. They truly are trustworthy men.

"You're right that troubling things started happening when the man came exploring the wilderness with his dog. Lester, our leader, went to check on a campfire we had been following for some time. He had no idea there would be a dog until it was too late. The dog sensed his presence and came charging at him and was going to cause him harm. He had no choice but to end the attack. Not long after that, we saw campfires coming again. I flew out to check on them and was almost killed when a dog sensed my presence."

"I'm thankful you weren't hurt," says Cap.

"Oh, I was hurt. My den was counting on me to learn as much as I could without the men knowing I was there. I was ashamed to tell them the next morning. We had to make a decision, and the only answer was to kill the dogs and men."

Cap and Jackson look at each other and frown as Fuzzy talks about killing men. They aren't afraid or angry, but struggle with the thought of men dying. They look into Fuzzy's eyes and feel his thoughts. He regrets having to kill anything, just like them.

"We killed the dogs, and when the men saw they were dead, they disappeared into the wilderness. We searched and finally found them hopelessly lost. We decided to let them go. I doubt the three of them will survive long in the wilderness. They're now in a very wild and dangerous place."

Cap looks at Jackson.

"When these men passed by our farm, there were four of them," says Cap.

Fuzzy's expression changes and sadness fills his eyes. The tone of his voice changes as worry returns about the hunting party.

"Are you sure there were four men?"

"Yes," replies Jackson.

"How could we have made such a foolish mistake?" says Fuzzy solemnly. "This means at least one of them may return to civilization, and more trouble will follow."

"Now I'm glad our den has decided to leave their cavern. We have two dragons searching for a safer place far from civilization. It's just a matter of time until man proves we exist. When that happens, they will not rest until they have made all the silver they can at our den's expense."

"Fuzzy, we're sorry your den is in this predicament because of the ambition of a few bad men. I feel guilty just being human," says Jackson hanging his head.

"Don't feel guilty, old friends. You aren't like these men. Life will reward you in better ways than it will the selfish ones. I want you to know I will miss you once we leave because I will be too far away to come back and see you. At least now I can go before my den and they will know I speak the truth as I impress on them that you and your family are not to be harmed. Many dragons will be furious with humans if any member of our den is hurt. There's a chance many men and dragons will die before we are able to find a new cavern. I will do all I can to protect your family."

Cap and Jackson grit their teeth, and their eyebrows wrinkle as suddenly they realize their family is in just as much jeopardy as Fuzzy and his den. Even the two wonderful women they are just beginning to know and love are in danger. The brothers are trapped. All they can do for now is help Fuzzy and hope he can keep their family safe.

"We feel the same way about you and your family. If we need to help or warn you, we will come to the wilderness and build a huge fire. We will tie red ribbons around our arms so you will know it's us. Tell the other dragons we are on their side," says Cap.

"I will tell everyone as soon as I return. We must help each other." He bows, flaps his wings, and lifts into the sky, continuing to rise until he is above the clouds. The brothers watch until he disappears.

"After what we just heard, I'm worried. Our family and the girls need to know about the danger and the ribbons, but we can't breathe a word about it," says Cap.

"We're trapped again, knowing something unbelievable, and yet we have no choice but to stay quiet and act like this never happened," says Jackson.

"Well, let's finish these chores and try to get on with a happier evening," replies Cap as they walk out of the woods.

Working hard to keep Fuzzy off their mind and complete their chores, it isn't long until they're on the trail heading toward the Brittain's.

"Poor Fuzzy. I wish he and his den could live in peace out there in the wilderness," says Jackson as the horses trot along.

"Just think how emotionally and physically hard it's going to be for them to leave their ancestral cavern and move far away," replies Cap.

Jackson shakes his head. "Don't talk about Fuzzy anymore. I want to be in a better mood by the time I see Sandra."

Riding in silence, a cold fall breeze blows toward them, making their cheeks turn red. The chill adds to the emotional discomfort they endure.

By the time they dismount at the Brittain's, they're shivering. Janice sees them and calls for Sandra. Together they run out to greet the brothers. The women are happy and talkative, and their presence mellows the mood the two men have fallen into. Cap savors his greeting kiss and this time Jackson gets a hug from Sandra.

It's too breezy to sit on the porch, where they can be alone, so they move inside. Candles are burning, giving off a smell of honey as they flicker around the cabin. A warm fire dances in the fireplace. It's cozy but there's nowhere for them to talk without the parents hearing every word they say. Jackson is self-conscious in front of Sandra's mom, and with the burden of Fuzzy's dilemma on their minds, neither brother is as talkative or affectionate as they normally are. Janice and Sandra try to cheer them.

"Sandra and I prepared supper tonight," says Janice, smiling.

Cap looks toward the table, raises his eyebrows, and smiles. "Everything looks delicious. If it only tastes half as good as it looks, it will be wonderful."

Everyone gathers around the table. After Jackson's first bite, he raises his spoon and gestures delight. Cap smiles at the cousins and nods, closing his eyes as he chews. They feel better after eating and smiles mixed with conversation comes easier. The cousins are happy and talkative as ever.

When the meal is over, Cap and Jackson insist the girls let them help with the dishes.

"This is supposed to be my time with you," protests Buck.

"Please excuse us this one time. We thought it would be fun to help the girls clean up," says Cap, glancing at Janice.

Buck nods wisely and asks Flavie and Mary to join him while the young folks clean up the kitchen.

The adults sit around the fire and talk, as laughter fills the kitchen from time to time.

Jackson would distract the cousins while Cap put dishes that had just been cleaned back on the wash table. When they catch Cap, and are looking at him, Jackson hides their drying cloths. It takes a long time to clean up the kitchen when you're playing around and kidding each other. By the time the work is done, it's time for the brothers to leave. Jackson and Sandra hold hands as they say goodbye.

174

"I would like to see you tomorrow if I can," says Jackson softly.

Sandra smiles and squeezes his hand lightly. "I would like that. Come with me and I will ask."

Jackson is nervous and blushing as they walk in to the room where the Brittains are talking.

"Mom, uncle Buck, do you mind if Jackson comes back tomorrow and spends the day?"

"Of course not, you're only going to be here until Thursday," replies Mary. Buck smiles in agreement.

Jackson is relieved. Any one of them could have said no and that would have been the end of it.

Riding home, Cap and Jackson are thankful the wind is at their backs.

"I feel sorry for Fuzzy and his den. Men will never give up until they capture or kill them," says Jackson.

"Let's not worry about Fuzzy tonight. The dragons may be okay for a long time. They may even move to a new cavern before any hunters return."

They ride quietly for a little while.

"After such a wonderful supper, I'm even more impressed with Janice and Sandra," says Jackson.

"They're both pretty wonderful," replies Cap.

<>

As the brothers sleep, Virgil and Ron ride by, struggling to stay on the trail, lit only by pale moonlight. They don't make a sound because they hope the Murrays never find out only two of them returned from the wilderness. Riding side-by-side they don't talk. They're too tired after riding most of the night. Adding to their misery, the cold breeze continues to blow in their face. Close to Blade Town, Virgil can take no more.

"We must find a place to rest."

"I'm so tired. I wonder if I can walk when we stop," replies Ron.

They turn off the trail where the brush isn't very thick, and it leads to a small meadow where they camp. The sky begins to lighten as Ron pulls blankets out of the packhorse's saddlebags and throws two over to Virgil. Nether one speaks another word, and they quickly fall asleep. The sun is directly overhead when they begin to stir again.

"Build us a fire and make some tea," says Virgil, still bundled in his blankets.

Ron groans as he limps around for a second, but he makes himself get going and builds a fire. Ron sits by the fire rubbing his hands, feeling better.

Virgil tries to get up. His face is full of pain. "I have never felt so sore in all my life," he says, stretching and walking slowly. Are you this sore?"

"Just a little," Ron lies.

"Let's clean ourselves up a bit."

"I sure will be glad to see Blade Town and civilization again," replies Ron.

"Me too, but don't mention anything about what we have been through or why we were out here to anyone. We don't want a bunch of men going into the wilderness trying to catch our dragons."

"I understand. I want to get on home as fast as we can, too," replies Ron, shaking his head in disbelief.

Virgil is quietly thinking about how to get back to the wilderness as soon as he can.

<>

On his way back to the den, Fuzzy is troubled. His friendship with his old friends and the safety of the den he

loves is forefront in his mind after his conversation
with Cap and Jackson.

As soon as he lands, he heads for Lester's special
place. It's time for the den to know what he has hid from
them all these years. He calls out to Lester before he
enters.

"Please come in and visit, Fuzzy."

"I have news and a confession to share with our
den," he says, bowing longer than usual.

"I will call the den together tomorrow. I look
forward to hearing what you have to say," replies Lester.

Early in the morning, Lester walks to the entrance,
where Fuzzy is waiting.

"Ureeeeee," he calls loudly.

Fuzzy is nervous and hopes he can find the right
words to say. The den is on the verge of hysteria,
worrying about having to leave the cavern of their
ancestors. He will have to be careful explaining his story.
He's glad his fellow dragons respect him, and know how
much he loves his den. Everyone waits quietly until he's
ready to speak.

He begins confidently and in the kind manner he is
known for. The den is surprised when he tells them that,
as a childish young dragon, he befriended two human
children and they had played and enjoyed being together.
He chose his words well, and they understand why they
became friends. He explains how as time passed they
began to communicate with each other and he discovered
these young humans are kindhearted as well. The mood
and demeanor of the crowd is very quiet.

"My father discovered my secret and told me what I
was doing could hurt our den, and I never went back.
Years later, as young men, these humans tried to find me
and became lost in the wilderness. I saved their lives and

helped them find their way home. I told them not to come back; we could never see each other again. They were very grateful and swore to never tell anyone about us."

Lester groans. "You can't trust any human. You know that, Fuzzy."

He looks at Lester and hopes to regain his trust.

"Not only can I communicate with them, I can tell what they are thinking. I know when they are telling the truth. I have discovered there is a big difference from one man to another. Some men are the kindest creatures on earth and some are cruel and thoughtless. These young men are good men, and we need their friendship. They told me four hunters and two dogs passed their farm headed into the wilderness. Now we know there is one man, and possibly another, we can't account for, and they will return to civilization."

Calamity spreads among the den as fear, and noise erupts. Fuzzy raises his wings, asking for calm. He waits until it's quiet again. "If it weren't for my old friends, we wouldn't know this. These men and their families live on the fringe of the wilderness, and I want all of you to promise you will not harm them. They and their families will be wearing red ribbons around their arms to let you know they're on our side."

The dragons are troubled and skeptical. They know how kindhearted Fuzzy is. But from past experiences, they know Fuzzy is wise and known for being right most of the time.

"It's not a good idea for dragons to ever trust humans," moans one of the dragons in the group.

Fuzzy doesn't reply. He bows longer than usual to the others in deep respect and moves back to his place in the cavern. He knows they will think about what he said.

Some of the dragons begin to talk with one another. Others, considering what he said, are quiet as they slowly disappear into the darkness of the cavern.

<>

On Monday morning, Jackson is searching for his best pair of pants. Cap is watching him as he dresses to go see Sandra. He laughs to himself as Jackson combs his hair and straightens his clothes before he leaves. The wind and the trail will undo all his primping.

"Today is your day, and I hope things keep getting better for you and Sandra."

"Thanks, brother. I know you will have to work harder today because I'm gone."

Jackson feels carefree as his horse trots along toward the Brittain's house. He realizes this really is his day. Normally, he would be starting his work at the farm, but not on this wonderful morning. Filled with a new emotion, he has no control of, he thinks, I like this feeling, love is the only real magic in this world. His senses peak, they're more alive than ever. The grass along the trail is greener, and the sky is bluer. Life is so worth living on a day like today, he thinks as he turns off the main trail and heads up the path to the Brittain's.

Jackson is tying his horse to the hitching post when Sandra and Janice come out carrying fishing poles and a pottery bowl of worms.

"Are you going fishing?" he asks smiling.

"No. You and Sandra are going to catch some fish for a fish fry supper."

Jackson loves to fish, and the thought of fishing with Sandra is too good to be true.

"I will see you when you get back. Be sure to go to the rock on the creek. You will know it when you see it."

Jackson and Sandra carry the fishing gear in both hands as they walk close to each other. They follow a little trail beside the creek in search of the rock. In front of them, a little meadow appears and the creek bank is clear of brush.

There, on the edge of the meadow, under a big shade tree, a large smooth, creamy white rock juts into the creek. It's just high enough above the water to comfortably sit on and fish. There's room for two to sit and lay out all their tackle. Water pools quietly in front of the rock, making it easy to drop in their hooks and relax.

Jackson's senses are still alive from his ride on the trail. He looks around at all the beauty surrounding them. The smell of wilderness flowers drifts pleasantly by as the breeze follows the creek, lingering over the pool. The water is crystal-clear as he kneels looking over the edge. He can see little round pebbles lying on the sandy bottom and fish lazily swimming all around. Closing his eyes, he hears the rocky creek song gurgling upstream.

Opening his eyes, he sees Sandra smiling. Her presence is more wonderful than this place.

Jackson reaches over to hold her hand as she sits, and then he settles beside her. He baits his hook and drops it into the water. Sandra scratches for a worm and hands it to him as he holds her hook. The worm slips through his fingers, and he accidentally pricks her finger. It hurts so badly a tear slides from her eye. She grits her teeth but tries to keep a smile.

"I'm okay. Getting stuck is just part of fishing."

As he holds her hand to clean her wound, she feels tender love and concern flowing through his fingers. That special moment melts her heart, and she knows Jackson is a deep and kind man.

When he finishes dressing her wound, she kisses him the moment he looks into her eyes. He flinches and is not affectionate; making her wonder if she should have taken the chance. Her emotions had surprised them both.

Realizing what happened, Jackson feels a pleasant tingle from the top of his head to tip of his toes, a feeling he never knew existed. He leans over and passionately kisses her lips, and their hearts discover a feeling they can never live without. They brim with smiles as they walk back. Buck is waiting to help Jackson clean the fish while Janice and Sandra set the table and hang a big pot filled with lard in the fireplace. The fish fries up to taste wonderful and everyone eats their fill. Soon they're all on the porch enjoying the evening.

"I hope I'm not keeping any of you from doing what you had in mind when Sandra and Mary came to visit," says Jackson.

"Of course not," replies Flavie.

Mary contemplates his remark, "Why do you ask, Jackson?"

"If you don't mind, I would like to come back tomorrow and take Sandra to my family's farm to meet everyone."

Mary smiles. "As long as I can go along, too."

Jackson is in heaven. He wants Mary to meet his family. He's proud of them and knows she will be pleased.

"I will pick you up early tomorrow morning so we can spend the day together. He turns to Sandra. "You will finally get to see Homer." He beams. They hold hands as they walk to his horse, and she kisses him goodbye.

Riding home, he is in a daze of happiness. His only concern is how to tell his mom. On his way to the barn, he sees a candle burning and knows his mother is sewing by candlelight. He tries to find the right words to say as he walks toward the house. He takes a deep breath and opens the door, walks over, and sits beside her. She stops and looks at him, knowing something is up. Normally, he would have said goodnight and gone straight to bed. "This must be important for you to sit beside your mom." She smiles.

"I invited Sandra and her mom, Mary, to spend the day with us tomorrow." Her mouth drops open slightly. "I will have to get things cleaned up before they get here. Why didn't you tell me sooner?"

"I would have, but it just happened. She will be leaving Thursday so tomorrow is the only day she can come meet you."

"The *it* that just happened. What would that be?" she asks, looking into his eyes.

"Mom, I can't lie. I'm in love, and I think she feels the same about me. You will love her and her mother."

Inez reaches over and squeezes his hand lovingly. "I know it's time for you to find your true love. I will be ready when she arrives."

Jackson happily walks into his bedroom. Cap's almost asleep.

"Cap! I have to tell you all about what happened at the rock on the creek. I'm going to bring Sandra and her mom to visit tomorrow."

Cap knows what that means. "I'm happy for both of you. Sandra is a wonderful person. Wait… Can't Janice come, too?"

"That would be even better! I'll ask as soon as I get there."

The next morning, as soon as there is enough light, Cap and Jackson grab the broom, rags and soapy water, and head out to the wagon. They clean it like it has never been cleaned before.

"I'm going to put some hay in the wagon so whoever has to sit back there will be comfortable," says Jackson.

Cap laughs. "Don't just put some hay, put a lot. Janice and I will need a warm place to snuggle while you and Sandra sit on the cold bench."

Jackson shakes his head and rolls his eyes. He wonders if he should offer the seat beside him to Mary and let Sandra and Janice ride in the back.

"I see that serious look on your face. Just go get everyone. Everything will work out," says Cap.

"See you in a couple hours. Try to have all my work done by the time I get back."

Jackson has never been happier when he arrives at the Brittain farm. Sandra and Mary are ready to go.

"Good morning," he says as he locks the brake on the wagon. "Before we load up, would you mind if Janice comes along to spend the day with Cap?" asks Jackson.

"How nice of you to think about Janice. Please run in and ask her," replies Mary.

Jackson knocks on the door. "Hey," says Janice as she opens the door wearing her usual pretty smile.

"Can I get something for you?" she asks.

"I would be pleased if you would come with us, and Cap would be even more pleased."

"Thank you! I would love to come along." Janice is ready in minutes, and they load up to leave.

Jackson enjoys driving the wagon and listening while everyone talks about Brittain family relatives he hopes to meet one day.

When the wagon pulls up to the Murray's house, Inez is on the porch wearing a pretty dress she has just

finished making. Miles and Uncle Matt are wearing
their best work clothes. Cap's dressed in soft leather pants
with no stains. He plans to spend the day with Janice.

Jackson introduces everyone before calling Homer
to meet Sandra. He barks until Sandra speaks to him with
a kind voice and pets his head. In no time at all, they're
best friends.

Everyone settles in chairs on the porch. Homer lies
on the floor between Jackson and Sandra.

Mary looks at Miles. "Tell me about this beautiful
farm."

Miles smiles from ear to ear. He's proud of what his
family has built and glad she's interested. He tells her all
about it.

Inez speaks up. "It's time to get ready for lunch.
Mary would you like to help me in the kitchen?"

"I would love to."

Mary and Inez make their way inside to freshen up
and set things out for lunch.

After eating, the young people are ready to leave
the porch. They saddle the horses to ride around the farm.
They trot along, having fun heading toward the north side
of the farm to a knoll where they can look over the
wilderness.

"No man lives in the wilderness as far as you can
see from here," says Jackson.

The ladies gaze into the distance. "Not even one
person is trying to start a homestead in all of that vast
area?" asks Janice.

"As far as we know, there is no one," replies Cap.

"It's beautiful but kind of scary," says Sandra.

"We call that respect for the wilderness," says Cap.

In the distance, a porch bell rings.

"Mom is calling us to supper," says Jackson.

After supper, the couples laugh and talk on the porch. Inez and Mary talk inside while Miles and Uncle Matt finish the rest of the day's chores.

When time comes to load up the wagon, the brothers hate to see such a wonderful day end.

"I can drive the wagon," says Mary, climbing into the front seat. "Jackson, you and Sandra sit in the back and enjoy your ride."

Jackson feels happy inside. Sandra's mother is in such a good mood and a smile is on her face. It's obvious she's pleased with everything she has seen. Sandra is in a good mood, too. She is more affectionate than ever, and Jackson can see contentment in her eyes. Cap and Janice doesn't know the rest of them are in the world.

It's just cold enough to sit close and hug all the way back. They discover there's something special about riding in a wagon full of hay, at night with your girl. When the wagon comes to a stop and Mary sets the brake, no one wants to get out. Mary stands and hops to the ground.

"I had a wonderful day Jackson. You have a nice family and I would like to visit them again sometime." She smiles and goes into the house leaving the couples to say good night.

I'm sad tomorrow is the last chance for us to see each other," confesses Sandra, as they walk to the door. "Let's pretend tomorrow will never end," he replies. Sandra kisses him. "I will try."

Jackson hurries to the wagon. Cap flips the reins, and they head home.

The conversation on the way is about riding with the ladies in the back of the wagon filled with hay.

Chapter 15

Virgil is exhausted, and quiet. The horses walk on and on until, finally, familiar landmarks begin to appear along the trail.

"It won't be long until the buildings of Water Town come into view," says Ron, breaking the silence.

"Never in my life have I been so glad to be home," moans Virgil as a building on the edge of town comes into view. "If I only had better news to give Mr. Peeler and his friends, I wouldn't dread meeting with them."

"How much silver do you think they traded for gear and supplies so we could go hunting dragons?" asks Ron.

"I don't even want to know. Fortunately, I have one more night to decide what I'm going to tell them. I will come up with a story that will make them have enough confidence in us to invest more silver." He sighs as he rides and thinks. He looks at Ron. "We know for sure there are dragons out there now. I just have to convincingly explain that I personally saw dragons twice, even if the last time they were flying away with our dogs in their claws."

Ron tries to look interested as they turn up the trail toward his farm.

"This last quarter mile is the only thing between me and my bed," says Virgil, feeling triumphant over the dragons. They have failed to keep him from returning home alive.

When they ride up to his porch, Virgil dismounts without saying a word. Ron knows he can't rest until he puts the horses in their stables.

The farm sits on the edge of Water Town. Virgil has enough silver to keep it looking nice without having to work all the time. His family has plenty of silver because they have operated a leather shop in Water Town for years.

Many times, his dad tried to persuade him to stay around and work full-time at the family's shop, but he is part of the new generation raised in Water Town.

Virgil plops in his favorite chair the minute he slips off his vest. He rubs his tired eyes thinking about the defeat the dragons gave him. After resting, and being surrounded by the comfort of his home, he begins to regain his confidence.

By nightfall he sees it as a temporary setback and convinces himself before he retires for the night that the time he spent in the wilderness--and even the lost battle-- has made him a better dragon hunter.

He sips a glass of wine to ease his pain, pulls the covers to his chin, closes his eyes and drifts into a beautiful dream about catching dragons and amazing the people of Water Town. He smiles in his sleep as he hears everyone cheering for their new hero, calling him a brave and cunning hunter.

In the morning, feeling confident, he dresses in a new set of clothes and heads to the mill office. The mill is the biggest business in Water Town. It's one of many businesses powered by the river flowing through town.

He is going to see Mr. Peeler whose father built the mill and who now runs the business. He has lots of silver and friends with lots of silver.

In Water Town, the more silver a person has, the more opportunities are available. Peeler looks up and is glad to see Virgil walk through the office door. He smiles broadly and stands as he enters.

"How did it go?"

Virgil wants to sound positive right from the start. "We have found the dragons! I personally saw one on the

ground near our camp one evening and two days later
we all saw two flying high in the sky"

"Did you bring any trophies back?"

"We came close. The dragon near our campsite was
beautiful. We shot at it but it flew away. The two we saw
later were too far away to shoot."

"That sounds great. I didn't expect to see you today,
and I'm already late for a meeting. Bring your men with
you tomorrow. I enjoy hearing a story like this more when
the entire hunting party is interacting with each other."

Virgil loses his positive smile and squirms. He
hesitates for a second.

"I can't bring them until they return."

"What do you mean?"

"Jess and Steven got lost in the chaos after the
dragons attacked us and killed our dogs."

Peeler looks into Virgil's eyes as wrinkles grow on
his forehead. "This doesn't sound like the story you just
told me. Now it sounds like two dogs, and possibly two
men may be dead."

"I'm sure they will find their way back in a few
more days."

"How about Ron? Did he see the dragons?"

"No. The undergrowth was so thick, we had to
leave Ron camped with the horses while Jess, Steven and I
continued on foot."

Peeler knows hunting can be unpredictable.

"So, no one but you at this time can claim to have
seen the dragons?"

Virgil, with a sick feeling, hangs his head. This
story is sounding all wrong so he doesn't reply.

"Tomorrow, I want you and Ron to come back. I
hope Jess and Steven will be with you. I will have a

couple other investors here, and we will want to hear your story before investing any more silver."

They shake hands, and Virgil is already rethinking his story. He's determined to do a better job of explaining things tomorrow.

Virgil heads toward his family's leather shop. The second his mom sees him, she runs to hug her son.

"Thank goodness you're home. Your father and I are always worried when you go on one of these adventures."

"Did you catch a dragon?" one brother-in-law asks, with a smile on his face as he looks over at Virgil's other brother-in-law.

His mother can tell they're making fun of him.

"This is something neither one of you need to be discussing at work," she snaps.

They return to what they were doing. When the two of them are alone they will vent some of their resentment. Virgil's two sisters look at each other and continue working.

The next day, Virgil and Ron sit nervously in front of the mill. They made sure to arrive earlier than they had been told.

Mr. Peeler walks out dressed in fine clothes. He takes a breath of fresh air and thanks them for coming back. "I hoped Jess and Steven would be with you," he says.

They follow Peeler quietly as he leads the way to his office. He opens the door and two well-dressed men are already inside. They're sitting in beautiful chairs Virgil hadn't even noticed the day before. The two men smile but the atmosphere is stuffy and intimidating.

"Virgil, Ron, these are my most trusted business associates, Mr. Bridges and Mr. Ferree. Virgil, tell us what happened when you saw the first dragon. The one you were close enough to shoot at."

"We were sitting around our campfire, preparing our equipment for the next day. The dogs popped up and barked, then the hair on their back stood up, and they howled ferociously. Suddenly, they leaped into the woods." Virgil's eyes light up, as it appears the three men are on the edge of their seats, and in his mind's eye he's reliving the excitement. "We jumped and ran as fast as we could after them. Jess was in front and could see the dragon. He raised his bow, released an arrow, ran a few steps, then released another."

Bridges looks excited, analyzing the story, and Ferree is looking interested. To Virgil, feeding on his own story, the room is filled with excitement. He smiles and uses his hands to emphasize events and goes into detail describing them. Bridges interrupts. "Did Jess hit the dragon?" Virgil is surprised he has to stop and explain. "He thinks one of the arrows hit the dragon." Bridges squints an eye, in analytical thought. "Did you find any blood in the morning? or look for dragon tracks?"

"No," replies Virgil.

"Didn't you think to measure one of the tracks and maybe even draw a picture of it to bring back and show us?"

Virgil's mind is back in the office, he doesn't know what to say, and all the excitement he tried to create is fading away. He hadn't taken anything to draw with. "We were too excited. We thought for sure it wouldn't be long until we would have a dragon caught or killed and we would have all the proof we would need."

Ferree is troubled. He's not a hunter, and in his business, things are written down, drawn out, and studied. The two men turn their attention to Ron.

"Tell us what you saw, young man."

Ron looks threatened. He has never been in a meeting. He's just a farmhand, and now two men dressed in some of the finest clothes he has ever seen are staring at him.

"I didn't go into the wilderness as far as the others, but it was terribly scary watching the horses alone."

Virgil's heart sinks. Ron's presence is worthless.

"Tell us what happened to the dogs?" asks Peeler looking back to Virgil.

"We didn't exactly see their encounter with the dragons. We first heard a yelp and a fury of barking, then a sound like a blast of air. We ran as fast as we could to see what was happening, only to stop in our tracks when we saw two dragons flying away with them gripped in their claws."

"That's when we saw the forest in front of us on fire and it was spreading rapidly. We ran for our lives, looking back at the fire and fearful the other dragons would swoop in at any second and snatch us off our feet."

"These other dragons. How many were there?" asks Bridges.

Caught in a situation where a lie would be and easy answer Virgil quickly decides to tell the truth, fearing he will be caught. "We only saw the two flying away but we just knew there would be others," he explains, looking like a liar.

Ferree has a glare in his eyes and becomes aggressive. "How did you manage to lose two men if the dragons didn't even attack you?"

Virgil grows defensive and looks at him with piercing eyes. "We were running for our lives! The smoke grew thicker, and the dark of night was closing in. We got separated."

The investors shake their heads. The silver they invested hadn't produced anything of value.

"Thank you, Mr. Peeler, for giving me the opportunity to listen to this story. It is the best tale I have heard in quite a while. I will not be putting any more silver into this wild goose chase," says Bridges.

"I have heard enough. Good day, Mr. Peeler," says Ferree.

Mr. Peeler leans back in his chair and is quiet.

Virgil drops his head and turns away. He and Ron slowly walk out of the office.

Chapter 16

Jackson wakes with a sad feeling hanging over him. This is the last day of Sandra's visit, and even though a wonderful day lies ahead, he's already dreading the loneliness to follow.

Anxious and energetic, he saddles his horse and waits for the sun to rise. Soon, he's on his way. The trail is dimly lit, but it starts coming alive even before the sun breaks over the horizon. He's entertained as he watches small wilderness creatures playing in the safety of the light of dawn. The serendipity of the morning trail eases his mind as he rides.

Sandra and Janice are cleaning up the breakfast dishes when he arrives. Sandra hears his footsteps on the porch and smiles as she opens the door. She welcomes him with a hug. "I fixed a plate of breakfast for you," she says with a pretty smile. He's hungry, and pleased she thought about him, and they sit together at the table as he eats. "I bet Homer will be glad when I go home. He hasn't had much time with you lately."

"I'm sure he will get a lot of attention next week. I will miss you so much," Jackson responds softly.

Sandra reaches out and places her hand over his, squeezing it lightly. "Let's get out of the house."

Outside, they walk hand-in-hand and soon pass the garden. Janice is picking beans, so they stop to help her. They have fun working together. When the beans are picked they head for the porch to shell them. It takes longer to shell the beans than it did to pick them, and now it's time for lunch even though Jackson feels as if he just arrived.

After lunch, they pardon themselves. Everyone knows they want to be alone for a while. Slipping away, they hold hands and walk toward the rock on the creek. The whole world seems prettier and better when they can be together alone. As they walk quietly, they absorb contentment from each other's presence.

At the rock, they sit close together. Jackson wraps his arm around Sandra's waist. They listen as the wind makes the leaves dance in the trees. The sounds of water splashing in the distance and the birds singing combine forming an ensemble that can only be heard at the rock. He can tell by the feeling they share, and by the look in Sandra's eyes, that he can ask her anything. It's time to take a chance.

"Someday, do you think you would like to live out here near the wilderness, or do you prefer to stay near your village?"

She looks at him with a loving smile. "If you're here, then this is where I want to be."

His heart throbs hearing the perfect answer. He savors the same feeling inside he has only felt once before when they first kissed at the rock. "I know we just met, but in my heart, I know I don't want to be with anyone but you."

"Why don't we promise each other not to see anyone else, and one day we can get married," she replies.

Jackson's heart almost bursts with joy. He knows this moment is one of the most wonderful experiences that will ever happen in his life. He fights back tears of joy. They kiss passionately to seal their promise. He hardly has time to let it all settle in when the porch bell rings. It's time to go in for supper, and they stroll up the path toward the house.

As Mary looks across the field, she sees a peacefulness and rhythm in their steps that only lovers share. There is even a look of passion expressed by the way they hold hands. When they're close enough for Mary to see their faces, there can be no doubt. Jackson is the one for her daughter.

After supper, everyone sits on the porch talking. Jackson feels right at home as if the Brittains have always known him. "If I were to come to your village to visit, would it be hard to find your home?" he asks Sandra.

"Our family's blacksmith shop is right on the trail from Water Town to Blade Town. The shop is almost always open, and everyone in our village knows us."

Jackson sits quietly next to Sandra. They hold hands until it's time for him to head home.

As Sandra walks him to his horse to say goodbye, he asks her if he can ride to her village next Saturday to see her.

"Of course," she replies. "But I will worry about you traveling so far by yourself."

"I will be careful. I would never let something keep me from seeing you," he assures her.

As Jackson rides home, he dreams about Sandra's promise to him. It makes his trip pass quickly. In no time, he's back in his barn putting up the horse.

The moment Jackson sees Cap, he tells him about the promise he and Sandra have made. Cap smiles broadly, and claps Jackson's shoulder.

"Congratulations! You are a lucky man."

<>

Cap can hardly wait to see Janice, after hearing about Jackson and Sandra's promise. When Saturday morning arrives, his mind is only thinking about one thing, and he doesn't do a good job as he does the morning chores.

"If these boys don't stop courting so much, we're going to have to make this farm a smaller place," complains Miles to Inez.

Inez moves close to his side, and reaches for his hand. "Give it time, Miles. We might get more help soon." She pauses in thought. "We might gain one and lose one. Either way, they are fine young ladies."

When he arrives at the Brittains, Janice is sewing on the porch while she waits for him. Cap steps up on the porch and sits next to her. They're both content to sit and talk while she sews.

"Jackson told me he and Sandra made a promise to not see anyone else."

"I know. Sandra is so happy. She told me, too. I'm very happy they feel that way about each other."

He pauses and watches her sew. "Will you marry me?" he calmly asks.

Janice stops sewing. Lovingly, she looks him in the eye and gently touches his face. "You already know I will. I love you too much. All I can say is yes." Tears of joy fill her eyes.

"After supper, I will ask your dad."

Throughout supper, Cap is nervous. He isn't worried about Buck saying no, but this will be the most important moment in his life.

When the dishes are cleared from the table, Buck heads to the porch, and Cap is right behind him. Normally, he would stay and help in the kitchen. Buck wonders why, so he sits down and waits for Cap to start the conversation.

"I love Janice, and I would like to have her hand in marriage. Will you give us your blessing?" He asks straight-forwardly.

Buck quickly turns and looks Cap in the eyes. "Son, I have liked you since the first time I met you. I will be the one who is honored if you two wed, and so will Flavie."

When Buck tells Flavie, she cries and hugs Cap. "I love you like a son already. Welcome to the family!"

"Where are you going to live?" asks Buck.

"I would never want to impose on you, but I wonder if we could live with you until Janice and I can build a house not far from here toward my family's farm. I want to be where I can help you and my father."

Buck looks him in the eyes and nods with contentment.

Cap beams and dreams. He's as happy as a man can be as he heads home. He still hasn't come up with the right words to ask his father, and it's late so he decides to wait until breakfast.

He wakes, full of nervous energy. The kitchen smells of ham, eggs, biscuits, and gravy. He kisses his mom as he enters the kitchen. He forces himself to wait until everyone is seated, and then blurts out his wonderful announcement.

"I asked Mr. Brittain for Janice's hand in marriage last night."

"And?" says Miles in suspense.

"He said yes." Cap smiles.

Inez wipes a tear stands and hugs her son. "Where are you two going to live?"

Cap's smile lessens. His posture changes, and he's slightly tense. Miles knows the answer from his hesitancy.

"I talked to the Brittains, and they agree I can move in with Janice until we build a house between our farms. I will be able to help you both from there."

"I think that's a great plan," says Jackson.

Miles smiles, but Cap knows he's disappointed.

Inez is just happy for him. "Congratulations son. Janice is a fine young lady. I hope you will be as happy as your father and I have been." She wipes another tear and smiles.

After breakfast, everyone goes to the porch to talk and enjoy the happy moment. Work can wait a little while.

Inez and Miles sit closer than usual, holding hands. When it quiets for a while, Inez smiles and squeezes Miles hand. "Miles and I are going to Water Town on Friday. We're going to see what it's like to sell a cow for silver. We're looking forward to spending a couple days away." Miles looks into her eyes and smiles contently.

"While we're there, I would like to visit the shops. Especially the leather shop Virgil told us about. We might trade some silver for a few things we could really use."

Jackson perks up, he wonders about a possibility.

Chapter 17

In the depths of the wilderness, hopelessly lost under a forest canopy so thick the sun rarely shines through, Steven and Jess are still alive.

"I have never endured a hunger like this before. It has been too long since we have eaten real meat. I don't know how much longer I can eat bugs and lizards and still have enough strength to survive out here," says Steven.

"I can't believe our luck. We can't seem to kill anything large enough to make a decent meal. Every time I release an arrow, I either miss or the poor animal runs away with it stuck in their side to die where it will do us no good," replies Jess, shrugging.

"Hopefully the arrows you made last night will prove to be better," replies Steven.

"Baking them over our campfire made them a lot harder, and I managed to keep them straight as they cooked. Now we need to find something I can get a decent shot at."

Quietly, they ramble through the brush for hours without seeing a thing.

"Listen" says Jess, stopping. He places his hand behind his ear and turns, trying to locate the direction a curious sound is coming from. "I hear animals fighting on the other side of this hill."

Carefully, they steal through the brush making their way to the crest, where they spy three wolves, surrounding a boar. The wolves take turns tearing at the boar when it looks toward one of the other two.

"We must try to run the wolves off after they kill the boar," says Jess, feeling nervous energy flowing through his veins.

"We have no other choice, but to wait. This could be the break we need to survive long enough to find our way home," states Steven.

"This could end up being the death of us, too," whispers Jess.

The boar stops squealing, and the wolves engage in a ferocious battle over which one will eat first.

"Gather several good size rocks you can throw while I try to shoot one of the wolves," says Jess.

Steven slips away and returns with several rocks just right to inflict real harm if they hit one of the wolves. "I'm as ready as I'll ever be."

Jess nods. "Scream as loud as you can, and let's attack them."

They spring to their feet and charge the three wolves. The closer they get, the bigger the wolves look, but there's no stopping now.

"Stop and defend me. I'm going to shoot," yells Jess.

Steven stands close to Jess, who is surprisingly calm. He can't believe Jess's self-control as he pulls the arrow back. He releases and it singings as it streaks toward the wolf. *Thunk*, the creature shrieks and jerks its head around, clamping its teeth onto the arrow, trying to yank it out. It collapses and thrashes in the leaves. Death comes quickly. The other wolves aim their sights toward the men and charge.

"Throw a rock at one of them while I nock an arrow," yells Jess.

Steven flings the stone with all his might, and he can't believe his eyes. It strikes a wolf's shoulder, and it falls to the ground, whimpering mournfully as it struggles to limp away. The other wolf slides to a stop, turns, and runs, disappearing into the brush.

"Did this really happen?" screams Steven, jumping up and down so full of energy and excitement he can hardly breathe.

"Luck. Pure luck. But I will take it as meant to be," says Jess as his heart races. His hands are shaking now.

It's time to skin the hog and cut it up. Finally, they will use their small knives for something besides whittling arrows.

They build a fire and cut some of the meat into strips, quickly cooking and eating their fill. Then they cut up the rest of the boar and slowly smoke it for later. They will have food for weeks.

"Next time I will have rocks and a spear handy when we attack an animal," says Steven. They smile, feeling more confident than ever. "All you have to do to make a real spear is cut piece of hardwood the length you like and then harden it over the campfire," says Jess.

It has taken a lot of suffering, mixed with trial and error, to learn how to survive. Their shared hatred for Virgil gave them the extra strength they needed to reach this day.

As time passes, they learn to track and bait deer and boar. They start skinning their kill and using the hides for clothing and other needs.

"We have to kill a large deer. I think if we skin it just right, we can use the hide to make a hammock," says Steven. He is beginning to make improvements to their gear.

"I really would feel safer in the trees. There are too many large predators on the ground. I'm afraid if we don't get out of their reach at night, it's just a matter of time until we end up being their supper," replies Jess.

They spend more time hunting deer than walking, and soon they're rewarded. They plan every cut as they skin the large deer, shaping its hide into a hammock.

It's not long until they figure out how to hang the hammock high in a tall tree. Soon, with another hammock made, they finally sleep feeling safe at night. After several nights, they improve their swinging beds by hanging another deer skin above the hammock, turning it into to a tree born tent, sheltering them from the cold wind, and keeping their beds dry.

As they finish a meal around a small campfire, Steven arranges several stones where a flat rock can be laid across the top, hiding most of the flames.

"The fire doesn't give as much heat as it did before," remarks Jess.

"I know, but we can't forget dragons are out here, and our fire has to be less noticeable." Jess raises his eyebrows, and nods in agreement. He leans back to relax and looks up into the tree they chose to sleep in. He marvels at the sight of the hammock tents hanging above them.

"Steven, you're a genius. If it weren't for you, I don't think we would have a chance out here."

"You're the one who figured out how to make the arrows strong and straight. We're a team, and we're going to make it out of here."

They now have a routine they do without giving it much thought. Every day before they build their campfire, they search for a tree large enough to safely hang their hammocks high above the ground. It also has to have limbs situated so both hammocks can be hung close together. The task of tying them in the trees is always done as soon as the campfire is built. After eating, and well before dark, one of them places all their food in a leather pouch and hangs it high above the ground a safe distance from their camp. Any bones or scraps are carefully picked up and burned.

They begin to feel safer. Most nights are peaceful, filled with songs of tree frogs and crickets. The men relax in slumber. Until just before midnight on what has been another beautiful evening, Steven is woken by a clawing sound. He lies quietly concentrating about what the sound could be. Then he hears something leap and latch onto their tree with a thud. A pattern of crunches can be heard as claws dig deeply into the bark. He picks up his spear, turns the blunt end toward Jess's hammock, and punches him. "Jess! Jess!" He whispers quietly, his heart is beginning to rush. Slight jolts can be felt as claws continue to dig and pull into the bark.

"What," wails Jess, waking badly "I just had the worst dream."

"Wake up quick! This is not a dream! Grab your bow and get ready to fight for your life."

Jess fumbles for his bow, as he hears the clawing coming from the tree trunk. "What do you think it is?"

"All I know is this thing is big, and it's on the prowl."

It's too dark to see, and the tree is shaking more now as something powerful pulls higher. Jess's shaking hands set an arrow.

"Try to stay calm. I have my spear ready if I can ever see something," says Steven, breathing rapidly.

A fearful minute surrounded by total darkness frays their nerves while the animal continues to climb. They hopelessly strain to see as the sound of claws digging again and again into the tree grows louder.

"We're in trouble! I can hear that thing breathing. It's on the limb my hammock is tied to" screams Jess. His heart crawls into his throat, when his hammock jerks. He holds his breath. "Something is trying to pull my hammock loose!" he cries.

"Shoot through your cover in the direction of the tie strap," yells Steven holding his spear, trying to judge where the creature stands.

Jess feels another strong jerk. Aimlessly he lets an arrow fly, tearing through the leather cover.

A split second after the arrow rips through the cover, a dull thunk, and an ear shattering roar thunders in the darkness. The creature leaps onto Jess's cover, pinning him. The stench of a filthy, sweaty animal fills their nostrils.

Steven is forced to make a split-second decision. Stunned by fear and without any way to judge where to strike, he thrusts his spear in the dark. He feels the resistance of flesh and bone as it penetrates. Suddenly, it's too quiet. He pulls the spear back. There's no movement. He gasps.

"Jess?" he yells.

He's struck with horror and falls back in his hammock when he hears something slide from Jess's hammock. A heavy body crashes through the tree limbs falling faster, and faster. The sounds of breaking limbs and thuds last forever.

"Jess!" screams Steven.

He jumps to his feet when he hears struggling in the hammock. He prepares to thrust again. "What happened to the animal?" yells Jess.

Steven falls to his knees, his hammock rocks. "Everything is okay, I think."

Jess plops back in his hammock sucking in fresh air he had been unable to find a few seconds earlier. "You saved my life."

"I only stabbed in the dark out of fear for myself. I could have killed you," laments Steven, his eyes fill with tears.

"No, you saved my life."

They're so filled with adrenaline and energy that they have no desire to sleep any longer.

"I have a bad feeling about what I hear going on at the bottom of this tree," says Steven.

"I hear it, too. Please don't let it be another tree climbing animal."

The sound of fighting grows into a raging battle. Finally, a shriek echoes in the darkness, and they know a pack of wolves are beneath their tree. The sound of chewing and an occasional growl is less worrisome, but concerns the men.

"At least wolves can't climb trees," says Steven.

"No, but now we know wolves are all around us, and they're hungry."

The morning sun's rays begin to penetrate the forest, and the men have never been happier to have light. They look down and study the ground around their tree. No sign of the creature that attacked them can be seen. Steven climbs down while Jess stands on one of the lower limbs with his bow ready to shoot.

Steven looks around from the lowest limb and then jumps to the ground. He builds a warm fire and they feel better.

They sit around the fire talking about an unbelievable night.

"I'm glad we picked the tallest tree around last night," says Steven.

"That gives me an idea," says Jess. He hops up, walks over to the tree, and looks up. The top of the tree is higher than any of the surrounding trees. "I'm going to climb as high as I can and look out over the countryside."

"I'm right behind you," says Steven.

Slowly, they climb. The tree proves to be much taller than the others. Jess, who is above Steven, can look out across the top of the forest. The sun shines brightly and he shades his eyes as he looks around, studying for a few minutes.

"I don't see any smoke or signs of civilization," says Jess, holding on with both hands, and shaking his head.

"Let me up there," requests Steven.

They switch places, and Steven looks intently. In the distance, he sees a mound of trees standing above all the rest of the countryside.

"I wonder if that high place in the distance could be the plateau where the dragons attacked us. We probably would be closer to civilization if we were back there."

"We don't have a better plan. Let's head toward the high place," says Jess.

Every morning, they climb to the top of a tree and look for what they hope is the plateau. They concentrate and try to stay headed in that direction all day.

"I have renewed hope just knowing we have a plan now," says Jess as they wind through the forest several days later.

"At least this plan keeps us from going in circles. If we can get back to where the dragons attacked us, then there's a chance we can find the trail we made on our way out," replies Steven.

"I'm sure as many trees and brush as we cut down, the trail will still be visible. Then all we have to do is follow it back to Blade Town and try not to be eaten by a dragon."

As long as we don't lose our knives and we stay hidden, we have a fighting chance," says Steven, rubbing his knife.

Chapter 18

Jackson is in the kitchen early the next morning, neatly stacking firewood. He helps crack eggs and asks Inez what else he can do to help. She wonders why he's helping her so much this particular morning. Then he looks at her humbly. "When you and dad go to Water Town on Friday, may I ride with you as far as Sandra's village?"

She rolls her eyes, realizing why he has been so much help in the kitchen. "Do Sandra's parents know you're coming?"

"I asked her last time I saw her, and her main concern was for my safety traveling alone on the trail."

Inez smiles and looks into the eyes of another son she is about to lose. "Then by all means, you will ride with us. You will need to spend two nights at her house because your father and I will spend one night in the wagon. We're thinking of staying at the boarding house the second night."

Jackson is happy he just gained an extra night without even trying, and he smiles.

"Why don't you go help your father? He's already fixing the wagon with a tarp in case of bad weather. We will be glad to have you enjoy part of our trip with us. We had already planned to stop in Sandra's village to let her family know about Cap and Janice's wedding." She pulls the washcloth out of his hands now that he's ready leave the kitchen. "Be sure to tell Cap when you see him we can save the Brittains a trip to Sandra's village if they would like."

Jackson joyfully heads toward the barn to talk to his dad. On his way he sees Cap working near the barn.

"Cap, I'm sorry to leave you and Uncle Matt while mom and dad are gone, but I'm going to ride with them to Sandra's village."

Cap shakes his head. "I hope you don't run into Uncle Matt after he finds out you will be gone too."

"Don't think I don't feel bad about it. But I have to see Sandra when I can."

The next day, Cap rides to the Brittains and talks with Flavie. She writes a pretty invitation to Mary and Ed.

Inez and Miles finish loading the wagon so they can leave early Friday morning.

After a quick breakfast, Miles and Jackson head to the pasture. When the cows see Jackson coming, they move to the corner where he always feeds them. Miles has a rope ready and slips it over the chosen cow's head. Jackson leads it to the wagon and ties the rope to the right back corner.

Uncle Matt and Cap watch as Inez, Miles, and Jackson climb on the wagon and pull out. They wave goodbye respectfully one time.

Homer scampers along behind the wagon. After a few minutes, Miles stops. Jackson hops to the ground. "Get back to the house," he scolds the pup, chasing him toward the farm with a stick. Homer looks surprised and stops halfway. Jackson scolds one more time, and he trots toward the house.

Returning to the wagon, Jackson notices how happy his mom and dad look sitting together on the seat, and realizes how much they love each other. As they ride along, he watches them talk and hold hands, sitting side-by-side. It's obvious they love each other as much as he loves Sandra, even after all these years together. He has never thought about his parents that way before.

An hour later, Jackson is surprised to hear barking in the distance. "Stop a minute dad."

They all look behind the wagon, and there comes Homer, running with his tongue hanging out, but smiling.

Miles isn't mad. He shakes his head and smiles at Jackson. "You will have to look after him at Sandra's."

Jackson picks up Homer. He's panting, but hops out of Jackson's arms into the wagon. Homer lies down beside him and rests for a while. Soon he comes back to life. This is an adventure for him. He walks to the back of the wagon and puts his paws up on the tailgate. Full of excitement, he barks at birds and critters. He aches to chase them, but his only choice is to return to Jackson for attention. Jackson enjoys his company as they travel down the trail. He's dreaming of Sandra and occasionally watching the bored cow amble along behind the wagon. Between watching the cow, passing strangers, and petting Homer, time passes quickly.

The trail widens, revealing small farms scattered around the landscape. A nice building close to the trail becomes visible up ahead.

"I wonder if that could be the blacksmith shop," says Miles.

"It has two chimneys and one of them puffs smoke every now and then. It's definitely a blacksmith shop," replies Inez when she hears hammers clanging behind the building.

Jackson moves up behind his parents where he can get a better look. Straining to see, he reads a sign above the door. "Brittain and Sons."

Miles stops the wagon in front of the shop. "Hop out, Jackson, and see if Ed is working today."

Jackson hesitates. He's about to meet the father of the woman he loves for the first time. Wondering if Ed will be glad to meet him, he takes a deep breath and straightens his hair as he approaches the office door. He knocks and looks inside, but no one is around.

"They're working around back," says Miles as he motions to go around the building.

"He's nervous," whispers Inez.

Jackson proceeds toward the sound of hammers ringing. When he turns the corner, the shop appears before him. It's a big open area with a wall on one side and poles supporting the roof on the other. Several men are pounding metal atop anvils, while others pump billows, making the forges crackle and glow bright red.

One of the men notices Jackson. "What can I do for you, mister?"

Jackson clears his throat. "I would like to talk to Mr. Brittain."

He points to the oldest man who is busily pounding on a red-hot piece of metal.

Jackson carefully weaves through the other men who are busy working and stands beside the older man. The man glances at him, still pounding away. "I will be with you in a moment. I'm almost done with this piece."

Jackson feels lost for a minute. Everyone is banging and throwing pieces of metal around. He patiently watches Ed work. He looks a little like his brother, Buck. Mr. Brittain quits beating on the piece of metal, looks at it from a couple different angles and gestures satisfaction.

"What can I do for you, young man?" he asks.

Jackson reaches out to shake his hand. "I'm Jackson Murray. A friend of your daughter."

Mr. Brittain smiles and Jackson thinks to himself, that's a good sign. "Glad to meet you, Jackson. I wondered how long it would be until I had the pleasure of meeting you."

"Can you come out front and meet my mom and dad they're on their way to Water Town?"

"I would be glad to meet them." Jackson and Mr. Brittain walk around the building.

"Hello," he says, approaching the wagon.

Miles hops off and holds his hand out. "Mr. Brittain, this is my wife Inez you can call me Miles."

"You can call me Ed," he says reaching to shake hands. "I have heard good things about all of you," he smiles. "I have a note from Buck and Flavie." She hands it to Ed.

He smiles even bigger. "I knew this was going to happen soon. From what I have heard, Janice has made a good choice."

"We think Cap is the lucky one," Miles and Inez agree. "I hope you won't feel like we're imposing on your family. I know Jackson was supposed to come tomorrow, but we felt it would be safer if he rode with us today on our way to Water Town. We will be back for him mid-evening Sunday."

Miles picks up Homer. "There's one more thing. Jackson's dog followed us from home. Do you mind if Jackson keeps him here?"

Ed smiles. "That will be fine, I have heard a lot about Homer, too."

Miles hands Homer to Jackson. "See you Sunday evening, son," says Miles as he gently flicks the horse's reins and they are on their way to Water Town.

Jackson feels a little sad to see them leaving.

"Make yourself at home, Jackson. You can wait in the office. I will finish work early, and we will walk to my house together."

Jackson looks around the office while he waits. Everything is neatly arranged and displayed. There's plenty to occupy his time while he waits.

<>

Miles and Inez arrive at the edge of Water Town a little after mid-evening.

"I would love to spend the first night here in our wagon. You have fixed it so nicely. We can start early in the morning," says Inez as they look for a place to pull over for the night.

"That's a good idea. I don't know how we can pay for a room anyway. We don't have any silver. Tomorrow we will have all day to figure out how this new world of silver works."

<>

Ed enters the office; his face is filled with a pleasant smile. Our house is not far from here." Ed holds the door, and they walk out of the office.

Jackson takes a deep breath. He's still nervous, but ready to finish his journey.

"It's a pretty day to walk," says Ed, hoping to get Jackson talking.

"I want to apologize for arriving early. I told Sandra I would be here tomorrow. I hope I'm not intruding on you."

"Don't worry, son. How could you let us know? I'm sure everyone will be glad to have you here a little longer. Make yourself at home, and don't worry about Homer either."

Jackson quickly realizes Ed is easy going and in a few minutes, he feels confident enough to be himself. As they walk around a gentle turn in the path, a beautiful home comes into view. The yard is covered with grass, and the bushes are neatly trimmed. The main part of the house stands two stories tall, and there's a one-story addition on either side. "This is a beautiful place," says Jackson, taking it all in.

Jackson catches sight of Sandra working in the yard. Even in her work clothes Jackson sees her beauty. She's surprised when she looks up to see Jackson and Homer with her dad. Jackson is pleased to see a pretty smile growing on her face as he comes closer. She reaches out to him.

"I have missed you! I'm glad you're here early!"

"I'm sorry I couldn't let you know, but I'm glad we have extra time." He is pleased she acts the same toward him in front of her father as she does when they're with Janice.

"I'm going to run in and tell mom you're here."

She quickly returns with a different blouse and she has combed her hair.

"I look forward to sitting on the porch and talking with you after supper," says Ed. My sons will probably come by later and we can all get to know each other. "You and Sandra visit while I clean up."

"Let me show you our farm. It's not as large as your family's," says Sandra.

They walk around enjoying each other, and don't see much of the farm. When they come to Sandra's flower garden, Jackson is surprised. It's so pretty they have to stop and look at all the beauty. In the garden, just waiting for two lovers to enjoy, sits a bench made with a big flat yellow rock set across two smaller stones. This bench will last forever, thinks Jackson.

"I feel the same here, sitting on this rock surrounded by all your pretty flowers, as I do when we are at the rock on the creek," says Jackson.

"With you beside me, I feel it, too," she whispers. She snuggles close to him, and it's warm where they touch. She lovingly explains all about her garden and the different flowers. The more Jackson learns about her, the more intrigued he becomes.

Mary rings the bell on the porch to let them know supper is ready. Jackson is glad to see he and Sandra will be the only ones eating with her parents. He will meet a lot of new people soon enough.

After supper, Mary insists on cleaning up by herself and shoos everyone out to the porch.

"Jackson, I think we know each other well enough you can call me Ed."

"Thank you, Ed," replies Jackson feeling more at ease.

Jackson and Sandra sit in the porch swing. Ed is in a chair next to them. Mary joins them when she finishes in the kitchen.

Sandra's brother Fred arrives first. He's taller than his father. Otherwise, he looks a lot like him. They have the same smile. Fred looks at Homer. "Hello little fellow," he says in a pleasant tone of voice. Homer can't resist sniffing him. Fred slowly reaches over and scratches the pup's head and back. They became good friends.

Ed Junior rides up thirty minutes later. He's friendly, but not as talkative as his brother, and Homer likes him too. They make Jackson feel comfortable being around them without even trying.

As the sun begins to set, the brothers take their leave. Ed and Mary sit and enjoy talking with Jackson and Sandra a while longer.

"Sandra, show Jackson his room," says Ed.

Jackson politely excuses himself and walks with her, and they hold hands as they stroll to the spare bedroom. The bed has beautiful carvings in the headboard and tall poles at each corner. Even the tables on either side of the bed and the wardrobe have matching carvings.

"Homer can sleep in here with you tonight," she smiles and kisses him goodnight.

"Everyone is glad you're here, especially me," she says with a pretty smile.

<>

Miles and Inez wake early Saturday morning. They feel uncomfortable because a lot of people are passing by and they're not used to being around so many strangers. After speaking with some of them, they begin to feel better.

Miles decides it's time to find the place where they can trade their cow. A stranger points him in the direction of the sale barn. When Miles pulls up, he's sad to see a sign that reads, "Sale barn open on Tuesdays."

"The market is closed today, mister," says a man sitting outside the barn. "You can come back Tuesday or I will give you silver for your cow and sell it myself."

"What is it worth?" asks Miles.

The man walks around examining the cow. "I will give you forty silver coins."

Miles looks at Inez.

"Your guess is as good as mine, Miles. Whatever you think," she says.

"I'll take your offer, mister," replies Miles.

The man hands Miles thirty-nine silver coins and twenty copper coins.

"Why are some of these copper?" asks Miles.

"You haven't been to Water Town before, have you? Not everything sells for a whole silver coin. The copper coins make up the differences. Do you have a money pouch to put your coins in?"

"I didn't think about that," replies Miles.

The man leans over his wagon and pulls out a new money pouch with a string at the top. "Here's a pouch, and a word to the wise. Hide some of these silver pieces in your wagon where they will be hard to find or give some to your wife. Never carry all your silver pieces in one pouch."

"I'm lucky to have met you. There's a lot for me to learn about Water Town," says Miles.

"Water Town is an amazing place with a lot of good things, but also some bad things, too. The longer you're here the better you will be able to tell who you can trust and who you can't."

Miles and Inez decide to go to the leather shop Virgil told them about. Miles asks a lady standing close by for directions. She points toward it, then hurries on her way.

Miles and Inez discover a whole new world as they travel up Main Street. All the shops have big windows that open up to show what they have for sale, enticing customers to come inside.

Entering the leather shop, the smell of leather greet them, and they can't wait to explore. It's full of merchandise all neatly arranged so it's easy to see, and the people working in the shop are eager to help them.

"This is all too new to us. Let's not trade any silver in here right now," says Inez.

"It's very tempting in here. I can't promise because those gloves look like something we really need," replies Miles walking over and studying a pair.

"The boys do need some new work gloves. These look like they will last longer than the ones I make," says Inez.

"I want you to get a pair for yourself too," says Miles.

"Only if you pick a pair out also," replies Inez smiling.

"Uncle Matt!" They say at the same time.

"He's home doing all the work so we can be here."

They purchase five pairs of gloves. The clerk behind the counter looks for a leather pouch to put them in but can't find one. He turns and calls loudly into the back room for someone to bring a pouch large enough to hold five pairs of gloves.

Virgil steps out of the room behind the clerk and finds himself face-to-face with the Murrays.

"Virgil! I thought you were still in the wilderness hunting dragons," says Miles raising his eyebrows.

Virgil's mouth drops open in dismay, and he has a look on his face like someone who has just been caught stealing eggs. He struggles to get a grip on himself. He has to say something quick. "Don't mention dragons around here! No one believes there is such a thing."

The clerk behind the counter rolls his eyes, and moves on to another customer.

"We got off the trail on the way back and missed the part that goes by your farm. We were almost in Blade Town when we found the trail again."

Miles senses uneasiness in Virgil's manor as he talks. "Did you find any signs of what you were looking for?"

"No. I'm not sure there is anything out there to find."

Virgil's story doesn't sound right. He's too nervous, and keeps looking to see who all is witnessing this encounter. His face is turning red and Miles can tell he doesn't want to talk about it anymore. Miles looks into his eyes, wondering what he's up to.

"If you pass by our farm again on your way to the wilderness please stop and visit," says Inez.

"Thank you, I have to get back to work." He disappears through the door where he came from.

Miles looks at Inez. "He never once looked like he was telling the truth or glad to see us. Something isn't right."

Chapter 19

Virgil wanders among the shelves in back of the shop. He plops down on a stool and tries to regain his wits. He can't believe how bad his luck is. It's miles to the Murray farm. How can it be that without warning he came face-to-face with them in his family's shop?

A man shopping for dress shoes overheard Miles's conversation with Virgil. Intrigued, he waits for the Murrays to leave, then makes his way over to the clerk and asks if Virgil will come out and speak with him. The clerk finds Virgil sitting in the back. "Someone else would like to speak with you."

"What now," he mutters. Virgil steps through the door, expecting a complaint. He looks at the customer and waits to hear his problem.

"Can we go somewhere so we can talk in private?" asks the man.

Virgil isn't sure he wants to invest that much time in this conversation. "Whatever you have to say to me, you can say right here."

"You just told that other man a few minutes ago not to say the word I am about to say in public," he replies with a sly grin.

"Follow me to the back."

When they are alone, Virgil looks the man over. He's wearing a nice cloth coat and clean pants. The man's voice sounds commanding, and there's an air of confidence about him.

"My name is Mason Smith, and I will be in town next week with my traveling show. I have gathered exotic creatures from near and far and I employ excellent trainers who know how to make them do amazing things. We draw a crowd everywhere we go because people love to bring their families to watch my animals perform. I don't have a dragon, but I do believe they exist. Here is my card. Come and see my show." Mr. Smith turns and leaves.

Virgil is surprised, intrigued, and not sure the man isn't joking.

<>

Miles and Inez enjoy rambling through shops, discovering new things, but the only other thing they buy is a large bag of hard candy to share with everyone at home. They're having fun just being together. They rarely have a chance to be alone without some kind of work needing to be done.

"This could become habit-forming," Inez says as she reaches for Miles's hand. "I would like to come back again before too long."

When suppertime comes, they choose to eat at the boarding house. A young, neatly-dressed lady asks them where they would like to sit. Inez chooses a table on the side where they won't be surrounded by strangers. It's the first time they have ever eaten in a restaurant. After supper, Miles walks over to the long desk in the lobby. Behind the desk stands a friendly man wearing well-made black pants and a white shirt.

"How much would it cost to stay in one of your rooms tonight?" asks Miles.

"One and a half silver pieces," replies the man hoping to make a sale.

Inez lightly touches Mile's arm. "It's such a pretty night. Let's sleep in the wagon and save our silver for the next trip."

Miles thanks the man and places his arm around Inez's waist as they walk to their wagon. They sit close as they ride out of town looking for a quiet, but not too secluded spot. Tired and happy, they hold each other. Having fun together rekindles their love, and they drift away into slumber.

In the morning, they decide to return to the boarding house for breakfast.

"Let's ride around town and see if we missed anything yesterday, then we will head home," suggest Miles after they eat.

As they ride past the sale barn, the man who bought their cow recognizes Miles and hollers. "Come see what I have!"

Miles is curious so he pulls the wagon over, and there in the man's wagon lies a calf.

"This is what you need. Take this calf home, fatten it up, bring it back next year, and take your wife out on the town again."

"How much?" asks Miles.

The man rubs his chin as he thinks.

"For you--since you are new to this--I'm going to help you out. Ten silver pieces."

Something about the way he sounds makes Miles remember learning to be careful who to trust.

Miles winks at Inez. "Thank you, but I would only give six silver pieces for that calf."

"Man, you learn fast! Give me seven and take it."

The deal is done, and the Murrays head home with the calf in the back of their wagon.

<>

Saturday morning after breakfast, Jackson and Sandra return to the flower garden. He is content with her by his side. Even digging and pulling weeds feels nothing like work. He wishes plowing and planting crops could be this much fun.

Later, sitting on the bench Sandra takes Jackson's hand. "I want you to meet my granny named Daisy. She lives with Fred and doesn't get out much."

As soon as Granny realizes Sandra is there to see her, a big smile appears on her face. She takes in everything about Jackson as Sandra introduces him. A sparkle grows in her eyes as she gets to know him. He's polite and gentle around her. "Now, Sandra, don't you let this one get away. Kindhearted men are hard to find." Daisy has never been bashful.

Sandra blushes. "Don't worry, Granny, I won't."

Sandra and Jackson enjoy spending a couple hours with her. She is so glad to have company.

That night, Jackson lies in his bed thinking about what a wonderful day it has been. Every experience made him love Sandra even more.

The next day, lost in a world of their own; the day flies by. As evening approaches, they sit side-by-side on the rock bench.

"My dad is never late. He will be at your father's shop before your mom rings the supper bell," says Jackson sadly. He pauses a moment "I will build a bench like this at our house someday."

"And I will plant a flower garden around it," replies Sandra. They already miss each other as Homer sits beside Jackson, enjoying an occasional rub on his back.

"I will be at Janice's house next week to help her get ready for the wedding," says Sandra as they walk toward the blacksmith shop holding hands.

Sure enough, Mr. Murray is coming into view when Mary rings the supper bell. Jackson and Sandra stand in front of the shop.

"Hello, Sandra. You look very pretty today,"
says Miles as he comes to a stop. He hops off the wagon
and scurries around back. "Look what I have."

She walks over and takes a peak. "A beautiful little
calf, how cute."

Miles only looks at the calf for a minute. He's ready
to get back to his farm and hops back on the seat. "Tell
your dad it was a pleasure to meet him," says Miles,
fidgeting with the reins.

Jackson turns to Sandra, "I will see you Friday."
She kisses him lightly on the lips. He blushes, but he
doesn't care what anyone else thinks.

He hops into the wagon with Homer and the calf.
The ride home is filled with his mom and dad's stories
about Water Town. When they tell him about Virgil in the
leather shop, he shakes his head and decides not to worry
for now. He's too busy thinking about Sandra. The sound
of the wagon wheels, Homer snuggling, a calf squirming,
and his mom and dad's company keep him from having
time to be sad.

Before long, they're home. Uncle Matt is in the
yard waiting for them.

"You aren't any prettier than when we left, but Inez
and I are sure glad to see you," says Miles in a happy
mood. He reaches into the pouch filled with gloves and
hands a pair to Matt. "We brought you a little present from
Water Town." Uncle Matt is impressed by how well
they're made, and he's glad they remembered him.
Jackson hops out the back with Homer right behind him.
Uncle Matt looks relieved. "I was worried about Homer. I
had no idea what happened to him. I was afraid you would
blame me for losing your dog."

"I'm sorry. He followed us down the trail so far we
had to take him with us," says Jackson petting Homer.

"Next time, I will lock him in my room."

"I bought a calf while I was in Water Town," says Miles.

Uncle Matt looks it over. "This will replace the one you sold. That's a good idea."

Uncle Matt stays close to the wagon, looking anxiously for ways to help the family he has missed. He holds his hand out to Inez as she hops off the wagon, hugs her, then scampers around to Miles, surprising him with a hug.

"I have fixed supper. Come and tell me all about your trip."

<>

Lester, enjoying some time alone in front of the entrance and looking out over the wilderness, notices two dragons flying toward the cavern. Coming from the north, he's sure it's Shim and Tee returning.

Seeing them approaching rekindles worrisome thoughts. The dragon hunters could return at any time. There's no way to know how much longer until they cause trouble again.

He closes his eyes, remembering all the good times his family has enjoyed at this cavern. When he was a young dragon, his grandparents told stories about tragedies and triumphs the den shared hundreds of years before.

He looks back to the sky. The dragons are ten minutes away.

"Ureeeeee," he calls into the cavern. As the den emerges he tells them that Shim and Tee will land soon.

Shim and Tee land, out of breath. But in seconds, they're hugging their families. The den is impressed with how strong and commanding they look.

Lester and Fuzzy are just as curious and concerned as the nervous den members. Worry has made this a very trying time for the den, and what these two say will determine the entire den's future.

Tee steps away from his family and speaks to the den. Instantly, they quiet.

"We're happy to have wonderful news to give you. About a hundred miles north of here, we found a cavern bigger than this one. It meanders precariously deep within a beautiful mountain covered with fir trees and tall rock cliffs. From the entrance, there is a breathtaking view looking across the countryside, much like our present entrance. Unfortunately, the opening is partially blocked, but we managed to climb in and look around."

"There's a lot of work to be done before our den can move in," says Shim.

"How long will it take to get it ready?" asks Lester.

"It will take longer than this trip did, and we will need two more strong dragons to go back with us to clear the entrance and get everything ready. Most of the boulders are too heavy for two of us to lift and a lot of digging remains to be done. When the hard work is finished, we will still have to gather and store enough food to last a couple of weeks. When it's ready, one of us will stay to guard our new home while the other three returns to help the den migrate," replies Shim.

"The migration will be hard on our young and old, but it's doable. The young small enough to ride on their fathers' and mothers' backs will fare better than the young who are too large to ride. Unfortunately, we will have to spend a couple of nights in the open," says Tee, as he steps back.

Lester's eyes crease slightly, as he takes over. "You have done a great service for your family. My biggest concern is being more vulnerable to the hunters while our strongest dragons are away," says Lester.

"We have no choice but to do as they suggest," states one of the den members, and others agree.

Lester bows in respect. "Then it is agreed. Two more strong young members of our den will return with Shim and Tee to prepare the new cavern. Fuzzy and I will stay here with the den. The rest of you, go to each of your family's special places and decide who will return with Shim and Tee."

A sleepless night lies ahead for every dragon. The reality that they're going to leave their old cavern is sinking in. While the new cavern is being made ready, there will only be six dragons left with the den strong enough to fight and protect them. The other fifteen dragons are too old or too young to risk a fight, and one of the strong dragons will have to guard the entrance all the time. Only five can fly out to fight the hunters.

The next day, the den goes about its business as usual until midday. Lester makes his way to the area in front of the entrance, takes a deep breath, and tries to calm himself. The sun is shining brightly and the warmth feels good. He soaks in its rays for a few moments. He turns looking into the cavern and sings, "Ureeeeee." His call echoes down the walkways, throughout the cavern, reaching everyone's special place.

When everyone is gathered, he speaks with authority, but his tone is compassionate.

"It fills my heart with sadness to tell you we must leave this cavern that has been our wonderful home for hundreds of years. Because of the advancement of human civilization, we have no choice. Fortunately, nature has provided us with a new place, and I hope we can live in peace and prosper there for hundreds of years to come. Now it's time for two more volunteers to step up and serve."

The families of Leo and Vic place their wings on the backs of their heroes in a gesture of support and love. They pause a moment, then the two dragons walk forward and stand with Shim and Tee. Lester faces the four brave dragons.

"We are all in your debt, and your safety is our primary concern. Work hard and return soon. Your fellow dragons may be forced into mortal combat while you're gone, so wish the ones of us remaining here good luck and peace. I suggest all four of you leave at daybreak, which will give you one more night with your families. Anyone who wishes to see you off is welcome. I will not be addressing the den in the morning."

When morning comes, the dragons rise early. They're full of energy and life. They have a real reason to be alive and all four of them are filled with pride and determination. They will work hard and quickly prepare the new cavern, no matter what it takes.

With little fanfare, the four ascend from the plateau and are out of sight in minutes.

<>

Rising early Friday, Cap and Jackson are on a mission. They work together in hopes of quickly accomplishing their chores. Their hearts are set on leaving as soon as they eat lunch. They enjoy the challenge, and the teamwork pays off. Inez watches as they gulp down their lunch and clean up to leave. They rush out of the house and run to the barn. They search through the blankets, hunting for the prettiest ones, and then carefully spread them over their horses' backs, smoothing them out. Cap reaches for the best saddle, but it isn't hanging where it should be. Puzzled, he searches all around. Jackson waits until his back is turned, then reaches over, picking it up from where it's hidden.

Cap shakes his head, "That's alright, you need all the help you can get to look as handsome as me," then laughs as he reaches for another saddle.

"I can hardly wait to see Sandra," says Jackson, saddling up fast and bursting with a broad smile.

Cap watches him carefully strap the saddle in place, and when he isn't watching he gently slips the bridle off Jackson's horse and tosses it into a stall nearby.

Now he's smiling broadly. "See you later, slow poke," replies Cap, hopping on his horse and heading toward the open barn door. "I will be there before you get halfway down the trail." He bumps his horse and springs to a gallop.

Jackson is surprised and jumps on his horse only to discover there are no reins. He slides back off, grabs a bridle, pops it in the horse's mouth, leaps in the saddle, and rides through the barn door too fast. He catches Cap in a minute, and they race.

"Enough racing!" yells Cap as Jackson aggressively tries to pass him in a place that's too narrow at such speed.

"You give up!" yells Jackson, full of energy.

"I give up. I can't take a chance of getting hurt being silly at a time like this."

Jackson understands, and they settle to enjoy their ride.

"After you're married, I think it would be nice if we gather to eat supper at mom and dad's every Saturday," says Jackson.

"I hope you and I can spend more time together than that. We've had a good childhood, and a great mom and dad."

They ride past a mound of honeysuckle vines draping over a fallen tree. They're in full bloom, and the smell fills the trail. Bees and butterflies hop back and forth, busily gathering the sweet nectar. The brothers savor the honeysuckles fragrance for a moment, then nudge their horses and move on faster. Moments later, they're trotting up the trail to Janice's house. Janice and Sandra are watching for them and reach them by the time they finish tying the horses.

Jackson notices Sandra shows him the same amount of affection as Janice conveys to Cap. He longs for the moment he can confidently ask Ed for her hand.

A crowd has gathered. Some are cooking, and the smell is divine, others are cleaning and washing pots, dishes, and even some clothing. There's hardly any room to stand in the house.

The couples want to be together, away from the chaos, so they walk to the rock on the creek. The air around the creek is filled with energy just waiting to be absorbed.

"I love the feeling I get out here," says Janice looking at the crystal-clear water. She closes her eyes and takes a deep breath. A gentle breeze filled with the smell of sweet wilderness flowers is always blowing along the creek.

Sandra sighs. "It's a flower garden you don't have to plant."

"I hope we can all live close to this place and enjoy the fringe of the wilderness for all of our lives," says Jackson.

The bell rings. Flavie has prepared fried chicken, slaw, green beans, and bread. Everyone has been working hard, making for a hungry crowd.

"Everything looks delicious, Aunt Flavie," says Sandra as the families gather around tables in the yard. "I will try to help you more from now on."

"Poor Cap will miss this fine meal tomorrow," says Janice.

"Wild horses couldn't keep me away," replies Cap.

"No one has told you?" asks Flavie. "It's our family custom that the man to be wed doesn't see his bride the day before the wedding."

"That's so Cap can take a bath Saturday," says Jackson, joking and grinning.

"It wouldn't be a bad idea for you to stay home tomorrow and clean up, too," replies Cap.

"Flavie, can I come back tomorrow?" asks Jackson.

"Sure." Everyone laughs. They can tell he's serious.

The next morning, Jackson is rushing around trying to feed the animals, spilling corn, and throwing hay where the cattle are not accustomed to finding it. Cap chuckles. "I will be here today. Go on and enjoy being with Sandra. I will finish what has to be done." Jackson thanks him and takes off running toward the house. Soon, his horse is trotting toward the Brittain farm.

Sandra doesn't see him ride up. All the women are in the house, bustling here and there. He finds her busy sewing and makes his way over to where she's working.

"Hey. I'm sorry I didn't see you ride up. There's so much to do, I lost track of time," she says holding needles and thread as she helps with Janice's dress.

"Don't worry about me. I will be outside when you have a chance to visit."

Jackson understands why the man to be wed doesn't need to be there. He walks around aimlessly until Ed spies him. "Jackson, it looks like you have plenty of time on your hands. Come have a seat." Ed's sitting where he has a view of the creek. "I never have a chance to travel out this way, close to the wilderness. It looks very peaceful, but I wonder how dangerous it is out here."

"My family has never had any trouble, and I have lived here all my life. But we are always careful to respect the wilderness."

"Have you ever thought about learning the blacksmith trade?"

"I help my dad in our shop when we need to fix things. I would love to learn more about it, but I prefer farming with my dad."

"There's nothing wrong with being loyal to your family. That's a good thing." They enjoy talking for a while, but then Ed sees an old friend he hasn't seen in a while, and leaves to talk with him.

After a while, Jackson tells Flavie and the girls good night. They have plenty to do without him being there.

Slowly riding home, he thinks about his conversation with Ed. They're comfortable around each other, and Ed is starting to ask questions about his future. He's tempted to take a chance after the wedding.

<>

Virgil's eyes sparkle, and energy fills his steps as he ventures toward Mr. Smith's show. He can only imagine what kind of wonder lies in store. His excitement grows when it becomes obvious a crowd of people, full of enthusiasm, are tramping in the same direction. Flags come into view first, then there's a spectacle of tarps, all laced together and held up with poles. They are arranged to secure an area large as a corn field. The entrance is buzzing with excitement as people file into a large tent, but it pales in comparison with the huge tent standing tall and majestic in the middle. He studies the tarps as he approaches. They're made of leather. When he is close, he rubs the tent. It's made of thick fabric. Everything is brightly colored, but nothing catches his eye like the red, gold, and black striped flags flapping in the wind atop every pole. He smiles as he stands in front of the entrance, soaking it all in. Arched overhead hangs a large white sign with red letters and a yellow border. It reads, "The Exotic Creature Show." A man wearing a fine red and black suit, embellished with gold tassels, stands in the entrance behind a podium, collecting silver from those who wish to enter. Virgil presents the card Mr. Smith gave him.

"One silver coin," the man holds out his hand, disregarding the card.

Virgil is surprised but digs out a coin.

Stepping inside, he's overcome by the festive atmosphere. Young couples hold hands, enjoying each other as they venture into the unknown. Adults are as excited as the children, and parents cling to their children's hands, struggling to see the animals while their children try to pull loose and run. People huddle in front of cages, talking and looking in amazement. Obviously, everyone's having a great time. The place is full of strange and dangerous creatures, the likes of which none of them have ever seen.

Virgil forces himself to stop gawking at the creatures. He has to see what this is all about and find Mr. Smith. After a few minutes trying to make his way through the crowd, he has to admit this is the most amazing spectacle he has ever seen, and he's caught up in the excitement again. A dozen wagons with cages built on top of them are on display in a roped in area with a man at each cage, keeping people outside the rope. Several cages contain very large cats. Some lie around, staring at the bars or sleeping, while others prowl back and forth with vicious, disgusted looks on their faces. Some cats have stripes, some are covered with spots. One is black as the night. Virgil has never seen anything like these, and he shudders at the thought that some creatures like them might be prowling around in the wilderness. The sight of those long sharp teeth and curved claws are forever burned into his memory.

He wanders into an area were a couple round cages have been put together and fastened to the ground. They're large enough for the trainers to get inside with the animals. Benches are placed in front of these cages, and people stare as a shirtless trainer locks himself in one of the cages. All he has to defend himself is a long, black leather whip. A small door flips up, letting a large striped cat hop inside. It's agitated. The trainer shows no fear. He twirls his whip, making the cat sit. It opens its mouth showing a glistening white row of sharp teeth. The cat is just waiting for the right moment to pounce on him. The trainer doesn't seem to care. He raises his whip and with a quick flip, he makes it pop an ear shattering crack so loud the audience flinches in their seats. Then he picks up a large metal hoop, holds it waist high, and the cat, looking unhappy, jumps through. Everyone cheers, and the trainer turns to the crowd and bows, taking his eyes off the cat. It creeps toward him and the crowd screams. Just in time, he cracks his whip again and the beast drops to the ground in submission.

Virgil is impressed but is ready to move on. Ahead is a pathway twenty feet wide with small tents on both sides. Some contain games, and some have sweets for sale. Between some of the tents stand wire cages holding snakes, lizards, and lots of birds.

At the end of the midway, people line up to go into the biggest tent he has ever seen. Virgil starts to go inside, but a man dressed in a red and black suit like the man at the main entrance says, "Ten copper pieces to see the show."

He can only imagine how much silver all these people are giving to be entertained as he pulls out ten copper pieces and hurries inside.

The tent has several rows of seats around the outside and is filled with people watching a show in progress. A pretty girl is riding a tall animal with a hump in front of her and another behind. A trainer wearing a hat with a veil attached to the back is leading the animal in a circle.

Virgil spies Mr. Smith at the animal entrance. He's dressed in a black suit with a red stripe sewn to the pants, running from his hip to his shiny black boots. In his right hand, he holds a cane he uses to push the animals around. Virgil makes his way over to him.

"Quite a show, don't you think?" says Mr. Smith, recognizing him and gesturing to the show.

"I have never seen anything like it."

Mr. Smith looks into Virgil's eyes. "Tell me for sure. Do you know where we can find a dragon?"

"I don't want to discuss business here with all these people around," he replies calmly.

"That's a good thing, young man. It tends to make me believe you more. Come to the boarding house in the morning. I'm in room number three. We will talk seriously then. Now go enjoy yourself."

After the show, Virgil is confident he has finally found the right man to help him catch a dragon.

The next morning, Virgil knocks on door number three at the boarding house.

A young man with bulging muscles and a square cut chin answers the door. He's well-dressed and confident in his manner. "What is your business here?"

"Mason Smith is expecting me," replies Virgil confidently.

"If this is about traveling with us, you're wasting your time."

"Tell him the dragon man is here," he says more confidently.

The young man discerns he's serious, and a dragon would be of upmost interest to Mason.

"Wait here."

Mr. Smith comes out smiling and ready to shake his hand. "Call me Mason. I have been thinking about how to get started with you in our quest to capture a couple dragons and bring them here to travel with us."

Mason sits at a table in his room and offers the seat on the other side to Virgil. They are both cunning and need what the other has to offer. They study each other as the conversation unfolds.

"First thing. Virgil, tell me why you are so sure you know dragons exist." Mason is curious to see how Virgil will react to this direct question.

With unwavering confidence, he answers. "It all started when I heard a story about a man losing his dog to a dragon," he says, being careful about how he tells his story. "I found several men who would go with me to check it out."

"Did you go out into the wilderness?"

"I can't disclose where we went at this time. I don't know you well enough. We succeeded in finding where the man was attacked," says Virgil coyly.

"But did you see a dragon?" interrupts Mason.

"I am getting to that part. We were getting ready to bed down for the night when our dogs ran into the woods, chasing something. We all jumped up and ran after them. I saw the dragon with my own two eyes as it was running away. We shot at it but missed."

"You swear this is true?" asks Mason, looking for any sign that Virgil is lying.

"Of course, I do." Virgil's thoughts turn on his mind's eye, and he's no longer in the room. He's back in the wilderness. "I have never been so excited and scared at the same time." His voice changes as he explains how the dragons caught his dogs and flew way with them in their claws. Almost in a rant, he tells about running in fear and hiding as darkness approached. "We were all afraid the dragons would find us in the dark and carry us off like the dogs."

Mason listens with his elbow on the table and his chin in one hand. He's glad to see Virgil becoming emotional about his story.

"That was the end of our hunt. We all just wanted to go home. Unfortunately, two of my men were lost in the panic and have not been seen since," says Virgil, sadly.

"I have heard of tragedies like yours happening just before we caught some of our fiercest animals. I believe everything you have said is true. Your emotions told me more than your words. Mason paces back and forth thinking to himself. "Do you want to be partners or do you want paid for your services?"

"I would like to be partners."

"Good, I prefer you have silver invested in this endeavor since this is an animal almost no one believes exists."

Mason stands, slides his lips to the side, while raising an eyebrow and walks in a circle several times. He's lost in deep thought.

"Virgil, I have friends who have helped me figure out how to capture other dangerous animals, and they know how to build amazing weapons and all kinds of traps. I will put them to work on our quest. With their help, there will be no problem we can't overcome. The whole process will be thought out, and soon they will start building equipment and weapons like you have never seen."

Virgil is too quiet. He's listening but there's no smile on his face. Mason realizes he needs to feel more important than just being a guide. "Virgil, you will be rich and an important man in this town when you return with our dragons," says Mason in a reassuring tone.

Virgil's smile returns. He can taste the fame already. He wants to go tell everyone what's happening, it's so exciting.

Mason sees mentioning fame brought a smile back too easily. "Virgil, you can't speak a word about this to anyone. We don't want a bunch of thrill seekers hunting our dragons."

Chapter 20

The wedding day arrives, throwing the Murray farm into a flurry of activity even before the sun rises. The chores are done, and everyone except the brothers are dressed. The wagon is filled with food for the celebration, and Homer is locked in the barn.

Inez and Miles climb onto the wagon as the first rays of light streak through the trees. Uncle Matt rides up beside them. Cap and Jackson are in the house, dressing as the wagon pulls out. They plan to saddle up and ride their horses fast enough to catch up with the wagon on the trail.

Jackson pats Cap on his back as they walk out the door for the last time as roommates. "I love you, brother, and I wish you and Janice the best of luck and happiness." They hurry to the barn, saddle up, and soon catch up with the family. Miles and Inez smile. This is a happy day for their family as they ride together to the Brittain farm.

When they arrive, tables stand ready in the yard, and the place is taking on a festive atmosphere. Several of the men are laughing and mingling with friends. They carry little cups and are sampling spirits from each other's jugs. Everyone brags about their brew, but after sampling each other's too many times, they're getting loud. Several women march over and take their jugs away. The women talk and show off their dresses they made just for the wedding. Everyone is lighthearted and happy.

When Janice hears the Murrays are in the yard, her heart says to run out and hug Cap, but her mother looks at her with eyes that leave no doubt she is to stay in her room and out of sight.

The moment the wagon stops, Inez begins unloading presents and food. Jackson doesn't help. He takes off searching for Sandra, and Uncle Matt checks out all the food on the tables. Miles and Buck find each other, and soon they're laughing and telling stories about their wedding days. Two more wagons pull up with friends from Blade Town. Everyone is busy or visiting and time vanishes. It's time for the ceremony.

Buck steps up on the porch and rings the bell two times. People in the yard quiet and those in the house file outside.

"Friends, family, and future family members, we are gathered here today to publicly show the fathers' approval for the joining of the Brittain and the Murray families. Our families are being united today because of the love and mutual respect that has grown between my daughter, Janice Brittain, and Miles Murray's son, Cap. If any family member has any objection to this union, now is the time for you to speak."

He waits in silence, and with no objection voiced, he invites Miles and Cap to the porch. He smiles at them and proceeds inside.

On his way to Janice's room a tear slides down cheek. He opens the door, wipes the tear away, smiles and takes a deep breath.

"I cannot say I am giving you away. My heart won't let me, but I promise never to interfere with you and Cap in any way. Janice wipes a couple happy tears. They compose themselves, and he offers his arm. She gently locks her arm in his, leans her head against his shoulder for a second, and then they stroll to the porch.

As she approaches, she and Cap begin to feel each other's presence, their love is strong. A wonderful feeling of happiness consumes her, and it radiates to everyone as a beautiful smile. Her dress is the whitest, most beautiful thing Cap has ever seen, and there is nothing scary about his wonderful feeling anymore.

She stops, almost touching Cap. Buck takes a deep breath. "I am pleased to have my daughter and Cap Murray be united," he says with a clear voice.

Miles smiles at his son. "I am honored to have my son and Janice Brittain united. And by their love, may our families be united forever."

Cap and Janice lean toward each other and kiss in the presence of their families, and it is done.

Sandra and Jackson hold hands tightly. They kiss when Cap and Janice turn toward the crowd.

"Looks like we're going to have another wedding before too long," says one of the guests near them.

All the guest start moving, some toward the couple while others head for the food. The crowd is jolly for a while, then grows quitter as time passes, and before long, people begin to leave. They have to be home before dark. The friends from Blade Town leave first, then Fred and Ed Junior. Ed and Mary say goodbye, and as Jackson escorts Sandra to her wagon, the joy of the day is fading fast. His heart aches as he thinks about how far apart they will be tonight.

Jackson can't control himself, and he doesn't intend to. He approaches Ed. "I know this is not the best time, but could we talk in private for a minute?"

"Sure, Jackson." Ed smiles.

They walk away from the wagon. Jackson is nervous and excited. He keeps telling himself to be careful about what he says and how he acts.

"I can't love Sandra any more than I do right now, and I know she loves me. Will you agree if I ask her to marry me, and she says yes?"

Ed looks Jackson in the eye, and then looks away in thought for a second. "I like you a lot Jackson," he says looking into his waiting eyes. "Come see me at my house next Saturday. My only concern is you have not spent enough time together. I love my daughter very much, and I need time to think about this."

Ed shakes Jackson's hand to reassure him and show respect. Jackson feels relieved. He had asked. He had obeyed his heart. He had not been told no.

Ed and Jackson walk back to the wagon. Sandra kisses Jackson goodbye. The kiss is wonderful, but she knows something is troubling him.

He waves one last time just before the wagon disappears from sight.

All of the members of the newly-joined families are sitting around the yard talking. Janice can tell how sad Jackson feels after Sandra leaves.

"Sandra is missing you as much as you are missing her," whispers Janice. "She will find a way to come back soon. Don't worry."

Jackson decides to wait a day or two before telling anyone about his weekend plans.

It's finally quiet enough around Cap and Janice for Mr. Murray to talk to them.

"Your mother and I are going to give you and Janice a cow to sell in Water Town. Please try to be there at the auction on Tuesday so you can see how it works. Use the silver you receive to have a good time and stay in the boarding house."

Buck speaks next. "Janice Murray, in our hearts, you're still our little girl. Your mother and I are going to give you and Cap the wagon he earned long ago, and a horse to go with it."

The Murrays are happy and content as they finish loading up and begin the ride home. But everyone notices Jackson has a lot on his mind.

The next morning is a new beginning for both families. Cap and Janice wake early like they're used to, but they snuggle a little longer. "I can't believe we can be together all the time from now on," says Cap.

Janice rolls over, hugs and kisses him. "Good morning, Mr. Murray," she says, holding on a little while. After breakfast they ride to the Murray's. Cap plans to borrow Miles's wagon, and help his father catch the cow."

When Cap and Janice arrive, everyone stops their work and sits on the porch talking to the newlyweds until lunch.

After eating, they catch the cow and hook the horses to Miles's wagon.

Cap goes to his room to see if there's anything he might have forgotten. There on the window sill sits one of the stones he and Jackson found at the old mine. He picks it up, rubs the dust off, and places it in his pocket. Someone in Water Town can tell him if it's of any value.

He takes one last look at the room. Everything still looks as if two brothers live there. Slingshots and toys Miles and Uncle Matt had made for them when they were children still lie on shelves, untouched for some time. Looking at those toys makes him remember the happy times when he played with Jackson. He had enjoyed a wonderful childhood in that room.

Inez walks in and hugs him. "I miss you, son. Even if it has only been one night." He feels a new feeling of love for her, knowing she's the one who will always remember him as he was when he was her little boy.

Chapter 21

As Mason strides toward the leather shop, he's thinking about what he's going to discuss with Virgil. As he steps into the shop he puts on his business face and makes his way over to the clerk.

"Young man, I would like to talk with Virgil."

"He's off today, but you can find him at his farm if you care to go over there."

Mason would rather talk business at Virgil's farm anyway, so he asks the clerk for directions. Virgil sees him ride up. He's intrigued as he makes his way toward the house. Mason catches a glimpse of him, "Do you have a little time to talk business?"

"Of course," Virgil replies, eyes brightening. "If it's alright with you, I prefer to sit at the kitchen table."

Inside, Mason spreads out drawings and notes.

"The first thing we need to tie down is our business agreement," says Mason, not wasting time. Virgil nods in agreement. "I'm willing to put up half of the silver for equipment and pay for my men. Will you agree to put up the other half of the silver?"

"That sounds fair."

"Great, we will split the profit as it's made." Mason looks directly into Virgil's eyes while cocking his chin to one side.

"And?" says Virgil, wanting to get whatever it is out of the way.

"I just want to be sure you realize not all the silver we take in at the entrance of my show is profit."

Virgil looks at Mason giving him slight smirk. "I know the difference between gross and profit."

Mason smiles. "There's one more thing. I will not be going into the wilderness. You will lead ten of my men and allow them do what they're trained to do."

"I never thought you would. You look more like a business man than a hunter."

Mason leans back, relaxing. "It won't be long until you see why I have a lot of confidence in these ten men. I always use them when we go after a dangerous new animal."

Virgil starts to make a comment, but before he can get it out, Mason starts talking again.

"I know this will probably be the most dangerous creature we have ever hunted. Because of that, I am going to have my people give everything about this trip a lot of thought."

Virgil sits closer to the table and props his chin on his right fist.

"Next Saturday, meet me at my barn. It's the first building on the right, just past the river bridge on the main trail. I want you to tell me if the cage I have started building will hold one of the dragons you saw. You're going to be excited when you see all of the surprises I have in store for you. We will be ready to engage these monsters sooner than you think."

Virgil has ideas to share, but he becomes hypnotized by Mason's voice. His head fills with visions of the equipment that's being described. Overjoyed and excited, he can't sit still. He's ready to start packing his saddlebags. "I will definitely be there first thing Saturday morning," he replies.

"Good. See you there." The meeting went better than Mason had hoped. Whistling, he hops energetically on his horse.

As Virgil walks back to his barn, filled with confidence, his courage swells and he daydreams about the excitement that lies ahead. He's finally going to be properly prepared to venture into the wilderness in his quest to capture one of the most perilous creatures alive.

<><

Cap wakes with his love's face inches from his. She opens her eyes and their day begins with a smile as they peer into each other's eyes. Overflowing with energy and happiness they prepare to leave on their honeymoon. Thoughts of doing whatever they please, without anyone telling them otherwise, and with no chores to worry about, add passion to their burning love.

As they walk out on the porch, Buck and Flavie stop them. "I want a big hug from Janice and a promise from Cap that he will take special care of my girl," says Buck, reaching for Janice. "This will be the first time she has gone to Water Town without us." She hugs them tightly, then bounces out to the wagon.

Eager to go, they begin their trip even though they can barely see where they're going. The air is cool and the grass is wet with dew.

"I never knew I could be this happy," says Cap.

"I have never been this excited about going to Water Town," replies Janice.

"Our whole life together lies ahead of us," says Cap, putting his arm around his wife. "I promise to try to make our journey through life as much fun as this honeymoon." He feels happy to be a man taking on new responsibility.

As they travel, the sun brightens, displaying a beautiful dark blue sky with wispy white clouds drifting overhead. From their seat, the trail looks like a blue and green tunnel running through the forest.

"I'm beginning to see the beauty of wild flowers that Sandra always talks about," says Cap pointing to a patch of violets with the greenest leaves he has ever seen surrounding purple blooms.

"The trail can be hard to deal with sometimes, but with pretty weather and a wonderful woman like you beside me, it's a beautiful thing today."

They're in a magical mood and snuggled next to each other when they arrive at the auction. It's open, and they are spellbound by the size of the place. It's almost as large as Blade Town. Log barns, corrals, and fences are everywhere. In the middle stands a tall, open building with seats along one side. People are everywhere. A man sees them pull in and points them in the direction they need to go. They stop behind two men on horses, each leading a cow. The men look back and nod hello to Cap and Janice. When the men move on, Cap pulls up next to a man sitting at a table tall enough they can speak face-to-face. He asks Cap his name, then hands him a number carved on a square piece of wood and a collar with the same number on it. "Slip this collar around the cow's neck and keep this piece of wood until you're paid." A worker waiting ahead takes the collar, slips it over the cows head and leads it away. Cap parks his wagon, and they walk hand-in-hand toward the large building.

"Let's find a good seat and wait for our cow to be sold," says Cap. He's quiet when they first sit, but slowly he discovers it's fun to watch people getting excited when their animals come up for sale. Slowly, the uneasy feeling of, being surrounded by more people than he has seen in his entire life fades. The auction turns into entertainment, as a talented auctioneer begins to work his magic. Talking

fast, and with a silly grin, he describes every animal
that comes up for sale as the best he has ever seen. Then
he jokes about his wife's cooking and his dog. Everyone
laughs a lot.

It isn't long until one of the workers leads Cap and
Janice's cow to the center of the arena. Janice holds her
breath.

"I can't believe how excited I feel watching them
auction off our cow," says Cap.

It's over in minutes. The high bid is 75 silver
pieces, and when several men standing around them say
it's a really good price, they hug each other. Even though
they're having fun, they decide to go to the cashier and
collect their silver.

"Hand me your number, please, and sign this." The
cashier pushes a paper showing that Cap is owed 75 silver
pieces minus three silver pieces and 15 copper pieces.
"That's the auction's fee, five percent of the sale price."
states the cashier, seeing there is a question on Cap's face.

"Thank you." Cap understands and nods.

"Next please" calls the cashier.

Cap gives Janice half the silver, and she hides some
in the wagon.

"I feel sad for our cow, but I'm glad it's gone. Now
we can concentrate on having fun," says Cap as his
thoughts turn to adventure.

"Let's rent a room at the boarding house," suggests
Janice.

After settling in they realize they're too tired from
the trip to enjoy shopping, so they decide to relax and
spend the evening alone.

When the sun lights the room the next morning,
they're ready to explore.

The leather shop is in the back of Cap's mind. He wants to look inside to see if he can figure out which clerk is Virgil. Being on his honeymoon, he doesn't want Janice to wonder why he would be looking for someone there. He smiles when she sees the shop and is intrigued, so they walk in. The women's shoes catch her eye. "I will find us a clerk," suggests Cap. He walks over to a nicely dressed man helping a couple. "Pardon me. Is Virgil working this morning?" The man cocks his head studying Cap. "I am Virgil. Do I know you?"

Cap blushes. "I am Miles Murray's son. I didn't get to meet you when you came by our farm headed into the wilderness." He holds his hand out to shake, but Virgil cuts him off. "I'm helping these customers. Someone will be with you in a moment."

Cap raises an eyebrow and backs away. Seeing a clerk talking with Janice, he returns to her side. The next time he looks around for Virgil he is nowhere to be seen. Janice likes several shoes, but wants to think about them, so they leave and walk around.

One of the largest shops comes into view and Cap stares with his mouth open. "I have never seen such a large hardware store in my life. Do you mind if we have a look around in there?" She happily agrees. There's plenty she is interested in, too.

The first thing they see grabs their attention. There, neatly stacked in a row, are some of Uncle Ed's wheels. Janice beams, proud of her family.

A couple shops later, beautiful jewelry is displayed in one of the shop's windows. The color and beautiful designs make Cap stop to look. Janice is quietly admiring the display. They look at each other, and step inside to browse. "I would like to buy you something pretty so every time you see it, you will remember our honeymoon," says Cap with his arm around her waist.

"I do see something I like," she says picking up a broach made of silver. It's the size of a silver coin, shaped as a five-petal flower. Each petal has a red stone attached leaving only a sliver of shiny silver outlining it. In the center stands a clear stone sparkling. Even though it's not very expensive, she and Cap think it's the prettiest thing in the shop.

The clerk behind the counter is helpful and friendly, and when he says he will take three silver coins for it, Cap feels he is getting a good deal. As he pulls the coins out of his pocket, the rock from the old mine falls to the counter, landing with a *thunk*. It glistens, catching the clerk's eye.

"May I show this to the owner?" he asks.

Cap agrees, and the clerk marches over to a well-dressed man in the back. Janice is not paying any attention to them. She is enjoying herself looking at all the pretty merchandise. Cap studies the interaction the owner is having with the clerk. He holds the stone up to the light turning it from side to side. The owner asks the clerk a lot of questions, and then quiets. They quickly return, stopping close to Cap.

"Where did you find such an interesting stone?" the clerk asks.

"It was given to me by a man who visited our family farm several years ago." He squirms. It's hard for him not to tell the truth, but he doesn't need trouble on his honeymoon, and Janice doesn't know the story about the stone, anyway.

"Why did he give it to you?" asks the shop owner.

"I like collecting rocks. He gave it to me because I thought it was pretty."

"Did he find the rock near your farm?"

Cap knows now that there's something special about this rock. He hates to keep lying, but he's stuck. "He told me it came from somewhere south of Water Town."

The owner backs off. "There is a silver mine south of here. I hope you thanked him. This stone is worth ten copper pieces. It's almost pure silver."

"He was a very nice man, and all he seemed to care about was finding pretty stones," replies Cap.

"I would like to have it. Will you trade it for a silver coin?

"No, but thank you for the offer," says Cap smiling.

"Come in and see us next time you're in Water Town and buy your girlfriend something nice."

"Thank you. We look forward to coming back soon," replies Cap.

Cap opens the door and breathes a sigh of relief. He's glad to escape the lies he has just told.

Cap and Janice walk hand-in-hand with a rhythm of happiness in their step. They look so alive. There's more than just a pleasant smile on their faces. Their love grows deeper as they take in all the sights and make memories they will cherish for the rest of their lives.

Early the next morning, they're up and enjoying breakfast at the hotel.

"I want to go to a food store we passed by yesterday to purchase some of their sliced meat and bread. We can stop at Sandra's and share a picnic with her on our way home," says Janice.

"Water Town has been a lot of fun, but I'm ready to head back to the country," says Cap.

They stroll to the wagon. Cap holds her hand as she hops up to the seat, then hurries around to sit beside her. He leans over and kisses her, flips the reins, and they're on their way home. Cap decides to ride by the sale barn to see if he can buy a calf like his father had done. Sure enough, a couple of men are sitting out front with calves for sale. Cap bargains for two of them.

The ride home is cool with the wind blowing out of the north. Janice reaches under the seat, pulls out a blanket, and spreads it across their laps. Content, they slide closer and quietly hold hands. Soon the blacksmith's shop is in front of them.

Janice hurries around to find Ed. "We wanted to stop on our way back from Water Town to say hello and talk with Sandra and Aunt Mary," says Janice.

"I feel honored you stopped to see us on your honeymoon. Sandra is dying to see you, anyway," replies Ed, smiling.

Janice hugs her uncle. She and Cap head toward the house.

Sandra hears the wagon coming and dashes out. The cousins greet each other like they did when they were little girls. They're lost in conversation as they stroll into the house, almost forgetting Cap is in the world.

"Tell me everything about your trip," says Sandra.

Cap knows to be patient. He gathers the picnic box and sits in the swing on the porch while the women share wonderful experiences and happy expectations.

"Jackson is going to ride out here to visit Sandra this Saturday," is the first thing Janice says as she and Sandra barge onto the porch.

"Jackson must really be in love to ride out here so soon after seeing Sandra at our wedding," says Cap. He silently hopes things will work out for them so they will be as happy as he and Janice are.

When the picnic is finished, it's time to leave. Sandra stays close as they walk out and stand beside the wagon. With teary eyes she hugs them both long and hard, leaving no doubt she is just as much in love as Jackson.

That night, Sandra sits quieter than usual on the porch close to her father. After Mary says good night and goes inside, Ed is surprised when she reaches over and gently takes his hand.

"I have had the best childhood anyone could ever wish for, but I love Jackson so much that, even though I'm with you and mom, I'm lonely every day."

Ed looks lovingly into her eyes, "We just need to know him a little longer and a little better."

"In my heart, I know the real Jackson. I don't need any more time to know what kind of man he is."

Ed rubs his forehead. "I love you more than anything in this world, Sandra. I will think about what you have said."

Saturday morning, Jackson hops out of bed early and works as hard as he can. He hates to leave so much work for Uncle Matt and his father. They already have more than they can do with Cap gone. He quits working well before lunch and passes his father on the way to the house.

Miles frowns and rumbles in an unkind voice. "You boys are trying to kill me and Uncle Matt." Those words are hardly past his lips, when he feels remorse for saying them. "Son, I'm sorry. I know there are things you need that your mother and I cannot give you. You and Sandra have my blessings. I know soon Matt and I will adjust. Go obey your heart. You're only young once."

Jackson hugs him. "I will be right here helping you and mom even if things work out between me and Sandra. You can count on that."

Miles smiles inside and out after hearing Jackson's reassurance.

Jackson is on the trail by lunchtime, and he rides faster than usual. It's a cool day so it won't be too hard on the horse.

As the sun begins to slip behind the tree tops, he sees the blacksmith shop ahead.

His nerves tense up and he bites his lip. What if Ed has already made his decision and it doesn't matter what he says? He ties his horse in front of the office and walks nervously inside. Ed is at his desk.

"Have a seat, Jackson. I just have one more line to add up, and then we can talk."

Jackson's heart speeds up, and he doesn't know if he should continue standing or sit down or watch him work. He decides to sit quietly out of the way.

Chapter 22

Ed lays his paperwork aside. Jackson fidgets nervously in his chair. Ed leans back, appearing relaxed and full of confidence as he looks Jackson in the eye.

"Young man, I have made my decision."

Jackson swallows so hard it's painful.

"Sandra had a long talk with me the other night right after Cap and Janice stopped to visit on their way home from their honeymoon. She explained why she cannot live any longer without you. That leaves me no choice but to say stop worrying, you have my blessing. Let's have a wonderful weekend together." A genuine smile spreads across his face.

Jackson can hardly breathe. He's so relieved his body struggles to handle the sudden drop of tension. He never dreamed things would work out so fast. Ed stands just in time for a grown man with tears in his eyes to grab him. Jackson squeezes him so sincerely. Ed is surprised, but he understands. Jackson releases and takes a deep breath.

"Thank you." He wipes his eyes with his sleeve.

"Let's head toward the house. Walking will help you calm down," says Ed.

They talk like old friends as they walk up the path.

Sandra has been watching for Jackson and runs out as soon as she sees them.

"Sandra, Jackson has something to tell you," says Ed patting Jackson on the back. He continues into the house so they can release all the passion and emotion lovers experience at this wonderful moment.

Jackson steps over to Sandra. She puts her arms around him and kisses him before he can say anything. It's so wonderful; he surrenders and returns equal passion. When Sandra pulls back Jackson speaks softly.

"Will you marry me, Sandra?" She stands motionless for a second to be sure this is not a dream.

"Yes!" she replies. They kiss again, only longer. They hug until they compose themselves. Jackson reaches for her hand and they stroll to the porch swing.

Ed and Mary come out shortly with a pitcher of tea and glasses.

"I'm pleased to have you become part of our family, Jackson. I know you will take good care of Sandra," states Ed as he takes Mary's hand.

"I promise to do everything in my power to make both of you proud of us," replies Jackson.

"Where are you and Sandra going to live?" asks Mary.

Jackson looks into Sandra's eyes before he speaks to be sure she agrees with what he is about to say.

"We have talked about going to my family's farm. Mom and dad need our help so they won't have to live alone. Even though Uncle Matt is there, they're all getting older."

Sandra smiles and squeezes Jackson's hand. "I love both of you, but I have fallen in love with a man from the fringe of the wilderness," she replies looking at her mom and dad.

Ed has a pleasant look on his face. He's in deep thought as he looks at Mary. They move close together, and he puts his arm around her waist as she lays her head against his shoulder.

"I can't lie. I will be sad to see Sandra move so far away, but I'm happy for you both. She has fallen in love with you, and I love you like a son," says Mary.

"We will just have to let the boys run the shop a little more so we can visit the fringe of the wilderness often," says Ed as his smile returns. "I'm pleased Jackson loves his family and wants to take care of them. That's the kind of love I want for my daughter."

Mary holds Ed's hand tightly as they agree to have the wedding on Sunday in two weeks.

Sandra is streaming tears as she lovingly hugs her father and then her mother. She backs away, wipes her eyes, and smiles. Now she and Jackson can be in love and not worry about trying to be together or wonder if this is real love. They excuse themselves. They want to spend some time in Sandra's flower garden.

<>

Saturday morning Virgil quickly saddles his horse. It's going to be special day, and he's eager to see and touch the equipment Mason has talked about. His horse trots all the way to Mason's shop. As he walks up to the barn he looks up at the roof high above his head. "This has to be one of the biggest buildings in town, even before the blacksmith shop was built on the side," he thinks.

The barn is constructed out of large, heavy logs. The space between them is filled with hewn saplings and mud. Along each side, windows are evenly spaced and stretch from one end to the other. Every window has a hinged door on one side so it can be opened to allow light to enter or easily shut to secure the building.

Hammers are clanging inside the blacksmith shop. He knocks on the door leading into the large barn, but no one answers. The door isn't locked, and he has been invited to be there, so he slowly meanders in.

Inside, he's struck by the sight of a wagon twice as long as a farm wagon with wheels heavier than any he has ever seen. Its bed is actually the bottom of a cage enclosed with vertical bars from the floor to the ceiling, and there is plenty of headroom inside. He walks to the back and studies the latches that secure the door. It can be lowered, making a ramp to the floor. He closes his eyes and pictures a large powerful dragon being loaded.

The sound of footsteps makes him open his eyes. Headed toward him is a blacksmith dressed in a dirty, burnt leather shirt and wearing long thick gloves. His pants are protected by leather coveralls that are as worn out as his shirt. On his head, rests a red cloth folded to be thick as it crosses his forehead, then tied in back. He's carrying a part he has just made.

"Good morning. Are you Virgil?" he asks.

"Yes. Is Mason here?"

"He will be soon. Make yourself at home." He lays the part against one of the other wagons, marks something to change, then heads back to the blacksmith shop.

Virgil turns back to the wagon and imagines how exciting it will be to have a dragon locked inside.

"Is it large enough to haul a dragon?" Mason's powerful voice echoes from across the barn, startling Virgil.

"Oh, yes. This is big enough for a dragon. I see it has a roof to keep its captive dry."

"This wagon serves two purposes. When we travel in dangerous places, we can all sleep inside and be safe and dry. When it's occupied by an animal we can still sleep underneath and stay dry."

Virgil rubs one of the bars, and looks toward Mason. "Isn't this wagon too heavy to pull through rough terrain?"

"We can hook up to ten horses if needed, but we won't try to pull it very far into the wilderness. This wagon is designed more for safety on the journey home."

He points to a second wagon with a pole in the middle that is securely mounted to its floor. It isn't as wide as the first wagon. There are no bars or roof, only side planks about three feet tall. The pole and floor have metal straps and hooks bolted to them.

"This is the one we must pull into the depths of the wilderness to bring a live dragon back. Once we have several ropes around his neck, we will pull him up on the wagon. Metal bands with chains attached will be bolted around the dragon's legs and fastened to the hooks on the floor. Next comes the most dangerous part. A metal muzzle has to be slid over his mouth and chained to the floor up front. Then his tail will be chained to the floor in back. The pole in the middle is offset to one side so we can put a chain around his body and hook it to the pole. He will be restrained to the point where he won't be able to move, keeping him in the middle of the wagon. This wagon is pulled with a couple horses, but more can be added if needed."

"Why is there no seat on this wagon?" asks Virgil looking at all the hooks and straps lying on the wagon floor.

"It's removable. When we catch a dragon and chain it down, the seat will be pulled out, and the driver will ride the lead horse. We don't want him sitting close to an infuriated dragon. Once we reach good trails we will move the dragon to the heavy cage, but we won't take the muzzle off."

Virgil isn't a very kind man, but the way the dragon is going to be treated sounds distasteful and cruel. Mason watches with pride as Virgil examines his creation for a minute, and then leads him to another room.

Virgil is speechless when he enters.

"In this room, Virgil, we have equipment you won't find anywhere else." In one corner stands dozens of metal shields. Virgil is drawn to them first, and tips one forward to get a better look. "These shields are beautiful, but they feel light to me."

"They're more than just pretty and light." Mason picks one up and jumps around, holding it in various positions, pretending he's protecting himself from dragon flames. "These shields are not to stop arrows, they're made light so you can jerk them around quickly and protect yourself from a whirlwind of fire."

Beside the shields, standing at attention is a long line of brown and white bows made from aged Yew tree wood. Virgil pulls one out and looks it over. With one end on the ground it's taller than him. He wrinkles his forehead and looks at Mason.

"They're long and a little harder to carry, but easy to pull back and when you release the arrow, it travels so fast you can't see it until it hits. These bows are made to bring down large creatures.

Virgil picks up one of the arrows. They're perfectly straight.

"Beautiful, aren't they?" says Mason picking one up to admire. "These arrows have iron points made in Blade Town. They're the best there is."

Mason beams as they move to the next room. "This is the surprise I told you about.

Virgil gasps. A crossbow so large it has to be mounted on a wagon, sits before him. He marvels at the beautiful workmanship.

"This weapon is not just big and powerful, it's easy to aim in any direction with little effort. The bowman can sit comfortably in the seat behind the weapon and use his feet to spin around in either direction. At the same time,

he can lean back and the bow will point into the sky.
As high as he chooses. A dragon can be easily followed as
it flies around," explains Mason, pointing upward.

"You're a genius," says Virgil, shaking his head
solemnly.

"No, I just know how to find men who are genius at
what they do. These men love figuring things out and
enjoy working with each other. There isn't anything they
can't make."

"Look at the workmanship put into the crossbow."
Mason gestures to mount the weapon.

Virgil climbs up on the wagon to look it over.

"Pull back on the cord and try to cock it," says
Mason.

Virgil pulls on the cord with all his might. "I can
only pull it back half way."

"Crank the little handle on the side several times
and see if that helps."

Virgil turns the handle. A ratchet and gears began
clicking, and the cord moves back, stopping when it's
ready for the arrow to be dropped in place. "Can I put an
arrow in the slot to see how it works?"

"Just don't cock the trigger and it will be safe."

Virgil pulls out one of the arrows. It's over four feet
long with a Blade Town tip on it.

"Now that I know how to load it, I think with a little
practice I could be ready to shoot in seconds," states
Virgil with a big smile.

"And practice you will," declares Mason.

Virgil is pleased with everything, especially when
he hears he would be practicing shooting the crossbow.

"Look behind you. There will be two large quivers.
One on the end where you picked up the arrow you set,
and one on the opposite end. You may be facing the other

way after shooting at a moving target. I hope I can find a leather shop capable of making us four or five quivers large enough to hold twenty-five of these arrows."

"I think I can help you find such a place," replies Virgil with a grin. He hops out of the seat and walks around the wagon.

Mason walks over and points at two pins.

"When the crossbow is not in use, you can pull these pins to lay the weapon down on the wagon floor. When it's on the floor, the wagon can pass through underbrush without much cutting to clear the trail. I'm so proud of this weapon. Let me show you how well it works." Mason pulls himself onto the wagon.

"See how easy it is to aim up and down?" He leans back and forth making the crossbow aim up or down. Then he spins around and around, like a child on a toy. He turns the weapon and aims at a target made of thick pieces of wood half way across the barn.

He winds the crank, picks up an arrow, sets it in the slot, and cocks the trigger. He adjusts his aim, and then pulls the trigger. The eerie squeak of air being ripped apart by the cord as it zips forward sends chills down Virgil's spine, while the arrow explodes into a blur flashing toward the target faster than his eyes can follow.

It crashes into the boards with a chilling *spelunk*, sending splinters flying. Virgil is so startled by the strike he flinches. Without saying a word, he walks over to the target and studies the impact area.

"The arrow penetrated the boards, and the point is in plain view from behind!"

"The accuracy is pretty amazing, too, isn't it," replies Mason.

"The arrow is touching the red center dot. I have never seen such a fierce fighting machine in all my life," says Virgil, amazed how well Mason has been able to get things done, and he's excited to be partnering with him.

Then the look on Mason's face changes for no obvious reason. He slides out of the crossbow seat and stands on the edge of the wagon looking down at Virgil.

"As we talked about earlier I have ten men who have gone on hunts like this before. I expect you to cooperate fully and let them teach you as much as they can. Your job is to get them to where they can do what they are trained to do," his voice is somber.

He hops to the ground. "You can stay here and look around as much as you like. I will come to the leather shop in a week and we will get together at that time. I should be ready to introduce you to the men and set a time to leave Water Town and begin the hunt. Good day, Virgil."

Virgil is shocked and grits his teeth in disgust. Mason is in total control and has no regard for his feelings. Virgil clinches his fist, and looks at Mason thoughtlessly walking away. Virgil nods yes to himself in resolve and determination to prove to Mason that he's just as important.

<>

Saturday morning, Jackson wakes to the wonderful smell of eggs, ham, gravy, and biscuits. He dresses and heads for the kitchen, where Mary greets him with a smile. She hands him a cup of mint tea and he has a good feeling inside.

Soon, Sandra and Ed can be heard coming. As always, Ed has a smile on his face. He looks at Jackson as he enters the kitchen.

"You didn't change your mind last night, did you, Jackson?" he jokes.

Jackson knows not to be kidding about that. "No, sir!"

Ed turns to Sandra. "I will hook the horses to our carriage and you two can have some fun riding around the village."

Ed brings the carriage to the porch and hands the reins to Jackson, who stands looking in awe. He has never ridden in a carriage before. The horse trots along as they make their way around the village. After a while they come upon a stream that crosses the trail. The horse stops to drink, and they talk.

"I wish I could stay here forever, but I will have to leave soon. I want to share our good news with Cap and Janice on the way home."

"I wish you could stay, too, but I can't wait for my favorite cousin to hear we're getting married."

"Knowing we will soon be wed makes me love you more than I thought possible," says Jackson just before they share a kiss sweeter and longer than any before. They hold hands as they ride home. After putting up the carriage, they head to the flower garden and say goodbye. Sandra watches Jackson ride out of sight. He turns at the last moment and waves one last time. She consoles herself knowing that, in one week, they will be back together.

Jackson rides contently thinking about his mother and father, they will be happy he wants to move in with them. That will solve some of father's problems trying to keep the farm going.

He greets a family with two young boys riding south. Seeing the boys makes him fondly remember all the good times he had growing up on their farm. Jackson hopes the farm and their way of life don't change much so his children can enjoy their childhood like he had.

As clouds and rain roll in, he pulls a leather poncho out of his saddlebag and slips it on. The drizzle can't dampen his happiness. He's excited about the future and grateful for the past.

He smiles in the rain when he sees Cap and Janice's turnoff.

Riding up their trail, his contentment grows deeper. He hops off the horse, bounds up the steps, and knocks on the door.

Everyone is enjoying supper, and he's glad when they ask him to join them. He's starving and fixes his plate. But before sitting down he blurts out, "I'm getting married! Sandra said yes and Ed said yes! Now we can be together forever!"

Cap jumps up and hugs him. Buck and Flavie stop eating and wait their turn. Janice's eyes fill with tears, but she's excited and smiling broadly "I am so happy for both of you and now my favorite cousin is going to live less than an hour away!"

"These Brittain girls are something special aren't they," says Cap as he releases Jackson.

"When is the wedding?" asks Flavie.

"Sunday in two weeks," he replies.

After eating, Jackson is anxious to go home and share the good news with his parents.

Climbing on his horse, he has a feeling of peace and happiness he hasn't felt in a while. The strange feeling that turned into burning love no longer causes him to wonder or worry. Now he knows the woman he loves feels the same way, too.

It's late, but he can't wait to tell his mom and dad the good news, hopefully their faces will light up.

The long trip back is finally over, and Uncle Matt is on the porch. Jackson waves at him on his way to the barn. As quickly as he can, he puts the horse away.

As he steps onto the porch, Uncle Matt gives him a look of disapproval. Uncle Matt can tell he hadn't done everything he should after such a long ride.

"Come in the house I have something to tell everyone," says Jackson, knowing he won't be in trouble long.

His mom and dad are waiting in the kitchen. They aren't going to bed without knowing their son is safely home. "Father, I'm here to ask your permission to marry Sandra," he says confidently, surprising them. Inez reaches over, taking hold of Miles's hand, and they smile.

"Yes, son, you have our blessing."

"I do have one request," says Jackson. "Will you allow us to move into my room? We would like to live and work on the farm. I have already talked to Ed, and he has agreed to let Sandra move out here."

Miles and Inez jump up to hug him, but Uncle Matt reaches him first. They hold hands and wait their turn. No one is sleepy anymore. Miles hugs Inez.

"Son, you will never regret staying here to help your family! You can't find a better place to raise your children." He wipes a tear.

"If I have all three of you to help me, I can't go wrong."

They share a wonderful peaceful feeling. Inez lights two more candles as Miles heads to his bedroom to retrieve a dusty jug of the best apple wine he has ever made.

Chapter 23

Steven and Jess miss their families as much as ever, especially in the quiet of night, but they no longer struggle to survive. The wilderness provides for them, and they are filled with respect for her. Some days, they walk a mile or more toward the plateau. But others are spent making things like clothing, shoes, or jerky. They're halfway back to the plateau and filled with hope. Earlier in the day, they stopped, relaxed, and watched two beautiful red-winged black birds playing. The day has been pleasant, and their evening fire is inviting as it sparks and crackles, roasting their supper. As they relax, watching it dance, Jess pulls out his small knife and carves a pocket in a rotten log lying nearby. He stands flowers he picked earlier in the hole, just to enjoy.

"Virgil would be surprised if he knew we're still alive and doing this well," says Jess, sharpening his knife on a round river stone.

Steven creases his eyes. "Did you have to mention that traitor's name? I will never rest until I get even with him for all the suffering we have had to go through." They finish the evening in the comfort of their airborne tents.

The next day, a damp musty smell is in the air and the sun fails to peek through the clouds. Few birds fly, and the forest is quiet. As evening approaches, a mist begins to fall and the wind is whipping through the trees. Darkness comes early. It's too wet and windy to build a fire, so, cold and wet, they tuck in for the night. They wake to a forest dripping all around, as drizzle gathers on limbs, forming big drops that make a popping sound when they hit the top cover. Dim light fills the gloomy wilderness as they climb to the ground. Everything is too wet for a fire. They will have to walk if they are going to stay warm.

Rain falls for the next two days and they trip, slide, and fall more than they ever have.

"I'm really tired of dealing with all this rain." says Jess crouching close to a tree as he tightens the straps on his leather poncho. He shivers.

Steven sits beside him and doesn't answer. They are quiet for some time. There is nothing interesting to talk about. They're tired, depressed, and cold.

"Even though it's midday, I think we should hunt a good tree and hang our hammocks for the night," says Steven, breaking the silence.

Jess points to a tall tree next to a stream they have been taking advantage of for several days. It zigzags through the forest, disappearing at times, but always returns. They're fond of it because it makes their lives easier. The water is clean enough to drink, and handy when they cook.

Steven climbs the tree and drops a leather strap to the ground. Jess ties the hammocks to it so Steven can pull them up. Rain falls harder, pelting them as they hang their hammocks. Jess shakes the rain from his poncho and finally slips into his shelter.

"I hate lying here wet," says Steven.

"At least we won't get any wetter," replies Jess. They nap and occasionally talk until night creeps in surrounding them with a gentle breeze and darkness.

"Even though the sun has set, it feels like it's getting warmer," comments Steven.

"Listen," says Jess. In the distance, he and Steven hear the sound of heavy rain drops beating against millions of leaves moving closer and sounding louder. A gust of wind shakes their hammocks, followed by a wave of pouring rain. "I'm glad we tied our hammocks close together. The rain is so loud I can hardly hear you talking."

"When the weather is stormy, I feel safer when we're tied close to each other," replies Steven.

"I wish we hadn't hung our hammocks so high in this tree. The wind makes them sway more way up here," says Jess, as the breeze picks up.

As they lay there, swaying back and forth, an occasional faint blink of light turns the trees of the foggy forest into flashes of silhouettes.

"I hope a thunder storm isn't headed toward us," says Steven. "How much worse can things get," replies Jess.

They have experienced storms filled with thunder and lightning before while lying in their hammocks, but this one seems different. The sound of breaking limbs, thunder and tortured trees rubbing against each other as they bow in submission to the wind roars in the distance. A feeling of energy fills the air and in moments it's on top of them. They're immersed in blinding rain, and rocking wildly. Lightning explodes over their heads, bursting into jagged streaks, followed by thunderous shockwaves so strong their tree shakes. Cringing they slither down into their hammocks, peek over the edge, and hold on. Thunder rolls across the sky for miles, echoing back and forth in the little creek's valley. They're blinded over and over as flashes of lightening streak across the sky from cloud to cloud, battling back and forth with each other.

Jess catches sight of Steven shivering with his hands folded over his nose and mouth in fear, his eyes squinted as he peers over his forefingers. Jess tries to hide his fear.

The sound of bouncing, pecking, pinging, and ripping leaves join the roar of the storm as hail stones larger than hickory nuts whip across them in waves, pelting everything in sight. The top deer skin protects them, but now and then, a stone squeezes through and stings them when it strikes. Suddenly the hail stops and they breathe a sigh of relief, but the storm morphs and all its energy is thrust into torrential rain. It drenches the valley so long their little stream is transformed into a raging river. Their gentle little stream roars angrily, as the storm rumbles.

Late in the night the rain begins to die down. Jess begins to relax and drifts off to sleep, but his subconscious instinct tells him something isn't right.

In slumber-laden thought, he analyzes his concern. *Is the tree literally rocking me to sleep?* He dreams. *This feels good.* Suddenly, with a jerk, his eyes pop open, realizing he's experiencing the worst possible reason for the pleasant swaying. He rubs his eyes and feels the tree lean toward the river.

"We're in trouble!" he screams.

Steven is too quiet. "Steven, are you okay?" yells Jess.

Steven's fingers are gripping the sides of the hammock tightly. "I can't swim." He says bleakly, shaking his head.

"The storm is almost over. The tree probably won't lean any further," says Jess, doing his best to sound encouraging.

An hour of gentle leaning passes, and then they feel a rhythm of pull and return, pull and return as the water pulls the tree further into the torrent.

"If the tree falls, crawl out of your hammock and hold on to a limb until it lodges on the bank," says Jess. Steven is still too quiet.

The tree changes its swaying rhythm again, and Jess knows it's going to surrender to the river. It leans so slowly and gently he thinks maybe they can ride along on top of it, but when his arm dips into the water, the pull is unbelievable and water shoots into the air over his body, yanking him into the raging current.

He's instantly in a battle for his life while blinded by darkness and choking on water. Frantically, he fights to free himself of sticks and logs that are bumping into him as he struggles to keep his head above water. The tree's roots snap and it spins perpendicular to the bank, racing down river toward him. It's picking up speed. He is in its path with no way to escape. He ducks under the trunk and it brushes over his head, pushing him frightfully deep in the water as it races downstream.

When his head pops up, he can only see when lightning flashes and he has to quickly decide which way to swim. He's being swept downstream rapidly, and he has only seconds to make the right decision. Desperately, he swims as hard as he can toward the bank. His chances of surviving are fading quickly. A limb hanging over the bank is bouncing in the torrent and hits him in the face. He desperately grabs it and pulls hard. His body rises out of the water like a skipping rock skimming across the surface as he pulls with all his might, trying to climb up the limb. He feels his strength dwindling rapidly. The limb bounces up lifting him out of the water for a second, and that's all he needs to pull his legs free of the current's grip. He wraps them around the limb and inches higher.

His mind is on Steven, even as he fights for his life. He hasn't heard a word from him since he hit the water.

"Steven! Where are you?" he screams as loud as he can in the darkness, but the only sound he hears is the frightful sound of raging water.

He desperately hopes Steven just can't hear him above all this noise.

Jess continues to climb and the limb grows bigger. He wrestles with it until he reaches a larger limb that's stronger and easier to hold on to. He manages to pull himself on top of it and shimmy over to the trunk where he is able to sit with his back against the tree. He will wait out the flood, but he's wet, cold, tired, and grieving.

He is thankful to be alive, but reality haunts him. There's little hope two men could have been lucky enough to make it out of that angry water.

When morning light appears, the water has receded enough for him to drop to the mucky mess under the tree. He wades a few feet up the bank to drier ground and sits. It's damp but more comfortable than he has been in hours.

The river is still raging and he's tired of hearing it. Exhausted, he slowly pulls himself to his feet and trudges up hill to a grassy spot where the sun is shining. He plunks to the ground. The sun begins to warm him through his wet clothes, and he doesn't move. Sleep takes him away from his suffering for a short time.

Pleasantly dreaming, he feels someone poking at him. Half-asleep, he smiles. He's glad Steven has found him. The next prod hurts and his eyes pop open. He jumps up, startled. A buzzard flaps its wings in disgust and hops back a few feet, then becomes threatening. Instinct tells Jess to charge the bird. He screams and lurches at the horrid looking creature. Dumbfounded, it squawks. With wings flapping furiously it takes to the sky and flies away. A new battle to survive has begun, and he must find Steven and food.

He searches along the river, looking for fish stranded in puddles by the receding water. Luckily, he still has his knife on his belt so he uses it to cut one of the fish into strips. He devours several pieces.

Looking down the waterway that is beginning to look more like a creek again, he sees devastation everywhere. Traveling along its side will be difficult. He cleans his knife and searches frantically at first. The further he wanders, the more he realizes the chances of finding any sign of Steven has passed.

In the evening, he finally finds the tree he and Steven were in. It's lodged against another tree in a sharp bend of the creek. He scrambles around searching frantically for any sign of Steven. Then he climbs into the tangled mess and pulls through every limb with no luck. Overcome with grief, he drops to his knees and sobs. Wiping tears, he gazes at the hammocks. They're still tied to limbs, but they are twisted and pulled this way and that. He climbs to them and unwinds one hammock and its cover. While he's untangling the hammock, he spies his bow. It's still where he hung it, but it's twisted within a clump of limbs. He carefully cuts it out and pulls on the string. It springs back, thrilling him that it will still work. It and the hammock are all that's left of their belongings.

He's thankful he will be back in the trees before night. He picks a tree close by and pulls the damp hammock into its sturdy limbs, preparing for darkness. This will be a sad, cold night.

After sunset, the hammock is cold and his body itches everywhere he's pressed against it. He would be more comfortable lying on the ground, but he can't give up the security he feels knowing he's safe from most predators. The chill of night penetrates to his bones, and he realizes if he is going to survive, he will have to build a fire in the morning to warm up and dry the hammock.

When the sun rises enough that most predators are not as aggressive, he climbs down. Luckily, there's a cottonwood tree nearby, and the fluffy seeds are lying all around. The sunny day after the flood dried them, and they are blowing around, ready to take flight. He gathers a handful of seeds and some small twigs and places them where he's going to build his fire. Next, he picks up larger limbs and piles them next to the twigs. He heads to the creek bank, searching for quartz rocks hard enough to throw a spark when struck together. He kneels, sits back on his legs, and lays the bed of seeds between his bent knees. He takes a deep breath, picks up the two rocks, and with determination strikes them together over the pile. Sparks fly into the kindling and produces smoke several times but he can't manage to start a blaze.

He begins to grow angry and feels a burst of energy, making him more determined to survive. He tries over and over until he finally obtains a little glow. He blows with all his might and it bursts into flames.

Very carefully, he places the tiniest twigs on the pile of blazing white fluff. Then he adds the smallest limbs until flames are dancing high enough for him to lay the large limbs on top. At last, he has a life-giving fire to dry his belongings and cook something.

As soon as his clothes are dry, he pulls them on and trudges into the woods in search of several small, straight poplar saplings. They will be used to make new arrows, and they're needed quickly. He places them beside the fire to bake until they're hard. He hopes to have a weapon again before dark.

Next, he searches along the creek for more trapped fish, but predators have already eaten most of them. He finally finds two, and with the first glimmer of hope, a little smile appears as he carries them back to his fire.

As the sun sets and now that he has a weapon and food, he dares to hope his luck will hold out. Maybe he still has a chance of making it back to the dragon plateau. He's confident he can find the trail they chopped out close to the plateau, and it will lead him home. He is determined to sneak past the dragons when he's close to their den again.

He makes a vow to himself to never forget Steven, and never to take anything in the wilderness for granted. Not even a beautiful little creek.

That night, from time to time, he feels Steven's spirit close by, looking over him. During one of the moments the feeling is so strong it makes his hair stand on end, Jess bows his head and speaks out loud to Steven with the wilderness as his witness.

"I will find your family and tell them what happened, old friend, so they can properly grieve and go on with their lives. I will miss you and always remember the hope you gave me out here. May you rest in peace." At that moment, a warm feeling inside reassures him that Steven is pleased.

<>

Saturday morning, on his way to see his bride-to-be, Jackson is on top of the world. Humming a tune as he approaches Cap and Janice's turnoff, he can't believe how lucky he is to meet them sitting on their horses at the top of their trail.

"Good morning. Are you going to Blade Town today?"

"No. If you will allow us, we're going to ride with you so you won't have to travel alone," replies Janice with a happy smile.

"That's right, brother. We would like to see Ed and Mary anyway, and we would enjoy riding along with you."

"I love both of you," says Jackson, and they head toward Sandra's village.

The trail is warming up and a gentle breeze puffs every now and then, making the wild flowers bow to the south. They lose track of time talking, and by mid-day they're in front of the blacksmith shop. Jackson and Cap go inside to look for Ed. Ed Junior meets them. "Ed is at his house," he says with a really big smile on his face. "Mary is making him fix everything she can think of. She wants everything to be just right for the wedding." He laughs.

When they trot up to the house, Sandra can hardly contain herself when she sees Cap and Janice are with Jackson.

"This is going to be the best weekend ever" she thinks to herself as she bounds out of the house to greet them. She's wearing the fragrance that smells like a bouquet of flowers she wore when she first met Jackson. He straightens his hair as she comes toward him, and they kiss.

"I'm glad you're here," she whispers, then turns and starts talking to Janice, and they head into the house.

Sandra's flower garden comes to Jackson's mind, and he can't wait to show Cap. Cap looks in amazement when he turns the corner and sees the beautiful garden. "Sandra is an interesting woman. Just like Janice. They stay busy all the time."

Cap strolls around, looking at all the different plants. With no one except Jackson around, it's the perfect time to tell him what happened at the jewelry shop.

"I took one of the stones we brought back from the old mine with me to Water Town. While we were in the jewelry store, I showed it to the owner and he was extremely interested. He asked so many questions I actually became a little uneasy and had to lie about how I got it. I told him a really nice man gave it to me. He said the stone is silver ore worth about ten copper pieces, and he offered to buy it. From the way he acted, I'm sure we can be very rich if we want to."

"I'm not sure being rich is what I really want," replies Jackson. "I think we shouldn't say anything about it until the wedding is over and we have settled into our new lives. We can get together when the time is right and discuss it with our wives."

<>

Fuzzy and Lester gather with Rah, Spar, and Auh in front of the den entrance. Preparations need to be done so the old cavern can be sealed quickly when they leave. They decide the most important thing that can be done without affecting the daily activities of the den is to search for the stones needed to fill the opening.

They go separate ways in search of suitable stones. Soon they are busy flying back and forth piling stones near the entrance.

The next day, Auh questions Lester and Fuzzy. "Why does it matter if we seal this cavern?" Rah and Spar are curious also.

"My instinct tells me we can leave an opportunity for our offspring if we leave this cavern where no one will discover it," says Lester. "Some of them may remember this place and want to return someday. The wilderness could possibly be safe again, and they will want their old home back."

Spar's face brightens. "I will be glad to do my part. I would love to see this cavern start anew with our offspring."

"We need to gather enough stones to do the job as fast as we can. The volunteers may return anytime," says Fuzzy.

All five of them work even harder.

Everyone is anxious. All day, the young dragons keep a watchful eye on the sky, hoping to see the volunteers flying toward the entrance. Every night, the adults take turns watching for campfires on the horizon, always fearing the hunters are on their way back. Waiting causes the den to grow gloomy and depressed.

Lester knows he has to say something to help his den be strong in their resolve. It's the instinct of a good leader. He talks with Fuzzy and he agrees to stand with him

"Ureeeeee," he hails. As he waits, he hopes he will find the right words. Fuzzy looks at Lester and assures him the words will come.

The den makes its way to the entrance. They stand in small family groups. Each family stays close to each other during this stressful time. The den is quiet.

"Beloved family, as I look at all of us gathered here, I am proud to be part of this den. The decision we have made to find a new cavern and start over so our offspring can prosper in peace and safety is an opportunity and an honor. I don't take the task lightly, and I'm proud of every one of you for the support you give each other in this difficult time. We are a den united in love and purpose because of the evil that has been forced upon us. We will rise to the challenge. The more we hear the stories of the wonderful past our den experienced here, the more united we will become. The new cavern will become just as dear to us and our offspring, but let us resolve that one day our offspring, if they wish, can return to a safer wilderness here at this cavern and start a new den."

"Yaheee. Yaheee. Yaheee," The den chants. The young dragons dance with pride. The adults, if only for a little while, feel more confident and glad that Lester and Fuzzy are their leaders. Lester and Fuzzy are pleased their den is excited and approve. They stretch their wings out proudly, humbly bowing in respect to the den. "Yaheee, Yaheee, Yaheee," Cheers the den. They're more united than ever in the fight that may come, and all they really care about is protecting each other. When they quiet, Fuzzy assures them that moving to the new cavern will open new possibilities. They can find a new cavern, but they can never replace the loved ones that will die trying to defend this one.

<>

Sunday morning, Cap, Janice, Jackson, and Sandra saddle horses and ride around the village and countryside. The landscape is made up of gently sloping hills with an occasional shallow stream.

"Everyone we meet seems to be so friendly," says Cap.

"This is a small village, and we all know each other. Several times a year, we help each other when someone has a big crop to harvest. It's a lot of fun because we all bring food and have a party when it's finished. Follow me," says Sandra as she turns onto a path between two fields. They ride to a rocky cliff where flowers bloom everywhere. It's a flower garden the way nature planted it.

Sandra hears the bell on her porch ring. "Mary is ready for us."

In the distance, they hear other porch bells ring as they return.

"Everyone knows the sound of their family's bell," explains Sandra.

After lunch, it's time for the visitors to head home.

On the way, they all enjoy talking, and soon they're at Janice and Cap's turnoff.

"I'm glad you rode with me," says Jackson. "Will I see you here Friday morning?"

"We will wait for you and the rest of the family. The fun can begin early for all of us," says Janice.

Once home, Jackson puts the horse away. Worn out, he heads for his room. As soon as he opens the door, reality strikes him. The room looks as if two boys live there. Cap's bed is made, and one of his favorite toys from his childhood lies on top, as if waiting for him to return. The curtain is faded. It's made of an old quilt that once was used on their beds. There's no space for Sandra's wardrobe. Jackson rubs his forehead. He has a lot of work to do before the most wonderful woman in the world moves in, and little time.

After supper the next day, he begins the transformation. The first thing he does is lovingly take down Cap's bed and store it in the barn. Inez starts making a beautiful curtain. The next day the atmosphere of the whole room changes when he hangs it. He smiles as he looks at the room cleaned up and ready.

Friday morning, Jackson wakes to a house abuzz. Inez has breakfast ready. He dresses in clothes he laid out the night before and heads for the kitchen. As he enters, his mother hugs him. The door swings open. Miles and Uncle Matt come in from feeding the cattle. They eat quickly and pack the wagon. Then everyone rushes around bathing and dressing.

They begin their journey with Uncle Matt and Jackson riding horses in front of the wagon carrying Miles and Inez. At the Brittain turnoff, Buck and Flavie are waiting with Cap and Janice on horses behind them. Everyone is glad to see each other on such a wonderful occasion.

The horses lead the way with the two wagons following behind. Janice rides between Jackson and Cap.

When they pull into Ed's yard, everyone wants to greet Jackson and tell him how lucky he is. He's not shy, but he's seeing a lot of new faces. People he has never heard of come up to inform him they have watched Sandra grow up. They complement how wonderful she is. In no time, he realizes people from her village are very fond of her.

Janice yells for Sandra, and that's the last he sees of them.

Ed and most of the men gather in the backyard where Ed is getting ready to prepare supper. He has a fire going in an outside cooker he built.

"This is a great idea," says Jackson, checking out the stove.

"I thought this was the best way I could help Mary. The kitchen is so busy. Even Fred and Ed Junior will help with the cooking out here."

Ed rings the supper bell and the women come out to eat with the men. Jackson and Sandra finally find each other. "Let's disappear for a little while," whispers Jackson, looking into the eyes of the woman he loves.

"There's nobody in the shed where the carriage is stored." She blushes.

They're careful no one sees them go inside. It's pleasant and quiet, and they are alone at last. They climb into the seat and hold each other. Laughing and talking can be heard outside, but it seems far away to them. In the dark, Sandra's fragrance smells wonderful, and after talking to strangers in the yard, he realizes what a prize she is.

"I will miss you tomorrow," says Jackson.

"Even though I doubt I will be alone for more than a minute, I will miss you, too," she replies.

They kiss and say good night. They walk back to the crowd, holding hands, and then reluctantly release their grip.

Jackson finds Fred. "I understand I'm supposed to spend the night with you."

"Yes, I told Mary I would like to have you stay with me. Granny Da reminded me every day for a week she wanted you to stay with us."

Jackson smiles as he rides to Fred's house. He has a peaceful feeling. This time tomorrow, he will be with his bride.

The wedding day arrives, and Jackson is up before the sun. He hears talking in the kitchen, so he heads that way. He's a little nervous, but the smell coming from the kitchen makes him forget he's queasy.

"Good morning," says Fred. "We will eat breakfast in a minute, and then you can have your privacy in here to bathe."

After eating, Fred prepares the bath for Jackson and shuts the door. Jackson feels uneasy undressing in an unfamiliar kitchen and quickly takes his bath, but takes his time dressing and fixing his hair. Fred smiles when he comes out all dressed up. He, Daisy, and his family climb into their wagon and head for Ed and Mary's house with Jackson on his horse beside them.

Just before what would normally be lunchtime, Ed walks up on the porch. He's dressed in his best clothing and is wearing a peaceful smile. The crowd is noisy as he reaches for the bell. He rings it two times. The crowd in the yard quiets, and everyone in the house files out.

"Friends and family, we are gathered here today to show everyone the father's agreement for the joining of these two young people, Jackson Murray and Sandra Brittain. If any member of either family has anything to say, let it be said now." He waits the customary ten seconds.

Everyone smiles when no one speaks.

"I will go to Sandra's room and escort her to the porch. Mr. Murray, please accompany Jackson to the porch."

<>

Ed walks through the house to Sandra's bedroom, remembering how his little girl had played as a child in every place he looks. As he opens the door, there before him stands a beautiful woman. Her hair looks like silk as it flows to the back of her head where it turns into a bun. The wedding dress Mary and Janice made compliments her womanhood in ways he has hardly noticed. A happy smile makes her look even more beautiful. Time has taken his little girl and replaced her with a grown woman.

Sandra lovingly looks at him. "I will always remember how much I loved being your little girl. You played rough and wrestled with my brothers, and they loved it. But when you played with me, you were always gentle and kind. You passed on the feeling of kindness and love, and I will pass it on to my children. You gave me a great gift."

Taking her arm, he escorts her to the porch, stopping near Jackson and Mr. Murray. He looks into

Miles's eyes. "It is my pleasure to give my daughter to your son, Jackson Murray," he says with a strong voice, so everyone is sure to hear, and then releases her arm.

Miles gently nods to Ed. "It is my pleasure to give my son to your daughter, Sandra Brittain."

Jackson and Sandra step closer and kiss in the presence of both families.

They feel a release of tension and worry. With that kiss, they're finally going to be together for the rest of their lives.

Jackson and Sandra disappear to Sandra's room. They hold onto each other for a few minutes and let their hearts settle into the new world they're entering.

After holding each other a moment, they kiss sweetly to begin their lives together. "Let's go see our friends and family," says Jackson.

Ed and Mary reach them first.

"We know you both will be very happy. You were made for each other. We want to give you a horse and wagon as a wedding gift."

Sandra hugs her mother as Jackson shakes Ed's hand. Ed, I will work hard every day to make you proud of us," he promises.

"If you love my daughter truly and take care of her, I will love you just as much as I love her."

Then the crowd presses in. Dressed in their finest, everyone wants to shake hands and wish them well. They can hardly speak to each other until the last well-wisher is finished.

Miles and Inez wait for them to be free. "Sandra, we are honored and proud to have you as our daughter. Our wedding present to you and Jackson is a cow, and we hope you will sell it in Water Town and use the silver to enjoy your honeymoon," says Miles. Sandra thankfully hugs him, and then Inez. "I'm honored you have allowed me to become part of your family."

They're both tired and relieved when the last guest leaves, and they stroll back to Sandra's room.

Chapter 24

Monday morning, Mason walks toward the leather shop. One concern is on his mind. He scratches his head wondering. Can a man like Virgil, who hardly works for a living, keep up with my seasoned hunters? They have experienced unbelievable hardship many times, and this hunt will test them again.

Well, he concludes. As long as he can take them to the dragons, that's all that matters. Things will just have to play out in the wilderness.

As he opens the door, Virgil stands in the sales area right in front of him. He's dressed neatly in clean, well-made clothes and his hair is combed perfectly. The shoes he's wearing are as nice as his own. "Mason, please follow me to the back where we can talk in private."

Mason glances at the shop's merchandise neatly displayed as he walks back. The leather goods are some of the best work he has seen. This is a prosperous business, he thinks to himself.

Virgil holds the stock room door for Mason then shuts it to discuss business.

"Good to see you, Virgil. I hope I have found you well today."

"I am well, thank you," replies Virgil, getting through formalities.

"All of my men are in town now and I would like for you to come to the barn tonight. It's time for us to have a meeting with them and introduce you."

"I will be there after supper," replies Virgil.

Mason starts to leave but turns. "You don't mind if they come by and get some gloves and boots to use on the hunt, do you?"

Virgil wants to say no, he pauses. "Of course not," he says, not wanting to cause trouble.

Mason tips his hat and leaves.

Virgil yearns to be excited but worries about how Mason's men might act toward him.

As he approaches the barn, he hears harsh talking from a group of unruly men. Laughter erupts and slowly dies down, followed by more talking. He stops, takes a deep breath, and opens the door. After his conversation with Mason, he figures the men will be expecting him. He walks in, trying not to look like he's lost.

The men are busy talking in little groups, telling stories everyone listening seems to be very interested in. It's obvious these men have worked together before and this is like a reunion to them.

They're dressed in a style he has never seen. Their pants are made of leather with deep pockets and loops on the sides to carry weapons. Over the front of their pants, a thicker leather cover is laced onto them, providing extra protection for their legs, but most of the men have taken them off and the tassels dangle. Their shirts are made of thinner leather, but lying next to saddlebags are thick leather vests and sleeves that can be laced onto the vests to protect their arms. These men are prepared for the going to get tough. Their clothing is designed to give them as much protection as possible from briars, limbs, and animals if they're attacked. Virgil can hardly wait to instruct his tailors at the leather shop to make him the same thing.

No one pays him much attention so he stands close to one of the groups and listens to their story. The storyteller is short and stocky, his skin is weathered, and he has a long, ugly scar on the left side of his face. As the tale spins on, he's reliving his experience, and he's close to the animal. "I leaped onto the striped cat and held on for dear life. It was a struggle for me to hold on as it ran, but I managed to grab one of his front legs, tripping him, and we rolled to the ground. I flopped on its belly before it could stand and held it down while the rest of the men ran up to help. I will never forget how the claws on that cat's rear legs were frantically digging into my side. They almost ripped my vest to pieces before someone slipped a rope over them. Then, the cat's glistening white teeth clamped onto my shoulder until another man pried them loose and wrestled a muzzle over its head, but I didn't let go until all his legs were securely tied."

One of the men listening blurts out, "That's not the way it happened! I definitely remember you running away as the rest of us held the big cat down. Lem tied his legs and mouth," he shouted loudly with a sassy sneer on his face.

The storyteller pounces on him, face red with rage, and the two men clamp onto each other. They flop around on the floor while the rest of the men laugh. Neither is able to get the best of the other, as they pull, grab, and strain. When they tire and gasp for air, and it's obvious they have had enough, the men watching pull them apart.

They lay on the floor for a few minutes. Then the intruder speaks up.

"Why did you jump me? You know I was just jerking your chain. We both almost got killed that night." The storyteller calms instantly, and they lay there laughing.

Virgil moves on and several times he tries to talk to some of the men. He begins to have a bad feeling. He's intimidated by their demeanor. None of them care if he has anything to say. He's half the size of most of them and looks like he has never worked a day in his life. He definitely isn't dressed like them.

Virgil's desire to be famous in Water Town is the only thing keeping him from running out of the barn and forgetting all about his quest to capture dragons. Their intimidation hardens his determination to eventually earn some respect from these goons.

<>

Mason is in another room and doesn't notice Virgil come in. When he sees him, he's not surprised to see the other men are too busy talking to each other to pay him much attention. Mason knows he will have to help as much as he can to give Virgil confidence in himself. He's afraid Virgil might decide not to join in this enterprise if the men don't show him respect.

Mason's voice is more than just commanding. It thunders when he's upset. "It's time for all of you to shut your mouths and listen to someone who knows what they're talking about!" His roar silences the crowd. He straightens his shirt and scans the room. "That would be me. And I'm unhappy to see you've shown no respect for my partner in this endeavor. He has faced a creature more dangerous than any of you can imagine!"

Several men look at each other and shrug. Others wonder what Mason is up to as he walks over to Virgil.

"This is my partner, Virgil. I want you to treat him with the same respect you would me. If he tells me you're giving him a hard time, I will cause you to experience anguish and a cut in pay. This is a serious adventure we're about to pursue. Quite likely, some of you, and even Virgil, might die trying to capture one of these monsters. Dragons are not dumb animals. With mouths full of long, sharp teeth, their bite is worse than anything you have ever hunted. They have longer and stronger claws than any creature you can imagine and while soaring in the clouds, they can spot you from far away. Without making a sound, they swoop down and carry you away, dangling helplessly from those claws. If impaling your body doesn't kill you, the fall will, and you will scream all the way to the ground."

The room is quiet. Mason's voice is strong and convincing. The men stand silently with a solemn look on their faces. No one moves. Every man has his eyes riveted on Mason trying to picture what they're up against.

"Virgil tells me the dragons are as big as four bears, but very agile. If none of this scares you, try to imagine a flow of liquid fire engulfing you, melting the meat off your bones."

He looks straight in the eye of every man, one at a time, making sure they get the seriousness of this trip. "I will be surprised if any of you survive this trip at all."

Some of the men look as if they're having second thoughts until one of them shouts. "These dragons are no match for the likes of us!" he cheers.

Mason smiles broadly. He had hypnotized them, and now they're coming out of it with discipline and determination. One by one, they began to cheer and reassure each other. He waits for them to calm down.

"I hoped you boys would feel that way." He looks at Virgil. "It's up to us to get these men equipped and trained well enough to survive and bring one of these magnificent creatures back. You will need to help us find any weaknesses in the equipment, taking into consideration what you experienced when you encountered the dragons."

"I will be here early every day to help, and I intend to work hard to get into shape like these men."

Mason looks around. "Come here, Cliff," he motions for a tall, strong-looking man to come to him. The man is quieter than the others. His hair and clothing look clean and neat.

"Virgil, this is Cliff, my head huntsman. He is skilled with bow, knife, rope, you name it. He can do anything. He's also the leader of these men. I suggest you become his best friend real soon."

"I will make it happen," says Virgil, surprising himself with the strength and confidence in his voice.

"Tomorrow, these men will come to your leather shop to pick up their boots and gloves for the hunt. Can you do that?"

"Yes, I can," Virgil replies.

"I suggest you stay and talk to everyone. You need to learn how they think. Your life may depend on any one of them later."

"Cliff, take this rookie hunter around and introduce him. I'm depending on you to make a man out of him and keep him alive."

Mason looks back at the group. "We leave for the wilderness in three weeks.

<>

Miles and Inez return to Ed and Mary's Monday evening with Jackson and Sandra's cow and spend the night. Early Tuesday morning, Miles ties the cow to their wagon.

It's a damp and foggy, but the newlyweds are warm inside and bright-eyed. The parents hold hands and smile as Jackson helps Sandra up to her seat. He hugs his mom and then his dad, and hops up next to her.

"Look after Homer for me," he says. Jackson flips the reins, starting their trip to Water Town.

A wonderful feeling sweeps over them, and they smile as they lean against each other, they're on their own and won't have to wonder when they will have a chance to see each other again. At this point in life, being together is the most important thing to them.

Not long after they arrive at the auction, the cow sells, and they can't wait to find the boarding house. After paying for a room, they decide to eat lunch there. In a lighthearted mood, they don't notice anyone around them until a friendly couple nearby stops to tell them how happy they look together.

"Those nice people noticed us because you're so pretty," says Jackson.

"I am sure I'm not any prettier than anyone else. I may be one of the happiest right now, though."

When they finish eating, they head toward the shops. The first place they visit is the jewelry shop. Sandra likes several things, but Jackson still has to make her let him buy her a necklace. "You are the prettiest girl in town now," he says, as they step out of the shop.

They stroll along holding hands, and only glance at most of the shops. When they come to the leather shop everyone talks about, they decide to look inside.

They enjoy looking at all the different gloves. Sandra picks out a pair to use when she works in her flower garden. Jackson decides he needs a nice belt for his dress trousers.

"I'm amazed to see how many pretty things can be made out of leather," says Sandra.

"And traded for a little silver," says Jackson.

The shop door swings open, and a noisy bunch of men barge in. The pleasant atmosphere disappears.

Jackson watches as ten very loud men act as if no one else is in the store but them. They aren't dressed like most of the people in town.

One of tallest men marches over to a clerk. The clerk looks nervous standing next to the big man.

"Go get Virgil," he says loudly.

The clerk relaxes. He's relieved this is going to be Virgil's problem and not his. He hurries through the door to the back, and Virgil comes out. Jackson recognizes him.

Virgil proceeds over to the men with a measuring ribbon and a note pad. One at a time, he makes them sit while he measures their feet. While he's trying to measure them, they continue to talk too loud and are throwing things at each other. Virgil turns red, stands up, and in a tone of voice the men never expected to hear from him, shouts. "Every one of you is going to have to shut up, stand still, and quit messing with everything!" This also surprises the other customers and clerks.

The first big man who came in looks at them sternly. He means for them to do what Virgil said, and they quiet. When Virgil finishes measuring their feet, they walk over to the gloves and pick up a couple pair each.

"Put this on Virgil's tab," says one of them to the clerk as they walk out. They all laugh.

Virgil acts as if it doesn't matter, Jackson can tell he's not happy. He glances at Jackson, but he has too many things on his mind and doesn't recognize him.

Jackson almost forgets about Sandra as he watched the interaction between Virgil and the men. He's deep in thought when Sandra bumps him.

"Why are you so interested in those men?" she asks.

"I just wonder why someone would give that much stuff to those men," he holds his chin.

Sandra doesn't mention it anymore, but Jackson is worried about Virgil, and can't get the men out of his head.

They leave the leather shop and walk around for a few more minutes. Sandra leans against Jackson while they stand on the walk, deciding which way to go. "We have seen enough of the shops today." She takes his hand. "I would like to go back to the boarding house and spend some time alone with you." She looks into his eyes with her beautiful smile. Jackson melts and all that matters is being with his bride.

The next day, the newlyweds sleep late. Jackson wakes first. He lies quietly in the dim light, watching the woman he adores sleeping beside him. As he looks around the room, he sees her pretty dress thrown across his trousers on a chair, and the sight gives him a deep peaceful feeling. He's content.

After they wake and hug a few minutes, they stroll to the dining room. People are eating and talking. Most of them are in a hurry to get somewhere. Jackson reaches over the table, and they hold hands until the waitress comes their way. They enjoy the experience of eating together, even though other people are around, they're alone.

"Breakfast was good, but not as good as your mother's cooking," says Jackson, being sure no one can hear him. "I think we should hop on our wagon and ride around the outer part of town."

Riding around is not a peaceful experience. New shops are being built everywhere. Wagons carrying wood, logs and rock bustle by. Ladders lean against buildings that are half-finished, and men are busy working all around.

"More people are earning a good living running shops and specializing in a few things instead of working to grow or make everything they need," says Jackson. "I respect all the hard work these people do, but I prefer living next to the wilderness and taking care of myself."

"It sure is a lot more beautiful and peaceful," responds Sandra. They spy a candy store, and people are in the window busily making candy. "I have to go in there," says Jackson. Inside, they're giddy. The shop has an aisle with barrels on both sides filled to the top with brightly colored candy and samples sit around in dishes for customers to try. After sampling all of them, they fill a big bag with the ones they like best.

Chapter 25

As they're leaving the candy shop, Jackson decides to stop at the leather shop on their way back to the boarding house. He needs tack for the horses and that will be one less thing he has to make when he's home. He lays the bag of candy in the wagon and wraps his arm around Sandra's waist as they head back.

Inside, the leather shop Jackson notices several very large quivers as he makes his way to the bridles. He motions for a clerk.

"What can I do for you?" asks the clerk, smiling as he makes sure Jackson sees he's wearing a pretty leather vest like the one the shop has on display in the clothing section.

"I am interested in a horse bridle, but I have a question." He points to the large quivers. "Why would anyone need a quiver that big?"

"Those belong to the shop owner's son. He and a hunting party are going north to the wilderness. They have made several powerful crossbows to hunt a large animal there. Those quivers will hold the special arrows they will need."

Jackson is stunned. He knows exactly what that means. Anxiety consumes his thoughts. He fights his emotions trying to keep his mind on buying the harnesses and bridles. He doesn't want to make Sandra curious about something that will upset her and be impossible to explain.

This is their last night in Water Town, and they plan to eat at the most popular restaurant. Once inside a waiter seats them at a table for two. Sandra wonders why Jackson isn't as talkative and carefree as he should be on a night like this.

"Are you not happy?"

"Of course, I am. I'm with you, and that joy will never end."

"I feel something is bothering you." She reaches over and rubs his hand tenderly. He sees compassion and love in her eyes.

"No. I think I just ate too much candy, that's all." He forces himself to smile. Talking to Cap as soon as possible is eating at him, and not being able to tell the woman he loves everything about his life bothers him deeply. He's anxious for things to change.

In the morning, they load their wagon and buy a calf to take home. "Maybe the calf will be big enough to sell next year on our anniversary," says Jackson happily.

Sandra tries to agree. "If I watch it grow up, I will have a hard time bringing it back to the sale barn."

They feed the calf and load it in the back of the wagon. Sandra places a mound of hay around it to make it comfortable.

Jackson's mind wanders from ecstasy to panic and back. He worries about Fuzzy and his own family if war comes between man and dragon. Torn between the happiest moment of his life and a horrific possibility, his nerves are shattered. He is only able to function because it's such a wonderful time for him and his bride.

They pull up in front of Sandra's home just in time for supper.

Ed and Mary bounce out and hug them both. They're filled with joy seeing the newlyweds are back safely.

After supper, Jackson and Sandra sit on the porch and share stories about their adventures in Water Town.

"It's a different way of life for the people who live there, and it grows bigger every time I see it," says Ed, relaxing in his porch chair. They sit and enjoy the evening together until time to retire for the night.

Ed and Mary are happy as they slip into bed because their daughter is happy and at home, even if it's for just one night.

Jackson wakes in the middle of the night in a cold sweat. No matter how hard it is, it's his duty to warn Fuzzy about the hunting party that's being organized. He and Cap will have to find a place to talk alone tomorrow. Maybe his brother will have an idea. He closes his eyes, but sleep doesn't come.

Jackson is wide awake at sunup, but he's content to watch Sandra sleep late. Hand-in-hand they walk to the kitchen for a late breakfast. "Dad, are you not feeling well today?" asks Sandra.

"I'm fine. I normally would have been at work, but," he pauses to compose himself. "I want to spend as much time as I can with you. I know when you leave this time; it might be a while until I see you again." His eyes are brimming with tears. Everyone can see the sincere expression of her father's love in those eyes. He's already thinking of reasons to visit his brother Buck so he can just happen to be close and drop in to see Sandra.

"Ed, if you don't mind, I could use your help loading some of Sandra's things onto our wagon." Jackson interrupts Ed's thoughts, and soon his happy smile returns.

"I expect to see both of you at least once a month," says Mary as she hands Sandra her special blanket. She carried it everywhere as a child. It's the last thing that can possibly be stuffed into the wagon. Sandra hugs her.

"I love you, mom. We will come back often."

It's time to leave and tears well in everyone's eyes as Sandra hugs one, then the other.

"I will always be good to Sandra. You will never have to worry about that," says Jackson, hugging Mary lovingly.

He climbs on the wagon, picks up the reins, gives them a flip, and they're on the way to their new home.

"I think we should stop at Cap and Janice's when we get to their turnoff," says Jackson.

"I think we should, too," replies Sandra.

As they trudge along with a bulging wagon load of precious cargo, they sit close, hold hands, and dream. Sandra thinks about her new home and a happy life with the man she loves. Jackson forces his worries about Fuzzy out of his mind. The end of this trip will be the beginning of real living with the woman of his dreams by his side.

Flavie is preparing lunch when the newlyweds ride up. She bounces out to greet them with hugs and a big, loving smile. "Everyone will be so glad to see you." She bolts to the porch and rings the bell. When Cap and Janice see the wagon, they run to the house. Cap claps Jackson's shoulder and shakes his hand while Janice hugs Sandra.

"Did you bring a calf home to raise?" asks Cap with a laugh.

"Yes, but Sandra's already attached to it. I may never get to take it back to the auction."

Cap smiles. "She is a very kind person. I kind of thought she would be that way."

Jackson looks around to be sure no one is listening. "We have to talk in private. Fuzzy is in danger."

Before they can find a place to talk, Flavie comes to the front door. "Lunch is ready. You boys come on in with the girls. I want to hear all about your trip."

After lunch, the brothers steal far away from the house so no one can hear them. They stop under a walnut tree and look back toward the cabin to see if anyone is watching. It's a beautiful day, but it's hard for Jackson to enjoy, and he hesitates to spoil it for his brother.

"Fuzzy is in real trouble this time. Virgil has assembled at least ten men who look like real wilderness hunters. They're rough and dressed in hunting clothes like I have never seen before. When Sandra and I were in the leather shop, they came in and he just gave them whatever they wanted. The next day, Sandra and I went back to the leather shop to buy tack for the horses. There on a shelf sat a huge quiver. I asked the clerk why anyone would need a quiver that could hold so many large arrows. He told me the shop owner's son has a hunting party going north to the wilderness, and they're building powerful crossbows to hunt a very large animal."

Cap drops his head, grits his teeth, and takes a deep breath. They both feel sick. Fuzzy's warning about angry dragons wanting revenge and red ribbons was frightening enough when it was only a possibility.

"Why did this have to happen now? The timing couldn't be worse. If only we could have been married a couple years before we had to tell Janice and Sandra about Fuzzy," moans Cap.

"Poor Sandra, what will she think about me?" sighs Jackson.

"How much time do you think we have?" asks Cap.

"A month at most, I'd guess."

Cap reaches for a limb and holds on, thinking and looking back at the house. "Let's get together Friday. We have to tell Janice and Sandra everything. I hope they love us enough to understand. I'm not sure they won't think we're crazy," says Cap. Jackson is so distressed he almost throws up. "I hope we can make the story believable. It will tear my heart out if Sandra thinks something is wrong with me."

"Bring your piece of hatching stone with you," suggests Cap.

"Now comes the hard part. We must go back and act like nothing is wrong," says Jackson, holding his stomach.

The wives are on the porch talking.

"Look, Sandra, we have found two of the most wonderful men in the whole world."

"That has to be some kind of women's intuition," says Cap.

They do their best to grin.

"I would love to stay and talk, but it's time to go home," interjects Jackson with a convincing smile. Sandra's tired and ready to go, too.

Cap suggests they come back Friday and go fishing. The ladies are all for it. Jackson is glad he won't have to hide part of his life from Sandra much longer as they aim the wagon toward their new home. The closer they are to the Murray farm, the more in love they become. Fuzzy fades from Jackson's thoughts.

Sandra lays her head on Jackson's shoulder as the house comes into view. She reaches for his hand and holds it lovingly. There's a fresh smell coming from the wilderness as a gentle breeze blows by. "I'm glad this is my new home. I love all the beauty I see in the wilderness around us. And now I have you to love," she says as she squeezes her husband's hand.

Jackson is proud and falling deeper in love with his kind and loving wife. The feeling they share in those last few minutes arriving at their new home together will live in their memories for the rest of their lives.

As they tie the horses, Inez rushes out and hugs them both. "Miles and Uncle Matt are still working. I think I will let them work a little longer. I want to cook a few more things now that you are home."

"I will be glad to help," says Sandra.

"You two go ahead and start moving into your room. I will be done soon enough," replies Inez.

Sandra's wardrobe is set where Cap's trunk had been, and a dressing table and trunk occupy the space where his bed used to be. When everything is in its place, they stop and look at their new world.

"I'm very happy right now," says Sandra.

Jackson hugs her and makes her feel good inside. She will be loved, safe, and cared for by this man.

"You can go help mom now if you like. I'm going to put up the horses and the wagon."

He's surprised to find his father and Uncle Matt built a shed on the side of the barn for his wagon. Jackson knows he has made a good decision to move in with his parents. Everyone will look out for each other.

<>

At the big barn in Water Town, Virgil has been training with Mason's men. He always comes in early, works hard, and doesn't ask anyone else to do his job. His respect among the men is growing. He has plenty of reasons to be motivated, but his biggest motivation is to show Peeler and his investors that they were wrong about him.

Cliff is busy working with a couple of the men when Virgil catches his attention and walks over. "I'm surprised and very pleased with your progress. Every day, I can tell you are getting stronger and able to work harder and longer."

"I just want to earn the respect of your men," replies Virgil.

"Some of the men are telling me you are a really good marksman." Virgil climbs on one of the crossbows and aims at a target set up for practice. The arrow streaks fiercely across the full length of the barn, slamming through at dead center. Virgil spins his seat around, looks at Cliff, and smiles. Mason walks in and is pleased to see Cliff and Virgil happily talking to each other.

"Virgil, you haven't met the most important member of our party, our cook, Ben," says Mason. Cliff smiles. He hoped Ben would go on this hunt.

"I would like to meet him this evening, if we can."

They saddle horses and ride to Ben's home. His cabin is small, but he has a big garden. There are fruit trees all around his yard and a patch of well-kept herbs grows close to the front door. Ben sees them outside and pops out to meet Mason and Virgil, inviting them in. The smell of a wonderful stew simmering on the hearth floats out the open door. Virgil takes a long sniff and closes his eyes in delight. The house is cozy with inviting chairs arranged neatly as they enter. Ben leads them straight to the kitchen. It takes up half of the house. Obviously, Ben loves to cook. The smell of the stew cooking and the lingering smell of things cooked earlier give the kitchen an atmosphere of culinary perfection. Virgil is delighted when Ben invites them to have a bowl of stew.

"Whatever you want or need to cook like this, I will do my best to get for you," says Virgil as soon as he savors the first bite. Ben smiles. He's not very tall, but he's a big man. He loves to eat. He has short curly hair, is clean shaven, and his clothing is neat and clean like his kitchen. "I can tell you and I are going to become friends," replies Ben, shaking Virgil's hand.

Mason is feeling better about Virgil going with his men on their quest for dragons. He's beginning to see real progress with the entire hunting party. There's just one more thing they need. It's time to meet with one of the best dog trainers he knows. Mason picks two men to hook horses to a wagon with a cage fastened to the floor and accompany him to the trainer's farm, a days ride south of Water Town.

As they ride up, the trainer is inside a corral made of split log rails. He has a whip, whistle, and strips of meat. A sheep dog and six sheep are inside with him. The dog is neatly groomed and is energetically running around, keeping them close together.

"Mason, I was wondering if I would ever see you again," calls out the tall, thin man. He's wearing soft leather pants and shirt with a red scarf around his neck. He hangs his whip on a hook made into his pants as the dog runs up to get its treat. He hands the dog a strip of meat and rubs his head, then walks over to Mason.

"Albert, good to see you are still hard at work. I have need of two of your best big game hunting dogs," says Mason in full business mode.

Albert's face lights up. "I have just what you're looking for. Two large but fast dogs that are accustomed to being together in cages. They pack well together." He and Mason walk past several barns with pups and half-grown dogs playing in fenced-in areas. A clean watering trough sits in each area, and a couple men are raking around one of the barns. Just past the barns, Mason can see several small sheds. They're only large enough to house two dogs each, and these buildings have a strong fenced-in area around them.

Two dark gray, short-haired dogs run over to Albert. He gives them each a strip of meat and tells them to sit. They instantly obey and look as if they await his command. They have very large heads with powerful jaws. Their eyes are almost black, and Mason can see they're studying everything around them.

"These dogs are accustomed to being around men and don't pose a threat unless you do something stupid like wear clothing that makes you look like an animal or act afraid and run from them."

"How much for these two?" asks Mason.

"Two hundred silver pieces."

"Two hundred silver pieces! Are you crazy?" replies Mason, shocked.

"Well, I have two more dogs that are older and might not bite your men if they're careful."

"If it weren't for your reputation of producing some of the fiercest hunting dogs around, I would leave right now." Mason shakes his head.

"It's really not how fierce they are, Mr. Smith, it is how obedient they are. That makes the difference."

Mason opens his money pouch and counts out one hundred and ninety silver pieces.

"Ten more," says Albert. These are the two best dogs I have.

Mason knows he must have the best dogs he can find to hunt dragons. They will be the hunting party's best defense at night in the wilderness, and the first warning they will have if dragons attack. He pulls out ten more pieces and hands them over to Albert.

"Thank you. I will teach your men the commands and help them get comfortable with the dogs tomorrow.

Chapter 26

Jackson wakes in his old room, but its different now, a hint of perfume and the woman he loves lies beside him gently snuggled to his side. It feels so right to be back working on the farm with his father. After breakfast, while he and his father are trimming fruit trees, they bump into each other. Miles hugs Jackson. It's quite a surprise. "I'm proud to have you here, working beside me now that you're married. It means a lot to your mother and even though he won't tell you, it means a lot to Uncle Matt, too."

Jackson is pleased, but he begins to worry. He and Cap must warn Fuzzy soon and he's afraid his family will lose some of their respect for him when he starts talking about dragons.

Friday after lunch, Jackson and Sandra saddle horses and head toward the Brittain farm. When they arrive, Cap and Janice are waiting on the porch with worms and fishing poles, ready to go to the creek.

A light breeze rustles the tall yellow grass growing beside the path, and grasshoppers pop up fluttering from top to top as the couples pass. Janice and Sandra are carrying picnic baskets, and they swing back and forth gently as they stroll along, talking all the way. Jackson and Cap almost stop worrying for a few moments as they listen to their wives enjoying being together. At the rock, everyone chooses an inviting spot to sit and lay out their gear. As the couples bait hooks, Cap and Jackson's distress grows stronger. Time is running out. They're sweating nervously and butterflies churn in their stomachs. If it were possible at all, they would forget about Fuzzy's problem, but they're too honorable. They can't abandon Fuzzy. He would probably die, and it's impossible to bear the thought of what will happen to the rest of the den if they do nothing.

Jackson has waited as long as his nerves will let him. He nudges Cap.

Janice and Sandra catch a glimpse and exchange blank looks.

"Tell us what's bothering you two," says Janice.

"It's a hard story to tell. And even though it's true, you will have to keep an open mind," explains Cap as Jackson nervously watches. "We love you both very much, and hope your love for us will help you understand."

Janice and Sandra forget about fishing. They lay their fishing poles down and wait to hear what kind of problem is at hand.

"When Jackson and I were young, our family journeyed into the wilderness to have a picnic and pick berries. We traveled further into the wilderness than we ever had. While our parents were busy picking berries, we wandered off while we were playing. We saw a beautiful creature and it appeared to be young like us," says Cap

"What do you mean creature?" asks Janice.

Jackson takes a deep breath. Cap's response will test their wives trust, and he fears the worst. His heart beats faster, anticipating their reaction.

"A dragon," responds Cap. He's careful to show little emotion. He doesn't want them to think he might be kidding.

The women crease their eyes in curious disbelief, but they're trying to be patient and see where this story is going.

"A dragon?" questions Sandra solemnly.

"He had an appeal I can't explain. He was friendly and interested in us. Before we knew it, he was playing with us. He would chase us, and then we would chase him. We were just three young kids having fun. We were lost in play until our mother discovered we were missing. She screamed so loudly for us, that he ran away."

"And you never told your parents?" asks Janice.

"Not exactly. We were afraid we would be in trouble, and we didn't think we would ever see him again, but he showed up at our farm a couple years later," answers Cap. "We nicknamed him Fuzzy. He was covered with dark blue fuzz except for a spot of red fuzz on top of his head. He only stayed a few minutes the first time he came to see us."

The women listen patiently. Janice has an attentive look on her face and Sandra relaxes and shuffles into a comfortable position. Cap and Jackson are too sincere to doubt, and they want to believe their husbands. Once Cap and Jackson see trust and a desire to know more in their wives' eyes, they feel less tense.

"We finally decided to take a chance and tell our family about Fuzzy, but they thought we were being silly and said not to tell anyone about seeing dragons again. We knew after that we would have to deal with our new friend all alone," says Jackson.

"How many times did he come to see you at your farm?" asks Janice.

"He came several more times, and we were worried we would get caught every time. Once, we played together for days, and after a while we realized he is as smart as us. The most amazing thing of all was that, from the beginning, we could communicate with him in a way we don't understand. When we're together, we can tell what each other is thinking. Sometimes we would forget and talk to him out loud, but he always knew what we were saying. The longest visit was in the middle of summer.

The three of us hid from our family and played for two weeks.

"Why has no one else ever seen a dragon except you?" asks Sandra.

"I guess it's because we live so close to the wilderness, and we were all children when our paths just happened to cross," responds Jackson. "We were too young to know what we were doing. We even made plans to see his cavern. He was going to fly us there. He gave us both a small piece of hatching stone to keep us safe while we were close to his den."

"Neither one of you were afraid to do such a thing?" asks Janice.

"I was, but I would have gone on anyway," says Jackson.

"It wasn't meant to happen," says Cap. "We tried to trick our father into letting us go. We asked him to let us go camping in the edge of the wilderness alone. He made it clear that we were too young."

"For some reason, Fuzzy left and never came back, and we wondered why for a long time," says Jackson.

"So, you never saw him again?" asks Sandra.

"Not until four years later when we finally talked mom and dad into letting us go into the edge of the wilderness, camping and exploring. We didn't tell them the truth. We planned to go deep into the wilderness. Far north of here, we discovered a cavern. You can only imagine how excited we were as we went inside. We hadn't been exploring long when we heard a loud noise. We ran to the entrance and were scared out of our wits to see a dark scaly dragon throwing sticks and rocks into the entrance. It only took a few minutes for him to trap us inside," says Jackson.

Sandra and Janice sit quietly with a distant look in their eyes. They're inside the cavern with the men they love.

"Frantically, we tried to dig out but we felt tired and breathless. We knew no one would ever find us, and we were out of air. We laid down and said goodbye to each other. Lying in cold damp and darkness, we cried thinking about the grief we had brought on our family. We both passed out and entered a deep troubled sleep," says Jackson.

Janice and Sandra are tense again. Tears fill their eyes and sadness creeps over them as they shudder at the thought of losing Cap and Jackson.

"Fuzzy saw what had happened and dug us out when the other dragon left us for dead. He carried our bodies into the woods where we slowly regained consciousness, and then he helped us find our way home," says Cap.

"This is the most unbelievable story I have ever heard," says Janice, slowly shaking her head.

"We were in an emotional storm. We were so thankful to him," says Jackson. "He made it clear this would have to be the last time we ever tried to see him, and we could never talk to anyone about the most exciting thing that ever happened to us. It has been hard to go this long and never talk about it. We will always owe Fuzzy for saving our lives."

Their wives slide close and hug the men, grateful they're still alive.

"Do both of you swear on our love that this is a true story?" says Janice.

"I love you more than life itself, and this is as true as my love for you," responds Cap.

Jackson looks at Sandra. "This is all absolutely true. Unfortunately, this is not the end of the story," he says without smiling.

Janice and Sandra are consumed with worry. It didn't take intuition to know the worst part of this story lies ahead. Fear returns to their eyes.

"There's trouble brewing for Fuzzy and his den. Not long after Virgil passed by, headed for the wilderness, Fuzzy surprised me at the farm. He needed to talk to us. His den had just gone through a deadly encounter with Virgil's hunting party," says Jackson.

"So, you talked to Fuzzy not long ago," says Sandra.

"Yes. He needed to be reassured we had nothing to do with any of the hunting parties. He could tell we have been true to our word before he heard our answer. We began talking like old friends, and in our conversation he discovered some of the hunters may be on their way back to Water Town.

"It wasn't until mom and dad happened to see Virgil in Water Town that we realized he had returned from the wilderness," says Cap.

Jackson looks at Sandra. "Do you remember the rough-looking men in the leather shop who came in and were unruly?" She looks at Janice and nods, assuring her what he says is true.

"That's the hunting party. I returned the next day and learned they have built special weapons to shoot dragons. Cap and I love you and Janice more than life itself, and it will be harder for us to leave and spend a short time in the wilderness than ever before, but we must go warn Fuzzy. He needs our help, and we need his. In our conversation with him, he mentioned something we had never thought about. If men harm or kill some of his family, several dragons could turn vengeful and cause even greater sorrow to our family. He assured us he would protect our family from angry dragons seeking revenge, and we promised him we would do all we could to protect his den. He returned and told his den we will be wearing red ribbons around our arms if we come to warn them. Do you have anything we can use?"

"Yes. I have an old red dress," replies Janice.

"I can understand how you became friends with this dragon but I can't understand why your friendship is worth dying for. Are you sure warning him will really make a difference?" asks Sandra.

"We have no choice. Our debt to Fuzzy must be paid, and we need his help protecting both of you and our family. The sooner we warn him, the sooner we can get on with our lives," says Cap.

"You are too kind and dependable, and that's one of the reasons I love you so much," says Janice.

Sandra cries and holds Jackson's hand. She stands, trembling and hugs him.

Cap and Jackson wipe tears from their eyes. They are deeply troubled because they don't know how to explain all this to Buck. There's no way they could ever make him understand. It would be best to let their wives tell the Brittain's they had to go into the wilderness for a few days and they will explain why later.

Cap hands Janice his piece of hatching stone. "This is the stone Fuzzy gave me. Put it in the sun during the day, and at night it will keep you warm until I return. Please be patient with us. We'll only be gone four or five days. We love both of you dearly."

Janice quickly runs to the house and returns with several pieces of red cloth. Cap and Jackson kiss their new brides goodbye.

Cap and Jackson trot toward their parents' house. Sandra stays with Janice and tells Buck and Flavie their husbands have to go into the wilderness for several days.

"It seems strange they didn't stop to say goodbye," says Buck, he shakes his head, and goes back to his shop.

Sandra and Janice cry all night. Seeing and hearing their precious girls suffer breaks Buck and Flavie's heart.

When Cap and Jackson reach their house, they see Miles and Inez sitting on the porch.

"Cap, I'm surprised to see you instead of Sandra with your brother," says Miles.

"Jackson and I have to go to the wilderness for a few days," replies Cap.

"I can't imagine why?" says Miles, curiously expecting an answer.

"Dad, in a few days we will explain everything, I promise," says Jackson. Inez starts to speak, but Jackson cuts her off. "We can't explain it right now. Please, pack us some food while we get the rest of what we will need. We have to leave first thing in the morning."

All night, Cap and Jackson suffer as memories of almost dying in the wilderness haunt them, and when they shut their eyes, visions of the cold dark cavern and how hopeless they felt are too real. But the hardest part of the ordeal is the heartache they endure knowing they have given their new brides a reason to worry.

They lay in Jackson's bed, looking at the ceiling. It's uncomfortable, and it feels strange for them to be in the same bed. They're both too full of worried energy.

Cap and Jackson rise before the sun. Every candle in the room is burning as they pack their saddlebags. They're tired from lack of sleep and are trying to be as quiet as possible. Then they hear Inez building a fire in the kitchen. Miles steps into their room.

"I know you aren't going to tell me anything, but I can't imagine a situation you couldn't explain to me and your mother. You owe us at least enough to make us feel a little better about what you're up to."

"Dad, I'm sorry. We just can't get into it right now," says Cap, hoping Miles won't continue to pursue an answer.

Miles's face turns red. "You boys have responsibilities now. You can't just run off and do anything you want to. There are two women at the Brittains' who are probably worried sick wondering what this is all about."

"You'll understand soon and I think you will be proud of us," states Cap.

Chapter 27

"If I could stop worrying about Sandra, I would enjoy being on an adventure again," says Jackson as the horses trot along. The smell of the wilderness fills the breeze as it gently puffs by. Jackson closes his eyes and takes a deep breath. The essence is refreshing.

Cap looks at him. "You need to stop worrying and daydreaming. We must be mindful of the respect the wilderness will demand of us. This trip is dangerous"

"Surely this trip will go a lot faster than last time, and we will see Fuzzy before long," says Jackson.

"I hope so, but if we stay focused, we will get done quicker. Worrying about what our wives think can only be fixed by us getting home safe and soon."

Cap smiles and points toward limbs and saplings lying on the ground. Their brown crunchy dry leaves mark where Virgil and his hunters cut a path through the underbrush.

"What a pleasant surprise. I think we'll be able to travel far enough into the wilderness by sunset to try building a big fire for Fuzzy to see," suggests Jackson.

"Tonight will be as good a time as any to give it a try," replies Cap.

Luckily, they stumble on a good place to spend the night before the sun sets. It's a perfect campsite with a jagged rock cliff 20 feet tall protecting them from behind, and a large boulder sheltering them on their right. They have plenty of time to gather enough wood to last through the night. They want Fuzzy to recognize this is more than just a campfire. They take pleasure in knowing they will have a warm fire to sit beside as they wait. Shortly before the sun disappears, the fire is burning and the brothers relax as best they can. All they can do now is wait to see if

Fuzzy will show up. Occasionally, they check their ribbons to be sure they're ready. After half of the night passes uneventful, they're disappointed. They're tired, but to be cautious, they decide to take turns keeping watch. They will try again tomorrow night. As light begins to fill the forest, Jackson rekindles the fire by throwing several short pieces of wood into the center were coals are still hot, and soon they burst into flames. They enjoy the warmth and a hot cup of root tea with their breakfast.

"I'm a little surprised Fuzzy didn't show up," says Jackson.

"He should have noticed our fire, but I will only be concerned if he doesn't pay us a visit tonight. We will be a lot closer to the plateau when we try again."

Before nightfall, a knoll covered with large rocks comes into view. They decide to veer from the trail and build the fire on top of it in an open area surrounded by large rocks. There's room to camp and build their fire. It's exactly what they're looking for. After gathering plenty of wood, they work until flames are leaping into the air, then they settle in for the evening.

There's plenty of light between the rocks close to the fire but just beyond them it's dark in the forest. The fire pulses and flickers, making the brothers' shadows dance across the surrounding rocks. Quietly waiting, they hear a tree limb snap and several frightened birds flutter into the dark. They look at each other and listen intently. The sound of dry leaves crunching grows louder as something heads toward them. A cold chill sweeps over them, making the hair on their arms stand up, even with the fire blazing.

"I think my heart is going to burst out of my chest," whispers Jackson, rising to cautiously peer in the direction of the sound.

"Check your ribbons," says Cap in a strong nervous voice.

They glance at each other. Whatever is moving around in the dark is very close now. Sweat and beating hearts tax their bodies, but they grit their teeth, fight their fear, and try to stay calm.

"How fast can you grab your bow," asks Jackson, standing very close to Cap.

"If it's something other than Fuzzy, I think I can get a shot off. I would go ahead and set an arrow, but I'm not sure I want to be holding an arrow pointed toward a dragon while it's trying to decide if we're on his side," replies Cap.

The creature is a few feet away. They hold their breath as tree limbs not twenty feet away push out of the darkness toward them. Lester pushes through first. Cap starts toward his bow. "Stop! It's Fuzzy," yells Jackson. Fuzzy is right behind Lester, and Jackson grabs Cap's hand.

Fuzzy immediately speaks to Lester. "These men are no threat. They are my friends."

<>

Janice and Sandra try to stay busy at the Murray farm. They decide to make a quilt for Janice and Cap. Buck fastens hooks to the ceiling of Janice and Cap's room so they can hang the quilting frame. Once the frame is hung, there's barely enough room for the cousins to use the bed. With nervous energy, they sew most of the time, but fingers get tired after a while.

"I can hardly bear to stop working. I start worrying about Jackson every time I rest," says Sandra. She hasn't slept well.

"My biggest problem, until last night, was trying to believe the story our husbands told us. Cap gave me what he called a dragon hatching stone the dragon gave him. I laid it where the sun would shine on it all day like he told me to, and last night it stayed warm in bed next to me almost all night. I was amazed," says Janice

"I have Jackson's hatching stone, too. Why didn't you tell me until now?" asks Sandra.

"Truth is, I thought it might worry you more."

"Their story was hard to grasp, but I wanted to believe it. I have felt something honest and dependable about the Murray boys from the moment I met them," says Sandra.

"I wish we could help my parents understand what's going on. It worries me knowing how they must feel, and there's no way I could ever explain this to them," says Janice.

"Don't you dare tell the story. It wouldn't matter how hard you try, no one will understand why the boys are doing this. If Jackson hadn't been the one who told me about dragons, I wouldn't have believed it either."

"At least we have each other. We have to stay together until this is over," says Janice.

"I have faith that every passing day brings our husbands closer to being with us again," says Sandra.

<>

The fire burns brightly. Lester and the brothers study every detail about each other. Lester is the same height as Fuzzy, but he's covered with dark blue scales that shine in the firelight. Lester looks at the men and senses their uneasiness. "Can you understand my thoughts?"

"Yes," replies Cap, looking over at Jackson.

"I can, too," responds Jackson, feeling better.

Lester is pleased. "I wouldn't have thought we could communicate so easily with humans."

"This is not the first time these men have talked to dragons. They grew up talking with me. I think their good nature helps, too."

"Why would you risk your lives coming out here like this?" asks Lester.

"We have no choice. Fuzzy has been our friend for a long time, and we owe him our lives. We have come to warn you," says Cap.

Lester senses their sincerity and bows with respect.

"We have discovered a man in Water Town who has put together a well-equipped hunting party. He has assembled at least ten experienced and trained hunters, and they're coming to find your den," says Cap.

Lester feels the sorrow in his thoughts. "How long do we have?"

"Not long. They could be on their way now."

Lester looks at Fuzzy, and the brothers feel the sadness in their thoughts. They quietly ponder what they heard, and then turn back to Cap and Jackson.

"We need to take you to our den so you can tell everyone what you have told us and meet our family. You are our friends and we don't even know you. It's important the other dragons have the chance to see that some men are good. Soon, they will see men trying to harm us, and they need to know all men are not bad," states Lester.

"We also want them to see what you look like. It's important to us to keep you safe. Neither you nor any of your family must ever be harmed by our den," says Fuzzy.

Lester squats as low as he can. "Get on my back near my neck," he says as Fuzzy squats for Jackson."

The brothers feel a tingle of fear. Holding on to a flying dragon is going to be dangerous and exciting beyond words.

"You won't fall off," says Lester feeling the men's fear of heights.

The brothers hesitate.

"You will be okay and we will bring you back here in a couple of hours," encourages Fuzzy.

Cap climbs on Lester and discovers he can hold on with his legs. Jackson hops onto Fuzzy. Lester vigorously flaps his wings and air gushes back onto Fuzzy and Jackson. As Lester picks up speed, air blows Cap's hair and makes him squint to see. His heart and mind are stimulated with a rush of excitement more intense than he could ever have imagined. He senses the power of the dragon beneath him as Lester gently flaps his wings. When the wings pull up, Cap feels Lester's body drop slightly. As they push down, he's pressed into the dragons back, and it feels solid as a rock. Then Fuzzy takes off. Jackson is so excited; he loses all fear of height and worry about holding on. He just wants to fly as long as he can.

They realize this is an honor the dragons have bestowed on them, and it makes the trip worth the danger. Even with all the euphoria they're experiencing, they still are mindful of their wives at home, worrying.

In minutes, they're circling over the cavern entrance. The experience becomes even more exciting when the dragons lean to the inside of their spin as they descend. Cap and Jackson are being pushed into the dragons' backs, taking away any fear of falling off. The landing is as exciting as the takeoff, except for their ears popping several times.

They're catching their breath when Lester startles them by turning toward the cavern entrance and bellowing, "Ureeeeee." The sound echoes loudly from the depths of the cavern.

They're a little shaky and their world is still spinning. Slowly it stops, and they look around. They can barely see as the other dragons appear from the cavern to hear what Lester and Fuzzy have to say. The men stand close to each other. It's noisy and intimidating as the large dragons move around on the stone floor, trying to get a good look at them. Cap and Jackson squint trying to see. The dragons are so close they can smell fish on their breath. Fuzzy realizes the brothers are uneasy, and remembers they can't see in the dark as well as dragons.

"I'm sorry. I know you feel uncomfortable being surrounded by my den while being unable to see what is happening."

He asks several dragons to gather dry wood for a fire and place it in a pile where they're gathered. Soon, it's ready to light, and Fuzzy spews a tiny stream of fire, igniting it.

"Thank you, Fuzzy," says Jackson, looking around at all the dragons. In the dim light, their bronze-colored eyes glow.

The fire grows fast and its light flickers and bounces off the cavern walls. Cap and Jackson feel better. They study the den. It's made up mostly of young and old dragons. Only a few of them appear to be in their prime and capable of fighting. The little ones stay close to their parents, but they're curious.

Lester steps beside the men. "Every one of you must take a good look at these men. Fuzzy has known them since he was young, and they have risked their lives to warn us of approaching danger. They can be trusted because they are our friends."

Lester steps aside to let Fuzzy continue. "These are good men, and I have promised them no one in my den will ever hurt them or their family. You must honor my word and protect them with your life. They have proven themselves worthy by coming here tonight."

The den, from the youngest to the oldest, relaxes their demeanor, and a look of acceptance appears on their faces. They sense and understand these men have kind hearts.

The brothers are humbled when the entire den bows in respect to them. Fuzzy places one wing on Cap and Lester places one wing on Jackson. The den then circles and touches wings signifying unity with the men.

Cap and Jackson are deeply touched they have been accepted into the den. The act makes them feel even more responsible for the safety of this dragon family. They feel the bond growing with the dragons deep within their hearts.

Cap feels very emotional. He raises his hand, requesting to speak to them. "My brother and I will defend and help you any way we can. We do not approve of what these hunting parties are trying to do. We believe the world would be a better place if men and dragons would respect each other. My brother and I have deep respect for you and are honored you have accepted us."

The dragons pull their wings back when he finishes speaking and wait to hear from Lester or Fuzzy.

"We don't have much time until we will start seeing the hunting party's fires getting close. Cap and Jackson have told me this hunting party is much better prepared than the last and could be deadly. They have built special weapons to hunt us down, and as you know, this couldn't come at a worse time. Until our volunteers return, our defense will be weak. I hope Cap and Jackson will join us so we can think like men but fight like dragons," says Fuzzy.

Lester steps forward. It's time to end the meeting. "We are thankful for what Cap and Jackson have done for us. For now, Fuzzy and I must take them back to their horses."

The den can be heard talking amongst themselves as they head back into the cavern. They're impressed these men are brave and kind enough to risk their lives for them.

Cap and Jackson follow Lester and Fuzzy as they walk away from the fire. Lester explains that four of their strongest dragons are preparing a new cavern for the den and will not be back until it's finished. The den has no idea how long they will be gone, but there's a good chance they won't be back in time to help fight.

"Jackson and I will help you however we can, but we cannot kill other men. We know men will die, and we will understand when there is no other choice. I think we can live with that. We just can't kill a man or a dragon," says Cap.

"I know. That's part of being a good man, and I respect both of you," says Fuzzy.

"How many fighting dragons do you have?" asks Jackson.

"Six, but one of them will never leave the den entrance, so only five are left to do battle. There are fifteen old, young, and female who will not fight unless the situation becomes hopeless," replies Fuzzy.

All the events of the last two hours have made Cap emotionally endeared to Fuzzy's den.

"We will be here with you when the battle starts. We will bring our bows and help protect the entrance. We will have to do what we have to do to protect the old and the young."

Lester stands still and looks at the brothers. He opens his wings and bows to them. He's so touched to hear them promise to help his den. Folding his wings, he looks sincerely at them. "It's time for us to fly you back to your horses. If need arises, you can rest assured we will protect your family just as you have agreed to protect ours." Cap and Jackson feel contentment as they climb on their friend's backs.

"You're in luck; the moon is high and bright tonight. You will be able to see the countryside from high above the wilderness," says Lester

The brothers feel much more confident in dragon flight. They're looking forward to the excitement of flying back to their horses. As they lift into the sky again, their senses are more receptive to all the new feelings they're experiencing. The night is warm and the air rushing past their faces is refreshing. The flight will be short so they try to see as much as they can.

"I could get used to this!" yells Jackson, looking at Cap.

Cap smiles and opens his mouth. The rushing air pushes a breath of fresh air into his lungs, and he smiles.

There's enough light for them to see hills and valleys and silhouettes of mountains far away, fading into darkness.

"Look at the creeks and lakes," yells Jackson. The moonlight dances across every ripple, making them look like they're covered with twinkling stars.

Fuzzy and Lester take their time. They're pleased the men are happy for a little while. The dragons circle again and land next to where the campfire had been. The horses are spooked badly, but when Cap and Jackson call out to them, they calm down.

"Thank you for that amazing ride. It's something we will always remember," says Cap, feeling anguish.

"What is bothering you, Cap?" asks Fuzzy, feeling he wants to ask something.

"We need your help before we can come back and help you."

"Of course, I will do everything I can."

"Jackson and I have mates now, and they are understanding women. But they cannot picture what we have tried to tell them about you being our friend. I'm afraid to ask but, respectfully, would you come to our farm? It would be so much easier for our families to let us help you if they can see what wonderful creatures you are. I'm sure they will be true to their word and promise never to tell anyone about you."

Fuzzy feels hesitance in Lester's thoughts.

"Lester, I know a little about their family, and they love each other much like the members of our den love each other. They need to know we will take care of Cap and Jackson.

Lester grimaces. "If I didn't know from past experience, I would say you're too kind, but hidden in your request I'm sure is wisdom, as usual. I just hesitate to let any more people see us."

"I understand, but we will all be gone soon. It can't do any harm now. We owe this much to their families.

Lester thinks silently for a minute. "You're right. It will be hard for their family to let them leave to fight with us."

Lester's statement thrusts the men into reality. They have been so caught up in the moment they haven't seriously thought about how much their family will worry when they leave again. Deep down inside, they're sure the dragons will be able to keep them safe.

"Give us three days to travel home. On the evening of the third day, we will build a large fire at the farm. One of you needs to come and show our family what we are fighting for," says Cap.

"Fuzzy and I both will come. Be sure there's no one other than your close family there," says Lester.

The brothers agree and bow in respect.

<>

In Water Town, Mason and Virgil meet at the barn. They're pleased as they look at a very large cage built in the barn to hold the dragons when they are brought back. Practicing on the crossbows and using the shields has been completed, and all the men, especially Virgil, have mastered the art of shooting the large crossbows. Every man knows his job once they reach the wilderness, and all the food they need is loaded.

The men had been promised a week off before leaving if they worked hard, and Mason is satisfied they have earned it.

Virgil is so confident he can already feel the excitement he will experience when he returns with the first dragon men have ever seen. His mom and dad will be proud of him. He's always been the adventurous one in their family.

Mason puts his arm on Cliff's shoulder and guides him to his office in the barn.

"When our men return next week, make them rest for a couple days. We don't want any drunks or worn out men starting this trip. This will be the most dangerous and important hunt we have ever taken. I'm counting on you to get the job done without half of them being killed. Just put up with Virgil and let him have his moment of fame.

We will make our money on the shows to come, and I will take care of you when the silver starts pouring in.

Chapter 28

Jackson and Cap ride home, carrying a heavy burden. They can't possibly explain what lies ahead to their parents.

"This is going to be a trying time for us. Everyone is already upset and thinks we're crazy," says Cap.

"It's probably a good thing we won't have much time to tell them what to expect," replies Jackson, thinking there's no part of their story their parents could believe. "We will have to suffer through lots of scolding, questions, and disbelief while we gather fire wood."

"I can see it now. They will think we are absolutely crazy as we pile it higher and higher," adds Cap.

"My biggest concern is Uncle Matt. Even though he is a man of his word, I'm afraid he will get too excited and tell someone in Blade Town about the dragons. Do you think we can trust him to keep this to himself?" says Jackson.

"Uncle Matt already believes in dragons. He may be the least excited one when he sees them. We only have to look him in the eye and make him promise us he won't tell anyone.

The first night on their journey home, they're exhausted. They build a quick shelter out of dead logs by leaning them against a bolder. Then, before crawling in, they throw a tarp over the top, making it warm and dry.

The second night, knowing their journey is almost over; their thoughts are about home and their wives.

"I miss Sandra more now than any time since we left," says Jackson.

"I miss Janice, too. I hope she will understand we're obligated to keep our promise to Fuzzy and his den."

They sleep hard and rise early. It's going to be a trying day. The sun is barely above the horizon as they mount their horses to finish their trip. When the farm comes into sight, anxiety grows, and their stomachs feel as if they're tied in knots. Things have to happen fast, so the fire will be built before sunset. They'll still have time to explain to everyone what is going to happen. There's nothing they can say to prepare the family they love that will lessen the shock they will experience when Lester and Fuzzy land. It will be chaotic for a few minutes.

The day is half over by the time they ride up to the house. The first thing they do is go inside and hug their mom.

"I'm almost too mad to hug you, but I can't help myself," she says as she hugs them like she will never let go.

"You are grown men now, and you have responsibilities. Your wives have cried for almost a week. Buck and Flavie are mad. They're trying not to say anything about Cap in front of Janice, and you both have a lot of explaining to do to all of us. I just hope your father doesn't try to discipline you like he did when you were young." The tone of her voice is scolding, and she doesn't have a pleasant smile. "Mom, please stop. Jackson and I have a lot to do before sundown. This ordeal is not over, and we absolutely have to gather wood and build a large fire burning before dark. Please be patient with us until the sun goes down. Then you will understand everything and forgive us. I promise," explains Cap.

"Jackson, go ring the porch bell," says Cap. "Mom, talk to dad and Uncle Matt when they arrive. Try to calm them down as much as you can. If you ever loved us, trust us now. We need your help."

Inez shakes her head and hugs them again, she's trying to understand. She regains her motherly look and attempts to be patient. "You just don't know how worried we are," she says softly.

The bell rings on the porch and Jackson returns.

Inez meets Miles and Uncle Matt on the porch and tries to calm them. The boys can hear their father talking angrily, and it's obvious by the tone of his voice that things aren't all right.

Miles is too mad to listen to Inez. Cap will have to try to end their hostility as fast as possible. He's able to muster up a confident look and walks out the door, not looking guilty about anything. Jackson is behind him, trying to be strong, too.

"Give us the benefit of the doubt for a few hours, and you will understand what's going on," says Cap.

"You better start explaining right now, mister! I'm ashamed to look Buck in the face."

"Janice and Sandra know what's going on, but we have sworn them to secrecy. Give us enough respect to wait until sunset, and then you will have no more questions. You will understand," pleads Cap.

"I hope understanding means a little more help around here. Your dad and I have done all the work for months, covering for you boys," says Uncle Matt, so irritated he can't stand still.

"Time will fix all of that. We realize how much both of you have had to do," says Jackson.

"We will make it all up to you, but right now Jackson and I must get ready for sunset. Mom, will you fix supper a little early tonight? We're starved."

"Yes, but if this thing is not resolved tonight, I will be ashamed of how you two have treated your new wives." Cap and Jackson hang their heads but rush toward the barn.

"I hope with all my heart that after tonight everything we have put our loved ones through will be made right, and they will forgive us." Jackson sighs.

Sadly, they know too well the real danger and even stronger worries are still to come.

They hitch the horses to the wagon so they can load a lot of wood. The fire needs to be really big and bright. It's important for Fuzzy to see the fire and know the brothers are home and ready for them. They work hard, and an hour before sunset the pile of wood is ready to light. Jackson is on his way to lock Homer in the barn when he notices Miles and Uncle Matt looking at them from a distance and talking. He shakes his head. *"At least it won't be long now until they forgive us,"* he thinks.

He returns to the fire, and stands next to Cap. Then the bell rings on the porch.

"I thought supper was never going to come," says Jackson.

Supper is the best ever, even though there's almost no conversation. "Thank you, mom," says Jackson as he gives her a hug. "How much longer can you boys wait to go see your brides?" she asks.

"We're going to see them tonight for sure," replies Jackson. Inez knows it's too late to start on the trail and shakes her head. Miles and Uncle Matt say nothing. They decided earlier to leave the brothers alone until nightfall, like they had requested.

"It's about time to light the fire. Come with us, and when the fire is burning, we will tell you what to expect," says Cap.

Cap and Jackson look at the sun as they lead the way to the pile of wood. The time they have anticipated is here. Jackson lights a mound of small twigs at the base of the pile. The fire quickly climbs to the top and leaps into the sky. The brothers look at each other and smile, the brighter the fire is when the dragons arrive, the better everyone can see their magnificent friend.

"It would be best if you tell the story," says Jackson.

"Everyone, please listen and be open-minded about what I say. Try to let me finish before you start asking questions or disagree." He looks at Jackson for support and takes a deep breath.

"When Jackson and I were children, we became friends with a young dragon. We tried to tell you, but we were so young you never took us seriously. We have played and visited with each other several times over the years, right here at the farm. Tonight, you're going to meet him and the leader of his den,"

Miles's face turns red. In disgust and he starts to walk away. He takes two steps and turns gritting his teeth. "I can't believe you would tell such a stupid story at a time like this. Surely you realize I don't believe one word of it, and it only fills me with more anger. I promised your mother I wouldn't get mad, so I am trying really hard to keep my word."

Inez looks at Miles with a determined face. She glares at him for a second. "Calm down, Miles! If this story isn't true, these boys have gone to a lot of trouble to be proven wrong. I don't think they could tell such an outlandish lie at a time like this. I will give them the benefit of the doubt for now."

Uncle Matt feels he should share his thoughts since everyone else has. "I have done a lot of kidding about dragons as the boys grew up, if one comes here tonight, I will be excited and terrified."

"That's the reason we're telling you now about our friend and what is about to happen. When you see them coming, please don't be afraid and run. They will not harm us, so be as calm as you can when they land. These dragons are just as smart and sensitive as you and me," says Cap.

"If things go like they always have, we will be able to understand what they're thinking well enough to talk to them," says Jackson, trying to help the family believe Cap.

Miles is growing restless and has a look of disgust on his face. "You two have always been so sensible. How can you come up with such nonsense now? Dragons that speak our language! I'm not sure I'm going to sit here and let you make a fool out of us any longer."

"Just sit still and don't say anything else until they get here. It won't be long now. This will be the most exciting day of your life in just a few minutes," says Cap.

"After you see the dragons, and understand what's going on, you will be completely satisfied," says Jackson.

The sun begins to set and there's a light glow remaining in the west. Everyone is looking at the sky. Before long two objects can be seen flying toward the farm. At first, they appear to be birds, but as they come closer, everyone can see they are large creatures. Fear fills Miles, Uncle Matt, and Inez. They can't take their eyes off them. Half-squinting and with wrinkled worried brows, they stare and are quiet.

Trying to give them confidence, Cap speaks in the calmest voice he can muster. "Don't worry. These dragons are our friends. When Fuzzy first saw you at our farm long ago, he was afraid of all of you."

Jackson hears Homer barking in the barn. He knows something is happening.

Lester and Fuzzy land gently in the grassy field and lower their wings. They walk with determined steps toward the fire, stopping near the speechless family. Their bronze eyes glow and flicker in the firelight and their horns look ominous silhouetted against the last red glow in the sky. Inez moves over and leans against Miles, and he places his arm around her. Uncle Matt has his mouth open in awe.

Cap and Jackson turn toward the dragons and bow in respect.

"Thank you for coming, old friend. We needed our family to see you more than you can imagine," says Cap. Everyone watches and breathes a sigh of relief when the dragons bow in return.

Cap and Jackson move aside so the dragons can have a good look at their family. The fire burns brightly, and they can see them well. The dragons bow in respect.

The Murrays, with wide eyes, bow as Cap and Jackson had done. Cap introduces his family to them.

Fuzzy speaks, and everyone is astonished. "This is Lester, our leader, and I am Fuzzy. I have been to your farm many times and have grown to respect your sons as much as any dragon."

Inez wants to show hospitality, but is at a loss to know what to do. She is so excited, she speaks with a higher pitch than usual. "I can understand what you're thinking, and you are a noble creature worthy of our respect."

Lester's heart is touched, and he's glad he agreed to meet this family. He knows Fuzzy made a wise decision, and this is the right thing to do.

"I like these people, and I trust them. How can it be some humans are so much different than others? If only all humans were like these good people, we wouldn't be hunting another cavern."

Uncle Matt beams. "I have always wanted to believe in dragons, but I never dreamed you could be so intelligent."

"Most dragons are kind-natured, but as you can understand, some of us are not," replies Lester. Neither dragons nor men can ever make all their kind be good creatures. One bad man or dragon can ruin wonderful possibilities for both man and dragon.

Miles has a smile on his face for the first time in days. There's a look of amazement and respect for the dragons on his face, and he marvels at their stature. "I'm honored you have come to meet us and proud of my sons for becoming your friends. I'm beginning to understand lots of things that happened in the past that I couldn't figure out at the time. I now know my young boys really did see a dragon with red fuzz on his head, and blue fuzz covering the rest of his body."

Fuzzy smiles. "Lester, let's take these nice people for a ride. Cap and Jackson seemed to enjoy flying so much the other day, and I feel their family will trust us even more after the experience."

Inez bows to the dragons. "I'm too old for that, but grateful to you for offering. Let the men go if they wish."

Miles and Uncle Matt look at each other. "We're too old," says Miles, "but if I don't go, I will regret it the rest of my life."

Cap and Jackson smile. They know after the ride of a lifetime they will never have to worry about dragon talk ever again. They walk over, hand them each a safety rope they made, and help them up. "Place the rope under the dragon's neck, then slip each hand through a loop and hold on. If you fall off, the rope will spin around on the dragon's neck, and you will be dangling below. Just hold on until he lands.

The dragons lift off more gently than they did with the brothers. They sail smoothly in the twilight making a big circle so Miles and Uncle Matt can see the farm in a way they could never have imagined. Miles and Uncle Matt are so excited, they yell to each other as they ride. They have never been so excited in their lives. Fuzzy and Lester coast back to the fire and land so gently the men are surprised it's over.

Uncle Matt and Miles are speechless and grateful. They know they have experienced something almost no man will ever be able to do. The only thing they can think to do is bow humbly with thanks and respect.

Cap looks at his family. "I know you have a lot of questions, but time is short. Fuzzy and Lester have to fly us to the Brittains so we can explain everything to them. Now you have the burden Jackson and I have had since we were children. You can never tell anyone about the most exciting thing that ever happened to you in your whole life."

"Don't worry, you'll get used to it in a couple days," says Jackson.

Cap and Jackson hug their family.

"I will return with Sandra. There's a lot more to explain, and I will talk to all of you in the morning. Cap will stay with Janice," says Jackson.

Grabbing the two safety ropes so the Brittains can ride, Cap climbs onto Fuzzy, and Jackson makes himself comfortable on Lester. The dragons take off and disappear into the darkness.

The flight is short and the dragons land far from the house so no one will hear them. The landing is scary to

Cap and Jackson. They can hardly see. The dragons are accustomed to landing in the dark and land safely.

The men are shaky and nervous as they slide off their backs.

"Please wait here. We will return in a few minutes," says Cap.

They trudge toward the house. There's going to be a lot of emotion released when they reach the door. They worry about the moment Buck and Flavie see them. They will be angry. It's dark, and they're in a hurry to see their wives. They suffer as they pull and trip over briars. Ahead, candles are burning inside the porch window. At least they can tell which way to go as they stumble along. Cap and Jackson are so excited by the time they reach the steps that they're shaking. They step up on the porch and walk quickly to the door. As Cap knocks, he calls out loudly. "It's Cap and Jackson."

Their wives scramble to the door, fling it open, and run out to hug their husbands. There's kissing, crying, and tears of joy. Except for Buck. He has a mean, piercing look on his face and only good answers will satisfy him. He doesn't speak. He will wait his turn. Flavie doesn't care. She's glad to see her daughter happy again.

Buck decides he has given them enough time. "Boys, I need to talk to you outside right now," he demands.

"Before we talk to you, all we need is ten minutes to show everyone the answer to all your questions. Please, trust us," says Cap confidently.

"Father, give them ten minutes before you get mad. I think I know what they have to show us," says Janice.

"I can wait ten minutes," he replies.

"Jackson and I would never do anything to hurt any of you so try your best not be afraid of what we're going to show you," says Cap.

"Light us all a candle so we can see to walk in the field," says Jackson.

As they start out the door, Jackson can't wait any longer. He wants to be forgiven and return to his happy life.

"Cap and I rode here on the backs of the dragons we told you about. It was incredible," he says to Sandra.

When Buck hears the word *dragons,* he shakes his head and creases his eyes, sulking. Cap is hurt deeply, and wishes Jackson had waited just five more minutes.

Buck is stewing. He takes Flavie's hand. "How can these boys even say such a crazy thing as much trouble as they're already in." He stays in the back, but Cap hears every word. "I can't believe we're letting these two take us out into the field to see something that doesn't exist." Flavie turns and quietly shushes him.

As they move further into the field, they begin to see four small bright spots reflecting candle light. The reflections look like deer eyes, but they're too high off the ground. Slowly, the candles cast light onto the dragons' bodies.

Buck, Flavie, and even the wives gasp at the sight. They stop in their tracks. Buck and Flavie back up slightly. Cap holds Janice's hand tightly and Jackson pulls Sandra close to his side. "Everything is okay, you're in no danger. Be calm and bow in respect when we get close. It's customary. Then, they will bow in respect to you," says Cap.

The Brittains bow in front of the dragons. It's hard for Buck to take his eyes off them for even a second as he bows. Everyone watches and is somewhat relieved when the dragons bow in return.

Buck is the first to speak. "I'm sorry for doubting you," he says sincerely. He's so filled with emotion his eyes fill with tears.

"We certainly don't blame you. I regret we couldn't explain what we were doing," says Cap. "You are about to experience an amazing thing. They will understand what I say, and you will hear what they think as well as you can hear me."

Cap introduces Janice and Sandra to Lester and Fuzzy, explaining they are their mates.

"It is an honor to meet you," replies Fuzzy. "Lester and I can feel the love they have for you."

Janice and Sandra are speechless, as they bow. Cap motions for Flavie and Buck to come forward and introduces them. They're more at ease and bow respectfully.

"I am Fuzzy, an old friend of these young men. And this is Lester, our den's leader." Buck is in shock, realizing he understands the dragon's thoughts.

"We're grateful to your families for your understanding and sacrifice. These men have done us a great favor by warning us about a dangerous hunting party coming to harm us. We will be forever in your debt because of what they have already done," says Lester.

Fuzzy speaks. "Unfortunately, half of our strongest dragons are gone, searching for a new cavern. If battle comes, we will be weaker than we should be. Cap and Jackson have promised to help us defend our old and young dragons, and use their human creativity to combat and understand what the hunters might be planning. We will try to keep the fighting away from them and our vulnerable family members."

The Brittains are on an emotional rollercoaster. They have just started to feel better, and now they're plunged back into the depths of fear.

Cap and Jackson see the smiles on their brides' faces quickly turn into disbelief. Flavie leans against Buck's shoulder, surrendering to worry.

"We will be in the cavern, and all the fighting will be in the wilderness. The dragons will protect us, and we'll be fine," states Jackson.

"Lester, I know it's dark, but could you take our wives for a ride and let them become more confident in your ability to keep us safe?" asks Cap.

"Sure," says Lester. "As you already know dragons can see at night better than humans anyway."

Jackson pulls out the two ropes and shows Sandra and Janice how to slip their hands through and hold on.

"Now, all you have to do is climb on the dragons and enjoy an experience you never dreamed possible," Jackson explains.

Janice pulls onto Fuzzy's back and Sandra slides into place on Lester.

The dragons take off fast and soar higher with the young women than they did with the old men. Janice and Sandra are breathless as the dragons sail around, then lean and spin in circles. Both women are very brave and thrilled, even when the dragons dive toward the earth and the acceleration pulls their hair straight back. They feel weightlessness for the first time in their lives. Fuzzy and Lester pull upward at the last minute and gently touch down. Sad the ride is over, they slide to the ground. They're breathless with excitement and can hardly believe this is not a dream.

Fuzzy looks toward the Brittains, "Cap and Jackson have been my trustworthy friends for a long time. Your family is fortunate these women have united with their family. They're true and honorable people."

Buck and Flavie hold hands. "Thank you for your visit. Meeting you has made it a little easier to let the boys go and help defend your den. Please, keep them safe, and may you find peace and contentment at your new cavern," says Buck.

Lester and Fuzzy bow in respect for such a kind family.

"We must let the dragons depart. I will stay here with Janice until they come back for me. Jackson and Sandra will fly back to the Murray farm tonight."

Fuzzy and Lester prepare for Jackson and Sandra to hop on their backs.

"I hope the battle never comes, but if it does, we will be ready to help," says Cap to Fuzzy and Lester.

"We will watch the hunting party's campfires. If the hunters come too close, we will have no choice but to come back and ask for your help," says Fuzzy.

"It will be hard for a large hunting party to make much progress in the wilderness. Hopefully your den will be gone before they arrive. It's only right that you and your den can one day be free to live like dragons once again," says Jackson. He and Sandra climb onto the dragons. As they rise into the sky, Jackson yells. "We will come see you Saturday."

Sandra feels lucky to enjoy an extra ride on Fuzzy. She's amazed how quickly they return and land softly at the Murray's.

"If only men could respect other creatures, especially dragons, what a wonderful relationship that would be. Why do men have to interfere with every creature they find?" she asks Jackson. As they walk toward the house, she realizes dragons are too powerful and smart to ever allow man to have his way with them.

"I wish we could have flown longer together, but I'm looking forward to being with you tonight," says Jackson, holding her hand.

"I would never have believed I could love you more than I did when we got married but worrying about you and missing you so much has made my love stronger," she replies.

After breakfast, Jackson tells his family about his and Cap's promise to help the dragons defend their old and young. A lump aches in his throat when his mom, dad, and Uncle Matt cry.

Chapter 29

In Water Town, the hunting party anxiously prepares for their final briefing. They're less than an hour away from taking the equipment outside and starting their adventure. The men are glad to be together. They're laughing and talking as some of them saddle horses and others throw harnesses over the horses that will be pulling wagons. There's energy in the air and a festive atmosphere fills the barn.

Mason is happy as he looks over the equipment one last time. Satisfied everything is ready, he climbs on the wagon with the pole mounted in the middle where everyone can see him. With his announcer's voice, he calls Virgil.

"Come up here beside me." He extends a hand.

"Gather around, men. We have a few things to discuss before I send you on your way."

The men tie the horses. Several talk with their buddies as they head toward Mason, but they all make haste. Once they reach the wagon, they stand quietly.

"Virgil, these are the best hunters anywhere, and they tell me you have become a really good marksman on the crossbow. I respect you for all the hard work you have done. Please understand there are a lot of things these men have learned the hard way. Listen to their suggestions. It's very important to know what to do and when to do it. Cliff has a gift for that. Taking advantage of his talent and experience will help you be successful on this trip."

Mason looks to Virgil for a response.

"Thank you for allowing me to learn things I would have never had the opportunity to experience anywhere else. It will be an honor to follow Cliff's leadership."

Mason looks out over the men and smiles at Ben. "I'm sure all of you were glad when you heard Ben will be your cook."

"Grumpy old Ben, the best cook you'll ever find in the wilderness," says someone. "That's because you won't find another cook in the wilderness," yells another. Everyone laughs, and Ben knows they're fond of him or they wouldn't have said a word.

"I don't have to tell you he's a good cook and will keep all of you fed well. But he likes everyone to brag about his cooking and help him clean up. You will eat much better if you do what I just told you."

Mason motions for Cliff to climb on the wagon.

Cliff walks over with confidence and pulls up onto the wagon with ease. He stands a head taller than Mason. He looks around and speaks calmly in a strong, deep voice.

"I know we have been over what I am about to say but listen up one last time." He eyes the men to see if everyone is paying attention. Not a soul is talking. All eyes are on him.

"As with all our hunts, some of us may die. If something happens to me, Lem will assume command. All of you have hunted with him before."

Mason looks at the men. "Is that right, men?" he summons loudly.

They give a yell of approval.

Cliff smiles and begins again. "Besides being second in command, Lem will be a crossbowman, and by his side on the other crossbow I want Virgil. If something happens to me and Lem, then Aaron will take over and remain in charge of the archers."

Cliff peers frankly into the group. "If you lose the three of us, it will be time to run for it. Get out of there and head for home as fast as you can. Leave any equipment that will slow you down."

Cliff looks around. "Any questions?"

One of the men yells from the back. "Whose job is it to put the muzzle on the dragon? All the men smile and listen for Cliff's reaction. "If we're successful catching a dragon, that decision will be made in the field, but we must force it on as quickly as possible.

Cliff pauses. No more questions are asked. "Mason, this hunting party is ready to go," he proudly announces.

Mason steps to the center. "Good luck to all of you, and I hope you return on your feet and with all your arms and legs attached, but you better return with a dragon."

"Extra silver for every man if you succeed!" he shouts loudly. "If you bring more than one back alive, even more silver!"

"You might as well go get the extra silver!" yells one of the men as the group breaks into cheers and revelry.

The hunting party is filled with energy, and excitement lights every face. Some of them even place bets they will be the one to get the first dragon. They're all confident they will succeed.

"Open the barn doors!" commands Mason.

The wagons and men on horses begin to move out. In front of everyone, riding on the finest horses are Cliff and Virgil. The heavy bar cage pulls up behind them and is driven by one of the archers. The wagon with a pole in the middle is behind the heavy cage and has an evil look with straps and muzzles securely tied down ready for the bumpy trip ahead. Next is the wagon with a tarp stretched over wooden bows. It carries hardware and weapons. Everything in this wagon has been packed with much thought. Two horses pull the hardware wagon with one archer driving.

The fifth and sixth wagons carry the large crossbows. The holding pins have been pulled and they are laid down for easy traveling. One horse with an archer on each pulls them.

The seventh wagon has a lighter cage mounted to the floor. This wagon will be used to transport a dead or badly wounded dragon. The two hunting dogs lay in the cage for now. One archer rides on one of the two horses pulling it.

The eighth wagon is the cook's wagon. There's enough food stowed in it to last the men for months as long as they catch some game along the way. Ben smiles as he pulls out. His wagon looks like most farmers' wagons, except for a barrel made of wood strapped onto its side to carry water.

The last position is the rear guard, Glenn. He has a smaller bow and quiver than the rest of the hunters. It's made to hook onto his saddle where he can grab it quickly if there's trouble.

Cliff looks back at the hunting party, and when everyone is looking at him and waiting, he raises his hand and motions the group to move ahead.

The hunt has begun. Virgil feels proud to be in front with Cliff. Everyone will know he's one of the leaders.

The men don't do much talking while they're moving. They're too far apart and there's too much noise from squeaking wheels and horse hoofs clomping along.

The men in the back of the line grumble because they're eating a lot more dust than the ones in front. Everyone from the third wagon back ties their bandanas over their noses.

The train of wagons moves along swiftly while the horses are fresh. They don't pass many people on the trail, but when they do, the people watch in amazement as the equipment passes by. Some of them try to ask what's going on, but Cliff motions for them to move along.

The party passes through Sandra's village as sunset nears.

Virgil rides close to Cliff. "It's about time to stop for the night. Why don't we stop here?" he asks.

"We can't stop near a village. Too many people will come asking questions, and we don't need that. Sometimes people will even want to follow us." He has already started looking for a place out of sight to spend the night. They move on for a while.

"Here is more like what we're looking for," says Cliff, looking at an overgrown path into the forest. He stops everyone and rides over to take a closer look. It leads to a clear meadow far enough into the brush to be hidden from anyone passing. He motions for the hunting party to follow him. They circle around in the meadow and stop. Cliff rides back over to Virgil. "This will be a night to remember. The first night is always the best. Everyone will have more energy tonight than they will from here on in."

Ben unhooks his horses and a couple of the men take them to feed and tie up for the night. Two other men help him fix supper. Within an hour, the smell of ham and beans fills the air making the men's mouths water. He rings a bell on the side of his wagon and everyone rushes over to fill their plates.

"Ben, you're the best cook any hunting party ever had," yells one of the men as he flops down with a full stomach and feeling good.

"Don't lie back yet! Get up here and help me clean up and get ready for the morning," yells Ben.

"You know I don't know anything about cooking."

"This has nothing to do with cooking. Get over here and start washing things up." The man decides he isn't going to help wash dishes. Cliff stands up and marches over to him. "Get up. You and I are going to help Ben tonight." The man hops up, smiling. "I was just having some fun."

Virgil realizes he will have to take as many turns as anyone helping with chores to keep the party's respect.

The men sit around the campfire telling stories from earlier hunts. Everyone is trying to outdo everyone else with their story. When Cliff finishes helping Ben, he joins Virgil and leans back to listen to the entertainment.

"This is the way it is every time we go out on a new hunt. The stories grow more amazing every time they're repeated. And the longer they talk, the more unbelievable they get," says Cliff.

"I bet you have some really good stories, too." says Virgil. "Do you ever tell them while everyone sits around like this?"

"I have learned it's best for me to act like very little has surprised me. It gives the men a little more confidence in me," replies Cliff. "Just enjoy all these stories. The men will start quieting soon. Watch Ben. When he starts digging out jerky for breakfast, you'll know it's time to bed down."

"I thought we would have a big breakfast in the morning," says Virgil, surprised.

"No. I intend to get back on the trail at first light."

After everyone's asleep, Virgil walks through the camp. The fire is dying, but there's enough light for him to take in all the sights and sounds. This is the first time he has been on a hunt with this many experienced hunters, and he doesn't want to miss a thing.

That night, as he lays thinking about the day, he's proud of himself. He has figured out how to put together another adventure most men only dream about.

As soon as there's enough light to see, Cliff stands, brushing himself off. "Time to get going," he says loudly as he walks over and pulls a blanket off the first man he comes to.

"Time to get going," he says again, looking around to see if anyone is moving. He claps his hands and walks around the camp. Most of the men are awake and start moving as soon as Cliff approaches. Men stretch and dust off, then disappear into the woods for a minute. When they return, they're ready for breakfast.

Ben picks up the basket he filled with jerky the night before.

"Here you go boys. Good old beef jerky for breakfast. It's good and so tough you'll still be chewing on it when it's time for lunch," he yells loud enough for everyone to hear.

The men quietly gnaw on the jerky as they prepare to line up. Ben is the last man to slide into his seat. Cliff watches until he picks up his reins, and then motions for the hunting party to move out.

The group moves along at a good pace until Cliff pulls them over just before Blade Town. He rides to the middle of the train and addresses them loudly.

"Don't speak to anyone in Blade Town. We're going to pass through without stopping. If it's necessary to talk to someone, I will do the talking. I want all of you to pick up the pace so we can pass through quickly without attracting a crowd. If any of the town's people follow us, the rear guard will send them back. Is that understood?"

Cliff looks up and down the line. Everyone appears to be satisfied and is ready to start going again. Cliff returns to the front of the party and motions for them to move ahead.

"Look, Virgil, just as I suspected," says Cliff as they reach the outskirts of town. People are casting curious looks in their direction. "They want to know what's happening. They could hold us up for half a day if we were to let them."

Virgil is pleased to see all the attention they're receiving. He wonders how they will react when the hunting party returns with something really exciting to see. He tips his hat to some of the people who wave.

Cliff just wants to hurry through town. It's midmorning by the time Blade Town disappears behind them.

It isn't long until a small clear stream becomes visible down a little path, not far from the trail. The men water the horses and fill the barrel, then relax on the bank, drinking out of dippers made of little gourds until they quench their thirst.

Once they start moving again, it doesn't take long to reach the Brittain farm turnoff, but no one sees them go by.

Shortly after midday, the hunting party sees the Murray farm in the middle of the trail ahead.

Virgil tells Cliff to stop the hunting party for a minute. "This is the last farm on our way to the wilderness. I camped near their barn and talked to these people about going to hunt dragons. They will know why we're passing by when they see me. I would rather not talk to them again. They don't trust me, and I do not trust them."

Cliff rides to the middle of the train, and shouts. "We're going to pass through the farm ahead. No one is to stop or talk to these people." That's the way he wants it anyway.

Cliff returns to the lead and motions to move on.

All the Murrays quietly watch as the train of equipment and men go by. Inez stands on the porch, looking at the men as they pass. None of them offer to wave at her, and she doesn't wave at them.

After the hunting party is out of sight, Inez rings the porch bell. It's lunchtime anyway. Jackson and Sandra reach the porch first with Miles and Uncle Matt right behind them. They have a lot to talk about before they go inside to eat.

Jackson has a bad feeling in his gut, but he doesn't want to act as if he's worried.

"You boys better think twice before you run out into the wilderness to fight those men," warns Uncle Matt. "They look dangerous, and that's a large hunting party."

"All the men were dressed for the wilderness and most of the wagons are built for only one purpose: to haul dragons back," says Miles.

Having just seen the hunting party and hearing Uncle Matt and Miles makes Sandra feels sick to her stomach. "I felt pretty good about the reassurances you gave me after Fuzzy and Lester left, but after seeing all of those men..." She breaks into tears. Inez is no longer as sure about the safety of her sons either, but she doesn't mention it in front of Sandra.

"I know the hunting party looks impressive, but none of you really know how powerful the dragons are. Cap and I do. We'll be alright.

No one enjoys lunch while their heads are filled with worry and their hearts and stomachs tremble.

Everyone is ready to return to what they were doing, knowing work will help keep their minds off what they have seen.

After supper, the men gather on the porch to talk. They're worried and don't want the women to hear them talking about a battle Cap and Jackson could be involved in. Miles rubs his forehead like he always does when he's troubled. Uncle Matt is uncommonly quiet. Jackson feels he should say something to take some of their anguish away.

"With all the wagons and equipment the hunters are moving, I figure it will take a long time for them to reach the den."

"I think the fight will start much sooner than that. If I were one of the dragons, I would want to keep those men as far away from the den as possible," replies Uncle Matt.

"I would guess Lester and Fuzzy will be back for you in less than a week," says Miles.

The door opens and the women come out to sit. No more is said about dragons or fighting.

Everyone works quietly the rest of the week and tries not to talk about the hunting party. Sandra stays close to Jackson all the time. The family notices, but no one mentions it.

When Saturday evening arrives, Sandra and Jackson saddle two horses and leave for Cap and Janice's.

"I love you so much, Jackson. I hope we can enjoy life together after this is over. I want to live on a quiet little farm with you and raise our family."

"Don't worry. A year from now, we will be living perfectly normal lives again," he assures her.

"I'm afraid you will ride off, and I will never see or hear from you again." she says softly, wiping her eyes.

"Don't let yourself think things like that. The hardest, most painful thing out there for me will be the pain I endure from missing you."

They reach out and hold hands as they ride along. When they reach the Brittains', Flavie is finishing supper.

"Let's not mention the hunting party until after supper," says Jackson remembering how lunch tasted after he and Sandra saw them go by.

As they're eating, the question comes up about how much longer it will be until Fuzzy and Lester come back for Cap. Sandra and Jackson don't say a word, and everyone enjoys their meal.

Buck and Cap stroll to the porch after supper. Jackson prefers to stay inside and help clean up. He wants everyone to hear about the hunting party at the same time. Sandra and Jackson, holding hands, walk behind Flavie and Janice. They sit side by side not releasing their grip. Everyone notices. Janice sits in a chair beside Cap, Buck and Flavie are in the swing.

"I have news to share with all of you," says Jackson. Everyone holds their breath.

"The hunting party passed our farm a couple days ago."

Janice reaches for Caps hand and holds it tightly. As Sandra watches her, she understands all too well the emotions stirring in her mind.

"How bad did it look to you?" asks Cap as he squeezes Janice's hand lightly.

"It looked like there were ten or eleven men," explains Jackson, everyone's eyes are fixed on him. He describes the wagons and the men that passed. No one is surprised when they hear Virgil is one of the men leading the group and he didn't stop at the farm.

Cap is quiet for a few minutes, thinking about what he has heard. "How long do you think we have until we have to leave with Fuzzy?" he asks.

"I would say about two weeks, but dad and Uncle Matt think the dragons will come sooner."

Everyone sinks into a somber mood, and not much more is said. They just rock and hold hands. Flavie makes a pot of mint tea with honey, and they sip and are glad to be together.

<>

The wilderness fights to protect its children from the intrusion of man. Thick underbrush, biting insects, and rashes from heat and poison vines combine to slow the hunting party to a crawl. Cliff is determined to speed things up. He watches the men swinging axes and blades. They lift their blades slowly, and then quickly slam them to the ground tearing the vegetation into mulch. Sweat trickles down their faces, wetting their clothing.

"Virgil, it's time to park the heavy cage wagon. The men are beginning to complain for good reason. They're all suffering and most of them have too many blisters." He yells for them to stop for the evening.

After supper, there isn't much talking. The men lean back, resting, and some of them already have their blankets pulled across them.

Cliff lies down near Virgil. "In the morning, the men will be sore from all the work they did today, and there will be a lot of complaining. I'll think of something to get them going again," he says, pulling his blanket up.

Everyone except Ben is still sleeping as the sun breaks over the horizon.

"Alright, I know all of you are sore, but its time get up and get going," Cliff makes his round waking the men like he usually does. "It's time for some real chopping today."

"I have done too much real chopping already. I am an archer not a wood chopper," complains one of the men.

"I have done enough chopping to last me a lifetime," yells another.

"What's the problem? We have chopped trails before," says Cliff.

"I have cut twice as much as some of these other men, and I can't keep that up day after day," says the man who complained first.

Two other men agree they can't chop without resting every now and then.

"Ben!" yells Cliff. "I'm going to break these men into two groups. Can you time them so everyone takes the same amount of time on the axe?"

Ben reaches into his wagon and pulls out a small pot with a hole in the bottom side. It's his cooking timer.

"I will fill this pot halfway up with water, and every time it empties, I will call out for the next group to take their turn cutting," he says.

Cliff sees rebellion on their faces. "Men, I know all of you are working harder than we planned. It's taking a lot more cutting than Mason or I imagined. I know most of you are having second thoughts about this trip. Let's try the timer. We'll leave the heavy cage wagon chained here so we won't have to cut as much. I will make sure all of you have a chance to rest a little more."

Virgil is surprised how much good his talk accomplishes. Most of the men seem to be willing to give it a try. They pick up their axes and are ready to start.

The men become grumpier as the day wears on, but now they know everyone is doing the same amount of work. They begin to work as a team, and Cliff is pleased. A week passes and Cliff is vigilant to keep an eye on the men so he can judge when to stop for the day. They make good progress every day, but it has been hotter today and everyone has worked hard. Before the men start complaining, he rewards them by stopping early.

After supper, Virgil throws his blanket and gear next to Cliff. "I think you made a good decision to stop earlier this evening."

"The men are working so hard, I'm concerned they're getting too tired. They want to sleep as soon as they eat supper. It's dangerous for everyone to sleep so soundly out here," says Cliff.

They discuss having a couple men sleep during the day, and stand guard at night. "We're getting close to the dragons anyway, and after tonight we have to stop building camp fires," says Virgil.

Cliff looks at Virgil. "It's time for you to address the men. You're the only one who has any experience out here with these creatures. I will pick the guards in the morning, and at lunch I want you to talk to the men about the campfires. You have worked alongside all of them so don't be shy tomorrow." Virgil is pleased Cliff has shown him respect, and he won't let him down.

After lunch the next day, Cliff yells for the men to gather.

Cliff moves over beside Virgil, and when the men are ready to listen he looks toward him, and nods.

Virgil speaks loudly with newfound authority. "Men, we have reached a point where we must not build anymore campfires. The dragons can spot a fire from miles away. They're close to the plateau ahead, and if

they're up on top of it, they probably already know
we're coming. We must make it harder for them to find
us, especially at night. From my experience, they will try
to protect their den when we are close, and we don't want
a dragon visiting us while we're asleep."

"How will our guards see to protect us if we don't
have a fire?" asks one of the men.

"If we don't build a fire, their night vision will be
better, and their sense of hearing will be keener. Each
guard will keep a dog beside him and sit on opposite ends
of our camp. At least without a fire we won't be sitting
around all lit up, making it easy for the dragons to study
everything about us. Let's make it harder for them to see
us."

The men listen, and they talk among themselves.
"I'm going to sleep with my bow beside me ready to pick
up and shoot," says one of them. "This is just one more
inconvenience, but at least now I'm feeling like we're a
hunting party again instead of wood choppers." states
another.

Cliff looks around at the men, and they understand.
"It's time to start cutting again. Some of you help Ben
clean up." says Cliff.

"That's right. If you do a good job, I will cook your
supper beans while it's still light and keep them warm.
They'll taste better tonight in the dark if they aren't cold."

That night the guards stand in place, and without
light, the camp is quieter. Every man has his bow close by
his side. The hunting party is in survival mode. They
know the dragons could come on their own hunting trip at
any moment.

Chapter 30

Atop the plateau, Fuzzy and Lester stand side-by-side, waiting to see the hunter's evening fire. When it doesn't appear at dusk, they pace around to pass the time until it has been dark for a while. They sadly agree it's a bad sign, and the men are probably beginning their hunting strategy. It's time to ask for Cap and Jackson's help.

Lester ambles to the cavern entrance. "Ureeeeee," he hails loudly. It's time for the den to know the hunters are close at hand. The den quietly files out, gathering around their leaders. Everyone knows this will be unwelcome news.

Lester speaks in a calm, authoritative voice. "Fellow dragons, it's time for us to be strong and prepare for battle. From this day forward, be a little more understanding with each other. Everyone will be edgy until the battle is won. Work together as we gather extra food to store in the cavern. It will be too dangerous for us to venture out in a few more days, so bring in anything you think we may need. Tomorrow evening, Fuzzy and I will be leaving to try and persuade the two young men who promised to help, into returning with us. I beg of you to be as considerate of them as you would one of our own.

Lester waits to see if everyone agrees. He's pleased to see one of the dragons in front bow in agreement, followed quietly by a wave of bowing heads moving from front to back.

Lester bows, and the meeting is over.

That night, the mood in the cavern is quieter than usual. Everyone's apprehensive about things to come.

Morning light finds Fuzzy and Lester standing in the entrance, watching the sun rise. Lots of things need to be done, but they're depressed as they accept the fact that a deadly chain of events is beginning. By nightfall, it will be undeniable to every member of the den with Cap and Jackson there. Reality fills them with anxious energy, and it taxes them. They decide to return to their special places and spend the day with their mates.

Mid-evening, when Fuzzy and Lester sail from the ledge, hardly anyone notices. They circle far away from the hunting party in hopes of not being seen. If they had a choice, they would wait until dark to fly, but they must pick up the men and be back at the den before dark. Cap and Jackson need to be able to see well enough to settle in for their first night in the cavern. In a short time, they land at the Murray farm.

Inez sees the dragons land and her heart aches as she walks to the front porch to ring the bell.

Miles and Uncle Matt stop plowing. Seeing the dragons crushes their spirit, causing them to wipe tears as they make their way toward the house. Jackson and Sandra stop their work and look toward the house. They see the dragons in the backyard. They turn and wrap arms around each other and hold on tightly for a moment.

Jackson quickly walks inside and grabs his bow and quiver. He slips on his pack filled with the supplies, and he's thankful Inez keeps the food and blankets in it fresh. He carefully straps his knife to his leg. He's ready to go, but stops when Inez takes his arm and checks his red ribbon. She is quiet, and cries as she lovingly tugs the ribbon.

He hugs her first, then Miles and Uncle Matt. Last, he embraces the woman he loves and kisses her passionately. He turns and walks to Fuzzy, ready to climb on his back.

Fuzzy stops him. "Wait. We're humbled that you are coming with us, and we must remind your family to wear their ribbons until you return." Fuzzy and Lester bow in deep respect and so do the Murrays.

Jackson climbs on Fuzzy's back.

"I will keep Jackson safe for you," promises Fuzzy. As he flaps vigorously, the Murrays cover their eyes. Wind gushes past them. They sail into the sky and are gone in no time. The family puts their ribbons on and vows to wear them until Jackson is safely home. It's too much for Sandra to bear. She retreats to her and Jackson's room for the rest of the evening.

As the dragons soar into the sky, the sun glows above them. Jackson looks down, watching the family he loves fade into tiny dots and disappear. The house and barns all fade away into the surrounding forest. The sky is bluer than he has ever seen, and the green of the forest fades to a greenish gray. The bright sunlight makes Fuzzy's deep dark blue fuzz glisten as it flows across his body. The red bristles on the top of his head are iridescent, and with the sun penetrating them, they glow. The excitement only lasts a few minutes until Fuzzy leans to one side and they're circling over the Brittain farm.

Jackson can see his brother as he looks down. The house and Jack's workshop all look like he had imagined, but he's surprised to see trails from the front steps of the house connecting the out-buildings and heading toward the fields and the creek. It gives the farm character he has never noticed. Cap is working in the yard and sees them coming. If it wasn't such an emotional moment, he would have marveled at the sight of Jackson riding on Fuzzy's back.

The moment they land, he walks over to Jackson with a restrained frown on his face.

"I hoped this day would never come. I respect the dragons, but I only wanted them to find a new cavern. In my heart, I yearned for them to just leave and everyone would be safe from harm." He hugs Jackson dearly. When he pulls back, his eyes drip several tears. He takes a deep breath and wipes his eyes. "I will grab my pack and be right back."

He makes his way to the porch and into the house where Janice and Flavie are sewing.

"The dragons are here, and it's time for me to go with them," he says in a calm voice even though his heart is breaking. He tries to act as if everything is going just as planned.

The women lay their needles on the table and go with him to gather his things. Cap slips on his pack and Janice hands him his knife. He can see she's trembling, but trying desperately to control herself. She hugs him with a grip in her hands that tells him she hates to let him go.

When Cap emerges from the house, the dragons bow in respect to the Brittains and Janice for letting Cap help them. Cap hugs everyone and kisses Janice goodbye.

Janice wants to tell Cap so many things as he ties his red ribbon, but it's impossible to talk while she's still trembling inside, and her vocal cords are pulling so tightly they can't possibly vibrate.

"I love you, Janice," is all he says. He tells his family to put on their ribbons, then bounds off the porch, hops on Lester's back, and settles into place. He looks at his loving family. "Be strong! Don't worry about us. Fuzzy and Lester are very wise. Jackson and I will be alright."

Lester and Fuzzy turn head-first into a breeze gusting from the north, hop forward, flap their wings rapidly at first. Then with gentle strokes, they rise higher and higher. Cap looks back toward the people he loves, longing to return to the life he has just begun, and in a few moments, they fade out of sight. Cap knows Lester and Fuzzy can tell he's about to cry. They can sense everything the men are thinking.

The wind and the mountaintop view from Lester's back soon turns the moment into an exciting experience and helps ease Cap's mind.

"I have always wanted to see the other side of a cloud. Would it be possible to fly over the clouds to the west of us?" asks Jackson.

Fuzzy and Lester look toward the formation of fluffy clouds floating peacefully to their left. They agree it probably will be a good idea to fly above them anyway. They soar higher until they're in a white, wet mist. Cap and Jackson lose sight of each other. The mist begins to grow brighter until they can hardly see. Then their heads pop through and the sun shines brilliantly. Cap and Jackson cover their eyes until they adjust to the light. The sight is breathtaking, clouds cover a vast area, and they look like pearl cotton balls floating in an ocean of air. It's such an awe-inspiring sight, they forget to be sad for a few minutes. They begin to shiver. They had no idea it would be this cold above the clouds.

The dragons start to circle, and the men know they're above the den. They feel almost weightless as they descend to the ground. The warmer air feels wonderful.

The flight ends with a slight bounce, and, sadly, they slide to the ground, landing lightheaded but on their feet. They're in a new world. A world where loved ones with broken hearts are behind them and the fear of battle and possibility of death lies in front of them. The change makes them feel sick to their stomachs as they try to grip the reality of being in front of Fuzzy's cavern.

Fuzzy wants to reach out and hug his friends. He understands the flood of emotions they're experiencing. "I would be honored if you will spend the night with my family," he says.

As they walk inside, the light grows dim, but they can see through openings in the hallway well enough to observe other families together and an occasional youngster staring at them. They follow Fuzzy into his family's special place, and he introduces Liz to them. The men bow in respect to her. She is a beautiful female with soft, smooth features. Her muscle tone is not as pronounced as Fuzzy's. As they hear her thoughts, they're astonished. Her tone is conveyed in a feminine manner, softer and kinder than that of the males they have communicated with. She's very gracious and proudly introduces their two young dragons, Lee and Kim.

The more time they spend together, the more the dragons and men like each other.

"My family finds it easy to trust and communicate with you because they can tell you are sincere and honorable," says Liz.

"Mankind is in a struggle within itself. It's a struggle between good and evil," says Fuzzy. Cap and Jackson know man's obsession with silver and the things it can buy is mostly to blame.

As the next three days pass, the brothers are treated kindly by the den, and they grow to respect the dragon family.

Chapter 31

On the fourth day, Cap and Jackson are saddened to hear "Ureeeeee" echoing thru the cavern. Battle is eminent. The hunters are close and the dragons have filled the cavern with as much food as they can. The den assembles and everyone is somber. They see the resolve to protect them on their leader's faces.

The brothers stand quietly in the back, unsure what to expect.

Lester speaks earnestly with a strong voice. It echoes from the cavern walls as he speaks to the quietest group he has ever addressed.

"It is time to choose the dragon that will have the honor and great responsibility of guarding our entrance. He will stand guard all day, watching for anything that appears suspicious. If the entrance is attacked, he will call out a warning cry to us and fearlessly defend and repel the attackers. Only at night will he be allowed to rest while other den members, two at a time, assume his duty," says Lester.

Everyone looks at Leonard. He grew up with Lester and Fuzzy and is a highly respected member of the den. Everyone feels safe when he's around because he is fearless yet comfortable showing his love for the den.

Leonard bows in acceptance and beams with pride.

"Leonard, you will be the entrance guard from this day forward. You have been honored by your den. You will be the last defense between the hunters and our loved ones hidden in the cavern," says Lester "Cap, you and Jackson will stay behind him. He will protect you, too. If you choose, you can help him if it becomes necessary."

Cap and Jackson quietly hope nothing ever happens, that will make them have to hurt any of the men.

They suddenly realize they will have to do whatever has to be done. There's no way they can let the young or old be taken or killed.

Reality sinks in as Leonard assumes his post in front of the entrance. The battle has begun for him. "This is it, Jackson. We're in a situation where a life or death decision may have to be made in an instant. There's no backing out now," sighs Cap.

<>

Cliff decides the time has come to allow the dogs to prowl around, anticipating they will soon pick up an interesting scent. Hopefully that of a dragon. There's always the possibility they will flush one out lurking in the woods. From now on, an archer or two will keep a close eye on them and be ready to shoot in an instant. Watching the archers ride close to the sniffing dogs makes Cliff realize an attack or even a dragon flushed from its hiding place could occur at any moment. "Virgil, it's time for you and Lem to occupy the crossbow seats. Keep them cocked and ready to fire. It's up to you two to keep us safe while the rest of the men chop."

Cliff cautiously studies everything, keeping a keen eye on the surroundings, looking for any signs that indicate which way to go.

Moving ahead is very slow now with only a few men chopping. Cliff senses they're close to a sighting.

That evening, the dogs become excited and their bark sounds different, as if they're trying to warn the hunters. Cliff understands they have picked up an intriguing scent they have never smelled until now. "Be careful and stay close to the dogs," he yells to the archers on horseback.

"Don't let them run off by themselves! That's how I lost the last two dogs," screams Virgil.

The dogs turn from the direction they have been going and steadily sniff the ground. Instinct is driving them crazy. The more they sniff, the faster they trot. They head northwest of the hunting party. They pause as if contemplating their next move.

Suddenly, they break into a run. The archers on horseback turn with them in an attempt to remain close. They're able to keep up until the dogs crouch low and run through brush so thick the archers have to stop. They quickly circle around the thicket. One turns right, and the other gallops to the left. The dogs are unprotected.

The thicket is wide from left to right, but thin from front to back. The dogs are running blindly, with limbs and briars slapping them in the face. It only takes a second for the dogs to streak through to the other side, where the vegetation stops and a large meadow opens up. There, lying in wait, filled with anticipation, and bellies churning with gas, two dragons seethe. The dogs pop into the open so suddenly they don't have time to focus on what lies in front of them.

The dragons unleash a blast of fire, blinding them and engulfing their bodies with blue and yellow flames. As they tumble through the flames, the stench of burned flesh and smoke fills the dragon's nostrils.

When the archers come around the thicket into the meadow, it's too late. They fill with anger when they see the dragons have incinerated their dogs. They dig into the sides of their horses, making them gallop as fast as they can.

The dragons are shocked to see the archers on horses barreling in their direction with arrows set and aiming at them. They frantically leap into the air, knowing the arrows can reach them long before they will be close enough to spew fire over the archers. Their only hope of surviving is to quickly flee.

Both archers shoot and arrows streak through the air fast as lightning, hitting one of the dragons. The arrows sink deeply into his body.

The other dragon, seeing his companion is wounded, quickly turns, lowers his head and knocks one of the archers off his horse while continuing to fly toward the other archer. Seeing anguish in his companion's eyes causes his anger to explode into rage and energy. He peers into the eyes of the terrified archer on horseback, who trembles, as he tries to set his arrow. A split second before the arrow is released, his claws slice into the man's body, yanking him into the air, He quickly releases him, and the archer tumbles to the ground.

The archer butted off his horse is badly hurt, but stumbles to his knees and sets an arrow to defend himself. The dragon stays clear of the threat, and returns to his wounded partner.

The wounded dragon struggles, blood streaming down the arrows and spilling onto the ground as it returns to the den. Cliff watches as it heads toward the cavern entrance, disappearing over the edge of the plateau.

The other dragon flies away and hides.

Cliff turns to see two of his men carrying the lifeless archer over to Ben's wagon. As he looks in anguish at the torn clothing drenched in blood and ripped flesh dangling, his personality changes. His face turns red and the blood veins in his neck bulge as he fills with bitterness and curses the dragons. From now on, even though he and his men came to the dragons with intentions of causing them harm, the only fact that matters is that a man has died at the hand of a dragon. In the minds of

Cliff, Virgil and their men, the dragons deserve whatever pain and punishment they can give them.

Virgil and Lem aim their crossbows where the wounded dragon passed over the ledge. They can't see the cavern entrance, but they each fire a large arrow in that direction. The arrows barely pass above the ledge as they disappear where the dragon was last seen.

"Wiiiiii," screams several devastated dragons. The den is in terror when the large arrows bounce around the entrance, making a clanking noise. They're already unnerved because one of them is dying, and now they know the men have found the entrance.

"I fear we're up against an insurmountable foe," says Cap, staring at the dying dragon and his frantic den. He holds his breath.

"Things look really bad, especially for the confrontation to have just begun." Jackson is in shock.

The wounded dragon's name is Auh, and he's taken inside the cavern to be cared for. "Wiiiiii," the dragon's uncontrollable sound of deep mourning echoes over and over as it's repeated throughout the cavern.

"I have never felt so helpless. There's nothing we can possibly do to help this dragon," says Cap.

"I don't think any of the dragons will think we could do anything," replies Jackson as he covers his ears.

That night, with his closest family and friends by his side, the noble dragon takes his last breath. Many dragons mourn. "Wiiiiii," can be heard continuously as one dragon, and then another, sobs.

Cap and Jackson are just as sad as the other dragons after feeling the mourning and hearing the wailing for so long. They realize what a loving den they're with. The dragons feel genuine sadness coming from Cap and

Jackson, and realize the brothers are beginning to act like members of the den.

As a new day breaks, Fuzzy and Lester console the den and ask everyone to be quiet. Fuzzy steps out, raises his wings, closes his eyes, and speaks. "Auh, we know you are here with us. We can feel your spirit. You have loved and served our den well, and your sacrifice will help us win this battle. We release your spirit and honor you as you depart to fly with our ancestors in eternal peace." A gentle cool breath of peace settles in the place, and all is quiet. With tears in his eyes, Fuzzy lowers his wings.

Most of the dragons turn and head back to their special places. As they pass, Cap and Jackson can tell they have no feeling of ill will toward them.

"I believe these dragons are more emotionally civilized than mankind. They understand that just because we are men, it wouldn't be right to punish us for what other men have done," says Cap.

Deep in the cavern, as the two men talk, sounds of quiet sobbing and mourning can be heard.

"I have to do something to prevent the men and dragons from having to suffer like this. They both will endure great sorrow and pain if this confrontation continues," says Cap.

"Cap, we're helpless compared to these dragons and hunters."

"I'm determined to at least try to save lives on both sides. I'm going to make a white flag and wave it at the entrance. I have to take off these red ribbons and go down there and have a talk with Virgil. He needs to understand these aren't just animals. I have to do it for their own good as well as for the dragons," says Cap as his energy and emotions stir. In his mind, it's the right thing to do.

"You need to stop and think before you rush into this situation. You're too emotional right now to make a decision like this," pleads Jackson, He grabs Cap's hand and holds on. "I won't let you go. I fear Virgil will harm you. He's not like us. I have a bad feeling when I am near him." Cap forces his hand loose.

"I must try. When I talk to him man-to-man and explain how intelligent these dragons are, surely he will have to understand. I will also explain to him that most, if not all, of his men will die in the battle ahead."

"Our family will blame me for not stopping you if you don't come back," says Jackson trembling with tears in his eyes.

"I will be fine. I will climb right back up here if he won't listen to reason."

Cap walks away, searching for a branch to hang his white flag on. He finds one and breaks it about five feet long and ties a white rag from his pack on one end. There's nothing Jackson can say to stop Cap. He's already made up his mind.

"You better be careful. They have no idea a man is up here," says Jackson.

Cap moves cautiously with the flag held as high as he can. Leonard meets him on the way to the ledge, and motions for him to stop. "Is this why Fuzzy and Lester brought you here?" he asks.

"I hadn't thought about that. This is the civilized thing to do," replies Cap.

A crossbow arrow zips over the flag and clangs in the entrance. In the distance, Cap hears Cliff yell. "Hold your fire! I think I see a man up there."

Cap moves to the edge where he can look down on the men below. The hunting party is closer than before. A hard climb lies ahead for them if they try to storm the entrance. Cap studies the steep slope below the ledge. Descending will be dangerous and hard work. He has to be sure the tree limbs and bushes he reaches for will hold as he climbs down. Several times he slips and frantically grabs for something stronger to stop him from tumbling to the bottom. Finally, he reaches a level where the slope tapers enough he can walk, and he trudges toward the men.

The men gather in front of him with dirty faces and weapons in hand. Not one of them looks reasonable as they look him over. Off to the side, he notices a tarp wrapped and tied tightly around what can only be a corpse. He fears one of the men has been killed. Dead men and a lust for revenge will make reasoning with them even harder.

Two angry looking men nock arrows and aim at him, and their eyes are cold and evil.

"I would like to speak to Virgil," says Cap. Virgil cuts his eyes toward him and studies the man who knows his name. He recognizes him instantly and marches hastily up to his face.

"You and your family knew about the dragons all the time, didn't you?" he yells aggressively. His eyes are piercing as his nose stops within inches of Cap's face. Cap backs away slightly. "Yes. I have been friends with one of them since I was a child."

"If you had helped me when I first came out here, none of the men I have lost would be dead," rails Virgil, clenching his fist.

Cap is in a state of shock, he had no idea he would have to be defensive before he even begins to negotiate. Sweat runs down his neck as tired looking hunters stare at him. His guts squirm inside, and his hands begin to shake. He's at the party's mercy. With his confidence destroyed, he is at a loss for words he so desperately needs to convince these men to give up their quest. With little certainty in his voice, he pleads. "These dragons are very smart. All they want is to be left alone."

Cliff stands beside Virgil. His eyes are more piercing than Virgil's, and neither man is interested in hearing about how smart an animal in the wilderness is. They sneer, remembering the blood and torn flesh the dead archer is covered with, and their tempers boil.

"If they're so smart, ask one of them to come down and we'll take him back to Water Town to be trained. They're no smarter than our horses. Once they have been properly trained, they will be of value to mankind," thunders Cliff.

"You don't understand. They're as smart as any man. It's important to realize that you and all your men may die hunting them because they're willing to fight for their freedom just like you or me."

One of the men behind Cliff speaks up. "I didn't even think we would find a dragon much less a dragon lover. There will be no reasoning with him."

Cap realizes there's nothing he can possibly say to change their minds. "I wish none of you any ill, and I hope no one else in your party dies. I will go back to the den and talk to them about what you have said. I already know they will not let one of their family members surrender and come down here. They're very loyal to each other."

"I don't think that's the way we are going to play this game, mister. If the dragons are so smart, then they can come rescue you from the cage I'm going to lock you in," says Cliff.

The rest of the archers, with revenge in their eyes, nock arrows and aim at Cap's heart. He has never experienced fear any stronger than he does at this moment.

Cliff grabs Cap by the arm and pulls him over to the small cage. Another archer opens the door, and Cliff roughly pushes him in and slams the door. As the door latches, the sound makes Cap sick. He has himself to blame for making the wrong decision to try talking to men like these.

Cliff walks around and looks at Cap. "I think you will make pretty good dragon bait. If you don't cause any more trouble, we might feed you tonight."

Jackson is hid where he can peek over the edge and sees Cliff throw Cap into the cage. He's trembling with fear as he pulls back to think about what he has seen. He blames himself for not finding the right words to stop his brother from going down to talk to Virgil.

Leonard is also watching and leaves his post to tell Fuzzy and Lester about what has happened. Fuzzy is shocked and fills with disbelief. He runs to the entrance to see, but Leonard grabs him before he reaches the ledge. "You will be a target if you show yourself." Fuzzy pulls loose and stumbles back toward the cavern. Filled with intense grief, Fuzzy lowers his head and turns to Lester, who places a wing around him. "I promised their families I would not let anything like this happen," sobs Fuzzy, tears dripping to the floor. "I knew these men might try to talk to the hunters."

"You can't blame yourself. We have been in mourning, trying to console the den. I had no idea Cap was going to go down there," says Lester.

All the dragons feel sorry for Jackson when they hear the story. They suffer from his sadness when they're close to him, and they quietly bow their heads in respect. Fuzzy approaches Jackson, searching for words to express his sympathy and guilt.

"Don't blame yourself." Jackson stops him. "I want to be alone for a while to think. It will take a little time before I will be able to function again," says Jackson humbly. Fuzzy bows in respect and leaves.

In the cage, Cap gropes with helplessness as the day passes. He discovers a bowl of water and is thankful for it. He doesn't realize it had been put there for the dogs. After the men eat supper, one of them flips a piece of jerky into his cage as he passes. Cap thanks him but there's no reply. He slides back in the middle of the cage and lies down, wondering about his brother. He can only imagine how upset he must be. He hopes Jackson will be strong and stay hidden in the cavern where there's a chance he will be able to help Fuzzy. As he closes his eyes, Cap can't help wondering if being locked in the cage isn't a safer place to be than in the cavern.

Early in the morning, the sun is up, and the men quietly eat. Cap sees Virgil and Cliff looking toward the plateau and talking to several of the men. They point at the entrance, and everyone has something to say. Cliff stops talking and looks closely at the plateau as if he' studying a suggestion. Cap can tell he responded, "Let's try it." He's distressed because he can't hear what they're saying, even though he's unable to do anything about it.

In a few minutes, two men pass the cage. They're smeared with mud from head to toe. They have their bows and quivers tied tightly to their backs and are completely camouflaged with small limbs and moss. They walk toward the bushes growing at the base of the plateau. They ease slowly to the ground and disappear into the underbrush.

Cap has to look long and hard to occasionally get a glimpse of the men moving ever so slowly. They're being very patient and careful. Cap begins to sweat in fear, knowing they probably wouldn't be detected by the dragons until it's too late.

They crawl and pull all morning, inching up the steep slope toward the entrance. Virgil and Lem lean back in the crossbow seats with the weapons cocked and ready to fire. If one of the dragons looks over the edge of the plateau, there's a good chance it will be shot. Cap grits his teeth and tightens his lip, worrying Jackson will come over to the edge to check on him.

At midday, the men are more than halfway up the side of the plateau. Cap's nerves are frayed after watching helplessly all morning, and he begins to panic, fearing the dragons have no idea the men are climbing up the steep grade. He wants to yell and warn them, but he can't yell loud enough to be heard in the cavern. Cap is about to explode, and sticks his arm out of the cage, motioning up and down, hoping Leonard will get a glimpse of him and take a closer look down the cliff. He draws the attention of one of the archers in the camp. "Look at our dragon bait," he says to Cliff.

Cliff smirks at the sight. "Why don't you give him something else to think about before he starts yelling at his friends?"

Quietly, the archer walks up behind Cap. He sticks one end of his bow through the bars and jabs him in the back as hard as he can. The pain burns like fire up and down his spine. Shocked, and with his eyes tightly closed, he can hardly breathe.

"That will take your mind off your friends for a while," says the archer.

Cap restrains himself, but when his eyes open they show anger, and the archer jabs him again in the stomach. "That's for our friend your dragons killed," he growls.

As the archer walks away, Cap tries to rub the wound, but he can't reach it. All he can do is wait for the pain to subside. He soon forces himself to forget the pain, and carefully crawls where he can search for the archers again. Frantically he struggles, searching the incline with tears in his eyes, until he sees movement. He's disgusted with himself. There's nothing he can do. Mental anguish grinds at his soul, but something inside him refuses to give up.

Caps heart aches as he watches the men reach the ledge. Looking to the left, he sees the first archer pull up on the ledge in a spot hidden from Leonard. Slowly, he moves to a rock where he can sit and remain hidden, as he pulls an arrow and nocks it.

The other archer is crouched under a bush on the other side where he can step out, and his arrow is set. They're prepared to ambush Leonard. If he spies one of them and heads in his direction, the other archer will shoot him in the back before he can reach the archer he sees.

Seeing what's about to happen, Cap screams without concern for himself, but it's useless. The archer on the left whistles at the same time and steps around, taking aim at Leonard. Leonard jerks his head toward him, screams a warning that echoes into the cavern, then with a flash he scrambles toward the archer. Jackson grabs his bow and jumps to his feet. The archer behind Leonard lets his arrow fly. Jackson hears a high-pitched *zing* and a *thunk* as the arrow penetrates Leonard's neck.

Leonard doesn't even flinch as he continues his attack. The sight of Leonard charging, faster than expected, and only a few feet away, terrifies the archer in front of him, causing him to fumble his arrow. Leonard grabs him. The arrow zips out over the ledge, as Leonard's sharp claws penetrate the man's chest, and with a mighty jerk he tears him in half.

A second shot from the archer behind sinks into Leonard's back. This all happens so fast Jackson has only begun to take aim.

In uncontrollable anger, Jackson releases an arrow. It streaks thru the air toward the archer, striking him in his right side. He drops to his knees and slowly falls face down onto the cavern floor.

While racing toward the entrance, Fuzzy sees Jackson kill the archer.

With pain and sadness in his eyes, Leonard stagers toward Fuzzy, blood oozing from his mouth. Jackson, already in shock is hit with another emotional blast as he hears the big dragon's only regret. Leonard leans against Fuzzy. "I'm sorry I will not be able to protect our beloved den anymore." He slowly sinks to the floor.

Some of the den members coming out behind Fuzzy see Leonard's lifeless body, and they begin to scream, "Wiiiiii," over and over as mourning overtakes the den again.

Jackson drops his bow, weeping uncontrollably. He's overcome with emotional pain.

Leonard's family emerges from the depths of the cavern shrieking and convulsing. The sound of Leonard's family suffering is heart-wrenching for Jackson. He tortures himself, wondering if he is at fault for not shooting sooner.

The shrieking spreads to all the den members until, slowly, one by one, they begin making a low moaning sound of deeper sorrow, and the moans synchronize into rhythm. The dirge is more than painful to Jackson and all the dragons because they feel the pain deeper inside, in the same way they communicate with each other.

One of Leonard's brothers, filled with anger and grief, rushes past Jackson to the entrance, drops beside Leonard's body, and sobs. The moment causes him to explode into uncontrollable rage, and he sails out of the entrance, diving toward the men below.

Virgil is caught by surprise but manages to shoot his crossbow. The large arrow misses. The dragon is too fast. Lem spins around in an attempt to follow the dragon as it streaks overhead. His shot misses, too.

The dragon grabs an archer from his horse and carries him high into the air before dropping him. The bowman's lifeless body spins as it crashes to the ground.

Virgil misses another shot, but it's close. Lem takes a deep breath to calm himself, and as the dragon comes back around toward the archers, he shoots again. The arrow slices through one of its legs. The wound causes the dragon to pull up and climb higher. The pain fills him with even more rage and he dives at the crossbows. This time, there are too many arrows aimed at him. Four archers on horses and the crossbows are ready.

Two arrows hit him. Virgil waits a second, then pulls the trigger on his crossbow. The large arrow smacks into his body, going almost out of sight.

The dragon falls to the ground, lifeless. His body crashes close to the archers, making a *thud* on impact.

The men cautiously wait to see if he will try to get up. When there's no movement, they cheer. They finally have a dragon to skin and take back as proof.

One of the archers dismounts and runs to the dragon's body. He bends over and pulls its head up to look closely at their prize.

The dragon's heart stops just as the archer looks into its eyes. Death releases all body functions of the dragon, and the churning gasses inside explode through his open mouth, engulfing the archer. The force of the blast lifts his burning body off the ground and he tumbles with burnt clothing falling apart as he rolls.

The other archers jerk back in horror. They quickly shoot three more arrows into its body, but the dragon is dead. The burnt archer continues to scream in agony before their eyes.

That evening, Cliff calls the men together. "I have never in all my hunting adventures had such an emotionally and physically exhausting day," he says, hanging his head, bewildered. "We need to eat and keep guard at the same time this evening. Decide which half of you archers and crossbowman are going to eat first, then switch places.

No one cares who eats first. They're too worried about the coming of darkness, and everyone is jittery thinking about sleeping only a few feet from where their friends have been killed. Fear is already haunting the camp, and night will cast its spell of fear, fueling imaginations that will gnaw at them until daylight. Ben does his best to get some hot food dished out.

After the men eat, Cliff calls on three of them to skin the dragon. "We have to start drying the hide to keep it from rotting."

Cap watches the most barbaric thing he has ever witnessed. He has seen other animals skinned and their hides tanned, but they weren't noble intelligent creatures like the dragon. He's ashamed of what humans are capable of doing because of their love of silver and entertainment.

When the men finish, they stretch the hide between two trees. While the men clean up the mess they made skinning the dragon, Ben cleans the supper dishes. He scoops up a cup of food and sits it in the cage next to Cap. Cap thanks him, but Ben isn't in the mood to reply. He continues on his way to the stream that flows nearby to wash the cooking pots. As he bends down at the water's edge he hears the gravel lying along the stream crunching behind him. He turns to see long claws in his face. A dragon hidden in the bushes lifts him as he squirms.

The men cringe as they hear Ben's screams. Two archers run to help, but there's no sign of Ben or the dragon. A couple pots and other utensils lie in the stream with water splashing around in them.

Full of anger, one of the men turns around and walks to Cap's cage. He reaches in and grabs the bowl of half-eaten food and throws it at Cap.

"You'll never eat again," he shouts.

Cap, already emotionally worn out, curls up into a submissive ball. He closes his eyes and thinks about Janice. They could have had the most wonderful life together. They were so much in love. All that's lost. His soul aches. His bad judgment is going to cause her great sorrow. He lies in the cage, crying quietly.

Few men sleep that night. More than half of them sit with their bows ready. Cap overhears Virgil and Cliff talking almost all night.

"We don't have many men left. I think we should take our hide back and get more men and equipment," says one of the men.

"I can assure you from past experience, if we don't bring one or two live dragons back, there won't be any silver for our troubles. Mason wants something he can make real silver showing. Most people will think the skin is a fake anyway," states Cliff.

"You're probably right. I figure some young, helpless dragons are hiding up there. We only have to kill several of the strong ones to reach them. There can't be many big ones left," says Virgil.

Cap can't believe how cruel some humans can be. The thoughts of what these evil men might do to Fuzzy's den and Jackson make it impossible for him to sleep.

In the morning, Cap sees the rear guard has been replaced by Cliff. Glenn is now one of two archers who have started inching up the face of the plateau like the others had done yesterday.

The guard dragon learned from what happened to Leonard, and in the dark of night he hid on a ledge where he can look back toward the entrance.

When the first archer crawls over onto the plateau, he flies out from behind the crossbows' line of sight and snatches the archer before he can stand. The crossbows hesitate to shoot with the archer squirming in its claws, and the dragon flies high above the hunting party.

The second archer watches in horror as his partner squirms. He doesn't see Lester behind him. Lester spews fire all over the poor man. Blinded by fire, and in excruciating pain, he stumbles over the ledge, rolling and bouncing down the incline toward the camp.

Fuzzy hears the confrontation and dashes out to the entrance to see what has happened. He and Lester are relieved to see no dragon has been lost this time.

The guard dragon is still flying over the men with the archer in his claws. He's high above them and is confident he's safe from the crossbows below.

Lester watches from the entrance as two crossbow arrows sail into the sky, heading straight toward the soaring dragon. Lester jerks as if he feels the pain when arrows slice through the man and plunge into the dragon's body. The guard dragon stops flapping his wings and drifts into a death spin as his body twirls all the way to the ground with the man still in his claws.

Lester and Fuzzy follow the falling dragon until it disappears out of sight below the ledge. Their hearts ache as they move back away from the ledge. They don't speak. They're frozen in fear. Moments later, Lester looks at Fuzzy with tears in his eyes. "You and I are all that's left between those men and our beloved den."

"There are a couple older dragons that may be able to defend our little ones," replies Fuzzy.

"No, I am afraid they will be easy prey for these men."

Fuzzy and Lester look at Jackson. He has been subservient ever since he shot one of the hunters.

"Old friend, we know you're under a lot of stress worrying about your brother and the man you had to kill, but our situation is grave. The crossbows have become lethal, and they hardly miss when they shoot. Please pull yourself together and help us think of something we can do to save our family. Awaken your human gift of creativity. We need a different plan. We have used brute force and followed our instinct, but now we have lost too many of our beloved den members. We're running out of ideas," says Lester.

Jackson looks devastated. "I thought all along I would be able to think of something, but now that time is running out, my mind is blank,"

"You're under too much stress," says Fuzzy. "Try to relax and something may come to you. Have faith in yourself. We and your brother are safe for tonight. There aren't many men left, and they will wait until daylight before they try anything else.

Jackson leans back, trying to think. All he accomplishes is to sink deeper into animosity. Why does no idea come?

Fuzzy and Lester watch at a distance. Jackson's eyes are wide open as he stares at the ceiling. Tears slide down his cheeks and he wipes them from time to time. They can tell he's consumed by distress, and they feel sorry for him. They feel a twinge of guilt having brought the two brothers into this confrontation, and now both of them are probably going to die.

"I will guard the entrance until midnight. Then, if you're able, you can watch until sun rise," says Fuzzy.

"Of course. Be careful, old friend."

The day is almost over, and Jackson has lost his appetite. Not even the smallest pleasure exists for him as he dreads trying to sleep. He's trapped like a prisoner by the long dark night ahead.

<>

The three remaining men are cold and hungry. Cliff and Virgil search through Ben's wagon trying to find something to eat while Lem sits in his crossbow seat, guarding as the last light of day fades. Cooking is out of the question so beef jerky will have to do.

Cap watches the men gnaw and complain about how tough the jerky is, but it looks delicious to him. None of the men offer to give him water or food, and he has done without all day. He can't understand why they think he should suffer. It's obvious he doesn't have much time left in the cage one way or the other.

"It's time to pack our saddlebags and make a run for it," says Cliff.

"Like I told you in the beginning, these are cunning creatures. They aren't going to quit now. They will hunt us down if we turn and run. They can't let us go home knowing we will return with more men and equipment," assures Virgil. "If we leave now, they will have the advantage out in the wilderness. There can't be more than two or three dragons left. With our crossbows, we have the advantage sitting here."

Cliff and Lem chew and think about Virgil's reasoning. They agree they're trapped in a win or die situation.

Cliff shakes his head as he smiles a little for the first time all day "We could get lucky, kill a few more dragons, and be able to capture some of the young ones to bring back to Mason and collect our silver. I will think of a plan tonight now that I know we're all in agreement and we really have no choice."

They try to settle for the night, but with the stench of death surrounding them, they sit wide-eyed with bows in hand, ready to shoot.

<>

Lester and his mate stay close. They're thankful for all the joy they have shared. They know there's a chance this will be the last night they can touch each other and enjoy the life they have built.

Fuzzy and Liz stand, side-by-side, looking at the starry sky like they have done so many nights from the cavern entrance. Worrisome thoughts drift through their minds, but they share affection, trying to support each other. They know all too well this may be the last time they will be able to enjoy this world together.

Jackson is wide awake. Haunted by thoughts of Sandra, and the life he may never have the chance to enjoy with her. He is at a loss to understand how Lester and Fuzzy have begun to accept their fate and find peace.

Jackson blames himself too much to think clearly, much less try to be at some level of peace. He forces himself to put the thoughts about the woman he loves aside and try to forge an idea that will save his brother and the rest of the dragons. He hears Fuzzy and Lester talking. Its midnight and they're changing guard.

"I'm going to fly Jackson away from the cavern to a safer place before the sun rises," says Fuzzy.

"It's not right for him to stay and die in a fight meant for dragons," replies Lester.

Hearing their concern for him makes him weep. He pulls himself up and walks to where Fuzzy and Lester stand. There's enough moonlight to see each other's face. The night air is cool, especially with the light breeze blowing across the entrance. Jackson speaks with the courage of a dragon. "You and your den are my family now. I will not let you take me away.

Lester and Fuzzy are deeply humbled.

Jackson stays in the entrance with Lester until the sun rises. When it's light enough to see, he walks over to the pile of rocks the dragons have placed at the entrance. As he sits, he knocks an unbalanced stone loose and it lands on his foot. The pain causes him to limp with a hop as he tries to walk it off. He sighs as he sits again and rubs his wound. He looks at the rocks for a moment, and his mind starts to work. He steps back and studies, they're all about the size of watermelons. He calls Lester and Fuzzy, and they see a ray of hope in his eyes. There's confidence in his voice and he's almost smiling.

"How well can you fly carrying one of these rocks?" He picks one up.

"We gathered them to use later, and flew back with no trouble," says Fuzzy.

"I think you need to use them now. We've got to take the battle out of here and outside to the hunters."

Fuzzy and Lester look at the rocks. They each pick one up, studying its weight. They decide one of them will carry a rock back into the cavern as far from the entrance as they can, then run as fast as possible toward the entrance. As soon as they're traveling fast enough to hop into the air and take flight, they will fly faster than they have ever flown. With a little luck, they will take the men by surprise and be traveling too fast for them to have good shot. As soon as they circle behind the plateau, they will climb higher than the crossbows can shoot. Then make their way back over the camp and aim their rock as best they can, and let it drop.

Jackson and the dragons fill with hope. They're pleased to have a plan. "Try to hit their crossbows first. Please, just try not to hit the cage wagon with Cap inside. When you need another rock wait until the other one of you is outside being watched, then dive back as fast as you can and grab another one. The hunters will be concentrating on whoever is circling with the rock and the one landing should be able to land safely," says Jackson. He pauses a second. "I wish I could fly and help you do this."

"I will try first," says Lester. Fuzzy touches his wing gesturing, good luck and support.

He hurries back into the cavern as far as he can and still have a straight run toward the entrance. He takes a deep breath and mentally prepares. He bursts into a run, accelerating as fast as he can. He's airborne before he leaves the safety of the cavern. He zips over the ledge so fast the men are completely caught off-guard. Their shots miss. By the time they reload, he's behind the plateau, circling higher and higher. Fuzzy peers over the ledge and sees they're concentrating on Lester. Before the men know what is happening, he's behind the plateau, climbing higher.

Lester takes aim at Virgil's crossbow. He has never tried dropping rocks at anything before. He lets go of his rock. In seconds, it's obvious he isn't going to hit Virgil. The most amazing thing happens. By luck, he hits the other crossbow. The rock destroys it and crushes Lem.

Virgil screams furiously, he shoots arrow after arrow at Lester, but the dragon is too high. Virgil begins to worry about Fuzzy flying high over him with another rock. He changes his aim. Lester dives into the entrance and lands safely, grabs another rock with his powerful claws, and is circling higher before Fuzzy lets go of his rock. Virgil cringes. At first, the falling rock looks as if it's going to hit him, but plunks harmlessly nearby.

Lester's ready for his second try as Fuzzy returns to the cavern.

Lester feels confident after his first try. Taking a deep breath, he takes aim at Virgil's crossbow and releases. It crashes harmlessly into the brush. Lester's newfound confidence fades.

When he returns to the entrance, he sees Jackson has tied two dragon safety ropes together and attached a small rock to one end.

"This will help you aim," instructs Jackson. Putting the empty end of rope in his mouth and showing him the small rock dangling below. When you look down the rope, wait until the small rock hides your target. That's when you let go, just be sure the big rock is beside the rope."

Lester snatches the rope and takes off.

Fuzzy misses every time he tries. And Lester had just been lucky the first time.

Virgil is sweating and shooting at dragons that are too high to reach.

"Calm down, Virgil, they're not going to hit us again. They're flying too high. When they hit Lem it was just a lucky shot."

Cliff looks at Virgil. "Take a break and wait until they start flying lower. They will get tired of flying around and missing."

High above, Lester looks down the rope aims the small rock at his target. He opens his claws and the stone plunges toward the earth. Cliff is still looking at Virgil when the rock smashes him into pieces that splatter all around as the rock continues crushing the horse beneath. Virgil's mouth flies open in horror and disbelief. "Cliff!" he screams. He jumps off the crossbow and runs to the mangled body mingled with crushed horse. The horrid sight is too much. He regurgitates the entire contents of his stomach in one blast. As he regains control of himself, he turns red. He's filled with mindless rage. Hate rules his soul now as his heart races. He shoots wildly at targets too high for him to reach, and soon he's out of crossbow arrows. He jumps out of his seat and dashes to Lem's crushed weapon, gathering all the arrows he can carry. He fills his quiver, sits down, and takes a deep breath. He's going to make himself wait for a good shot.

Fuzzy continues dropping rocks without much chance of hitting anything. He keeps Virgil busy watching him so Lester can safely land and reload. Everyone grows exhausted from the battle. Lester decides to take a chance, he flies a little lower and slower. Carefully aiming again, he releases his rock. Virgil watches as it plummets toward him. In shock, he realizes it's going to hit and he jumps a split second before the crossbow is smashed to pieces. He lands hard on the ground, face down as debris from the crossbow rains down on him.

Cap feels sorry for Virgil until he grabs Cliff's bow and an arrow. Filled with rage, he peers at Cap. He sets the arrow as he walks with a determined look on his face straight toward the cage. He pulls the arrow back aiming at Cap.

A million hopeless possibilities race through Cap's mind. He has more reasons now to live than ever before in his life, and he knows Virgil can't miss. Cap surrenders all hope, this is the end for him. Fuzzy and Lester are too high to help in time.

As the men lock eyes a flash zips past Cap and then there's a *thud*. Virgil squints and grits his teeth in mortal pain. In a split second, the look of death fills Virgil's eyes, and they slowly roll up sending chills down Cap's spine.

Virgil stumbles. The arrow he had set flips harmlessly to the side, and the bow falls to the ground. He grips the bars on the cage, one in each hand. As he slides to the ground Cap can see a crudely made arrow sticking out of Virgil's chest. Virgil's last sight had been of a thin, hairy man marching toward him, aiming.

Chapter 32

Fuzzy and Lester dive toward Cap. They're not sure why Virgil fell to the ground lifeless or who came out of the woods with a bow in his hand.

"Do not hurt this man!" Cap yells as loud as he can, seeing they're close.

The man looks up. Seeing dragons diving toward him takes his breath away, and his heart races. With hands shaking he tries to set an arrow.

Cap yells again, this time to the man. "Don't shoot! These dragons are our friends!"

The man stands paralyzed, not sure what to do. Fearfully, he peers at Cap. "What do you mean?" he shouts. "They won't hurt us! Please trust me!" Cap gestures for the man to lower his arrow.

The dragons land nearby, studying what is happening. They can see the man trembling in fear looks nothing like the hunters. "This man saved my life," explains Cap.

They bow in respect to the man and move back

"Mister, bow to them respectfully and you will be safe with us from now on," says Cap.

He bows in fear.

Cap looks at the thin, hairy man. He's strong and healthy, but he has a beastly appearance. His hair is long and knotted. It's hard to tell where the hair on his head stops and his facial hair begins. As he lays his bow down, Cap sees his scarred hands have almost turned to leather. He has suffered a long time in the wilderness.

The man walks over to the cage, releases the latch, and opens the door. The sound of hinges squeaking as it swings open is music to Cap's ears. He crawls to the opening. The man is so excited his hands shake as he reaches to help Cap step out. Cap looks into the man's eyes and sees a soul that has suffered. Cap struggles to stand at first, and then hugs him.

"Thank you, friend. You saved my life. I will be in your debt from this day on. What is your name?"

"Jess." he replies, hugging Cap. Cap sees he is thrilled to embrace another human. "You don't know how long it's been since I dared to dream I had a chance of surviving."

"I'm starving," says Cap. He runs toward the cook's wagon with Jess right behind him. They find cheese and jerky and eat until they can hold no more. It has been a long time since Jess has been really full.

Fuzzy and Lester sigh in relief and fly back to the den, leaving the men to eat and rest. They joyfully tell their families the danger has passed.

As soon as Fuzzy can free himself from his rejoicing den, he heads straight to Jackson. "Thank you, my old friend. Your plan saved my den!" Fuzzy bows as low as he can. "Cap is safe as well. I will be honored to fly you to his side."

Jackson bursts into tears. So much stress suddenly lifts off his heart, and he can't control himself. Fuzzy opens his wings and hugs Jackson. Soon, he's smiling and climbing up on Fuzzy's back.

Fuzzy turns and hops over the edge of the plateau. After a quick sail downward, he lands beside the food wagon.

Jackson slides off and runs to hug his brother like he has never hugged him before. They share a few tears and a feeling of relief from deep inside.

"I never thought I would see you alive again," says Jackson, beaming from ear to ear.

"You and I owe our good fortune to this man, Jess, for stopping Virgil from killing me," says Cap. "If he hadn't been here at just the right moment, I would be dead."

Jackson turns and bows like the dragons to show respect. "The dragon culture is wearing off on me," he says.

"I can't believe you really rode down here on that dragon," says Jess in awe.

"It's an amazing experience, and we're honored they have accepted us as their friends. You will soon discover they're very intelligent," replies Jackson as he looks at raggedy Jess. "Man, you have to get some clothes on."

He's almost naked. Only a few remnants of cloth and some animal hides are tied around his waist. They search the wagons for clothing. They don't like it, but Jess has to have something to wear.

The only thing they remove from one of the dead men's bodies is a quiver and some arrows.

<>

"Ureeeeee," hails Lester. The entire den is gathered, and the excitement of the victory has faded. Everyone is relieved, yet sad. They are all grieving. As Lester looks around, it's obvious the victory cost them dearly. There are hardly any young adult males left.

"It's time to gather our dead and grieve as a family. We will show our respect as we say good bye to our fallen heroes with mourning and ritual." Lester and Fuzzy lead the way to the entrance and take to the air.

Slowly, they gather their dead, including the remains of the mutilated dragon. Many trips are made to the cremation pit and a flood of tears fall as the slain dragons are gently laid on a neatly stacked pile of wood. The cremation pit is a sacred place to the den with ancient customs passed on from generation to generation.

<>

Despite what they have been through Cap, Jackson, and Jess feel grief for the dead men.

"We must gather their bodies and bury them so they can rest in peace," says Jackson. "They deserve respect."

"There is a sunken place near the cage wagon that will hold them," says Cap.

Cap, Jackson, and Jess lay the men gently side by side in the sunken place. They gather stones lying all around, most are the very ones the dragons dropped during the battle. There are enough to cover them well and build a mound where the sunken place had been. When the last stone is placed, all three men bow their heads in respect.

They are quiet that night. It has been emotionally hard to bury so many. As they drift into slumber under the cage wagon, they're glad this day is over.

In the morning, as the sun is rising, Fuzzy and Lester fly to the campsite. The dragons and the men sit together and talk.

"You have given our den a chance to live on. What you have done for us will never be forgotten and will be passed from generation to generation. The story will explain how good men helped make it possible for this den to continue our lives as free dragons," says Fuzzy.

Jess is awestruck. "I understood what you said. How can that be?" he asks.

Fuzzy looks at Jess, "You would have been afraid to take the time to listen until now. Living in the wilderness has made you understand how to live and think more like a dragon."

Fuzzy turns to Cap and Jackson. "Old friends, you have wives now and will start your families soon. I hope you can raise your children to be like you. You know what's important in life, but things are changing and temptations you didn't have to deal with will tempt your children. Man's quest for silver and fame could one day end all progress mankind has made. Only a few will choose to live like a dragon where family and simple life is all that matters and is fully enjoyed. Soon, our den will move deeper into the northern wilderness. We will be okay. We will survive in small numbers, and someday we may return. But for now, we must go so we can be free to live like dragons."

Cap and Jackson bow in respect as they say goodbye. The dragons return the gesture, and there is no more to be said. They lift off the ground and fly back to their den.

Fuzzy had offered to fly the men home, but Jess and the brothers felt sorry for the horses that would probably die in the wilderness and are able to catch three. As the men ride home, they tell stories of the trials they have been through and the hard lessons they have learned about life. They will all remember what Fuzzy said about living like a dragon. The more they think about it, the more they see real value in the dragon's philosophy.

The top of the Murray's barn comes into view.

"I will not stop to meet your family, but I promise to come back soon," says Jess, anxious to return home.

He nudges his horse and trots toward Blade Town, waving as he fades out of sight.

Cap and Jackson decided before they started the ride home, they are going to go back into the wilderness soon and cover the entrance to the silver mine.

They're choosing to live like dragons. If Water Town ever discovers silver is out there, they will lose their wilderness home just like Fuzzy.

About the author:

Fred J. Hoyle was born in 1947 in Lawndale NC a little town nestled in the foothills of the South Mountains. With few neighbors close by, he explored the woods and creeks surrounding his families' farm. His imagination helped him find adventure as he played in the woods where he fell in love with the beauty of nature. At age eleven his family moved to Shelby where he attended Shelby High School. Fred developed a love for track and field sports. He set a new Western North Carolina Athletic Activity Association record throwing Discus his senior year. In 1970 he met the love of his life and they are still in love and married forty-seven years later. He studied business administration at Gardner Webb College and later assumed the role of president in his families' business for twenty-five years. The business prospered and grew, branching into several endeavors. Now in retirement he has found that with pen in hand he can once again use his imagination to venture into natures beautiful woods, where endless dangers and triumphs await.